Praise for *Blood Red*:

"Lackey's long-awaited ninth *Elemental Masters* fairy tale (after *Steadfast*) will satisfy her eager fans.... The action and dialogue flow freely, mingling with beautiful descriptions of European countryside and just a hint of romance."
—*Publishers Weekly*

"How much did I enjoy *Blood Red*? Now I want to go back and read the previous eight books.... This is a story that's a comfortable read but slyly bubbles away with uncomfortable thoughts and concerns between the pages. Perfect."
—*Geek Native*

And for the previous novels of the *Elemental Masters*:

"This is Lackey at her best, mixing whimsy and magic with a fast-paced plot." —*Publishers Weekly*

"Richly detailed historical backgrounds add flavor and richness to an already strong series that belongs in most fantasy collections. Highly recommended."
—*Library Journal* (starred)

"Fans of light fantasy will be thrilled by Lackey's clever fairy-tale adventure." —*Booklist*

"I find Ms. Lackey's *Elemental Masters* series a true frolic into fantasy." —Fantasy Book Spot

"Lackey has delivered another fine entry to the *Elemental Masters* series.... The storyline and subplots are smoothly woven together and as usual, Lackey's character development is delightful." —Monsters & Critics

"All in fine fairy-tale tradition.... It's grim fun, with some nice historical detail, and just a hint of romance to help lighten things." —*Locus*

MERCEDES LACKEY

BLOOD RED

The Elemental Masters,
Book Nine

DAW BOOKS, INC.

DONALD A. WOLLHEIM, FOUNDER

375 Hudson Street, New York, NY 10014

ELIZABETH R. WOLLHEIM
SHEILA E. GILBERT
PUBLISHERS

www.dawbooks.com

First Paperback Printing, June 2015

1 2 3 4 5 6 7 8 9

To the memory of Donald "Tre" Chipman

Prologue

MUTTI and Vati were talking again. It wasn't quite arguing, and Rosa pretended that she couldn't hear it. Children were not supposed to hear when grownups were talking about them.

It wasn't exactly about her, anyway. It was about the fact that they were living in a cottage in the little village of Holzdorf in the Schwarzwald instead of in Wuppertal, as Mutti wanted. The reason, of course, was Rosa. Living in the city had nearly killed her; she had felt poisoned all the time, and was sick all the time, and it hadn't been until Onkel Hans and Tante Bertha had come to the house and told them about the magic that Mutti and Vati had understood that being in a city was just not going to be possible for Rosa until she was much older, at the very least. Maybe not ever.

Mutti and Vati had only a little of the magic, but they knew it was real, and Vati hadn't sent his brother and sister-in-law away with taunts of madness. But Earth Magic had never been in their families before; it had been two unbroken lines of Fire Mages until Rosa was born. A Fire Mage had no problem with living in a city. Some even found it pleasant.

But for an Earth Mage, well . . . no wonder Rosa had always felt as if she was being poisoned. She *was* being poisoned. All of the industries spewing filth into the air, the soil and the water, all of the smokes and the soots, all of the nastiness caused by too many people living too closely together—all that made the Earth sick, and that made *her* sick. So living in Wuppertal was no longer an option, unless they wanted to send Rosa away alone—and that plan had made Mutti even more unhappy than the prospect of leaving the city.

"It's so *lonely* here," Mutti said plaintively.

Rosa knew what Vati was thinking, that it would be less lonely if Mutti just tried a little harder to fit herself into village life. Her city clothing alone set her apart, and it wasn't as if Tante Bertha had not supplied her with the right costume and more than enough fabric to make more. Rosa thought that the black skirt and black laced jacket, together with the beautifully embroidered blouse and apron and shawl, looked wonderful on Mutti, but she would not part with her stiffly corseted, voluminous, and highly impractical gowns.

And it was not as if the women of the village would not have welcomed her! They felt sorry for the "junge Frau" who always looked so shy and sad. They were eager to share recipes and needlework patterns and gossip. They were always happy to see Rosa, and if she hadn't by nature had a modest appetite, she would have been as round as a Christmas goose from all the good things they tried to coax her to eat. Everyone here knew *of* magic, even if they didn't have any themselves, and they sympathized with the city folk who had exiled themselves here in order that their daughter might thrive and learn.

"Liebchen, you must try harder," said her Vati, wearily. *He* had fitted himself right into the life of the village almost as soon as they had arrived. Now he could not have been told from one of the locals until he opened his mouth, wearing his black suit, the long coat with red lapels and brass buttons, and his little round black hat. The village had lacked a proper schoolmaster; the local priest, a very old man, had served double duty in that regard for decades, and he was more than happy to give over the position to Vati.

And oh, yes … religion. That was another thing that made Mutti unhappy. The village was Catholic, mostly, and she was staunch Lutheran. Not that such a designation made any difference to the village. How could it, when there were Elemental Masters in their forest? Even the priest, gentle old man that he was, would have happily served Holy Communion to Mutti, as he did to Vati, without so much as a hint that she should convert, even though his bishop would probably have died of a fit if he found out. "We are all Children of the Good God," he would say. "The bad days that Master Luther railed about are over. We should accept each other in God's Peace and make no fuss about names and credos."

Well, Rosa had faith in her father. Eventually he would wear Mutti down, as he always did. One day she would put on the pretty black dress and hat bedecked with fat pompoms and go to visit the neighbors. One day she would meet the gentle priest and discover he was not a baby-eating ogre.

"Rosa!" Mutti called from the kitchen. "It is time to visit Grossmutter Helga!"

That was what Rosa had been waiting—a bit impatiently—for. "Grossmutter Helga" was not really her grandmother. Both of her *real* grandmothers had lived back in the city, and they were gone now. "Grossmutter Helga" was a very learned and very powerful Earth Master who was teaching Rosa her magic, because one day Rosa was expected to be just as learned and powerful—although no one knew yet what direction her magic might take.

Rosa was never happier than when she was sitting beside the old woman, listening so hard her face would ache from it afterward. And sometimes—sometimes she was allowed to do a very little magic herself. Or try. Sometimes it didn't work. She didn't seem to be very good at coaxing things to grow under most circumstances, or at healing. Grossmutter said that this was all right, that not every Earth Master was adept at nurturing.

And when Rosa was tired, Grossmutter would make her tea and give her a little meal and tell her stories. Many of the stories were about the Bruderschaft der Förster, the Brotherhood of the Foresters, the arcane guardians of the Schwarzwald; there were many dark and dangerous things that lived here, and the paths through the shadowy trees could be perilous. Rosa was very glad, listening to those tales, that the Brotherhood stood guard.

As Rosa entered the warm and fragrant kitchen, Vati ruffled her hair and left for the schoolhouse. The kitchen—indeed, the entire cottage—was the one thing that Mutti did like about their new life. Living space in the city was cramped, and Rosa remembered Vati always complaining about how expensive it was. Here, thanks to Vati's schoolmaster job, the spacious cottage cost them nothing. It had three rooms below, and the loft where Rosa slept above. The kitchen had a red-tiled floor, a spacious hearth with an oven built into it for baking, a sink, cupboards that held all manner of good things, a sturdy wooden table in the center, and real glass windows—it was ever so much nicer than the tiny little kitchen in their city flat. They had a real parlor and a bedroom for Mutti and Vati as well, where in the city flat they'd had to hide their bed behind a curtain, and Rosa had slept in a cupboard bed.

"I have your basket for Grossmutter," said Mutti, folding the top of the napkin that lined the basket over the contents. "Some lovely apple cakes, a nice pat of butter, and that soft cheese she likes so much." Mutti always sent Rosa with a basket to Grossmutter, as if Grossmutter needed someone else to do her cooking for her, although Rosa knew very well that Grossmutter was as good a cook, or better, than Mutti. But she was too polite to say anything, and Grossmutter always accepted the contents of the basket with grave thanks, so Rosa supposed that this was one of the many things children were supposed to be silent about.

Then Mutti tied Rosa's pride and joy about her neck—a beautiful bright red cape with a matching hood. Rosa always felt like a princess in this cape, which was a miniature copy of the riding capes that fine ladies wore when they went hunting. Mutti had copied the pattern from an illustrated magazine that Vati had brought from the city for her, and Grossmutter had sewed it for her.

"Now go and take your lessons with Grossmutter, and don't dawdle on the way," Mutti cautioned.

"I won't, Mutti," Rosa promised.

"And don't speak to strangers."

"I won't, Mutti," she promised again, although she could not imagine what strangers she could possibly meet on the path to Grossmutter's cottage. It wasn't a common route for travelers or people out to see the sights of the Schwarzwald. But Mutti had said the same back in the city every time Rosa went out to play on the doorstep, so she supposed it must be habit from that time.

"And if you are kept too late, you may stay with Grossmutter," Mutti concluded, albeit reluctantly. "I don't want you wandering in the forest at sundown. There are wolves. And bears."

Rosa stifled a sigh. Of course there were wolves and bears. Everyone knew that. That was why there was a wolf or a bear on practically every piece of Schwarzwald carving. And stags, but her mother never warned her to beware of stags, even though Grossmutter had told her that they could be just as dangerous as a bear. "Yes, Mutti," she said dutifully.

"Now off you go."

Finally Rosa was free to scamper out the door, through the vegetable garden that was Vati's pride, and out the gate to the path that led to Grossmutter's house.

The first part of her journey was out of the village, and through all of the village fields. She always ran through this part; the farm fields and small pastures held very little interest for her. The land had been tamed, controlled, and confined. Everything was neat, everything was regimented. She always felt a little stifled when in the village or on the farmlands. It was *nothing* like as bad as it had been when she'd lived in the city, but . . . well, it was akin to being forced to wear your Sunday Best all the time. You couldn't really be yourself. The land wasn't itself.

She was always glad when she got out of the farmlands

and into the water meadow. While the meadow and its pond weren't exactly wild, not like the forest, they were still much freer than the farmed land. Nothing grew in the meadow, or in the pond, that was deliberately planted. The village ducks and geese grazed here, and the village goats, but that was about the extent of the hand of man. She slowed to a fast walk as soon as the path crossed the boundary of the meadow.

Here was where she finally saw the first of the Elementals—other than brownies—that lived around the village. The village was *full* of brownies, of course, even if no one but Rosa and her parents were aware of them. It was a wholesome, earthy place, and brownies were the Elementals not only of Earth, but of hearth and home. Virtually every household in the village had at least one brownie seeing to it that all was well in the house, and that any accidents were small ones. Rosa's household had three, because of Rosa's magic.

But here in the water meadow was where she started to see the wild ones. There was a little faun that she thought lived here. Not like the ones in the woods, who were older, somehow more goatlike, and were always looking at her slyly out of their strange eyes. This was a very little fellow, shy, and often found napping in the sun. There was a tree-girl here as well, though she held herself aloof from the faun. There were entire swarms of the sorts of little creatures that were in picture books, little grotesques with fat bodies and spindly legs, or made with parts of ordinary animals, birds and insects. She didn't have names for them and neither did Grossmutter, who just called them "alvar." No matter how odd they looked, they were playful and friendly, and Rosa wished she had lived here when she was younger, because she could have run down here to play with them.

She was not free to do so today, though, so she waved at the ones she saw and plunged into the forest. "Plunged" was the right word; the Schwarzwald was a very old forest, and once you got onto the paths within it, you found yourself in a dark and mysterious place. Tree trunks towered all around, like pillars holding up a green ceiling high, high above. Here and there shafts of sunlight pierced the gloom.

The forest floor was thick with old leaves and needles, soft with moss, rippling with roots. And normally, it felt welcoming to Rosa. But today . . .

Well, today the forest felt . . . uneasy. Not so much near the village, but the deeper she got into it, the more it felt as if the forest was holding its breath, and that many of the animals and creatures that dwelled here were in hiding from . . . something.

Now, Rosa had had that same feeling in here before, now and again. Nothing had ever come of it, but when she asked Grossmutter about it, the elder magician had pulled a long face. "There are dark tales in the forest," she had said. "And most of them are true. Hurry your steps, and do not tarry when the trees hold their breath and the fauns hide in their caves. And never come there after dark until you are older and *much* more powerful." That seemed like good advice to Rosa . . . and she was heeding it now. Instead of sauntering along, stopping to look at something interesting now and again, collecting bird feathers and the mushrooms Grossmutter had taught her were safe, she sped up, gathering her little cloak about her, for suddenly the shadows beneath the trees seemed cold.

She was halfway to Grossmutter's cottage when she rounded a twist in the path, and was stopped dead in her tracks by the sight of a man she did not know ahead of her.

Now, the forest was very famous. And her village was well known for wood carving. Strangers were known to trek through the forest for pleasure, especially in the summer, although this was the first time that Rosa had encountered a man she didn't recognize inside the forest and not in the village, and she couldn't imagine how he had come to be on *this* path.

But there was something about this man she did not like, and she could not have said why.

Whether or not he had been walking before he saw her, he had stopped now, and was waiting; she could not go farther without passing him, and he watched her every move with eyes that gleamed with an expression she couldn't fathom. Slowly, and with deep reluctance, she approached him.

He was dressed like a hunter, leather trousers tucked into leather boots, green wool jacket, green wool hat, and game bag—but he wasn't carrying either a rifle or a bow. But maybe he was one of those foreigners. A foreigner would think that hunting gear was the sort of thing you should wear to walk in the forest.

The hat looked a little odd on his head; he had longish, shaggy hair of mixed brown and gray, although he didn't look all that old. He was clean-shaven, but his features were—well, she'd have called him ugly if she'd dared. But she was only a little girl, and children were supposed to be respectful of their elders. His eyes glittered beneath his hat-brim, a strange yellow-brown. She really didn't know what to make of him, except that if she hadn't been halfway to Grossmutter's—and if she hadn't been half-scared he would chase her if she ran—she'd have turned around and pelted all the way back home.

"Hello, little girl," the man said, when she finally stopped on the path, unwilling to get any closer. "What would your name be and where are you from?"

"Rosamund Ackermann, sir," she said politely. "I come from Holzdorf." He must be a foreigner. The only way the path behind her led was to Holzdorf.

He nodded approvingly. "And what is such a little creature like you doing out here in the dark forest all alone?" He didn't move, yet somehow he seemed to loom over her, and the place where he stood got a little darker.

Magic. It must be magic that I feel on him. Maybe he was Air ... Air and Earth did not get along, at all. She gathered her little power about her and inched a bit sideways, off the path, trying to move without looking as if she was doing so. "I am going to my Grandmother's house, sir," she said, still remaining polite. "Mother says that she is old, and it is hard for her to cook anymore." It was *very* important that a magician not lie! But this was not a lie. Mutti *did* say that, even though it was not true.

"And what does your Grandmother do, all alone in that cottage in the woods," the stranger asked, his eyes glittering. "Does she make potions? Does she have any strange animals about?"

Oh! Now she knew why she didn't like him! Grossmutter had warned her about men like this. They were looking for witches, and would hurt them if they found them! Grossmutter had even warned her that such men might have magic themselves, and not know it, or pretend they didn't, or tell themselves it was some sort of God-given power.

"She knits," Rosa said truthfully. "And sews. She made my red cloak. She has two little hens for her egg in the morning." She wouldn't tell him about the goat. "And she mends stockings. Mother has her mend all our stockings." Also true. Mutti hated mending stockings, and Grossmutter didn't mind.

The man looked vaguely disappointed, which made her think that her guess was right. He *was* looking for witches. "Why does she live by herself in the forest? Shouldn't she move to the village where it is safer?"

"My Mother says there is no room for her in our cottage, sir," she replied, which was not strictly true but also was not a lie. Mutti had not *said* so, but every time that Vati mentioned the idea, she made a face. It wasn't as if Grossmutter was Rosa's *real* grandmother after all, and Mutti always replied with "But what if your father or mine needs to move in with us?"

Rosa didn't think that was likely to happen. Both grandfathers were vigorously pursuing pretty, young widows. She knew that Mutti had gotten used to having her own little house with just her and Vati in it, and didn't want to share, particularly not with an old lady who might be demanding, interfering, or critical. Rosa might be very young, but there was a great deal she understood quite well.

The man made a stern face. "Your father—" he began, then shook his head in disapproval. Rosa began to inch her way around him. "Women should know their place," he told Rosa sternly. "It is for the man to say what is to happen in his own house."

"Yes, sir," Rosa said automatically. She was almost halfway around him, although she had to go a good five feet off the path to do so.

Fortunately, he was now so engrossed in his own lecture that he didn't seem to have noticed what she was doing.

"Women and girls do not have strong enough minds to know what is best for them," he said, looking thunderous. "Women and girls must be obedient to men in all things. They must confine themselves to the tasks that God suited them for. Work in the home, childbearing, and child-rearing. They are too given to emotion to make any good decisions — like your mother, child."

By this point she was all the way around him and back on the path, and this seemed to be the opening she needed to get away from him. She ducked her head. "And my father has said I must take these things to Grandmother, and hurry, and not dawdle on the way, sir. So I must be going. Good day to you! Holzdorf is just ahead of you!" And before he could respond to that, she turned and scampered up the path, putting as much distance as she could between herself and the unpleasant stranger.

She was afraid he might call after her, but he did not.

The forest, however, remained strangely dark, and unusually quiet, as if something in it was disturbing everything. She didn't see a single Elemental, which made her unhappy and uneasy. Then again, that stranger had left her very disturbed, and she could easily see him having that effect on the entire forest. He was just nasty — and if he had been going off the path, poking about in the forest a bit, snooping, well . . . if she had been an Elemental, she would have hidden too.

As soon as she was sure he wasn't going to call after her, or worse, chase after her, she slowed to a fast walk. Normally she took her time going through the forest, because she liked it so much, but today, well, she just wanted to get to Grossmutter's house as quickly as she could.

It seemed to take much, much longer than usual, as if the path had somehow doubled in length, although she knew that could not possibly be so.

She almost sobbed with relief when she finally saw the little branching path that led to Grossmutter's cottage. She ran again, ran all the way up the path, through silence that was so thick it felt like fog around her, ran until she reached the door, pulled the latch-string, pulled it open, and shut it tight behind her.

The cottage was very dark, darker than twilight. Something was not right.

"Grandmama?" she called into the dark.

The cottage was a single room, with Grossmutter's bed in a little nook at the rear, which was now deeply in shadow. Something stirred back there.

Something was very wrong. She felt it deep inside her, worse than when she had been in the forest. But how could that be? This was Grossmutter's cottage, the safest place in the forest!

"Rosa?" said a strange voice. "Is that you, child?" There was a cough. "I am not well. Come closer. Did you bring me something from your mother?"

Rosa took a cautious step toward the bed. It should be Grossmutter there. She couldn't imagine how it could be anyone except Grossmutter. "Grandmama? You sound strange."

"I took a chill," said the hoarse voice. "Come closer, child."

Another step. "Grandmama?" She could see Grossmutter's nightcap in the shadows around the bed. "Why is it so dark?" She peered anxiously into the shadows, her little heart pounding. A pair of eyes seemed to gleam in the darkness beneath the cap. "Why are your eyes so bright?"

"So that I may see you better, my dear," said the voice.

Rosa shivered at the shadows, clutching her basket. It felt as if an icy drop of water was creeping down her spine. "Grandmama? Something is not right . . ."

It was a good thing she was poised to flee, because whatever was in Grossmutter's bed suddenly heaved up and leapt right over the top of her; it might have pounced on her too, if she hadn't ducked and scuttled out of the way. It landed between her and the door.

"Enough!" howled the thing as she backed away from it. *"Die, vermin!"* It lunged for her.

She shrieked in pure terror. And the thing winced back, clapping its paws over its ears, an expression of acute pain twisting its features. That gave her enough time to run for the pantry, wrench the door open, slam it shut behind herself and lock it from the inside.

She could lock herself in, even though most pantries were made to lock on the *outside,* because Grossmutter had had it made that way—one safe place that she, or she and Rosa, could hide in, if something bad happened.

Something bad, very bad, like the horrid creature *but with the stranger's eyes,* a hoarsened version of the stranger's voice, the body of a man, and the pelt, paws and claws, and the twisted facial features, of something that was a half-man, and a half-wolf.

The door shuddered as the thing flung itself against the wood. She wanted, badly, to just drop onto the floor, pull her cape over her head and hide. But Grossmutter had taught her better than that. Despite her terror, Rosa twisted her fingers in frantic patterns as she made the wood come alive, knit itself into the doorframe, and start to grow at preternatural speed. At least that was what she was trying to do—she couldn't actually *see* what she was doing, but a moment after she made the magic, she put her hand on the door and felt the rough bark of a living tree instead of the hewn wood of the door. The wood vibrated under her hand, but no longer shuddered. She was safe for now.

But she was also trapped.

She felt along the shelves until she put her hand on the wooden box of candles. Beside it was the box of lucifer matches. Carefully, she struck one, and lit the candle.

And screamed. For sharing the pantry with her was the mangled body of Grossmutter.

She clutched the candle, and screamed, and screamed, and screamed, weeping with terror and loss.

She screamed until she ran out of breath, took another breath, and screamed more. From the other side of the door came the shriek of terrible claws rending the wood.

The bare tip of a claw gleamed in the candlelight, re-awakening her to her danger. Frantically, she put her hand against where the door had been and felt the talons tearing it away. Feeling the power drain from her, she made the wood grow again, and from the other side came a terrible howl of rage and frustration, and the sound of claws shredding wood with renewed fury.

She didn't know what to do! Somewhere out there, there

were people who could help her, but Grossmutter had not told her how to call them yet!

She didn't know why she did what she did next. She just *did* it, out of pure fear and desperation. She dropped the candle, which rolled and went out, leaned into the living door, put both palms against it, and cried out in terror.

HELP ME!

It was as if a shudder went through everything, and a moment after that . . . an enormous *silence.* Even the thing outside the door paused. It really *did* seem as if everything held its breath—

Then the monster howled in triumph, and every hair on her head stood straight up. She had thought she was frightened before. She was so terrified now she couldn't even shriek. She couldn't even breathe.

The creature redoubled its efforts on her door, and she kept trying to renew the wood, her little strength fading more with each try. She began to feel faint each time she made the wood grow. She hardly had the strength to stand upright, and supported herself against the rough bark of the door—

Then the cottage shook with a crash and a drumming of hooves.

The monster barked in surprise, and stopped clawing at the door.

There was another crash, and another, and the bellow of an elk. Rosa knew what it was because she had seen and heard an elk trumpeting one day in the forest. Then another crash, and the entire cottage rocked, the monster shrieked, and chaos erupted on the other side of her wooden barrier.

She fainted.

She could not have been unconscious for too very long, because the fighting was still going on, although it sounded distinctly as if the elk was losing. She curled her fingers into the bark of the tree and tried to will it strength, tears pouring from her eyes.

The elk was going to die. The horrible thing out there was going to kill it. And then it would break through the wood, and it would kill her—

And then, out of *nowhere,* the cottage rocked again; a

thunderous roar shook the walls. Rosa screamed. She couldn't imagine what it was—

And then she heard the voices calling her. "Rosa! Rosa!" muffled by the wood.

"Here!" she cried out, pounding her little fists on the bark. "Here!"

Then she fell into a widening gap as the wood parted; fell into arms that plucked her out of the pantry and pulled her up onto a huge, strong shoulder.

The cottage was no longer full of shadows. The door was *gone.* She got a glimpse of her savior, the elk, with its head hanging but still standing, hide gashed in dozens of places, being tended to by a woman with short-cut hair, dressed like the stranger had been, in well-worn loden-green hunting gear. She got another glimpse of the monster, a hole in its chest, head hacked off, and hid her face in her rescuer's shoulder.

And she cried, and cried and cried, while her rescuer carried her out into the woods, patting her back awkwardly.

"There, there," he murmured. "It's all right now, Rosa. You're safe."

Her rescuer carried her over to some horses, and somehow mounted without ever putting her down. She looked up for a moment through eyes streaming with tears, and saw the elk stumbling out of the ruined door, staggering a little, but looking determined.

"That's one fellow that will never become cutlets with mushrooms," said one of the other green-clad hunters mounting his own horse.

"Aye. Gilda will bring him back to the Lodge and he'll live to be a ripe old age, and die having fathered a hundred more like him," her rescuer rumbled. "And well-done he. If it had not been for him answering the child's call, we'd never have got here in time."

Rosa put her head back down on the man's shoulder, sobbing and clinging to him.

"Hans, Fritz," the man ordered. "Go to the girl's parents. Tell them we're taking her. It's clearly not safe for her to be with them anymore. The next time, the beasts may come into the village, and the Good God only knows what would happen then."

"Aye Hunt Master," said another fellow, and there was the sound of hooves trotting away.

Wait . . . It wasn't safe for her to live with Mutti and Vati? "Where are you taking me?" she asked, pulling her head off the man's shoulder, and scrubbing her eyes with the back of her hand. "Who are you?"

Again, the man patted her back. "Don't be afraid, Rosa. I am the Hunt Master of the Schwarzwald Foresters. We have been watching you, and watching over you, ever since you arrived. Your aunt and uncle told us about you. We are going to take you to our Lodge, where you will be safe, and learn about your magic all the time."

Rosa blinked, took a deep breath, about to object—and stopped. Because . . . this felt *right*. This was what she . . . wanted.

"But Vati and Mutti—"

"Will come visit you, all the time. Unless they wish to return to the city—and if they do, we know powerful men who will make certain that they are well taken care of." The man put his horse in motion; the rest of the group followed him. She could see the elk limping along at the end of the group. She put her head down on his shoulder, and thought.

Was it wrong that she loved her Mutti and Vati, and yet felt . . . as if they never really understood who she was and what she wanted? Because that was, indeed, how she felt. She could not explain it, but she had felt, instantly, more at home with this man whose name she didn't even *know*, than with them.

"You are very quiet, little one," the man murmured. "Are you troubled? Do you not care for what we have planned?"

"I—I am troubled because I *do*," she almost-wailed, softly, feeling a desperate sort of confusion come over her.

"Ah . . . that is because your magic speaks to mine. We are more alike than if you were my daughter and I was your father." He patted her. "I will gladly be a second father to you, child. If you would care for that."

The *moment* he said that, she knew it was true. This man,

this Hunt Master, *was* more like her father than her own Vati. He understood the hunger to learn about her magic. And he would be able to protect her as her own Vati could not.

She thought about that monster breaking into her own little home, and her blood ran cold. Her parents would have had less chance against that thing than Grossmutter.

Even if she *hadn't* liked these plans—and she did—she could not endanger them like that.

"I would care for that, Hunt Master," she said with a sigh, laying her head down on his shoulder and closing her eyes. "Please take me home."

THIS was not the Schwarzwald, but all forests were home to an Earth Master. Rosamund—who no longer called herself "Ackermann," but "von Schwarzwald"—was just as comfortable here in the depths of Transylvania as she was at home. The earth itself spoke to her, and she could no more have gotten lost on the deep forest trails in these foreign mountains than she could have gotten lost going from the front door of the Bruderschaft Lodge to her rooms.

She breathed in the cool air, inhaling all the myriad scents of leaf and moss, bark, a brook nearby. Different scents from home, yet not unalike. As an Earth Master, all places that were not cities were "home" to her, so she didn't feel any displacement or unease that the scents were not what she was used to. She had been here in Transylvania for a week, which was three days more than she needed to settle into a new place.

If she "borrowed" the nose of one of the forest creatures, she'd have an olfactory kaleidoscope to sort through, of course; her own human nose couldn't tell her nearly so much. That *might* cause a little disorientation. *But I think not*, she mused, allowing all her senses to adapt so she could begin her hunting. *No, although this is not home, it becomes more familiar to me with every moment.*

It was just as well she couldn't get lost, because it was almost midnight, and as black under the trees as the inside of a Guildmaster's pocket. Not that Rosa needed light. Not when every living thing, from the smallest blade of grass to the tallest tree, emanated its own sort of living light when she looked with the attuned eye, and the part of her that saw magic as shimmers of color. This was, to her mind, the most important gift of Earth Mastery, to see the energy created by every living thing. It was especially important for both her and Hans, because the evil they hunted walked exclusively by night.

The Brotherhood hereabouts was small, having suffered much depredation at the hands of witch-hunters, Turks, and zealots of various sorts. That was why they had finally begged help from outside their borders. They could not cope with the thing that had moved into the ruins of some long-ago noble's great old manor. There were no Masters among them, only mages, and one attempt to track the creature had already ended in the deaths of two of the four local hunters.

And now that she was standing here, on the trail her hosts said the creature habitually took to stalk its prey, Rosamund knew why they had been outclassed. She read the tracks that stood out, black with evil, against the moss of the path, where even the vegetation itself had lost its life energy beneath the press of those feet.

Her hosts had been mistaken, something she had suspected from the beginning. There was not one creature, there were two. Master, and servant.

She felt her lips curving in a thin smile. They would not be prepared for her. Back home in the Schwarzwald she had a certain ... reputation. Here, well, it was unlikely they would have heard of her. Or if they had, they would probably dismiss that reputation as being a tall tale. All the better.

Now, Rosa. Caution, not overconfidence. Assume the worst. Assume they know you are here and are ready for you.

You cannot afford to take anything for granted. She could almost feel her mentor gently cuffing her ear for her momentary hubris. The smile left her lips, and she eased herself down the trail, following those death-colored footprints.

As dark as it was, it did not matter what the colors of her clothing might have been, but she was clad in her usual loden-green wool hunting jacket, with dark leather knee breeches and soft leather boots that came over her knee, beneath the red, hooded cloak that was almost as much a part of her as her skin.

The cloak—well, in the darkness, it only registered as more darkness, even if by day she stood out like a flower bursting through cobblestones. She wore it always, in memory of Grossmutter Helga.

As for the rest of her clothing, it was certainly far more startling to common eyes than that red cloak. But no one was around to be outraged at her wearing a man's knee breeches instead of a skirt.

For one moment she greatly regretted not wearing her special leather gear—leather on the outside, with cloth of silver on the inside, between the leather and the silk lining. But she had not had any notion when she started this Hunt today that she would have need of it. *Too late for regrets.*

As for Hans, he was used to her hunting gear. The women of the Bruderschaft wore men's breeches often when needful, and the men had gotten used to that hundreds of years ago. The Bruderschaft was practical above all else.

She made less noise as she threaded her way along the forest track than a deer would have. Her boots had soft soles, not hard; they were like those of a Red Indian from America. She could feel everything through those soles, and the magic of the Earth was not impeded by thick, hardened leather and hobnails.

Around her the forest was silent and frightened, as well it should be, with such evil in it. The trail she followed veered away from a running brook—no surprise there, these creatures often found it difficult to cross running water without a bridge—then up a rise to a wooded ridge. And there . . . the two who had been together parted company.

And for just a moment, she hesitated. She wanted, oh, most fervently, to follow the spoor of the beast that took the left-hand way. But that loped off in the direction of the deeper forest. There was no one there who could be in any danger. Well, no humans anyway, and any Elemental creatures would scent or feel the beast coming with plenty of time to hide. The other footprints, however, went to the right, where she knew a small village lay. So the master was, indeed, seeking prey tonight, as was the servant. There had been no movement into or out of that old manor for the full week she had been here. They were being cautious, but that caution had probably made them ravenous. Too ravenous for niceties; both would kill tonight.

That decided her. That, and knowing that the wind lay in *her* favor for now, if she pursued the right-hand quarry, but if she went left, she would be downwind, and might become the hunted, not the hunter. After midnight, the winds would shift; the sylphs of the air had told her little gnomes as much. She could lie in wait for the beast and ambush it when it circled back to its master, sated with the kill, or still hungering and thinking of nothing but hunger.

Concentrate on the master. If we have to, Hans and I can hunt the servant together, later. It would be on its guard, but there would be four of them. She and Hans could take Matei and Gheorghe with them. And she and Hans would be doubly protected, for she would not forget her special gear a second time.

Knowing now which direction she needed to go, and guessing where the evil creature would probably head, she let the forest tell her the shortest path to the village, and she made all speed. Years of learning to trust her feet to read the trails, years of trusting the magic let her run without thinking of the track itself, only the spoor she followed. Now that the Master had parted from his servant, he was being more cautious, and the tracks were fainter.

Don't think. Don't feel. Hunt.

She paused in the shadow of the trees above the little valley that held the village. Down there, not a single light shone, and a damp, cool breeze with a hint of rain on it made her glad of her cloak. It was late, and these village folk were all abed by now. She sought, and found, a rabbit, quivering beneath a bush nearby, and "borrowed" its nose, smelling what it smelled, and immediately was struck with the scent of the thing that made the rabbit shiver. There was no doubt; what she sought was down in the village itself, its scent mingling with the myriad scents of the humans and their living. The scent of the thing held the effluvia of stale blood and age and evil, and she readied her crossbow, wondering briefly how Hans was faring, back at the ruins.

Hans is an Earth Master and experienced. He has been on many, many Hunts, as well you know, she scolded herself. *Let Hans tend to his Hunt, and you tend to yours.*

The scent was everywhere in that little valley now, although those poor villagers down below with their blunted, human senses would not even detect a trace of it, not unless the thing was atop them and breathing coldly into their faces.

Now that she was this close, she felt that familiar mix of excitement and fear starting to build. She needed both. Fear, to keep her sharp—excitement, to make her fast.

She slipped carefully among the trees, glad the moon was down, but aware that the thing she hunted had means of its own to see by dark. Still . . . it was without allies, now that it had left its servant behind. And she . . . was not.

At the edge of the village, she put her hand to the ground. *Oh, my friends, my little friends, please give me your wisdom. Where is the hunter, the slayer-by-night?* she asked silently. She waited patiently. The creatures of Earth did not move quickly, nor trust easily. But she was fairly certain which of the many sorts would answer her first.

Sure enough, after a while, she felt a tugging on her sleeve. She looked down. Glowing a little with a healthy golden energy was one of the little *alvar,* anxiously pulling on the button at her wrist. She smiled down at it, thought her thanks at it as hard as she could.

This one had an acorn-cap for a hat, a round head not unlike an acorn, but a spindly little body and spidery legs and arms, all encased in a garment that seemed to be made of moss. When it saw her looking down at it, it let go of her sleeve, and gestured, then scuttled away. She followed.

Here the life-energy faded to almost nothing, what with the streets being pounded earth, the houses being dead wood and stone, and only the outline of the few growing things and the patches of the gardens to give her anything to see by. The village was not very big, smaller than Holzdorf. Just two main streets, crossing the road. The little creature moved like a leaf blown by the wind, down one of them, its faintly glowing body barely visible in the darkness. She followed, staying close to the buildings, using what protection they offered her, keeping herself as close to the walls as possible, although she always ducked beneath any windows she passed. It might be very dark, but she had not gotten as far as she had as a hunter by being incautious. What good would it do to have tracked her quarry all the way to this village if it was alerted because some wakeful villager struck a light, saw a shadow cross the window, and raised an alarm?

She caught up with the *alvar*. It was huddling against the wall of a goat shed, and when she reached it, it pointed with a trembling arm down toward the water mill. There, outside the village proper, there were grass and growing things to give her light to see by again. The creature stood out blackly against the faint glow of Earth energies given off by the grass around the mill . . . in fact, it emanated its own sort of anti-life energy, an aura that pulsed hungrily.

She immediately saw why the creature had taken up a post at the mill. The sound of the millrace and the rushing water would cover any noise. It was too hungry to think of anything but draining the prey dry, and all it had to do to escape immediate detection was tip the body into the water when it was done. The victim wouldn't be found until the body had traveled far from the village—if it was ever found at all.

It's smart, I'll allow that. This is probably how it's kept people from knowing it's prowling their villages until now. If it hadn't been for the Brotherhood—well, the creature probably could prey at will for months before having to move on.

And almost exactly halfway between her and the creature was its intended victim; from here it was little more

than a white form stumbling toward the mill, but Rosa
knew it was almost certainly one of the village women or
girls, dressed only in the shift she went to sleep in, being
drawn by the creature's sinister magic.

Poor girl. The creature would have gone sifting through
dreams, looking for someone who was vulnerable. And . . .
well, expendable. The servant girl who was a bit of a slut.
The unwanted, plain daughter who would never find a husband. The widow who was a bit odd. Someone who, when
she vanished, would set heads wagging and tongues clack-
ing, but would *not* send friends and neighbors out on a man-
hunt.

*Probably the servant girl who is a bit of a slut. People will
assume she ran off on her own when she vanishes.* Rosa grit-
ted her teeth. *Not tonight, monster. Not this time.*

Rosa put her hand down to the *alvar*; in her hand was a
bit of cheese from her belt pouch. The *alvar* took it greedily
and scuttled away. That was all the thanks it needed, as most
of the Earth Elementals—the small ones anyway—were
always eager for a bit of "man-food." As soon as it had hidden itself, she moved.

The creature—the *vampir*—had all of its attention focused on luring in its prey. It must have been very, very hungry after a week without feeding—or feeding only on the
unsatisfying blood of what it could catch in the forest.

She took advantage of that preoccupation to slip up the
hill, staying in cover by making use of every bit of fence,
hedge, and wall. She moved as quickly as she dared, conscious that the clock, so to speak, was ticking away the precious seconds before the girl fell into its clawlike hands. She
had to reach the *vampir* before its victim reached it.

She slipped around by the back of the mill, and the noise
of the wheel, the falling water, and the river all surrounded
her with so much sound that it was impossible to hear what
was going on up ahead of her.

She didn't need to hear anything, however. The nearness
of the creature was like a feeling of sickness. And she was
close enough she could sense its excitement. The prey must
be very near.

She readied her hand-crossbow, with the special, oversized bolt made entirely of hardened holly wood, with a needle-sharp point in place of an arrowhead. It was one of the weapons she had made sure to have with her when the local Brotherhood had first called for help. Excitement and fear in equal measure boiled up in her, and every nerve was afire with both. With the bolt in the channel, the crossbow cocked and ready, she rounded the corner to confront the creature.

Just in time. Its victim was a mere ten feet away, swaying where she stood. The hideous thing had its back to Rosa and had no idea she was there. Its bloodlust and hunger were overpowering at this distance. Even an ordinary human with not a speck of magic would have felt it. It had no eyes, no thought, for anything but the prey in front of it.

With a silent prayer to Saint Hubert, she let fly.

The bolt flew clean and true, hitting the monster squarely in the heart.

Its victim dropped where she stood, unconscious, as the monster's control over her evaporated.

It didn't die cleanly, of course. The *vampir* never did. It thrashed and writhed and spouted half-rotten blood from every possible orifice. But at least it did so quietly, and as soon as it was safe Rosa closed in on it and drove the stake all the way through its body with a shove of her boot, pinning it to the earth. That finished it. With a final squirm, it died, mouth open in a soundless gasp.

The stench was appalling. She pulled a candle out of her hunting bag and struck a lucifer match to examine the monster.

It did not differ substantially from any other *vampir* she had killed in the past. Bald head, hideous face not unlike a goblin's mask, strangely wizened body, clawlike hands. Mouth *full* of nastily pointed teeth. Most *vampir,* if they didn't want to kill their victim immediately, would make a cut on the inside of the elbow or some other place it didn't show, and lap the blood like a dog. But most *vampir* didn't bother with niceties. They simply tore the victim's throat open, messily, and fed, and either left the body to be found later or disposed of it somehow so they would have a few more days or weeks to continue hunting.

She had heard from the Bruderschaft tales of very ancient and very cunning *vampir* indeed, who had secured a place and ruled it with terror and a crushing mental power. She thanked the Good God and Saint Hubert she had never had to come up against one such as those. It would take not just a Hunt Master like herself, but the largest Hunting Party possible to put such an evil down.

She reached into her hunting pouch again and removed the glass-lined flask of naphtha. Dispassionately she poured it over the body, then bent down and lit it with the candle, stepping back quickly as the soaked rags flared into instant flame. That was one good thing about *vampir,* the only good thing, really. They were tinder-dry and burned to ash quickly, even without the use of naphtha to hurry things along.

She blew out the candle and restored it to her pouch so as not to waste it, and went to examine the girl. She was still unconscious, but a superficial examination did not reveal any telltale cuts that suggested the beast had fed on her yet. Good, then she had not been given the *vampir's* blood in return; he had not been grooming her for his nest. She was vaguely pretty, and clearly poor. Probably a serving wench in the inn or a servant of some sort. Her hands showed she was no stranger to hard work. That sort was the easiest prey for the *vampir* to lure, with sensuous dreams and erotic magic.

Well, she would be all right. Of course, she would probably have hysterics when she woke up from the *vampir*-induced trance and found herself in nothing but her shift, beside the mill in the open and next to a pile of smoking ashes, but that was no concern of Rosa's. The local Brotherhood had brought her and Hans here for one reason and one reason only: rid the area of the *vampir,* its nest, and whatever servants it had acquired. It had not required of her that she do anything other than *save* the next presumptive victim.

Now to get to the next hunt, before morning came and the servant-beast hid itself among humans again.

Without any need to conceal herself, she trotted up the road and out of the village, heading for the ridge where the two creatures' paths had diverged as fast as she could, pondering what her next move should be. Straight hunt, or ambush?

I don't know these mountains, and the creature probably does. I would wager that the vampir *recruited it here so that the fiend had someone that could give it local knowledge.*

Now she felt a mingled thrill of dread, excitement, and anticipation. *Vampir* were pretty mindless once they had focused in on a victim, and this one had been operating with the same handicaps she had, since it was not a native to the area. But the native creature? It was hunting on its own ground. This was going to be a real fight, and she was at a distinct disadvantage. At home in the Schwarzwald, she would have been able to set up an ambush.

I don't know where to ambush it here.

She shivered, and pulled her cape around herself. *Not* going after it was not an option. Even with its master gone, it was a terrible danger to everyone here. Worse, because evidently the local Brotherhood had not known of its existence. It must have been confining its slaughters to the forest creatures—but that would not last, once it had allied itself with the *vampir.* Surely by now, as a reward, the master had let it taste human blood. Once that happened—

The pit of her stomach went cold.

She didn't dare send out a widespread call for Elemental help either; it was possible for the creature to be an Elemental Magician itself, and it would hear the call. She remembered all too clearly when the one that had attacked Grossmutter had heard her frantic, widespread call for help. To send out something like that right now would be very like painting a glowing target on herself.

But . . . there might be a way around that.

She knelt and put her bare hand on the soil, and sent out something that was more like a whisper. It was not meant to travel far. *If you fear the thing that walks as both beast and man, please come to me now.*

She waited. She sensed that there were things all around her, the local creatures of Earth, the wild ones, the ones far less inclined to help humans because of what humans meant to them. She had a good idea that they were debating among themselves. *Should* they come to her? Which represented the most threat to them—the thing that roamed the night, or she, herself?

Perhaps another Elemental Master might have tried to coerce one of them, but that was not the way of the Bruderschaft. She waited, patiently, and finally, as time seemed to crawl past (and yet went far too quickly), she heard hesitant hoofsteps behind her, soft thuds on the earth.

She turned, and looked into the strange, slantwise, goat eyes of an ancient satyr.

She kept her gaze on his eyes, because he was priapic, of course. A satyr could not be alive and in the presence of anything female and not be priapic. If she took notice of it, *he* would take that notice for an invitation, as satyrs always did, and then there would be a tremendous waste of time while she dealt with *that* particular complication.

He was very, very old; he might even date back to when the Romans were in these mountains. His gray beard and hair fell in tangled masses, full of leaves and twigs, down to his waist. His curled horns were enormous, and she wondered that he could even hold his head up beneath the weight of them. "By your courtesy, Elder One," she said politely, trying Latin first. "Could you bend your effort to ask of your Master to speak with me?"

He looked at her with his head tilted to the side, and she was about to try again in Greek, when he answered.

"You are bold, to wish to speak to the Lord of the Hunt," he replied.

"There is another, twisted hunter in his realm, as you know," she replied calmly. "I think He might wish to be rid of it, for surely it is preying on you, His children. Or if not now, it will soon."

Now the satyr bent his head, a very little, in agreement. "It is," he said. "The forest is troubled. And you can rid us of this troublesome thing?"

"I hope, with the aid of the Lord of the Hunt," she told him, truthfully. A magician must never, ever lie, for his lies could turn to bring him mischief. "This forest is not my forest, and I need the help of one for whom every leaf is familiar."

"That will be the Lord of the Hunt," the satyr said, nodding. And grinned. "For the sake of the cheese that I smell in yon bag, I will go to Him."

She was very, very glad that all he asked for was the cheese. Without hesitation, she took the wax-wrapped wedge from her hunting pouch and handed it to him. All of the Earth Elementals had a fondness for human foods; many were partial to baked goods, but it seemed this satyr had a taste for something more robust.

He took the cheese and even bowed graciously to her, then turned without another word and walked back into the forest. A moment later, he was gone. Quite gone; he had vanished as only an Elemental on its home ground could.

She waited again, concentrating on *not* being impatient. The Being she sought would not be impressed by impatience.

But to her relief, the Being she sought evidently was just as eager to get the beast out of his forest as she was. It could not have been more than a few minutes before the forest all around her fell absolutely silent. But not with the silence of fear—no, this was the silence of awe.

The forest before her literally lit up with the golden glow of Earth energies. Every leaf, every twig, every blade of grass or frond of moss was alive with light. And striding out from the heart of the light was the Lord of the Hunt.

He glowed like the harvest moon, golden and radiant. Crowned with the many-branched horns of a king stag, clothed in a tunic of hide and fur and breeches of rough-tanned leather, he wore a hunting horn at his side and his every step was marked by a faint trembling in the earth. His eyes fixed on Rosa, implacable, stern. His face was neither old nor young, but had the same watchful stillness about it as an ancient carving.

Her impulse was to bend the knee to him, but this was no being to show submission to. Cernunnos to the Celts, Woden in her own home forest, Herne in the isle of Britain, he was the ultimate predator. This was the Lord of the Hunt, and any display of weakness could be taken as a sign that you were prey. He had been a god once. Now, with no or few worshippers, his power was diminished. But by no means gone.

Instead, she kept her eyes on his as she nodded slightly, acknowledging that he was much her superior in power, but also displaying her stubborn courage. She waited, however, for him to speak.

To her relief, he sounded amused.

"So. The little female wishes to rid my forest of The Fell Beast?"

"It is *your* forest, Lord of the Hunt," she replied. "I am but a stranger here. Yes, I do so wish, for we both know the thing will kill and kill and kill your children, wantonly, as well as ravage the mortals of this place. It is the mortals who begged me to come to hunt, but it is your children that I most truly wish to protect."

No lies there. To a certain extent, she was... unsympathetic with a population that decimated its protectors, the local Brotherhood, then went weeping because there was no one there to protect them from the things of the night. But the Elementals of this forest had *not* had a hand in that, and did not deserve to suffer.

The Lord of the Hunt smiled faintly. "You speak wisely, as well as truly. But the aid that such as I may lawfully render is limited to such as you. Be plain; what aid do you think I may render to you?"

"These lands hold no secrets from you, but many from me, Great Old One," she said honestly. "The surest way I can rid you of this beast is to ambush it, yet I have no knowledge of these forests to do so."

The Lord of the Hunt pondered her words, then again, smiled, this time broadly.

"I have a solution that is both lawful and amusing, Earth Master," he chuckled. "Hold you still while I drink of your scent."

It took every bit of discipline she had to hold very still while the Great Elemental—who had, after all, once been a *god of fertility* hereabouts and was known for mating with his priestesses—came within a hands-breadth of her, and snuffed her all over like a bloodhound. The sheer *power* he exuded was enough to make her knees weak. And there were a great many alarming instincts awakening in her when she was in this close a proximity to him. Flight, for one; in the long-ago days, he had hunted men. Again, the urge to fall to her knees. And ... most alarming of all, and fortunately she had been warned of this many, many times, so she was not taken by surprise ... there was the urge to strip her clothing off and submit to him in *quite* another way, as if she had been one of those eager priestesses.

Of course she did none of these things. And from the curl of his lips, she knew that *he* knew all these things were going through her. But tonight, he wanted what *she* wanted, and she was safe from him. Yes, even her virtue.

He lingered just long enough over his task to ensure that she was wildly uncomfortable before backing away. "Go into hiding yonder," he said, pointing to a rock outcropping. "Be prepared to step out and take your strike, and make the first blow the fatal one when the beast is in reach. I shall go and lure it to you, with your own sweet scent." He chuckled again. "It is hungry. I think it will not be able to resist."

And with that, the Lord of the Hunt somehow folded the golden light around himself, and vanished.

She didn't hesitate a moment, because there was no telling how near or far the beast was; she got herself into place and pulled her coach gun from the sling on her back, under her cloak. She readied it, making sure both barrels were loaded with her special rounds.

And then, she waited. Because if the Lord of the Hunt did what she *suspected* he would, the beast would come swiftly, and not at all—

—a bloodcurdling howl split the night air—

No. Not at all quietly.

That was definitely a hunting howl. The Lord of the Hunt had deliberately aroused all of the beast's bloodlust, without a doubt by flinging her scent in its face and leaving a "hot" trail. A tiny expenditure of magic, for a Great Elemental. She was good at judging distances by sound—with what she did, she had to be. She judged the beast was less than a quarter mile away, and closing fast.

It howled again, and it felt as if every hair on her body

stood straight up. From the deep tone of the howl this one was big. The entire forest had fallen silent—and not the silence of awe, but the silence of pure fear.

She had to time this perfectly. She had to stay in "hiding" until the last possible moment. If the creature had already killed and eaten, it wouldn't be so ravenous that all of its ability to think was gone. If it saw her actually standing there, gun at the ready . . .

She needed to step out at exactly the right moment. Soon enough to trigger an attack, not so quickly that it saw the gun and could or would abort the attack.

Another howl, this one sending shivers all down her and making her legs want to run. Close. Very—

So close that now it scented *her,* and not the trail the Lord of the Hunt had left. The howl changed; not a howl any longer, but the shorter, harsh bark that signaled it had found its quarry.

She concentrated, stilling her pounding heart. About a thousand feet now. Five hundred. Less than a hundred!

She stepped out from behind the rock, her mage-vision sharpened. The creature stood out against the golden glow of Earth energy as if it was sucking up all available light. As she stepped out, it leapt—

As terror flooded her, she fired both barrels of the coach gun, braced for the kickback.

The gun roared in her hands, and kicked against her hip. The werewolf dropped dead at her feet.

She staggered back a few paces, and sat down hard, shaking in every limb.

Hans found her at first light, examining the body of the beast carefully. He took care to make plenty of noise approaching her; she looked up as he pushed through some overgrowth on the trail. "Did you find the nest?" she asked, as he grunted with surprise at the werewolf's body.

"Aye." He knelt beside her. "Two females. When you killed the male they froze up and started shrieking. Took them down in a trice. And yes, I searched the ruins for any new recruits, but he had nothing." Hans bent his white-blond head over the waist area of the body. He immediately saw what Rosa had found about the body that was interesting. "Huh. Belt?" He indicated a paler stripe of fur that went all the way around the "waist" area of the body.

"Belt," she confirmed. The presence of a wolfskin belt meant that *this* werewolf had been a magician of some kind, and had deliberately chosen to transform himself in order to kill. Oh, it was possible to transform for other reasons, but every magician she had encountered that had done so had used forbidden blood magic. And had been a murderer in both two- and four-legged form.

There were two kinds of werewolves that Rosa knew of; those that transformed themselves by magic, like this one and the one that had attacked and murdered Grossmutter Helga, and those who had been born with the ability to transform. She had *heard* that, allegedly, there was a third kind, transformed by the bite of another werewolf, whose transformative power was out of his conscious control. She had personally never seen one.

She had also personally never seen a benign werewolf, although her mentor insisted they existed. Then again, she only ever saw the ones she was forced to hunt down and kill, so perhaps her view of the beasts was skewed, and her skepticism that such a thing existed misplaced.

Or perhaps her mentor was wrong, and eventually the beast within overcame every werewolf.

There was more rustling in the undergrowth, and they both looked up to see one of their two hosts come pushing his way onto the path. By this point, the sun was up, mist had gathered down in the bowl of the valley below them, and the morning sunlight just gilded the tops of the trees. Matei looked relieved to see them both—then his eyes widened as they fell on the body of the werewolf.

In full light, it looked nothing at all like the half-beast that had terrorized Rosa and murdered Grossmutter Helga. It looked like an extremely large wolf, and nothing about it was out of the ordinary, until you got to the head. *Then* it was clear this was no common wolf. The head was much bigger than that of a proper wolf—or rather the skull was, which gave it a slightly misshapen look. The silver shot that Rosa had used, created specifically to kill werewolves, had torn its chest apart. Silver was the only metal that prevented the shape-shifters from healing. In fact, they couldn't abide having any of it on their bodies at any time, not even the ones who did their transformations by means of magic.

Which made the glint of metal under the fur around the beast's neck that much more out of the ordinary. As Matei drew closer, Rosa poked at the fur where she thought she had seen something shine with the tip of her dagger. Just as he reached them, the dagger caught on and dislodged a copper chain, with a pendant dangling from it. Somehow not one of the pieces of shot had cut the chain or damaged the little oval pendant. She seized the chain at the ornament, and yanked sharply, breaking it.

"Well, well, look here." She held out her prize to the others. The pendant was a medal—a saint's medal, that of St. Hubert, who was also the patron saint of the Bruderschaft . . .

Or more to the point, it was a medal showing St. Hubert's *stag,* the vision that allegedly turned the Saint to a life of piety. This was the same medal that the Bruderschaft wore.

With two differences.

The medal was copper, not silver.

And the crucifix between the stag's horns was inverted.

Her companions' eyes bulged as she held it up to the light, examining it critically. There was nothing on the back, which was interesting.

"Is it—" Hans ventured.

She was getting no sickening feeling of evil, nor any tingling of residual magic, and Earth Masters were particularly sensitive to such things. She shook her head. "Nothing. Just ordinary blasphemy, I think. But someone in one of your villages might remember a copper saint's medal, Matei. Such things are far from common."

She spoke fluent Romanian; languages came easily to Earth Masters, although the intellect tended to be the provenance of Air Masters. But Earth Masters "cheated;" when they arrived in a place, they would call up one of the house

Elementals native there, and coax it to give them the local tongue by magical means, overnight, while they slept. It was a useful talent and never more so than when an Earth Master was called upon to be a Hunt Master away from home.

Matei nodded. "Even the poorest hereabouts have their saint's medals and crucifixes of silver. The village of Rosia Montana has much silver, and gold, and many have worked the mines there. Even if the fellow never let anyone near enough to see the blasphemous image, people would remember a copper medal." He sighed. "If only someone showed it to them."

Rosa looked the fellow straight in the eyes. Like most of the folk hereabouts, he was dark and wiry, and he contrasted markedly with the two big blond Germans. "Matei," she said, finally. "This is not my land, and perhaps this is not my place to say these things to you. But I am a Hunt Master, and you called us here, so I am going to say them anyway. It is time you stopped skulking along the paths of the forest and showed those villagers down there just *who* it is that has been protecting them all this time. *Not* those good priests. *You.* You and Gheorghe."

Matei gasped and paled as Rosa bent and hacked off the wolf's tail, then thrust it, and the copper medal, at him. "You need to go down there to the villages with these," she said implacably. "You need to claim the ashes of that *vampir* I killed as *your* work. You need to be proud of it! No more skulking, hiding from the witch-hunters! Do you know what our villagers in the Schwarzwald do when the witch-hunters come? They *protect* us! Just as we protect them from what prowls in the night! Make them your friends! Go to church! Take Communion to show that you are no evil thing of the night, but a strong arm to protect them! It is long past time that you claimed your heritage, and gave those with magic in their blood a place to go besides the church or going rogue! Or do you want more like *this* beast to prowl your woods?"

Matei seemed to shrink into himself. "But . . . but . . ." he stammered. Clearly, he not only was not comfortable with the notion of talking up his heritage openly, the mere idea terrified him.

Hans gently cleared his throat, and Rosa looked down at him. "Eh?" she said.

"I was . . . thinking of staying here, and not going back to the Schwarzwald," he said, a little apologetically. "They clearly need the help. The villagers already know I'm here hunting the uncanny things, and they respect that. I could do it."

It was Rosa's turn to gape at her friend and colleague. "You—want to stay?"

Hans shrugged, the loden-green wool of his jacket moving only slightly. Hans was a big, well-muscled man, with strong arms from chopping wood, and strong legs from patrolling miles of forest trails. She could well imagine he inspired respect among the villagers. "There are plenty of us in the Schwarzwald. Almost too many, if you ask me. And with you about—truly, Rosamund, you are worth any five of the others, that's why you're the first woman Hunt Master we've ever had. I already had it in mind to look for a place that needed me more than the Schwarzwald, and I can't imagine a place that needs me more than here."

Rather than being put out, Matei seemed pathetically grateful for Hans's declaration. "We would more than welcome you, Hans Osterwald! Gheorghe and I would be honored if you would stay here! And take over the leadership of our Brotherhood!"

Rosa managed to get her mouth closed again. She had not expected any of this! But the part of her that always stayed calm, no matter how terrified or perplexed she was, nodded in approval.

And she could not help but think of her own situation, when her mentor had made her a Hunt Master, a position she had desired so much she scarcely dared think about it. Many in the Bruderschaft had been against it, even though her performance was impeccable. But he had supported his decision, and her, and now no one even thought twice about a woman being a Hunt Master.

Hans was an Earth Master. He had long ago earned the right to decide where he wanted to go and what he wanted to do. He could breathe new life into this nearly defunct Brotherhood, and bring new protection to these woods.

Hadn't she trusted him to hunt the *vampir* nest alone? And hadn't he done well?

She let out the breath she had been holding in a long sigh. "It is your decision, Hans," she said, handing him the tail and the medal. "But I think it is a good one, and I shall tell the Bruderschaft as much."

2

THIS was certainly the longest and most complicated trip Rosa had ever taken. Hans too. Hans had been very intimidated; Rosa refused to let anything like a *trip* intimidate her. People crossed three countries all the time, perfectly ordinary people who had no magic to help them. She reckoned she should be able to do as much without requiring her hand be held.

She *almost* wondered if half the reason that Hans had decided to stay in Romania was because he didn't want to take the trip back.

The trip out had been something of an endurance trial. First, they had been taken by coach and local train to Stuttgart, and then to Munich. Then they had traveled from Munich to Vienna, from Vienna to Budapest, and from Budapest to Bucharest by three separate trains. Then from Bucharest they had taken a series of coaches to get to the village where Matei and Gheorghe had met them with horses. It was rather telling that the journey had probably been more exhausting than the Hunt itself. It had involved learning two new languages as well, Hungarian and Romanian. Hans had been in a state of terror lest they lose their luggage and the special weapons they were bringing with them—not to mention the three sets of special leather gear, one for her, one for Hans, and one in case one of the Romanians would fit it. No matter how many times Rosa had pointed out that they *were* going to another Brotherhood Lodge, and presumably many of the same weapons—or possibly better—would be available to them, he had still fretted through every train change.

To an extent, not having Hans come along for the return trip will be a bit of a relief.

It had not taken her much effort to persuade Hans to go make his dramatic appearance, wolf tail in hand, crossbow and coach gun at his back and belt, just as the villagers were dealing with the hysterical girl and the mystery of the man-shaped burn spot at the mill. Hans had done very well, but then, when he wasn't fretting himself to bits that something would go wrong, he was quite imposing and had a flair for the dramatic. He had stalked into the village as the villagers were gathering around the ominous patch of ground, announced himself as the slayer of the *vampir* that had been stalking their streets that very night, and brandished the wolf tail and unholy medal declaring he had slain the *vampir's* consorts and servant as well.

As luck would have it, someone recognized the medal. There was a rush for the man's house—and lo, beneath the rug in the main room was magic circle painted on the floor, and a search of the place turned up all manner of nasty things and occult instruments.

And when Hans declared himself prepared to remain in the forest and guard the area, the villagers fell all over each other with gratitude.

Rosa had watched all this from a distance, of course. Those selfsame villagers who were lauding Hans, and by extension, Gheorghe and Matei, would have instantly branded a woman who dared to dress as a man as a witch. When she was certain that the situation was well in hand, she had returned to the Brotherhood Lodge to pack and wait for the others to return.

They finally turned up just before sundown. She had assumed they would probably return bearing all manner of gifts, and had not troubled to make any supper preparations other than putting out plates and so forth, mending the fire, and making sure everything was as cozy as you could get in a Lodge that was nine-tenths empty.

She certainly hoped Hans would be able to find some new recruits for the Brotherhood soon. The Lodge had been built to hold thirty comfortably. The effect of the huge main hall, with most of the rooms in the wings on either side closed off, was distinctly depressing. The glassy eyes of the heads of trophy stags, bear and wolves looking down from the walls did not aid the oppressive atmosphere.

But when the three men came merrily laughing in through the door, bringing with them the aromas of the many good things to eat that they had been burdened with, the atmosphere lightened considerably.

It wasn't as if the food was *needed.* But it was delightful to have been given it freely, in thanks. And the roast hen, the sausages, and the fresh *cozonac* were all welcome changes to the stews that Gheorghe and Matei seemed to live on. Not that there was anything *wrong* with stew, and they did vary the recipes, but still . . .

For the first time since she and Hans had arrived here, talk around the table was cheerful and full of laughter. It had helped very much that after discovering the identity of the shape-shifting sorcerer, Hans had had a flash of pure genius, and had led Matei and Gheorghe straight to the priest to ask for his blessing. *In* the church itself. All three of them had knelt right at the altar and the priest had outdone himself, making a miniature service out of the rite. That pretty much killed the notion that any of the three could be a witch.

"Make sure you all start going to mass regularly," Rosa said, waggling a drumstick at the three of them. "More than once a week! The more you are in the church, the better. *We* know, don't we, Hans?"

Hans nodded his blond head solemnly. "Oh yes. Since there are so many of us, it is easier for us, of course. Our hunting gear is a sort of uniform, like a policeman or a soldier. People just look for the row of hunters in the church and know the Bruderschaft is there, as always. They don't even look at our faces anymore, really. But that's why they protect us from the witch-hunters. You see, they've seen us in church, taking Communion, being blessed. We didn't burst into flames or fly out the window. They *know* us. So they protect us so that we can protect them." His face lit up. "And I know I sensed someone down in that village with Earth powers! So soon, I think, we will have ourselves another new brother!"

Rosa snorted a little. "Oh trust me, that will not be a difficulty when people realize the Brotherhood also lives quite well."

Gheorghe, who tended to be quieter than his friend, blushed. "Well," he said, slowly. "We *are* Earth Mages, and this *is* country where gold and silver abound. We never saw any reason why we shouldn't ask the dwarves and the treasure guardians if they would share with us."

"And so you should do," Rosa assured him. "So long as no one is greedy, we work *hard* to protect both the Elementals and the mortals of our forests. There is no reason why we should not be supported in doing so." She smiled. "After all, one can grow very tired even of noble venison and boar with wild mushrooms if that is all one sees, day after day."

Gheorghe nodded solemnly, and passed her the basket of bread. Then he slapped his hand on the table. "Bah. What am I thinking? The least we can do is make your return journey proceed in comfort!"

She was about to remind him that they hadn't exactly come by wagon, but he leapt up from the table and returned with a strongbox. He opened it, and began counting out heavy silver coins. Rosa tried not to let her jaw drop again.

"The dwarves are very good at counterfeiting," Gheorghe said conversationally. "Of course these are identical in purity to Romanian coins, identical in every way, really. They just never saw the inside of a Romanian mint. There."

The coins were not small, about the size of a German thaler, and they were marked "20 lei." There were several of them. She had never seen so much money in her life. "This should be enough to give you first class rail all the way to

Munich," Gheorghe said matter-of-factly. "And make sure you are treated like a noble the entire way."

"He is, without a doubt, right," Matei said, as Hans also stared at the money. "He is very good with money."

"But—" she started to object. Then stopped. That was no small strongbox. And he had hefted it as if it was very heavy. The Schwarzwald did not have the benefit of sitting atop fields of gold and silver, and there were no helpful dwarves among the Earth Elementals there to grant the Bruder-schaft gifts of precious metal.

And she had seen for herself the difference between first class rail travel and second class. *Other* people would see to it that her luggage was whisked, guarded, from one train to another. *Other* people would get her taxis to lovely hotels, and get her taxis back to the depot to catch the next train, if she needed to stay overnight. She would have a compart-ment to herself, with a real bed in it, if the train was a slow one, or if she took a night train.

The thought of sleeping in a *bed* instead of leaning against Hans's shoulder all night long, fitfully dozing, was as intoxicating as the wine the men were drinking. *I may never again get a chance to travel like this,* she thought to herself.

"If we could not easily afford this, I would not offer it," Gheorghe said simply.

"Then I thank you," she replied, and pocketed the coins. "Truly thank you."

There was a night train from Bucharest to Budapest, and Rosa was on it. Most of the cars—second and third class—were full of people who looked resigned to spending a mostly sleepless night. But she was going to be able to sleep!

She settled herself into the private compartment; most of her baggage was in the baggage van, she only needed to keep a portmanteau with her, with the things she needed overnight. She had taken the second special leather gear with the cloth-of-silver inside, the one that they had brought in case one of the Romanians could wear it. And some other gear of Hans' that was duplicated; an extra pistol and silver bullets, an extra silver dagger, the boar spear they could both use. The Bruderschaft could certainly use them.

She was just glad that no one was likely to want to look in those trunks. She'd have some explaining to do if they did.

The private compartment was about the half the size of her little room at the Lodge; it had its own window with red velvet curtains, a banquette sofa, a footstool tucked under a table beneath the window, a luggage rack overhead, and enclosed in a little cabinet was a basin with a ewer cleverly strapped in.

On the journey in, she had been too aware of all the other people she had been crammed in with to take note anything other than relief when the train had gotten far enough into the countryside to lift the pressure of *wrongness* she always felt in a city. Now she settled herself for the hour or so before dinner to examine ... things ... a little more closely.

There was a sense of slight disconnection from the Earth, which was to be expected when so much metal separated her from it. She'd expected more, actually, considering how fast they were moving. But if she closed her eyes, it was not that difficult to orient herself, and she got fleeting "glimpses" of the native Earth creatures watching the great iron serpent as it flew along the rails.

She'd expected more anxiety, and more of a sense of being walled away from her Element. But the car, though not *natural,* felt not that much different from a house in a small village. She opened her eyes with a feeling of a tightness inside her being eased. When the gong announced dinner, she was still watching the landscape flow by past her window, marveling at it all. This leg of the journey out had been in daylight, and she and Hans had been crammed in with a family of six that included a toddler who had wailed softly most of the time.

She indulged in a late dinner in a dining car ornamented with sparkling crystal and gilt woodwork, and returned to her private compartment to find a bed where the sofa had been, turned down and waiting, with her nightdress ironed and laid atop the pillow. What a difference money made!

It had been something of a hard journey to get to Bucharest to catch this train in the first place—no amount of money could improve a trip in common coaches. Well, other than being able to sit inside instead of outside. Coaches and horseback were still the most common means of conveyance in most of Romania, and she knew she was lucky to have gotten a coach rather than a seat on someone's farm wagon as early in the journey as she had. As a consequence, a bed had never looked so inviting, and despite the novelty and noise of trying to sleep on a moving train, she was not awake for very long. When she woke, it was to find that a maid had slipped in during the night and taken away her dress to brush, sponge and refresh it until it looked like new, washed her stockings, underthings and petticoat, ironed everything dry, and then returned it all, hanging up and waiting for her.

How the maid had managed that on a moving train without ever waking her seemed more of an act of pure magic than anything *she* could do.

She washed up, brushed out her hair, and put it up again—there was a ewer of warm water in the little compartment with the basin, and she managed with a minimum of splashing despite the swaying of the car. Then she donned her sober black gown again, packed up her night things in her portmanteau, and returned to the dining car, which looked just as splendid in the morning light as it had last night. After a hearty breakfast, she returned to her compartment to find the bed made, and a freshly ironed newspaper waiting for her perusal.

A porter came to get her bag just before the train was due to pull in to the station at Budapest. She had arranged the full journey at Bucharest, and now she alighted from her car to find a helpful conductor fluent in Romanian, Hungarian, and German ready to direct her to a special waiting room just for first class passengers where she could pass the time until she was ready to board the next train, this one from Budapest to Vienna.

If she had been anyone else, there was no doubt in her mind that she would not have rushed through this journey in such haste. Bucharest was home to many beautiful churches and the Royal Palace, and certainly would have been worth stopping in for a few days. And as for Budapest, well! A week would not have been enough. And then, Vienna, oh, Vienna . . .

But . . . she was an Earth Master, and even though she had shielded herself heavily, she was soon at the point of *needing* that coffee pot at her elbow, drinking cup after cup of the beverage, mellowed with cream and sweetened with sugar. Budapest etched away at her shields. She felt every wound made to the Earth on which it stood, felt sickened by every poison in its metaphorical veins. Individually, the great iron engines of the trains, belching smoke and steam, did not trouble her much, but crowded together in the station they made her feel ill. She could scarcely feel the Earth beneath all the stone and cement, and what she felt was unhappy. There might have been some Elementals here, but they were none of them *good*. They were not the sort she would ever attempt to contact.

She was only too happy when it came time to take her place on board the Budapest to Vienna train, although she really couldn't enjoy the lovely parlor car until the train was well into the countryside. She did not have a private compartment for this leg of the journey, but rather had a seat in the first class parlor car. The porter had taken her silence for shyness, or perhaps grief—she was, after all, wearing black and her ticket listed her as "Frau" von Schwarzwald. He had assiduously seated her in her own plush red chair in the back of the parlor car, with her own little table, set away from the groupings of identical chairs and settees that would encourage socializing. She was glad he had, and glad that her veil allowed her to study the car and her fellow passengers with a degree of anonymity.

Paneled in highly polished wood, carpeted in real Turkish carpets, with red plush curtains at every window and stained glass skylights inset into the roof, she imagined that the parlor car must be a reflection of what the parlors of the very wealthy looked like. She was glad that she was wearing what she had chosen for this journey, even though she had picked it for its imperviousness to travel and not for any other consideration. Her simple, sober gown of black had been lovingly stitched by Mutti after the fashion plates in her beloved magazines out of the very finest of alpaca and delicate linen. As Rosa covertly studied the women around her, it occurred to her with no little astonishment that Mutti's handiwork not only equaled that of the fashionable ateliers whose creations were worn by the well-to-do around her, it surpassed them. No one was giving her a second glance, because she fit in with the rest of the folk in this car so perfectly.

She had worn this selfsame gown on the journey to Romania as well, but it was likely that amid the crowding and the wailing of unhappy children and the general weariness of all of the travelers in second and third class, no one had paid any attention to its quality.

Or they assumed I was a servant that had been gifted a cast-off from my mistress. That happened quite a bit, actually, and not only in well-to-do families. In her home village, servant girls often got old clothing as an added benefit from a generous mistress.

She breathed a little thanks to Mutti, for without this gown, she would certainly have found herself embarrassed back to the second or third class carriages where she belonged.

A waiter and waitress moved easily among the tables, offering coffee and tea and plates of pastries. Now that they were well into the countryside, Rosa's appetite was back and she gratefully accepted both. But she watched carefully how the ladies about her ate, and copied them, cutting the pastries into tiny bites and eating delicately, rather than picking the good things up in an ungloved hand and biting straight into them.

The car seemed to be full of a mix of Hungarian and German speakers. The porter had put her portmanteau in a rack above her head, but after the little waitress in her black uniform dress and stiffly starched white apron had cleared away the plate and cup, the girl offered Rosa a selection of fashionable magazines, so there was no need of the book in her bag. She feigned studying the stories and the fashion plates as she actually studied her fellow passengers.

Some of her fellow Foresters had seen people—well,

men—of this class up close in the past, but Rosa never had. Wealthy men often came to the Schwarzwald to hunt, and the Bruderschaft sometimes acted as guides to keep them out of mischief. These men and women fascinated her. It made her head swim to think that the women would change their clothing four and five times in a day to match whatever social activity they were doing. More than that, if they happened to participate in what passed in their class for "sport." And they would keep a perfectly good gown for no more than a handful of years before discarding it as "out of fashion" rather than remaking it as Mutti did.

She eavesdropped on them shamelessly. Most of them were either returning from, or going on, "tours." She knew what these "tours" were—whirlwind sightseeing trips to major capitols, occasionally taking in some countryside by way of relief. They would whisk in and out of the agreed-upon series of "things worth seeing" without really seeing any of them.

She wondered why they did it at all. It wasn't for education. It wasn't to examine the beauties of these places, for as near as she could tell, *every* place was judged inferior in some way to what they had "at home."

Maybe it's just for something to do.

Certainly the women, at least, seemed to have very little to occupy them in the intervals between changing clothing. They didn't tend their own children. They didn't make their own clothing or cook their own food. They didn't clean their own homes, and didn't even direct the people who *did.* That was the job of the housekeeper.

She could not even begin to imagine living like that. Although it was wonderful being pampered and cared for on this journey, especially when you compared it with the slog that had been the outward half, she knew that too much more of being tended to hand and foot would drive her mad. Living in gowns like the one she was wearing would drive her mad. And above all, not having anything practical to do with her time would drive her mad.

As she came to that conclusion, a gong sounded softly. This was the signal that they were all to rise in a leisurely fashion, and make their way into the next car—the dining car—which existed for the *sole* purpose of being eaten in, by these people and no others.

Luncheon, like the other meals she'd had on these trains, was amazing. And it was even more amazing to bear witness to the sheer amount of food that the men, at least, were tucking away. Eight courses! For luncheon! Small wonder those elegant vests strained a little to cover the bellies beneath them.

Out of deference to her apparent mourning, she was given a table by herself, allowing her to eat as slowly as she liked while she observed those around her.

Then it was back to the parlor car, where watching her fellow passengers had grown boring enough—and their conversation unvarying enough—that she retreated to her book. She caught some of the women casting curious glances her way, and she suspected that they were surreptitiously trying to read the title. Not that the title would bring any of them any enlightenment. She'd taken it with permission from the Romanian Brotherhood's library, as they had a second copy, and the Bruderschaft didn't possess this work; written in Latin, it was a treatise on a subject rather important to her—werewolves and other shapeshifters.

Tea and coffee and more pastries were served in midafternoon; she declined the pastries but accepted the coffee. About the time when she would have been sitting down to supper at the Bruderschaft Lodge, the steward passed through the car, politely informing the passengers in a deferential murmur that they were about to enter Vienna.

Rosa had felt the nearness of the city for some time. It wasn't as bad as some German cities she had been forced to pass through; Vienna was well known for its green and growing spaces. But it was uncomfortable, and she was very glad that she would not be staying overnight there. She would be taking another night train all the way across Germany, and arriving in Munich in the morning. From there, she would take a train to Stuttgart, then a local train to Freudenstadt, and someone from the Bruderschaft would meet her at the station with her horse. She would be home, and everything would go back to normal again. Meals at the proper time, not the time these people took it. Meals that would be simple, not ones that left you groaning.

Of course, nothing was straightforward in these journeys. Vienna had more than one railway station. She would arrive at the South Railway Station, and would have to leave from the West Railway Station. When she had made the outward trip with Hans, it had involved the scramble of two modestly dressed people—in Hans's case, a man dressed in rustic clothing—trying to compete for taxis against people who were . . . well, not "rustics." It was a good thing they'd made sure to have plenty of time to make the exchange; in the end they had gotten a tired looking old man with an equally tired, old horse and a shabby thing that could barely be called a "taxi," and they had clomped along at a snail's pace.

But ah, today . . .

She alighted from the train carriage, and was directed to a railway employee whose sole job, it seemed, was to get taxis for the first class passengers. She joined the small group of her fellow "elite," who followed him, and were in turn followed by no less than five porters pushing giant trolleys of baggage.

It seemed that there was even a separate class of taxi for the well-to-do. She told their guide where she wanted to go, and he grouped her with others who were also going to the West station.

In almost no time, Rosa and three other travelers from first class were seated in a spacious vehicle. Their luggage was piled up on the top with great efficiency, and they were off. They arrived at the Western station in half the time it had taken her and Hans to get there. When all the little details of paying were taken care of, a porter appeared for her luggage and it was whisked away, leaving her to have a leisurely cup of coffee and a slice of *Sachertorte* before getting to the Munich train.

It would have been wonderful, and she would have enjoyed playing the *grande dame* to the hilt, if she hadn't been forced to expend so much energy on keeping her shields up that she was *starving* by the time that *Sachertorte* arrived. And rich as the decadent chocolate cake was, she could tell it was barely going to hold her until dinner in the dining car. But it did give her the energy to send a telegram, and it was with glee that she did so, because Gheorghe's bounty made it possible to send such things. Vati would be very surprised to get such a missive, but he would take the news of her arrival to the Bruderschaft, and she would not have to linger in Freudenstadt, waiting for them.

By the time she was seated in the dining car, she was very, very glad of the rich menu on offer—this was Vienna, after all, the culinary capital of Central Europe, and the railroad felt impelled to offer its first class passengers the equal of any meal they could get at any of the city's most luxurious hotels.

Using magic took energy and strength. This was one reason why she preferred to use physical weapons against monsters, rather than magical ones. Or rather, she kept the magical ones in reserve . . . And if she were in farmland or forest, she could draw on the energy of the Earth to augment her own. But not in a city.

Now, she did know of some Earth Mages who *could* work—if handicapped—in a city like Vienna at least, where there were islands of green to keep the Earth from being completely poisoned or shut away, but she was not one of them, and neither was Hans. So they had been forced to keep solid shields up the entire time they were in Vienna, and the hours they had spent there had been an ordeal. *I think we ate our weight in food.* Part of the reason they had looked so rustic was that they had come prepared for Vienna, and were carrying *bags* of food, one each. Sausages, fruit, cheese—bread rolls had been easy to come by, since nearly every station had carts from local bakers outside it. By the time the train had left for Budapest, half their hoarded food had been gone.

She left the dining car while the train sped through the countryside, feeling better again. In her compartment, which was identical to the last sleeping compartment she'd occupied, the bed had been turned down, her nightgown—freshened with lavender-water and ironed again—had been laid out for her. There was a pot of herb tea, a plate of *kuchen,* and a vase with a bouquet of flowers on the little table, and a clever little oil lamp, mounted to the wall on a gimbal that kept it level, burned above the head of the bed. Not feeling equal, after that sumptuous meal, to tackling that Latin book on shape-shifters, she resorted to the frivolous and sensational stories in the magazines that had been left invitingly on the bedside table. Then, she slept.

When she woke, she was ready for the most complicated leg of the journey. Munich to Stuttgart, then the small local train from Stuttgart to Freudenstadt. Even traveling first class, with porters and railway employees at her beck and call, was not going to be easy alone, but she was rested and ready for it. *Much* readier than she and Hans had been, although at least from Freudenstadt to Stuttgart, they'd had the help of two fellow Elemental Masters—a Water Master in Freudenstadt, and a Fire Master in Stuttgart. She probably could have sent telegrams to them, asking for their aid again . . . but money made that unnecessary, and she was reluctant to disturb them when she had much more mundane help at hand.

But then, the train began to slow. By the time she reached the dining car for breakfast, it had completely stopped.

"There is trouble on the line," the steward told her, as he handed her a menu. "Some sort of accident, I believe. We will be about three hours late, the engineer tells us." Then he smiled at her. "Do not concern yourself, good lady. This train is completely safe."

She made herself smile at him. *It isn't the train I am worried about,* she thought unhappily. *It's me.*

3

THE train had been stopped for an hour, and the steward kept coming around urging wine and beer, and even stronger drinks, on the passengers in the parlor car. To Rosa's mind, this did not bode well for whatever was causing the train to remain stationary. After about an hour, some of the gentlemen got up and went to the door of the car. By this point, Rosa herself was more than curious enough to do the same.

The steward was not brave enough to try and interfere with the men, but he did interpose himself between her and the door, as the first of the gentlemen demanded—and got—the door open and the steps lowered. "Dear lady," the steward said, trying to forestall her. "Please sit down, there is nothing to be concerned about."

"I am sure there is nothing to be concerned about," she replied, making it very clear with her posture that she fully intended to get down out of the car and find out what was going on herself. "But I am not accustomed to sitting about for hours at a time. I require some air. I shall have a little walk."

The steward looked very much as if he wanted to stop her, but what could he do? He was only the steward, and she had enough money to be riding in the most expensive way possible. If he objected, while the other gentlemen might support him, it was far more likely that they would support her on the basis of class. He let her pass, and she alighted from the car onto the ground beside the track. They were in the midst of a forested part of the land—possibly some great estate's private forest, in fact—and there was no sign of a road or so much as an animal track on this side of the train. But she immediately felt at ease; *this* was where she belonged, with proper earth beneath her feet, and nothing artificial but the train and its track for miles. There was little or no wind, and beneath the smell of hot metal and coal smoke was the scent of good, green, growing things. She heard the calls of dozens of birds—finches, sparrows, a raven, rooks, starlings, tits, warblers, pipits—there were probably more birds than that out there, but the chatter of the people going to see what was wrong drowned out their songs as she approached the gathering crowd.

She was by no means the only person on the train who was curious enough about what was going on to have alighted—in fact, the passengers from the more crowded cars seemed to have taken this as an excuse to escape the crowding. There were four men from the parlor car, and many other men and a few women from second and third class making their way alongside the stopped train on this side. As she passed the great steam engine, waves of heat radiated from it, and she looked up at the cab of the enormous construction to see the crew sitting at what must be rare leisure, only occasionally throwing on a shovel-full of coal to keep the fires stoked.

Then she was out in front of the train with the rest, and saw what had happened.

There was a tree down across the track—quite an enormous tree at that. It looked to be hundreds of years old, and its girth was tremendous. There were half a dozen men sawing and hacking at it, and teams of patient horses waiting to take the pieces away. It was very clear that the thing could not simply be cut in half and dragged off. It would have to be cut apart in several pieces, or the horses could never haul it away. It was obvious from the limited progress they had made that this was going to take a great deal longer than the three hours the steward had promised.

It was also clear—to her, at least—what had felled the forest giant. Smoke still rose from the splintered stump. It could only have been struck by lightning, but it must have been a massive blast. Now—that was very suspicious to her mind. She had spent most of her life in the Schwarzwald, and she had never seen a lightning strike that powerful that was directed to the *base* of a tree rather than the top. She wanted to get closer, but could not think of a way to do so without drawing the ire of the working crew.

As she stood there at the back of the crowd, staring in astonishment and growing suspicion, a low voice spoke in her ear. "If I might trouble you for a moment of your time, Earth Master?"

The voice was male, and spoke German, and the fact that the speaker had identified her as an Earth Master came as a shock. She turned quickly. Immediately behind her was a tall, lean, pale-blond man with a pronounced jaw, little round wire-rimmed spectacles, and an extremely worried expression. She identified him immediately—not that she knew him, but she knew *what* he was. The green swirls of Water Magic surrounded him in a simple shield. Too simple a shield for him to be very powerful.

Water Mage. Not a Master. Not that there was anything wrong with that! Plenty among the Bruderschaft were mages rather than Masters, and the specific and skillful application of a little power could get as much done as brute force.

Things were going a little faster than she liked. She hadn't even had time to analyze the downed tree, and here was an unknown Water Mage addressing her. On the other hand, maybe *he* had exactly the information she was looking for.

She nodded at him, and inclined her head back along the train. Once they got past the engine again, they were alone—everyone that was curious enough to go to the front of the train had gathered in a crowd there, drawn together by the universal urge of people who do not have to do a particular piece of manual labor wishing to watch someone *else* do it.

"What can I do for you, sir?" she asked politely. She was not particularly concerned for her safety; invoking lightning was not a Water ability. And given that he was, by her standards, a distinctly *weedy* young man, she had no doubt she could best him in a direct confrontation. His own sheer astonishment that she could and would deliver a good punch to the chin would allow her to get back to the safety of the parlor car before he recovered.

"It is what I can do for you, Earth Master," he said, looking as if he was trying very hard to be brave. "That tree coming down was no accident. It was meant to stop me."

She blinked at him. "And whoever it was needed to stop you so badly he stopped an entire train?"

The young man swallowed hard. "I was sent to Vienna to discover, if I could, the identity of an Air Master that had gone to the bad. I did so—but in the process, I myself was discovered. I fled on this train before I could send a telegram to the Master of the Munich Lodge, Graf von Stahldorf. I thought I had escaped, but it is clear the man intends to stop me before I can reveal his identity, and yes, he was fully prepared to stop an entire train, and perhaps even slay innocents in the process. I must tell—"

Evidently his intention was to tell her the man's name. She had a much better idea. "Say no more," she said firmly, and let her sense of the Earth find the nearest game trail. "Such a fiend is too dangerous to be left at large. We must deal with this now."

"But dear lady—" he began, startled. This, clearly was not what he expected to hear from her.

"Pray do not interrupt me," she snapped. "I am a Hunt Master of the Schwarzwald. I know what I am doing. I need but a moment. Follow me."

With that, she strode purposefully to the door of the parlor car. "Wait here," she ordered him, and mounted up into the car. Once there, she secured her portmanteau from the overhead rack—or rather, the steward hastened to get it down for her—and she retired with it to the bathroom.

Knowing that her petticoat and dress would be freshened by the maids on the sleeper trains, she had secured most of the useful objects she usually wore inside the hidden compartment at the bottom of the bag. She extracted them now, distributed them about her person where she could reach them despite her gown, and then returned the portmanteau to the rack. Or rather, allowed the steward to do so.

"We are likely to be here for much longer than two more hours," she told him, quietly. "If I sit here listening to the gentlemen bluster and the ladies fuss like a coop full of hens, I shall be strongly tempted to scream. I shall take another brief walk."

When the steward looked aghast, she added, "I am accustomed to riding hunters in the Schwarzwald for at least three hours daily. An hour walking will do me no harm."

At that, he looked both mollified and impressed. She knew that he assumed, of course, that if she was riding hunters, she must be very wealthy, and was riding them all over some vast estate. Once again, she spoke pure truth, as a magician must adhere to; she *did* ride hunters all over the forest, often for far longer than three hours at a time. It was not her fault he made some other inference from her words.

The steward made no other effort to prevent her from descending from the carriage. She walked very close to the car to prevent him from seeing she was with a gentleman— and the gentleman himself did the same. Only when they reached the baggage car did he come up beside her. "Your pardon, Hunt Master, but what do you intend to do? This man may be Air, which might seem insignificant to you, but he is immensely powerful. If he had not been—"

She interrupted him impatiently. "If he had not been, he could not have hidden himself in Vienna. Please do not tell me my job, sir, I beg you. I have been in the tutelage of the Schwarzwald Bruderschaft since I was ten years old. If he dropped that tree *here,* he cannot be miles away. He must have coerced some very powerful Air Elementals to bring him here ahead of the train so that he could ambush you.

He would know, of course, that you would recognize his handiwork and immediately get out of the vicinity of the train in order to protect the innocents."

Now that she knew what he was, she was "reading" him—just to be sure this wasn't some sort of two-tiered trap, intended to snare *her* rather than him. She was not as good at reading Water as she was Earth, but she thought he was just what he appeared to be. Only one way to be sure, however.

She let her sense of the Earth tell her where there was a game trail ahead of them; after a moment with her eyes closed, feeling the way that life threaded its way through this forest, she found that there was one, just past the end of the train. She led the way down to it, glancing back at him.

He looked like a worried hound, which would have been comical had the situations not been so serious. "Yes, that is so, and I was going to ask you to guard them as well—"

"They will be safer with both of us away from the train," she said firmly, parting the branches to show the trail. "Come along."

The real test of him would come if she could just find a stream. Even a little trickle of water would do. She let her senses move ahead and—yes. Only a few hundred yards away. She hurried, and he scrambled along behind her, obviously not used to walking in the woods. Well of all of the Elemental Magicians, it was Air and Fire that did best in cities—with Water not too far behind, provided it wasn't an industrial city. She reached the tiny thread of a brook well ahead of him, and waited to see what would happen when he reached it.

She was pleased to see that the little undines immediately reached out of the water for him, wrapping their naked arms anxiously about his ankles. *They* knew he was in trouble, and he looked down at them and smiled weakly.

"Act as if you were making a stand," she told him, and when he straddled the brook, in order to increase the amount of power he could draw from it, she added. "Don't try to hide."

"I'm not sure I could hide from him if I tried, good lady," the Water Mage said, his voice trembling a little. She didn't blame him. After all, he was facing a Master powerful enough to draw down a truly terrible lightning strike, one that had felled a tree with a girth of several yards. He was but a mage, and Water was not much protection against lightning.

And that was the point where she *felt* their enemy. He was coming through the forest, not from the train tracks. She hadn't expected that, but—fine. She stepped back toward the tracks so that the young Water Magician was between her and the approaching Air Master. She wanted him to concentrate on the young man, and disregard her. She hoped that he would not even notice she was an Elemental Magician, much less that she was another Master.

The Air Master wasn't being subtle. Long before he got close to them, wind began to make the trees around them toss in something that was very near to a gale. She readied herself, prepared if she was needed to cast her shields over them both. Earth shields were the strongest there were. No Air Master, no matter how strong or skilled he was, would ever be likely to crack them.

Holding the power of the storm in their hands, even the best-intentioned of Air Masters tended to arrogance. That was what she was counting on. He wouldn't be content to strike from afar. He would want to see his victim's face, and savor his terror. And as a female, it was likely that she would be utterly dismissed from his mind if he even noticed her.

Still, in case she was wrong, she attuned herself very closely to the feel of the earth under the young Water Mage. She knew from experience that before lightning could strike him, the ground around him would be energized. She should have just enough time, if that happened, to throw up her shields.

But she had read the Air Master's character aright. As the wind howled among the trees, he came sauntering up the game trail, looking for all the world as if he was taking a stroll in a Viennese park rather than what was essentially wilderness.

He was the sort of Nordic blond that artists used for models for heroic statues, but the expression in his eyes was enough to make her shiver. This man was a cold killer. And he enjoyed it. He was dressed conservatively, but well, which was wise of him. There was no point in being ostentatious when you were an Elemental Master who had gone to the bad, unless you were born to a title. This way he would blend in seamlessly with the rest of society, hiding in plain sight, and only using his powers when the only person who would see them in action would soon be dead.

The Air Elementals whirling around him bore expressions of pain, and their postures were tortured. That was the last thing Rosa needed to solidify her decision. This man was everything the Water Mage claimed, for only an Elemental Master who was truly evil would cause his Elementals to suffer so.

He raised an eyebrow at the sight of the two of them. "What, Fritz? Hiding behind a lady's skirts now, are you?" He glanced aside at Rosa, then let his look linger, and licked his lips slightiy. "Well I am glad you brought her. I shall enjoy her when I am d—"

He stopped speaking, and stared down with an expression of disbelief at the knife now quivering in his chest and buried in his heart. He had been so busy concentrating on his boastful speech he had never noticed her hands moving in her skirt.

The gale—stopped. The Air Elementals broke free of his coercions with gasps of joy, and fled. He brought both hands up to his chest, then held them out and stared at them, wet and red with his own blood.

Then he crumpled.

Rosa shook her head as the Water Mage—Fritz?—stared in as complete a state of disbelief as their enemy. "They never do think to guard against a simple physical attack," she said aloud. "Do take note, if you intend to be serving your Lodge in this way in the future."

She walked over to the corpse—as an Earth Master, she *knew* when someone was dead, and he had been dead before he finished falling. She removed her knife and wiped it carefully on his fine coat, making sure to get all the blood off. She sheathed it again in the sheath on her leg. It was where she usually wore her knife, but this gown had been tailored so that she could reach it through a special pocket on her skirt and a slit in her petticoat. She wondered what the maid had made of that—

Well, probably nothing. Some women, she had been told, kept most of their money in a purse hung beneath their petticoat rather than in their reticule. Presumably they, too, reached what they needed through cunningly concealed slits in their garments.

Then she put her hand to the ground, stilled herself inside, and called silently for a specific sort of Elemental. What she needed would be large and . . . somewhat amoral.

"What are you—" Fritz choked out. She glanced at him. He was as white as snow. Evidently he had never seen anyone die before. Or if he had, it had been genteelly, in a bed, with no violence.

Lucky Fritz.

"Hush," she said, gently, as she heard the sound of heavy hooves approaching. "It is not wise to bring yourself to the attention of what I am summoning."

The minotaur did not so much *appear* as *loom*. They had plenty of warning, hearing him crackling and thudding through the underbrush, but still, his appearance came as a shock. He seemed to somehow resolve out of the leaves and branches, but when he did, he was very *present*. He was roughly seven feet tall, and he gave off a scent of heavy musk.

But he bowed his heavy head to her, acknowledging her power as Master and Hunt Master. *"Lady,"* he rumbled. *"You call. I come."*

Behind her, she could hear Fritz's teeth chattering. Well, they should. Though a lesser being than the Wild Hunter, the minotaurs were similarly Great Ancient Things, and were not to be trifled with. Fortunately, what she was going to ask him to do would please him.

"Please to take this meat away," she said, gesturing at the body.

The minotaur took a long, slow look, and began to chuckle, with a sound like distant thunder. *"I have leave to do as I please?"*

"You have leave to do as you please," she affirmed.

The massive creature bent down, picked up the body, and tossed it over his shoulder as if it weighed no more than a sack of grain. He retreated again into the forest, and then—into wherever it was that such creatures dwelled, when they were not actually *in* the world.

At any rate, the footsteps faded into the distance much faster than they "should" have done.

Rosa turned to see that Fritz was staring at her, aghast.

"That was a—" he spluttered.

"Yes, and?" she responded politely.

"But—but—it's going to—" he could not bring himself to say it.

"It's not *human*," she pointed out, with impeccable logic. "It's not cannibalism. And now if that evil man had allies, they will neither be able to find out what happened to him, nor who slew him. Nor will the human authorities ever find a body or connect his disappearance with us."

It was cold, calculating logic, the sort that Rosa had been forced to many times as a hunter and Hunt Master. She was sorry she had to force it on this poor young man, but . . . well . . . he had to learn some time.

She read the thoughts as they passed through his mind on his face, and finally saw his expression settle into resignation. "I don't like it—" he muttered.

"I hope you don't think I do," she said tartly. "I would rather your enemy had been brought to answer for his crimes before the Court of the White Lodge. But this is why I am a Hunt Master; sometimes one is forced into positions like this, and when one is, one had better be prepared to cover all consequences."

He heaved an enormous, shuddering sigh. "I hope, then, I may never become one."

"So do I," she replied, sincerely. "So do I. Now I think we should go back to the train." She had a strong need for a glass of wine and perhaps a slice of cake.

It was well after dark by the time the train reached Munich, and she had long since given up any hope of catching the night train to Stuttgart. The steward had become increasingly anxious as the train had remained stationary and his monied charges had become restive. The cooks had been pressed into creating more food with what had been left on board, and the steward himself pressed more and more liquor on the passengers until the men, at least, mellowed. By the time they reached Munich, several were verging on tipsy. Rosa would have been amused, if she had not been concerned for herself.

Now, Munich was in Bavaria, and Bavarians liked their green spaces. Although Rosa could never have *lived* there, she knew she would be able to tolerate staying overnight. And once again, money would make things easier than if this delay had taken place on the outward journey; the fact that she was traveling first class meant that she would have plenty of help finding a taxi, and a hotel. But even with that help, this was going to be wearying at best, and would add one or two more days to a journey that was already too long.

She'd had several hours to contemplate her actions regarding the renegade Air Master, and no matter how she considered her situation, she could not come to any other solution than the one she had taken. So be it. He had not been the first rogue magician she'd been forced to kill in cold blood, and he certainly would not be the last. Her first had been when she was only fourteen years old; although she had been with a Hunting Party and was not even close to being a Hunt Master, it had been her hand that had struck the blow. She could not regret it. The Fire Master had been within moments of murdering her mentor, her second father, Gunther von Schwarzwald. The wretch had, as had happened time and time again, dismissed her as unimportant, a mere female child, and had allowed her to get behind him. The silver ax that took off his head from the rear didn't care whose hand wielded it.

She could not regret that, and did not regret this.

She descended from the railway carriage, already braced against the stifling weight of the railway station, and the faint sickness of the earth beneath it. She pitied any Air Master that had to pass through a station; the smokes and soot would be as nauseating to him as industrial and urban poisons in the earth were to her. But her shields were good, and she was as well rested as someone could be after a long journey, so for now the station didn't really affect her.

Taken impartially, the place was very dramatic—the great black dragons of the engines with their trains of cars, the smoke, the gas and electric lights reflected in the high, windowed ceiling—the people looking very small inside a place meant for "creatures" much larger than human. She wished she was an artist; such a scene would make for a fine, moody painting.

She waited patiently beside the parlor car as porters appeared with the first class passengers' baggage and the owners of said baggage sailed off to their carriages or taxis like generals leading troops. Eventually a porter appeared with her baggage on a trolley, and one of the conductors approached to give her much needed direction. At this point, she had no notion of where to go, and would welcome his advice—even if he was probably going to be paid by some hotel to recommend it. Any direction was better than none.

But then, something altogether unexpected occurred.

Just as the conductor began to give her advice on hotels, a handsomely dressed young man approached them both. He wore an immaculately tailored suit with a brocade weskit beneath it, a white shirt and conservative tie. He himself was lean and dark haired, with muttonchop whiskers and a small moustache. He stopped at her side, with a slight bow in her direction. "I beg your pardon for interrupting, dear lady, but would you happen to be Frau Rosamund von Schwarzwald?"

Blinking in utter astonishment—even more so when she realized this young man, by the energies flowing around him, was a Fire Mage—she acknowledged that she was.

The fellow clicked his heels together and bowed more deeply to her in the Prussian manner. "I am Graf von Stahldorf's private secretary. The Graf is a great friend of your father, Gunther, and would be exceedingly pleased if you would be his guest tonight rather than putting up with the dubious comforts of a hotel." He reached into his coat and produced a square of pasteboard. "My card."

Rosa took it. It certainly was the card of the Graf's private secretary, the Honorable Rudolf Weiss. At least, as far as she could tell. And the young man knew Gunther's name and certainly was a Fire Mage. She vaguely recalled that the Lodge Master of Munich was a count. "The Graf has sent his carriage," the young man continued. "If you would care to accompany me?" He waited a moment, then added, "The Graf also regrets to say that the Hunting is poor hereabouts, and hopes that will not deter you from becoming his guest."

Well that decided her. *The Hunting is poor* was the password from one Hunt Master to another to say that things in the area were quiet. (Conversely, *the Hunting is good* meant the opposite, and that any magician should take great care lest he attract attention he would not want.) "Thank you, Herr Weiss," she said with all the dignity she could muster. "The Graf's kindness solves many problems." With a nod of thanks to the conductor, Herr Weiss beckoned to the porter to follow, and they made their way out of the station.

Munich, it seemed, was even greener than Vienna. She felt a sense of relief pass over her as they reached the street and exited the enormous train station. The feeling of healthy, growing spaces all around her was palpable, even though she couldn't actually see much of them except for the silhouettes of trees in the dim lighting from the handsome streetlights. But there was a good, fresh breeze, blowing away the exhaust of the motor-taxis, and it carried with it the scent of flowers.

There was an *enormous* carriage waiting at the curb, looking old-fashioned and quaint with all of the motorized taxis about it. Another relief, since a motorcar would have caused her a little discomfort; being that close to an engine was difficult for Air and Earth Mages. The wooden carriage pulled by four beautiful horses was highly welcoming. The young secretary handed her into it, then went to deal with the porter and the luggage.

And she discovered as she entered the vehicle that she was not alone. In the warm light from a couple of lamps inside the carriage, the young Water Mage from the train waited. "I hope you do not mind that I spoke to the Graf on your behalf—" Fritz said tentatively. He looked worried, as if he was afraid he had overstepped himself.

She laughed in surprise and pleasure to see him and hear

his apology, and settled herself into a plush velvet seat opposite him. "Not at all, in fact, it is I who should thank you! You know, you never told me your full name. I am at a disadvantage since you already know mine, it seems."

"The *Graf* knows yours," Fritz corrected. "I only described you and he knew who I was speaking of." His voice carried tones of embarrassment. "We never actually . . . things happened so quickly, and you took charge of the situation so . . . I still do not actually know who you are."

Poor man! It had never occurred to her that this city fellow might feel the want of finer manners than she was used to showing in an emergency. And when she remembered his discomfiture at the way she had simply taken over the situation, she realized that he had probably never had a woman take charge of matters before. That made her laugh again, as the secretary came back around and entered the carriage with them, seating himself beside Fritz. "If you would be so kind, Herr Weiss," she said as he seated himself. "Would you give the two of us a proper introduction?"

The carriage moved smoothly off. "Well, I can see how meeting over a corpse would not exactly be much of an introduction," the secretary said dryly, causing her to like him very much. "Fraulein Rosamund von Schwarzwald, may I introduce to you Herr Fritz Bern?"

"I am much better pleased to meet you now than I was the first time, good sir," she chuckled. "And these are far better conditions. You said a moment ago that the Graf knows my mentor, the Lodge Master of the Schwarzwald Bruderschaft, Herr Gunther von Schwarzwald?"

"They are of long acquaintance, and the Graf has wanted to meet you for some time," the secretary replied, leaning back into the comfortable cushions of the carriage, as she did the same. "You have something of a reputation, Hunt Master."

Perhaps once on a time she might have blushed at the compliment and felt unworthy of it.

Now she shrugged, diffidently. "I have had the best training," she pointed out. "And I have little or none of the talents one normally finds in an Earth Master. I am of little use in healing the damage done to the Earth by mankind, and my abilities at nurturing flora and fauna are no better than that of a mere mage. It seems I was meant for more martial duties."

"Well, if all of us had the same talents, surely some of us would be redundant," he pointed out, as the carriage rattled a little over an uneven spot in the road. "The Graf is conferring with your mentor even as we speak, and is conveying to him the wish that you might spend some time here before you continue your journey. Partly Lodge business, partly pleasure." The secretary raised a finger before she could object. "We are not traveling to his city apartments. His estate is just outside the city boundaries, and Earth Masters have spent a pleasant time there before. I will say no more about what the Graf wishes to speak with you about, because it is not my place."

She thought about the trip that remained before her. At least another day from Munich to Stuttgart, she would have to overnight in Stuttgart, for there were no night trains to Freudenstadt. Then from Stuttgart to Freudenstadt it would take another day, followed by wagon or horseback to the Lodge. . . .

And there was this, the fatigue of the battle—however brief it had been—was just settling over her.

"I think that might be wise," she agreed. And after all, whatever it was that the Graf wanted of her, she always had the option to say "no."

"Excellent." The young man seemed pleased. He might be Prussian in origin, but he did not seem to have that rigidity of outlook that so many of his countrymen had. "Now, the Graf wishes for me to note down an account of the events on the journey while they are still fresh in your minds. Would you be so kind as to tell me, both of you, how the combat came about?" He extracted a pencil and notebook from his breast pocket, and seemed ready to take notes or dictation. It seemed he was well used to taking such notes in a moving carriage.

"I believe Herr Bern should begin," she said, when Fritz hesitated.

"I traveled to Vienna on the Graf's orders, as you know," Fritz began. "I will not trouble you with my initial fruitless searches; I only struck the proper trail when I began investigating missing slum children. That was when I pieced together the description of the Air Mage who styled himself as 'Durendal,' and eventually tracked him to his home. I commenced to follow him in the ordinary manner without using any magic powers, and deduced his true identity—Herr Doktor Erik Reinhardt. Which was when I discovered—by being attacked—that I had not been as successful in evading detection as I had thought. I fled to the train station and purchased a ticket for Munich. Unfortunately it seems there was enough time for Durendal to track me, although I was unaware of that fact. I detected the energies of an Earth Master unknown to me as we left the station, but as the energies were located in the First Class coach, I had no way to make myself known. Then the train was brought to a halt by an 'accident' on the line. I disembarked with others to see what it was, and to my horror, saw the signature of our foe."

"And that is where I entered the story," Rosa said, and explained her part. The secretary merely nodded, although Fritz looked extremely uncomfortable when she coolly described eliminating the rogue Air Master.

She could not help but notice that the carriage traveled so smoothly that the secretary had no difficulty taking his notes. Either *he* had some Elemental power that made this possible—she detected Air about him, and he might have coaxed sylphs to steady the carriage while he wrote—or this was an exceedingly expensive and well-sprung carriage.

Probably both.

"Thank you, Hunt Master," the secretary said when she had finished. He tucked notebook and pencil inside his breast pocket. "I doubt I shall need any more information for the Lodge report than what you have supplied." He smiled. "The Graf will be asking you more questions, I suspect, but this is for the report he will require me to write."

A few moments later, the carriage commenced swaying and bouncing over the road in the manner Rosa would ordinarily have expected, which answered her question. But that also told her something else; that both the secretary and his master considered the report to be of great enough importance that it warranted the use of magic to make sure he got every detail clearly. That the now-deceased Air Master had been a person of some note was only a little worrying. Whether he had been a medical doctor or a scholar, he certainly would be missed. But he had never taken any sort of mundane transportation to get ahead of them, no one but she and Fritz knew he had been in those woods, and even if anyone else *did* know, there was no way to trace "Durendal's" disappearance to them. Aside from calling the minotaur, there had been no use of magic on her part at all, and minimal use on Fritz's part.

"I do not believe that the Graf will object to my saying that was neatly done, Hunt Master," the secretary continued, confirming her belief. "I have been in my master's service a very long time, and I cannot foresee any way in which this can be traced to you and Herr Fritz. Additionally, disposing of 'Durendal's' body—ah—*elsewhere,* has muddied the trail past unraveling." The young man gave a nod of satisfaction. "You certainly live up to your reputation."

"Thank you," Rosa said, pleased that he was now regarding her with the sort of slight deference he would give to someone slightly higher in rank than he was. Technically, he almost certainly outranked her socially. He was private secretary to a Count, which meant he was university educated, very likely the younger son in some noble family or other, and even if he had no financial means of his own, she, as the daughter of a mere village schoolmaster, was far beneath him. But power and competence counted for a great deal among Elemental Masters, and she had proved herself in his eyes, which was no small accomplishment.

She was, however, rather at a loss for polite conversation after that point. Fortunately, she did not have to supply any, for before the silence became awkward, the carriage turned into what shortly became a beautifully graveled drive, and pulled up in front of a handsome mansion, lit up for their arrival.

4

IT was difficult not to be intimidated by the sheer *size* of the Count's home. There were castles in the Schwarzwald, of course, but Rosa had never been in, or even very near to any of them. To be literally driving to the front door of one was quite out of her experience, even if it didn't look much like the "castles" she was used to seeing at a distance.

Rather than being vertical—taking advantage of the small space on a mountaintop—and sporting pointed towers on various buildings all linked together, this was a huge edifice of at least three stories, built all of a piece, and of a unified architecture. Not a castle at all, really, but a palace, of the sort you would only find in a city.

This one—at least as much as she could see in the darkness—was built all of cream colored stone, probably in the previous century or the early parts of this one. It looked very modern compared to most of the black-beam-and-white-plaster buildings of her beloved Schwarzwald, most of which dated back hundreds of years.

To Rosa's surprise, the Count himself was waiting for

them on the steps of his palatial mansion. He did wait for
Rosa to be handed out of the carriage by a footman before
greeting her, but—again, to her surprise—he greeted her as
if she was a favorite relative, and not as a very young lady
much his junior and *considerably* inferior in rank.

In fact, he first bowed and kissed her hand, then kissed
her on either cheek. She managed to control herself to keep
from flinching back in shock, and returned the favor, but
this was not at all what she had anticipated.

"Welcome, my *very* dear young lady!" he enthused, before turning to Fritz, and shaking the man's hand and utter-
ing a few words of congratulations and welcome. This gave
her a moment to collect herself and examine her host.

He was something of a puzzle. His upright bearing suggested that like his secretary, he was Prussian—but his exu-
berance was typical of a Bavarian. His expensive and
immaculate silvery-gray suit at least told her that he had an
income to match his title, unlike some nobles who were rich
in rank and impoverished by extravagant ancestors or
crumbling estates.

For the rest, he had a thick head of snow-white hair,
proving he was at least as old as her surrogate father Gunther, a neat little goatee to match, a pair of merry eyes behind gold-rimmed spectacles, and moved with a smoothness
and agility that belied his years. Then again, that was typical
of Fire Masters. There was a faint scent of amber about him.

While she was studying him, he finished speaking to
Fritz, and the young secretary, on some unspoken signal,
escorted Fritz inside the mansion. The Count once again
turned his attention to her.

"Would you care to come speak with Gunther before
you retire for some well-earned rest, my dear?" he asked, in
a quite kindly tone. "I believe that would put both your
minds at ease, and I should very much like you to be at
ease."

Now, many Masters were able to communicate across
vast distances, but she was not one of them. She had never
yet conquered the magic of using an obsidian mirror for the
purpose, and to have a Fire Master offer to exert his talents
on her behalf was very reassuring. No less so was the fact

that obviously he would not have offered to do so if he was not everything that he claimed to be. She relaxed a trifle, and smiled broadly at him.

"Oh, sir! I cannot imagine anything I would like better, and you are too kind," she said fervently. "Can we do so at once?"

"Immediately!" he exclaimed, and offered her his arm, as if she was the grand lady she had pretended to be. She took it, and the two of them passed between the pillars of the portico in through the double doors of his mansion.

If she had been less weary, she probably would have been dazzled, for she had never in her life even imagined a place as grand as this. It was every inch the baroque palace, with murals of sky and cherubs on the high ceiling, gilt and carving everywhere, crystal chandeliers boasting a fortune in candles in every one—and that was only the entrance. But he swiftly whisked her through the opulent spaces that he probably used for entertaining, and up a curved staircase into his private wing. Marble, gilt carving, and more shadowy murals greeted them, and statues, enormous vases, ornate furnishings, Turkey carpets—but lit only by the occasional oil lamp, so she only got hints of the lavish surroundings. At length he brought her to a small study, with floor-to-ceiling bookcases and plush velvet-upholstered chairs, where a fire burned brightly. He closed and locked the door behind them, directed her to sit in one of the chairs facing the fire, then made a series of unobtrusive gestures. She sensed the flow of warm and surprisingly gentle Fire energies all around her—caught just a glimpse of salamanders dancing in the grate, and then with a start of happiness, saw her mentor's face peering anxiously out of the flames.

His expression cleared immediately, and before she could say anything, he exclaimed, "Rosa!"

"Papa Gunther!" she responded joyfully. "I have a great deal to tell you!"

She glanced aside at the Count, who had seated himself comfortably, and made a little gesture that she should continue. "I can hold this connection indefinitely, my dear. Make your report. As one Hunt Master to another, I would appreciate hearing it."

She composed herself immediately, and began, starting with the moment she and Hans had arrived in Romania. The Count leaned forward and listened with interest, nodding with approval as she detailed how Hans had dispatched the nest of *vampir* females, and she had slain the male. He appeared astonished that she had had the temerity to summon a Lord of the Hunt, and tilted his head thoughtfully to the side as she described how she had taken out the werewolf. He chuckled, and exclaimed wordlessly when she told her mentor what she had told the Romanians.

"Well said," Gunther agreed. "Where the people still believe in magic, we need them to understand that as we protect them from the creatures of the darkness, we need them to protect us from those who do not understand that magic is only a tool. But what of Hans? I have your telegram that he will not be returning, but why?"

"He said it was that he wished to help the Brotherhood, and that there was much need of him there," Rosa said, as Gunther's image within the flames looked puzzled and concerned. "But I think there was more to it than that. It is very true that he can help them. It is also true that neither of our Brothers there are fit to be a Hunt Master, and we both know Hans is a fine Hunt Master, but as long as he remains with the Schwarzwald Bruderschaft—"

"He is unlikely to see as much action as a Hunt Master should." Gunther nodded, though he looked a little sad. "He will always be playing second-fiddle to those of us who are older or more skilled. Still—"

"I think also . . ." she flushed a little. "Well, there were several pretty girls in that village that were looking very fondly at him and he was not at all unhappy about that."

Gunther's face cleared, and the Count laughed out loud. "Old friend," the Count said, waggling a finger at him. "You will never be able to offer the boy anything to compete with a village full of pretty maids who think they've got themselves a magical knight in shining armor. And not a bad thing either, it's good for new magical blood to come into one of these places."

Gunther shrugged, with a rueful smile.

"Now let me tell you, old friend, all the details of the situation your young Hunt Master solved for me," the Count continued, and launched into the story of the rogue Air Master.

It appeared that the situation had been even more dangerous than Fritz had revealed—or perhaps been privy to. As she listened to the list of attacks and murders the man they had known only as "Durendal" had been responsible for, she was aghast. And it made her wonder—if she had known the whole of it, would she have been so ready to step in and intervene? As the fire crackled and gave off a heavenly scent of applewood, she watched as her "second father" nodded and frowned in concentration as he listened to the Count.

"If I had known this fiend was such a threat, my friend," Gunther said, his mouth set grimly, "I would have sent Rosa to you long ago."

"I am pleased you did not," the Count replied. "And I will tell you why. I fear that Durendal, being a Master of Air, had his Elemental slaves overlooking our every move. I cannot fathom how else he managed to uncover Fritz so quickly. Had you sent her to us, he would have discovered her, and she would have had a much more difficult battle. And had it not been that your young Hunt Master was on that particular train, and completely unknown to Durendal—well, things would have gone very differently. I am tempted to see the hand of Heaven at work."

"Who am I to guess at the workings of the Good God?" Gunther replied. "I am only to give my thanks that things happened as they did."

"With your permission, my old friend, I wish to thank your young protégée by entertaining her for some time before I send her back to you," the Count told him with a broad grin. "I warn you, if you deny me this, I shall be sorely vexed with you."

Gunther narrowed his eyes at the Count. "You have something more in mind than mere entertainment."

The Count pouted. "Really, old friend, how is it I can never keep the least thing secret from you? Yes, I wish to introduce her to others of our kind, and in other countries than our own." His voice took on an edge of steel. "There are others who need to know of her strength and ability. You know that I am right in this."

To Rosa's alarm, her mentor looked—distressed. "But—" he protested.

"But me no buts, my old friend," the Count replied, and turned to Rosa. "Tell me, my young Valkyrie. You have traveled to Romania to destroy the scions of evil, and you have fought another scarcely a few hours ago. Would you rather go back to your Schwarzwald and remain there the rest of your days, or are you willing to face the darkness wherever it raises its head, even if it means you must go far from the mountains you call home?"

She knew her answer; it felt as if she had been waiting to give it since she first realized she was meant for the Hunt. "I will pursue evil wherever it is," she replied, and turned to her mentor. "I must do this, Papa," she told him, so earnestly it almost felt like a prayer. "If the Good God had not meant for me to do this, why would He have given me the power he has? I could have been an Earth Master like Grossmutter Helga, but no. I am a Hunt Master, and my gifts are to cleanse, not to heal."

Gunther gazed at her from out of the fire, and his expression was a mix of pride and sorrow. "Very well. I could not deny the justice of Hans wishing to remain in Romania. I cannot deny the justice of this. I will trust in the Good God to guide both of you."

Rosa felt her throat close and her eyes grow hot and wet with tears. "Thank you, Papa," she said, softly.

"Hear now!" the Count interjected. "No tears! I have not told you what else I have in mind! Such things are much more pleasant, and near to the heart of every female I have ever met!" He reached out and patted Rosa's hand, silently placing a clean handkerchief into it so that she could dab surreptitiously at her eyes. "From all I have determined, Gunther, she counterfeited the fine lady very well on this journey back to you. She may need to do so again, in more discriminating company. I have no doubt she is an apt pupil; I intend to give her a few lessons, and the wardrobe of a lady of rank, as another weapon in her arsenal." His eyes

glittered again, but dangerously this time. "Durendal underestimated her because she was female. Many others will do
the same, the more so if they think she is pampered and
sheltered."

Rosa and Gunther both nodded, and she was not at all
averse to some polishing atop what she had already learned
of how to conduct herself as a fine lady. Wardrobe, however? How could he manage that in a few days?

"Heinrich, I will be the last person in the world to attri-
bute any weakness to my Rosa, but I am wearying, and I did
not just spend the last day traveling and dispatching a foul
magician," Gunther said, interrupting her thoughts.

The Count applied the heel of his palm to his forehead.
"Of course! How churlish of me! We will speak again tomorrow night, old friend. Meanwhile, I shall see to it that
your protégée is properly tended to. Good night!"

"Good night, Heinrich. Rosa, trust my friend as you trust
me. Meanwhile, rest well!" Her mentor smiled, and slowly
his smiling face faded into the flames until there was nothing but the fire, dancing over the logs in the fireplace.

"Now, my dear, I shall ring for a maid to show you to
your chamber," the Count said, patting her hand and standing up. He pulled on a velvet bell cord, and a maidservant
appeared almost as if she had been waiting outside for the
summons. "Gretchen, take the lady to the Forest room."

The maid bobbed a curtsey, and turned to go. "Run along
after her, my dear, and I shall see you in the morning," the
Count said, and made a little shooing motion with his hands.
Rosa chuckled, and followed the girl.

Fatigue descended on her like night over the forest, and
Rosa realized as she followed in the girl's wake that the
energy that had sustained her all day was finally running
out. She could not have retraced her steps back to the
Count's study if her life had depended on it as the girl led
her down halls and up stairs, and it was a very good thing
that the journey was relatively short. But when the maid
opened the door on a bedchamber and Rosa stepped inside,
she was so astonished by the chamber she stepped into that
for a moment she completely forgot her fatigue.

If, as a child, she had been asked to create the perfect

bedroom, it would have been something not unlike this. The carpet beneath her feet was as soft as moss, and was the color of moss, with a design of tiny flowers woven into it. The walls were covered with murals of a forest, with small creatures and birds scattered in and around the trees. The four posts of the bed had been artfully carved to look like tree trunks, and held up a canopy and curtains not unlike the sort of pavilion she had seen in her books of fairy tales as a child. The rest of the room was half-hidden in shadows, but from what she saw in the light from the lamp placed on a little table at the side of the bed, this was a room that had been tailor-made to please an Earth Mage.

Her nightdress was already lying draped across the foot of the bed. "Let me help you with your gown, milady," the maid said, putting down her candle, and reaching for the back of Rosa's dress.

Oh yes. Of course. I am supposed to be used to having a maid of my own, or several. Mindful of the station she was supposed to be, Rosa tamely allowed herself to be undressed, then helped into her nightgown. After a moment or two of feeling very awkward, the experience became a pleasant one. It was *much* easier to get out of the gown and corsets and complicated underthings with someone to help. And it was lovely to have someone to brush her hair for her. When taken down, Rosa's hair reached to her knees, and when she was tired, it was tedious to brush.

When the maid was done with her hair, the girl turned down the covers of the bed, and Rosa all but fell into the featherbed. She was not even aware of the maid blowing out the lamp and leaving.

She was awakened the next morning at what she *knew* was a most unfashionably early hour by another maid with a breakfast tray. As she was used to eating, this was a proper breakfast; cheese, liverwurst and schlackwurst, jam and butter and warm rolls, a soft-boiled egg, fruit, and a pot of good strong coffee. Before she had finished the meal, the girl returned with one of her hunting outfits from her luggage, cleaned and brushed and smelling of lavender. When she was done, the girl took the tray and set it aside, and assisted her into the outfit. "The Graf awaits you in the morning room," the girl said in a soft voice once Rosa was clothed and her hair brushed out and put up, with her hat nestled at a jaunty angle atop the crown of braids. "I am to show you the way." She showed no sign whatsoever of shock that Rosa was wearing breeches, which Rosa took as a good sign.

She followed the girl, and now that she was properly awake, she was getting a good sense for where she was in the huge mansion. She recognized immediately that they were heading for the back of the building, and was not surprised when the "morning room" proved to give out onto a terrace that overlooked the gardens. The Graf was sitting out on that terrace, evidently enjoying the view and a cup of coffee. Another chair and a second cup awaited her arrival on the small table between them.

"Good morning, Count von Stahldorf," she said politely as she came out on the terrace. The Graf stood, bowed a little to her with a twinkle in his eye, and gestured to her to take a seat, resuming his own as she did so. He poured a cup for her, and offered her cream and sugar. She took both, and they sat in companionable silence for a little while they both savored the view and the beverage.

The gardens were nowhere near as regimented as she would have expected. Oh, they were neat, and well tended—but they had been arranged in something like a bit of artificial wilderness, with ruined arches and columns among them. She liked it. She liked even more that she could sense, even if she could not see, that there were Earth and Water Elementals down there. He had gone out of his way to make his estate gardens into a home for them.

"Well, Rosa—I may call you Rosa, I hope?" he said.

"Papa said I am to trust you as I trust him, so you certainly should," she responded. She had liked the Graf as soon as she met him, and that warm feeling was only growing the more time she spent in his company.

"And you—well, you may call me whatever you wish," he told her. "Perhaps, as Gunther is your 'Papa,' and we are like brothers, you might call me—Uncle Heinrich?"

She felt her cheeks warm a little, and smiled at him. "If

that would not be too forward of me, that would suit me well, sir." She flushed a little more, very much aware of the honor he was bestowing on her.

"Excellent." He beamed at her. "We are about to engage on an adventure, one I would not place before you were I not certain you have a backbone of steel. But I promise you, the first part of this adventure will be quite pleasant, provided that your sensibilities are not delicate."

She looked at him with her head tilted a little to the side. "And what will that be, sir?"

"As it happens, I have it within my means to outfit you in quite the extensive wardrobe in a remarkably short time, and I am reliably informed that the garments I am about to offer you are such that would gladden the heart of any woman," he told her. "There is just one small fly in this particular pot of ointment, but I do not think that it is one that you will find distasteful—since I believe you are as practical a lady as your mentor is as practical a gentleman."

"What 'fly' might this be?" she asked, warily. If he was about to open to her the wardrobe of a dead woman—well, he would find that her sensibilities were, indeed, "not delicate." Where she came from, one often inherited a wardrobe. After all, what use had the dead for clothing? And why waste it?

"Oh, not yet. First come and view the booty," he said, setting his cup aside and rising, causing her to do the same.

She followed him back into the building, to yet another bedchamber—or rather, suite of rooms, one that was very near his study, if she had the layout of this palatial building correct. She thought it a little curious that this time they were accompanied by no servants—but then, again, there was something *exceedingly* peculiar about this entire "offer," and perhaps he did not want any witnesses in case her reaction was not what he had anticipated.

The suite was—well "opulent" did not even begin to describe it. She was rather glad she had been given the room she had, because she could not imagine ever feeling comfortable in rooms like these. They had been fitted out in the fashion of Versailles, or at least, *her* notion of Versailles. Dainty furnishings, gilt and pink and white, cushions everywhere ... not to her taste, not at all. But when the Graf flung open the doors of a gilt-and-white wardrobe to reveal the contents, she nearly lost her breath. Because the gowns inside were very much to her taste, and would have made her mother turn pale with envy. Even the faint perfume that came from the wardrobe, something rich and mellow, was something she would have worn.

She stepped forward, hesitantly, to take one gown out, a magnificent creation in brown silk twill with tasteful, restrained trimmings in a deep wheat-gold satin. And every feminine cell in her body yearned for it with lust.

Every article of clothing in that wardrobe, from the ball gowns to the most practical riding outfit, was one she wanted with all her heart. All of them were in colors she would have chosen for herself. And as near as she could tell, they would fit her with minor alterations, mostly taking in at the waist, bust and hips. As she held a handsome walking-dress against herself, she turned to the Graf.

"And what, exactly, is the defect in these wonderful garments?" she asked. "Because I cannot even begin to imagine what it might be."

"For any other woman but one as practical as you are, Rosa," the Graf said, without a hint of embarrassment, "The fact that they belonged to the mistress I discarded a week ago would be insurmountable—"

Her mouth fell open in surprise as she stared at him with wide eyes. And then—much to his evident relief—she began to laugh. A proper lady would have been shocked and appalled, of course. Or—to be more precise, a proper lady would have fainted dead away at the mere hint that "Uncle Heinrich" had a mistress. She was very glad that she was not a proper lady!

"One condition!" she chortled. "You must tell me the circumstances!"

He flushed and shook his head ruefully. "My dear 'niece,' you are a cruel woman. But I shall. I found the lady in question disporting herself with someone else. I wished him good luck with her, and consigned her to the devil."

"The more fool, she." Rosa was not at all embarrassed at the revelation that the Graf had taken a mistress. She would have been more surprised to learn he had *no* women. Life with the Bruderschaft had long ago inured her to things that would have given most young ladies hysterics. She was just surprised that there was a woman foolish enough to have given so obviously generous a 'keeper' cause to throw her over. "Well her being foolish is my good luck."

"I have a seamstress coming to take your measurements later today," the Graf said with satisfaction. "Come along, then, shameless child. I need to find out just how well you can learn to suit those gowns."

By the time they sat down to luncheon, the Graf was pleased to discover that Rosa knew how to counterfeit the part of a lady quite well indeed. Partly, it was because she was very observant, and could pick up what others did very quickly. Partly, it was because every so often the ennobled and well-to-do came to the Schwarzwald to view the scenery or hunt, and she had paid very close attention how they conducted themselves in case she ever had occasion to need to fit in among them—either as a lady or as a servant. Gunther had impressed on her from the time she was old enough to understand that she could never be sure where a Hunt might take her, and that she must be ready for anything she could imagine.

"Just a little polish, is all, my dear," the Graf assured her. "That is all you will need. To be honest, I know duchesses with the manners of a pig, and princesses who are barely literate." He rubbed his hands in glee. "This will be amusing for both of us. And I shall teach you to dance, of course."

"You will have to," she admitted, and shook her head. "I can polka, of course, and do all the country dances, but I fear I romp like a hoyden."

"Then romp we shall," the Graf promised. "I greatly enjoy a good country dance. But you shall also learn to waltz elegantly, and hold your own with any lady in the room." He turned to the manservant who had just presented him with the fish. "Berthold, tell the butler you are to play for us in the ballroom this afternoon."

The servant bowed a little. "Very good, milord," he said, and came to offer the fish to Rosa.

"And I shall need privacy so that Fraulein Rosa and I

can speak with some of the other Masters tonight," the Graf added, much to Rosa's shock—so much so that if Berthold had not reached out to steady her hand, she would have dropped her portion of the fish on the floor and not on her plate.

"It shall be done, milord," Berthold said calmly. "Will you need any of us to maintain wards? Or is the Durendal matter successfully concluded?"

Rosa could only blink in astonishment.

"It is concluded," the Graf told him, with great satisfaction. "But it will not do to drop our vigilance. I should like four volunteers to maintain wards."

"Very good, milord," said Berthold, and left with the remains of the fish.

The Graf turned to Rosa. "These people are not just my servants, they are my friends and some are fellow magicians. Those who do not *have* magic at least know of it. We have a bond of magical brotherhood, as well as that of master and loyal servant."

"Like the village, and the Bruderschaft," Rosa said aloud, realizing instantly what was going on. "Is this what you have modeled your estate after?"

"Exactly. Or rather, it is what my grandfather modeled our estate after." He looked pleased that she had deduced that. "As a result, I make decisions that other masters would not. I would rather that the second parlor go undusted for a day than find that when I need Heidi to stand as Earth ward, she is too tired to do so."

Well, that certainly went a long way toward explaining why she had felt so perfectly comfortable and safe here. This estate was protected in the same way that the great Lodge that the Bruderschaft shared was protected. It seemed a wise way to live.

"This is not the norm," the Graf continued, his tone cautionary. "Most of us will find ourselves forced to conceal our nature from those around us."

She shrugged politely. "Uncle Heinrich, I have done that outside of our village for most of my life. I find that is not such a difficult thing with only a little care. Most people see what they expect to see, and would rather *not* be aware that there is a world beyond the one they know."

"Well put. And I will not lecture someone who has been trained by Gunther on the caution you must take around outsiders." At that moment, Berthold entered with the next dish. "Now, let us finish our most excellent luncheon and speak of mere commonplaces. Tell me about this young man you left in Romania!"

The next several days were quite the whirlwind of activity, but by the third one, Rosa knew exactly what was going on in the Graf's mind. He was testing her, without being obvious about it. The "dancing lessons" in reality were tests of her physical stamina, agility, and ability to learn physical things quickly. The lessons in how to ape the great lady were similar tests—of how quick-witted she was, and how quickly she adapted to her surroundings. He took her shooting at targets; he took her out riding cross-country. And only when he was completely satisfied that she was everything that her "Papa Gunther" had claimed for her, did he admit to testing her. By that time, she felt she had earned that elegant wardrobe he was giving her.

"Why did you not test my magic?" she asked, finally, as they sat together in his study after a week of strenuous work. Truth to tell, she had enjoyed it. It was the first time in a very long time that she'd had her abilities tested without actually fighting for her life. Today had been particularly challenging, for once he admitted that he was testing her, the Graf had truly put her through her paces. She was pleasantly weary, and had enjoyed a hot bath before dinner. Oh the great advantage of the Graf's fine house over the Bruderschaft Lodge!

He shrugged. "Anyone that Gunther made a Hunt Master is not someone whose magic I need to test," he said candidly. "But a Hunt Master is more than magic."

She stretched out her feet to the fire. "A Hunt Master is one who knows not only how to use magic, but when."

The Graf smiled. She knew he had been discussing her

privately with other Lodge Masters over the past several nights. She wondered if tonight was the night he was going to start introducing her to them.

She was not left to wait much longer.

"The Master of the White Lodge of Berlin wishes to see you for himself, if you are amenable tonight," the Graf said, gesturing slightly at the fire.

"Will he be terribly scandalized by my breeches?" she asked, mischievously.

"Probably," the Graf replied serenely. "So by no means are you to run off to add a skirt."

She laughed. "Then I am ready."

The Graf directed his salamanders to—well, do whatever it was that they did to enable him to speak through the fire to another Fire Master. She leaned forward, and suppressed another smile when the monocled gentleman peering out from amid the flames nearly lost his eyepiece in shock at her attire. But he was gentleman enough to say nothing, and she remained quiet while the Graf made introductions.

Herr Bjorn Herbst, Master of the Berlin White Lodge, quickly got over her breeches as he quizzed her on her past Hunts. And just as quickly, he was satisfied. "I will be pleased to add you to our resources, Fraulein," he said. "It will be good to have someone we may call upon if the Hunt goes past the bounds of the city."

She made a little bow. "And if it does, I shall be happy to assist."

With that, Herr Herbst's florid face faded from the flames. "That went well," the Graf remarked. "Better than I expected. Care to brave another?"

Sensing this was another test, she smiled broadly. "As many as you care to," she said.

By the time the Graf confessed himself weary, she had spoken with around half a dozen Lodge Masters. All had at least come around to regarding her favorably by the time she finished speaking with them—but she knew that the Graf would not have been so foolish, or so unkind, as to attempt to put her in front of anyone who was likely to be outraged at the mere notion of a female Hunt Master. No, she suspected he had been carefully sounding the depths of his fellows, and had carefully picked only those he knew would be accepting. Anything else would have been a waste of her time, and theirs.

"Well now," he said, as he dismissed his salamanders and the fire went back to being a mere fire. "Are you regretting your wish to be of service outside of the Schwarzwald, or looking forward to it?"

She hesitated, thinking about the question. "Both?" she said at last.

"A reasonable answer." He leaned forward and patted her hand where it rested on the arm of the chair. "I think, my dear, that I will sleep soundly tonight, even if you do not."

5

IT was a restless night. Thoughts spun through her mind, keeping her wide awake for far too long. The bed seemed too warm, but when she threw off the covers, she quickly chilled, and found herself trying to get warm again. The night sounds seemed louder than usual. When she shut her windows, the room was too close. When she opened them, the breeze kept making the curtains move at unexpected moments.

Rosa was a little surprised. It had been a long and exhausting day, and she really expected that she'd fall straight asleep. But her mind was turning like a wheel, thinking about how, suddenly, she was no longer a Hunt Master in a small Lodge in the remote Schwarzwald. Suddenly . . . she was known in Berlin. And Hamburg. And Munich, Salzburg and Zurich. And Brussels . . . and Paris and Milan— fortunately those Lodge Masters knew German, because she certainly hadn't known French or Italian. It didn't seem real, and yet, it was all *too* real, and now that she had time to think about it, entirely overwhelming. She was just a simple schoolmaster's daughter from a little village in the forest! True, she had quite a number of successful Hunts behind her, but—how did that measure up against what these Lodge Masters had seen and done? They were all from great metropolises. Surely their experiences were far more sophisticated than anything she had seen!

She tossed and turned, and could not get comfortable as her unease—and yes, fear—began to grow. How had she ever imagined she could present herself to these men as someone they would *need?*

Until now these great cities were only places she had known on a map. And until now, she had thought that going to Romania, and helping out a tiny, tiny Brotherhood, was as far as she was ever going to go. She had assumed that she would go home, settle back in the Lodge, and that would be the end of that. She would return to her old paths, hunting out the dark things that crept into the forest, rooting out the predators before anyone in the villages of the Schwarzwald even knew they were there.

She had not really had a chance to *think* about all this, because she had been preoccupied with the Graf's tests. The other Lodge Masters hadn't been real to her until she had seen them in the Graf's fire, and spoken with them. When Gunther had asked her if she wanted to present herself to them—well, truth to tell, she really hadn't ever *thought* about just who and what she was presenting herself to. Somehow, in the back of her mind, she must have been thinking of them as little more than glorified versions of Gunther, with, perhaps, a few more Elemental Mages than the twenty or so that lived at the Schwarzwald Lodge. Now that she was actually thinking about it, she realized that these men each must have as many as a hundred mages answering to them. Maybe more. And the cities they watched over were—huge. So big it made her head spin.

She stared up into the darkness as it all finally settled into place. What had she done? What had she agreed to? How had she dared to put herself forward like that? She had *said* that she wanted this, but now that she had been given it . . .

I'm afraid, she realized, recognizing that cold, hard knot that suddenly appeared in her middle. The bed that had been too warm now seemed like ice. She pulled the covers up to her chin, shivering. And it wasn't just the enormity of her hubris that frightened her. It was that something she had been counting on to help her all this time was going to be cut right out from beneath her.

My one good defense will be gone soon. Because she wasn't going to be the underestimated girl anymore, not once she actually started Hunting outside the remote forest.

It would be sooner now, rather than later, that she would have a reputation outside the Schwarzwald. Possibly *far* outside the Schwarzwald. Rather than being ignored as an inconsequential female, when the enemy saw her, he would know her for what she was. The tales of the female Hunt Master would spread, and not just to the other Lodge Masters. Everything that walked in the shadows would learn who she was too—and know to watch for her. The distinct advantage of surprise would be gone. Whoever she faced would know she was not what she appeared to be, and would know not only that she was a Hunt Master, but that he could expect unconventional attacks and tactics from her.

When she had told her mentor that she wanted this—she hadn't considered that aspect of it. Now she could hardly believe that she hadn't thought it all through clearly. *Somewhere in the back of my mind I must have assumed everything would go on the same. That no one would ever know who I was or what I could do, that there was no such thing as a reputation. Just like at the train. I would just walk in, be ignored, do the unexpected and walk away unscathed.* She took a deep, shaky breath. *How incredibly stupid of me.*

Perhaps it had been because the Graf seemed to think so highly of her—after all, he had tested her personally, and as far as she could tell, he had been impressed. Was that what had made her so absurdly overconfident? It must have been.

It is impossible not to believe in what the Count believes in. And somehow he believes in me . . .

But now she was terrified that his confidence, and hers, had been tragically misplaced. And it was too late to back out now. Or at least, too late to do so without making a mockery, not only of herself, but of the entire Schwarzwald Bruderschaft. She'd tar *everyone's* reputation, but most especially that of her beloved mentor, Gunther, for Gunther was the one most directly responsible for making her what she was today.

It was bad enough that he had made her into a hunter, when most Earth Masters—and almost all the female Earth Mages she knew—were not fighters, but healers, nurturers, people who cleansed the forest, not with weapons, but with their gentle magics. He'd be questioned for not forcing her into the "proper" role, no matter what her talents actually were. He'd be castigated for making a mere female a Hunt Master. Just as bad, no one would ever trust another female to *be* a Hunt Master for—well, a very long time.

She felt sick. No matter what she did now, she was in trouble, and so was everyone who believed in her.

She wished, lying there in the dark, that she could take it all back, until finally the sleep that had escaped her ambushed her in the darkness.

The Graf let her sleep longer than usual the next day; perhaps he knew that she was going to lie there, sleepless, for a very long time. Had he guessed she was wrestling with regrets and second thoughts? Did he know how frightened she was, once it all came home to her? As she breakfasted, she thought that surely, he must. He was one of the wisest men she had ever met. And yet, when she finally joined him on the veranda, everything seemed the same. He greeted her as usual, and invited her to join him for another cup of coffee.

And the view over the gardens was just as peaceful as ever. Last night, both the interviews and the restless fears and doubts, seemed all part of a dream, or a nightmare, and his own commonplace greeting merely reinforced the unreality.

She sat down, and the two of them sipped in silence for a while. Birds sang in the bushes nearby, and the dreamy peace and gentle warmth of the sun on the veranda was no different from every other morning she had spent with him. Finally, she asked, apprehensively, "So . . . when do people start asking for me?"

She *almost* expected him to ask what on earth she was talking about. She'd have been relieved to discover it had all been some sort of dream born of an overactive imagination and perhaps something that had disagreed with her at dinner.

But no. The Graf chuckled, and glanced over at her, a great deal of amusement in his wise old eyes. "Who knows?" he replied with a shrug that barely creased the shoulders of his elegant coat. "First, they will have to get used to the idea of a female Hunt Master. Then, they will have to have a situation they cannot control with only the resources of their own Lodges. Then they will have to nerve themselves up to asking for help. Possibly tomorrow. Possibly never. Probably at some point in between."

Rosa felt a sudden sense of mingled relief and deflation. Had she been tormenting herself all night for nothing, then? Relief was uppermost. "Oh—" she said.

"Well, really, Rosa, how often does the Bruderschaft encounter something *truly* evil that requires all their forces?" the Graf said, reasonably. "Usually you are handling the sorts of menaces that a single person, or two, can dispatch. And the Schwarzwald, by its very nature, tends to attract dark things. It is the same in the great cities, except for scale. Not that the evils are greater—just the numbers of them are greater, but so are the numbers of magicians who counter them. What do all of you at the Lodge do most of the time?"

She had to laugh weakly. Now that she thought of it . . . well, no wonder her reputation hadn't gone much beyond the forest. "We hunt for lost children and sometimes lost adults. We track down dangerous beasts and kill them if we must. We see to it that the good creatures of the forest are nurtured. Really, combative magic is secondary to what we do."

"There, you see?" The Graf nodded wisely. "It is much the same in the cities. The men of the Lodge remain alert for magical danger, but for the most part they go about their business. They tend to their professions, they enjoy their families, they do all the things that any man or woman does. Thanks be to God, the great evils do not appear very often, even in the cities. No, you will go back to the Lodge, and back to your usual duties, probably for quite some time."

After all her worries and tossing and turning last night, that seemed a very attractive proposition. A little bit of a letdown but not nearly so much as it was a relief. Last night, she wanted nothing so much as to run back to the forest, to Gunther and the rest, and go back to being quite unknown.

And it might be the Graf was giving her a little hint that she should do that. "Well then," she replied, putting her cup down. "I don't want to overstay my welcome, and you have been unreasonably hospitable to me. When would you like me to complete my journey and move on, back to my people?"

"It depends on when you get homesick, my dear," the Graf replied, and reached over to pat her hand. "Our first days were mostly work for both of us, but I find that I am enjoying having the company of an intelligent female about, one from whom I must hide nothing, and one who is not either utterly dependent on my attention, or scheming how much she can get from me. I have many male friends and protégés, but you are the first female I could call friend since my dear sister died."

Rosa stared at him in a great deal of astonishment.

"What, you thought because I am wealthy and have a title, I live a life from the ending of a fairy tale?" he said, his smile turning a little cynical. "Oh, do not mistake me, I do enjoy life a very great deal! But everything in my life that is important to me is bound up with my friends and fellows of my Lodge, and the management of my estate. The rest—" he waved his hand "—idle pastimes. Pleasurable ones, to be sure, but idle pastimes. Not nearly as much intellectual stimulus as I would like, and I will tell you the truth, my dear, I am far, far too old to successfully lead a Hunt anymore. My days as a Hunt Master are behind me."

"You have not needed to be one—" she ventured.

"Because I always knew I could count on the Bruderschaft," he replied, and turned his gaze out toward the distant orchard at the end of the formal garden. "Truth to tell,

I was planning on calling on the Bruderschaft over the matter of Durendal, until you yourself neatly solved that problem for me. I *might* have been able to track and confront him, but Fire against Air is a chancy proposition, and even with the support of my Lodge, things could have gone badly for us. No, I would have needed you of the Schwarzwald."

"And we would have come," she said, instantly. "I know Papa would never have let you down. But is your Lodge so small, then?"

"It is—that is, there are many in the Lodge, but few who have any great power." He shrugged. "For some reason, the only family here in Munich that has ever produced strong Masters is my own. My sister, who died a few years ago, was a Master in her own right, and married a Master in Stuttgart, and relocated there—her husband is a fine fellow, a brilliant scholar who teaches at the university. Their eldest son, my nephew, is not yet ready to leave his studies there and join me here." He put his cup down and waved off the servant. "I will be glad when he does. It will be much better to have another strong Master here. Much safer for everyone."

She wondered now why he had never married. Perhaps he had not found a woman gifted with Elemental Magic with whom he formed a bond?

"Fortunately, the lad is both a Fire Master and a good steward to whom I will leave everything. I need not alter my style of living merely to create an heir." He laughed then. "And I had *none* of the trouble of having to raise him myself!"

She set her own cup aside. "Children can be tedious little things," she observed with humor. "I know I certainly was."

The Graf gave her a little quirk of a smile. "I have very little patience for them, I fear. Another reason why I never married. There's a blessing for you! Really, I am quite a lucky man, I have had all of the advantages of having a wife with none of the troubles and inconveniences. And when an inamorata gets tiresome, I get another, without having to be Bluebeard and conceal a room full of bodies!"

She had to laugh out loud at that. She was quite beyond being shocked by him saying such things. Truth to tell, she found it as funny as he did.

As he signaled to the servant waiting patiently behind them to pour them both another cup, she considered when she should return home. "Was there more testing of my skills you wished to do, Uncle?" she asked. "Or more lessons for me?" On the one hand, although she was really, truly enjoying the pleasures of the Graf's estate and wealth, on the other . . . she missed her "Papa."

"Oh, you could use plenty of polishing, if only to make the manners of a great lady second nature rather than something you need to think about," he replied. "But you could practice that all on your own. I am greatly enjoying your company, and . . ." he thought for a moment. "What would you say to inviting Gunther here, and having some of the others of my Lodge from the city join us for a time? I have not hosted a gathering that was merely social for far too long."

She felt her eyes widening. "That would be—quite amazing, Uncle. I have never taken part in such a gathering."

"Well, there will be all sorts of people here. The house can hold quite a number." His eyes twinkled at the understatement. "If this were a 'proper' gathering for someone of my rank, it would be nothing but boring members of my own class, but fortunately it will not be anything of the sort. I shall have tradesmen, professional folk, farmers, even an entertainer or two as my guests. You needn't try to be anything other than yourself, and they will all be mages, so there will be no need to watch your speech. I find these gatherings highly entertaining, and if it had not been that I had my—lady-friend—installed here, and it would have been impossible for them to be at ease around her, or for her to restrain her shock at such a mixed and mismatched company, I would have had one long ago."

Rosa beamed at him. "In that case, oh, please! I should like that above all things!"

"I hope you will, my dear." There was something odd about the way he said that. She wondered what surprise he was about to spring on her this time.

It seemed that this, too, would be another test.

Rosa stood in front of the wardrobes and stared at the contents in dismay. Until now her clothing selection had been simple: either what she always wore, or her one good gown. And she had greatly enjoyed trying on all the wonderful things she had "inherited" for the fittings. But she was expected to tell her maid what she would want to wear to greet the incoming guests and she had absolutely no idea what to tell her.

The maid, Marie, who had been the lady's maid for the Graf's inamorata, entered the bedroom to find her still staring in confusion. Until now, she had not attended on Rosa; Rosa's few needs had been taken care of by one of the housemaids. And Rosa had been uncertain whether or not she was included in the Graf's "family" of servants—who were all aware by this time of what, exactly, she was.

But when Marie saw her standing in front of the open wardrobe doors Rosa felt a surge of familiar power from her—Earth energies—and Rosa turned to her in relief. Marie was one of them after all! "Marie!" she exclaimed, about to confess her problem. But Marie, it seemed, had already guessed. Rosa didn't need to get any further.

"We have plenty of time, my lady," Marie said serenely— and with a faint French accent. "I realized that the Count is insufficiently educated in the finer points of Service and Fashion both, and would probably not be aware that you needed both assistance and education, if you will pardon my audacity. If I may be so bold as to explain the proper dress for every occasion?"

"Oh *please,*" she begged, sitting down on the bed.

What followed was an enlightening education on a fine lady's wardrobe, as Marie deftly reorganized the garments in their wardrobes by purpose. "These are morning gowns; they are to be worn to breakfast if you do not break your fast in your room, and for giving morning instruction to your servants—that is mostly the provenance of the lady of the house," here her eyebrow raised, "which Madame Giselle was not. These are the gowns you would change into for luncheon. These are the ones you would change into to make calls or receive them. These are tea gowns; if you were serving tea at home, entertaining company at tea, or having tea in the garden, you would change into one of these. These are walking gowns. This is a tennis gown. You would wear a tea gown to play croquet, but not tennis or badminton. And these are dinner gowns. Madame Giselle did not hunt, so there is no hunting outfit, but there is a riding habit, here, which she never used." A little smile. "This last is a ball gown, meant only for attending an elegant evening party or a ball. Madame Giselle had many ball gowns, but she only kept one here, as the Count did not have balls here."

"I can see the differences now, now that you have organized them," Rosa said with profound relief. The morning gowns were a more substantial version of a nightgown—more frothy than the dresses Mutti used to wear in the day, and more expensive by far. The luncheon gowns were similar, but the trimmings were more substantial and less frothy. Walking gowns were distinctly plain and sturdy, very like the gown Mutti had made for her. The riding habit was obvious. The tea gowns were all, universally, pale and lacy, but more elegant lace rather than frothy. The ball gown—well it was so incredible she hoped she would never be asked to wear it. Not only did it look horrifyingly expensive, she was certain she would look an utter fool in it. "But for this—this house party—"

"If this were the sort of house party that was not consisting of magicians, you would wear gowns in the order I showed you. But the people here will expect you to be yourself, and not change gowns as if that were your sole occupation during the day. *This*—" she pulled out one of the luncheon gowns "—will do during the day unless you go walking or riding, when you should wear whatever you wish."

"You mean, my working garb?" she asked, surprised that it would be suitable. Marie didn't laugh, but her eyes did twinkle a little.

"I expect they would be disappointed if you did not," she replied. "Then for dinner, this." She reverently pulled out a gown of a sort that Rosa had never seen before. It was of a dyed and printed brown and green velvet and silk, and flowed and draped—and truth to tell, it looked a little like something from an ancient time. "*This,*" she said, in tones that Rosa would have reserved for worship, "is a gown by the great couturier, Fortuny. It is worth a fortune. Madame brought it back from Paris, then never wore it, because she deemed the company here in Munich too provincial. You would look magnificent in this gown, my lady."

Rosa gazed on the dress with longing, but reservation. It was one that had not needed to be fitted to her as it was meant to hang loosely. "I doubt that anyone here could be called provincial, except for me . . ."

"Trust my judgment, my lady," the maid said persuasively. "You are a Hunt Master. You must look like a queen."

"No matter how I feel inside?" she asked, dryly.

"Especially if you do not feel like a queen," Marie told her, firmly, and selected one of her ensembles from the Schwarzwald to meet the guests in. This one had, not breeches, but a cunning divided skirt. It was very difficult to tell that it was not a conventional walking skirt. The skirt was of deep green moleskin, and she wore her hunting jacket of loden-green wool, moleskin vest, and rather than her plain linen shirt, one of Madame's more delicate shirtwaists. Marie brushed out and put up her hair, and after several moments of consideration, pinned her loden hat on.

"There," the maid said with great satisfaction. "Now, your role at this party is to be a sort of feted guest, rather than the Count's hostess. You should go to the veranda and make yourself comfortable there. The Count will bring the other guests to meet you, as you are the more notable. Or at least, you have the cachet of novelty."

Rosa wasn't quite sure how to react to that last statement, so she just nodded, left Marie to tidy up and continue organizing the gowns, and adjourned to the veranda above the gardens.

But the first guest to arrive was not one to whom she was a novelty.

She sensed him approaching before he even entered the morning room, and was up and out of her chair, running in through the double doors, and into his arms before he could say her name. "Papa!" she exclaimed with glee, as he put his arms around her and gave her a bear hug. "How are Mutti and Vati?"

"Your father is proud of what you did in Romania," Gunther chuckled, kissing her forehead before letting her go. "Your mother is beside herself to hear you are being entertained by a Count. The first and last thing she asked me was if he had any eligible sons or nephews."

Rosa sighed, blushing. "It is a good thing you didn't tell her how Hans was my age, or she would have had me married to him in her mind."

"She almost did even after I pretended he was a graybeard, like me," Gunther rumbled with amusement. Rosa was glad that he was amused, because she was not. "Don't frown so, child. All mothers are like that. Mine was. When I finally settled down with my Bertha, she still was not content until we had produced grandchildren. She took it very personally, too. At least your mother only asks if there are young men your age about, she doesn't hunt down every boy she sees to discover his marital status and offer to introduce you. I was more afraid of her than anything I met in the woods, shape-shifters included."

Rosa stared at her mentor; he was a tall, burly man, not unlike a graying bear, with a neatly trimmed beard and salt-and-pepper hair. Like her, he wore the most elegant version of his working clothes, a beautifully made loden-green jacket, vest, and trousers. He looked as important as the mayor, at least. She could not imagine him being so intimidated by his mother.

Then again . . .

"And you, Rosa?" he asked anxiously. "Are you still so pleased with Hans's choice to stay in Romania?"

"More than ever," she replied firmly. "I do not like that he was living so much in my shadow. Now he will be the best Hunt Master in those parts for at least a generation. And I cannot help but think he will have a great deal more to do than he would at home. That is, more to do *besides* flirt with the pretty girls."

Gunther laughed and they went out to the veranda and took chairs. "Were there that many, then?" he asked in amusement. "Or was it just that our handsome blond Hans attracted them like bees to honey?"

"That many," she said, sobering. "The area has been

dangerous, and I wonder at the number of 'accidents.' There
is some conscription as well to take away the young men,
but the place is so remote that they can hide in the woods if
they don't wish to go. I think that not all the wild animal
attacks are truly wolves and bears, and not all the 'accidents' when young men are farming or hunting are anything of the sort. As for the women, there is a reason why
the *vampir* chose that place. With so many unmarried young
women there, it was a fine place to find prey. Where there
was one *vampir,* there is probably more. Hans will be busy
for some time. You might want to send one or two of the
Bruderschaft to join him."

"I know just the ones." Gunther nodded. "Ulrich Bern-
wald and Walther Vogel."

Rosa smiled. Those were good choices, friends of Hans,
also single young men and the sons of Lodge members who
would be pleased to see them somewhere they would do
more than merely patrol the forest for weeks and months
on end. Like Hans, they were handsome, sturdy blond fellows who would be very attractive by reason of contrast to
the dark Romanians. It would do Hans no end of good to
have to compete for those young ladies too. "I like your
plans, Papa," she said. "Though Hans may like it less when
the maidens see how handsome Ulrich and Walther are."

Gunther might have said more, but at that moment the
Graf appeared with another guest. This one was someone
that Rosa was immediately comfortable with; he was
dressed like a gentleman farmer, and Gunther greeted him
heartily. They, too, were old friends, it seemed.

The more people that arrived, the more comfortable
Rosa became, rather than more apprehensive. The "gentleman farmer" proved to have a title as well as a fine manor
and a great deal of property, but he put on no airs at all.
Then came a medical doctor and his wife and three lively
children, a real farmer who was dressed no differently than
the fellow with a title, a handful of professors and scholars,
several also with titles, from the University in Munich, another family, this time of a lawyer, some artists, and some
musicians, Fritz Bern from the train, and Rudolf Weiss, the
Graf's secretary. Now she saw what Marie meant. None of

these people were anything like the well-to-do aristocrats on the train. They were here because of what they all had in common; they were all members of the Graf's White Lodge.

They all knew each other, and greeted each other with varying degrees of warmth; some effusive, some cool and calm, which only made sense. Not even all the people in the Schwarzwald Bruderschaft *liked* each other; there were some cases where people merely tolerated each other. But not all of them lived in the Lodge as Gunther and Rosa did. The Schwarzwald was very large, and those who did not get along with the others lived in their hometowns and villages, either with their families or by themselves—or out in forester cottages completely alone.

As Rosa watched the guests arrive, it occurred to her that the Graf was very lucky he had enough people in his White Lodge that liked each other well enough to supply such a big party as this one was.

It was grand that everyone here got along well enough to spend several days together. Those who did not get along in the Bruderschaft tolerated each other just long enough to gather for a Hunt and immediately departed—which tended to be just as well. It wasn't only *old* men and women either.

Of course, not everyone who chose to live outside the Lodge was someone who didn't care for his fellows. Perhaps once it had been possible to physically fit everyone in the Bruderschaft into the Lodge comfortably, but that was no longer the case. You would need a palace as big as the Graf's to do it now.

Rosa's morning and afternoon were spent in engaging in commonplace pleasantries with the others—where was she from, who were her parents, how long had she known of her powers. The children of the group were watched over by a nursemaid, and the Graf had seen to it that there were plenty of things for them to do. The laughter of happy children sounded over the grass—and they were far enough away from the adults that the *shrieks* of happy children merely made people smile rather than wince.

This was something she had never actually experienced before: an *extended* party. There had been parties and celebrations in her life of course, and many of them; the Bruderschaft was not a dour, grim lot. Christmas and New Year's Day were the most prominent times to celebrate, but there were plenty of other occasions for a feast or a cake, and *everyone* went to the villages for Oktoberfest and Maifest. But there was always a sense of *we must pack as much into this hour, this afternoon, this day as possible.* This was leisurely. The party had just begun, and there would be several more days in which to enjoy themselves.

Rosa found herself the object of attention from several young men; Fritz and Rudolf, and some of the students, artists and musicians. This was extremely flattering and, she found, very pleasant. None of these fellows were (as yet) intimidated by her despite her reputation, as her friends her own age were, probably because none of them had ever seen her at work, as the young men of the Bruderschaft had. All this might change the more they learned about her, but for now, she was going to enjoy being treated as—well—a *girl.*

Luncheon was alfresco in the garden. The afternoon was spent in croquet and tennis; Rosa had never played either, and was not sure enough of the rules to attempt tennis, but the croquet was a great deal of fun, since everyone played a friendly-but-cutthroat game, frequently sending balls flying out into the hedges and flower beds. The older children were allowed to join, and the best game of the afternoon for Rosa was one where she was partnered with a bright young girl with Water talent who reminded her a great deal of herself.

"My mother thinks a girl shouldn't go to university, but I am going," Hedwig said boldly. "They are giving girls degrees now! I want to study science so I can understand Water Magic better."

Rosa did not insult the child by warning her she must never talk of her powers in public. At her age, especially living so closely with those who knew nothing of magic, that would be second nature to her. "If I were to be able to do it over again, I would do the same," she told the child. "My father is a schoolmaster, so he taught me everything the boys learned, but I would like to know more about science.

Our powers have rules and logic, and the better you know how to discover the rules, the easier it is to do as much as you can with what the Good God has given you."

Young Hedwig beamed, and Rosa continued to encourage her—and made sure to let her know it was all right to say "Fraulein Rosamund said . . ."

She changed for dinner actually looking forward to it, whereas this morning she had been nervous and apprehensive. Marie came to help her, and put up her hair with a feather and bead ornament. "The rest of the servants say you are quite the toast of the party," the maid observed, then reached for a rabbit's foot and a little box on the dressing table, and to Rosa's astonishment, brushed powder on her face. Oh, she knew all about cosmetics from the advertisements in Mutti's magazines but she had never, ever used them before. Marie paused at the startled expression she must have been wearing. "Would you rather I did not—"

"Well . . . I suppose I had rather you taught me how," Rosa said after a moment. "I mean, I believe even the grandest ladies do this for themselves."

"So they do, and I knew you never had, since the cosmetics had gone unused," the maid replied. "Here, turn toward the mirror, and watch."

Rosa watched studiously, as the maid applied powder and added a little flush to her cheeks, a touch of red to her lips, darkened her lids a little, and lined her eyes. "Do I *need* to do this?" she wondered aloud.

The maid considered that. "Not here. But in some circles you might stand out if you do not, at least for dinner."

She could hardly recognize herself in the mirror. She thought she looked like some sort of creature from a tapestry or ancient mural. Marie seemed quite pleased with her handiwork, and Rosa didn't blame her.

"I am a work of art," she declared, "And you are as much an artist as any of the guests who call themselves as much."

Marie flushed with pleasure. "Thank you, my lady. May I say it is a positive pleasure to help you."

"You are making things that are very difficult, and foreign to me, ever so much easier." A thought occurred to her that made her frown. "Marie, now that your mistress is gone, what happens to you? You won't be dismissed—" A vague idea crossed her mind of hiring Marie herself. Though what she was to use for Marie's wages—and what she was to *do* with her at the Lodge was a real problem.

But Marie only laughed. "Oh, I am in the Count's employ, my lady. I serve all his ... companions. He does not trust the maids they might bring with them; really, how could he, considering what sort of household this is? I shall remain in his employ as long as he is the head of this household, and when his nephew inherits, I shall become the lady's maid to his wife when he takes one. Do not concern yourself for me! Seldom has there been a maid with a more secure position than mine."

Rosa breathed a sigh of relief. She should have known better, really.

"If I have a complaint, it is that I wish that the Count would find a proper *bride* for himself—" she shook her head. "I am very weary of serving spoiled and pampered fool after spoiled and pampered fool, not one of whom has the sense to see what a paragon our Master is." She gave Rosa a speculative look. "I don't suppose you—"

Rosa was scarcely the sort of girl who lived on romantic novels and was appalled at the idea of marrying a man old enough to be her grandfather. Heavens, Madame Giselle had probably been not much older than Rosa herself. Good marriages, especially in magic circles, were made between old men and young girls—and less commonly, old women and young men. But that was not why Rosa shook her head. "I'm sorry, Marie. First, I do not think the Count has any liking for the settled life. And second, what I do is decidedly not suited for the settled life."

Marie made a little face. "I cannot see why a woman would risk her life as you do. I could not do it," she declared. "Not for any amount of money or fame or—"

"But that is not why I do it, Marie," Rosa exclaimed. "I do it because it is something I must do, like the great old knights of the stories! *Noblesse oblige,* as they said in the ancient days."

"Well, I don't understand that," Marie replied after a moment. "But there it is, then."

The gong sounded for dinner, and Marie made a little shooing motion with her hands. Rosa turned with a care for her finery, and left the bedroom, relieved that Marie would be cared for, but wondering just what Marie *really* thought of her.

6

THERE was a new guest at dinner, a dark young man, ill at ease in a formal suit, who the Graf placed next to her at the table. The wonderful aromas wafting from the dishes on the sideboard were very distracting, but not so distracting as another handsome young man.

"I don't believe that I know you, sir," she said, as the manservants came around with the soup. She nodded at the fellow to indicate she accepted the soup, as she saw others doing.

"That is because I only just arrived," the young man replied, his hand twitching a little as if he would have liked to loosen his collar. She recognized his accent with a start as Hungarian. It seemed an age since she had last heard Hungarian, and yet it could only have been two or three weeks. "I came to make a request of the Count, but as I come from a remote region, I left more than a week ago and had not been able to communicate with him once I had his permission to visit. I gather that was before he called this gathering. I have been forced to borrow this clothing."

"Mine is equally purloined," she whispered in a conspiratorial manner, making him smile. There was something about this young man she liked immediately, although she did not know why. There was a faint sense of Earth Magic about him, but there was something else too, much stronger, that she couldn't identify. Whatever it was, the magic was actually part of him, the way it was part of an Elemental.

"I have no idea why the Count wanted me here tonight," the fellow continued, looking perplexed, as he accepted a modest portion of the soup. "I do not usually take part in entertainments like this. They are not what I am accustomed to. A good, big wedding perhaps, or a harvest fair would suit me better. I have never even worn a suit like this one before." He looked about to see which spoon the others were using before taking one up. "I am glad to be among friends, else I would surely be a laughingstock."

"I, too, am more accustomed to bratwurst and beer in a *bierhalle* at Oktoberfest," she agreed. He shared a relieved smile, and when the farmer on the other side of her said, "I would not turn down a good plate of sauerkraut and wurst right now," all three of them laughed.

The Graf must have had the sharpest ears in the world, for he spoke up from the head of the table. "Be content, my friends. I think you will enjoy this dinner, even if you are not accustomed to this sort of dining, and tomorrow dinner will be good, hearty fare and we will have our own little *bierhalle*. Complete with brass band! My people have a fine little band, and have consented to play for us all."

The farmer and the stranger both brightened considerably, and the three of them happily discussed peasant festivals they had attended in the past, joined not only by the *Landsknecht* who looked as ill at ease in his suit as the stranger, but by the musicians and artists. Rosa had the sense that the same sort of conversation was going on all around the table, but she could only hear those nearest her.

It did seem strange to be eating asparagus and duck cutlets and other delicacies while discussing the merits of the gallop over the polka, and the charms of sausages, beer, and various rustic cheeses.

When the dinner was over, they all adjourned to the

music room to listen to the performances of three of the guests—a remarkable pianist, a violinist, and a soprano who sang so beautifully it brought tears to Rosa's eyes. By that point, Rosa considered the latest arrival to be her new friend. They had been properly introduced, they seemed to have a great deal in common, and she knew his name was Markos.

"Markos Nazh," he said, which she knew was the proper pronunciation of what was spelled "Nagy," and literally meant, "the Great." He blushed when he said it, and she laughed.

"Do not take blame upon yourself for the *hubris* of your ancestors," she teased as they made their way to the music room. The new gown flowed around her in a delightful manner, soft and luxurious, making her feel unexpectedly pretty. She really was not used to thinking of herself in those terms, nor to trading banter with young men that was not identical to the sort she would have if they were her brothers. Was this "flirting"? If so, it was very exciting!

"My ancestors were not known for modesty," he replied, blushing still harder. "Bloodthirsty, yes. Hunters of *vampir* and other deadly things, so I suppose that both the pride and the bloodthirst are excusable."

"And you?" she asked, as they entered the room, and looked for empty chairs. The room itself was gorgeous, like the inside of a jewelry box, all gold and velvet and polished wood. A piano, some music stands, and chairs were arranged at the head of the room, with velvet drapes closed over the windows behind them and a huge harp pushed to one side.

"I would like to think I have the accomplishment without the overweening pride, though it is nothing to yours." They were taking their seats for the impromptu concert by that time, and it seemed rude to continue conversing, since the musicians were taking their places. Rosa did not often get to hear music, not even of the sort that the musicians in the villages played, and she settled herself to make the most of the opportunity, focusing all of her attention on the musicians.

And after the concert, they all retreated to a comfortable room, neither too big nor too small, too imposing nor too plain. There were comfortable chairs and settees with side tables scattered about the area, and servants kept them all supplied with things to drink. Rosa noticed that, while no one was abstemious, no one was getting tipsy either. This wasn't a room she had been in before, but it overlooked some of the gardens and the windows were open to a pleasant breeze. One of the professors and two of his students claimed her company before she could resume her conversation with Markos, and she realized that as the "prize" guest, she needed to spread her attention about. So with regret, she left Markos talking to the Graf and Gunther, and discussed Romanian customs—or at least the little she had seen—with the learned man and his protégés.

The servants came around again with drinks; Rosa was glad she had a good head for alcohol—which rather came with being German, she supposed, since beer was served at every meal but breakfast. "I prefer the Count's affairs to any other," said Professor von Endenberg, with a sherry in one hand, as his pupils invited her to sit with them. "One is not required to retire with the other men to the billiard room for cigars and port after his formal dinners. I dislike cigars, I have no taste for port, and I am bad at billiards."

"Is that what one does?" she asked, taking that proffered seat and settling back into the cushions of the sofa. "This is a new world to me. I have lived in the Schwarzwald for most of my life. I have never been at an affair such as this."

"Are you likely to be again?" the professor asked, looking alert, as if she had greatly increased his interest in her.

"The Graf seems to think so," she replied, and shrugged helplessly. "I am feeling very much the fish out of water."

"And I shall be happy to place you back in water." He all but rubbed his hands together in glee. "You have unearthed my private hobby, my dear young woman. I have been studying Society as if it was a foreign culture for quite some time now—though I dare not write up my findings, or I might just discover I have incurred the wrath of people who could make my position at the university very uncomfortable!"

"If this is no imposition—" she began.

"On the contrary! You give me an audience!"

The professor was now aware of her background, and shortly she learned just how happy he was to explain to her what a "dinner" entailed in any other establishment than this one—and everything else he could think of as well.

The professor had not exaggerated, for he proved to be the embodiment of everything she could have asked when it came to explaining how the Great and Wealthy did things—and why. This was a gentleman whose entire life was composed of studying, explaining, and understanding customs—and for her benefit he utilized all his expertise to analyze the customs of Society, and explain them to *her*, with the eager assistance of his pupils. She could not possibly have imagined a better education in the lives of the "upper crust."

The Graf and Marie had been a great deal of help in getting her started, and she already had an outsider's knowledge of Society, gleaned from her mother's magazines, romantic novels, and the newspapers—but she did not have the knowledge of Society from the inside. The professor and two of his noble pupils *did*.

She listened intently, mentally filing it all away with the other information she had, and rewarded him afterward with a minute description of the *vampir* she had destroyed in Romania, and how he had differed from other *vampir* she and the Bruderschaft had hunted in Germany.

"Chiefly in his nest," she said. "The one in Romania hunted to kill, and kept only the women he had brought with him. He ranged widely and alone. I am not sure what the women were preying on—animals perhaps, but more likely, minor Elementals. The *vampir* who had settled in the Schwarzwald stuck close to his nest, and rarely missed a chance to convert a girl to one of his consorts. The only time he did not, it was because he was interrupted in feeding."

"Were you ever able to save those girls?" one of the students asked, looking a bit disturbed. "The ones that the *vampir* didn't slay outright, I mean."

"If he had not made them drink of his blood, yes," she said, but it was with a frown. "The problem is making them understand that once they have been prey to a *vampir,* they can be called by any other, and the call is very seductive, like the call of the drug to an opium fiend." She thought it was not a good idea to tell these respectable gentlemen *why* this was so. That the call, and being fed upon, was quite *literally* seductive and literally addictive. *Vampir* magic—whatever it was—persuaded the women that the *vampir* was the best lover they had ever had, and after that, human lovers failed to satisfy. Formidable as her reputation was, she didn't think it would be enhanced by describing such a thing to these men. To the Graf, to Gunther, there was no question that she could speak the truth, and they would not think the worse of her for being so bold, even crude. But for these gentlemen—better the information come from another gentleman.

"What on earth sort of magic *is* that?" the professor wondered.

"I am not certain it is magic at all, at least not of a sort that I can recognize," she had to say. "While the Romanian *vampir* did have strong traces of blood magic about him, the German ones did not."

"Perhaps it is a psychical resonance?" suggested one of the students. "Some special power of the mind."

That triggered a discussion of powers of the mind that was entirely new to her—she had never been aware there *were* such things until now—that she listened to, rapt with attention, drink forgotten in her hand, until she found herself fighting off yawns. Looking around, she realized several of the guests had already excused themselves and presumably sought their beds.

As soon as an opportunity presented itself, she did that herself, made her goodnights to Gunther and the Graf, and went off to her room. She considered saying goodnight to Markos, but he was deep in conversation with the artists and the singer, so she didn't want to interrupt him.

She had chosen a moment to leave when the rest of the guests had either already gotten to their rooms, or were still deep in conversation. The vast building was curiously silent and mostly dark. During the day there was always work to be done, and always servants doing it, for the Graf believed in the saying "many hands make light work," and preferred that his staff have enough leisure to keep what magical abilities they possessed sharp as well as attending to their duties. Most of the staff had already gone to bed, and those that were still awake and serving would not be required to rise at dawn. As a consequence, the enormous manor seemed unpopulated, with only the few lamps showing the way to the guest rooms providing pools of dim light. She could have been wandering the rooms of the palace of the Sleeping Beauty in the old fairy tale.

She realized, as she reached her room and found her bed turned down and waiting, that she was both exhausted and elated.

For a moment, she could not imagine *why* she should be exhausted, until she realized she had been thinking harder tonight than she had in a very long time. Thinking was exceptionally hard work, harder than most people who got by on very little thinking realized.

As to why she was elated—well, that was easy. Although she liked almost all of the Bruderschaft, and loved many, not even her beloved Papa was intellectually challenging. Tonight she had been among people who were her equal or superior in intelligence. She'd had the most intellectually stimulating discussions tonight that she'd ever experienced.

As she stood there, just inside the door to her room, Marie appeared as if she had been magically summoned. That might have been mysterious, or given rise to suspicion that the maid was somehow spying on Rosa, but now that Rosa knew Marie was also an Elemental Mage, that ability to merely appear when wanted was no mystery. The maid could even have been napping on the settee in the sitting room, but the moment she sensed Rosa's powerful Earth energies nearby, she'd have awakened.

Marie stood beside the dressing table, and Rosa moved to her, and into the pool of warm light created by the lamp that stood beside the mirror. "I trust the evening was fruitful, my lady?" the maid asked, as she removed the hair ornament and helped Rosa out of the dress, leaving her in her shift, then helping her into a confection of a dressing gown made of silk lace.

Rosa took her seat on the padded stool in front of the

mirrored dressing table. "My head is full," Rosa replied, a little ruefully. "I had no idea from the stories in newspapers that Society was so complicated."

The maid laughed. "It is, for those who are born into it, and more so for those who are elevated into it. It is more complicated for females than men. Men can and do overlook whatever differences in class, education, and rank they choose to. Women do not have this luxury, for the doyennes of Society will see to it that they pay and pay dearly, if they dare to transgress."

Rosa wrinkled her brow at that, but a moment later, it became clear to her. These "doyennes of society" were no different at bottom than the leading dames among the gossips of her own village. Within that little "society," their word was law, and the law was *respectability. She* had escaped their tongues because the only times she appeared in the village she was dressed as demurely as any of the other maidens, she kept her eyes downcast and she spoke little. So far as the gossips knew, she was in service elsewhere—it was not wise to allow people outside the Bruderschaft to know you were a member. You could bring great danger on your family that way. As far as the villages were concerned, the only members of the Bruderschaft outsiders *knew* were Gunther and one or two of the eldest. The rest were shadows in the forest, people you knew were out there, but never glimpsed.

The professor had explained all this as best he could, but he had done so from a male perspective, not a female one. Possibly this was a side of Society he had not truly seen.

So, now thanks to the professor, Rosa had more tools to dissect Society with, and she saw that the queens of Society were like the female tyrants of the villages. Rosa understood that, and she understood why. In the rest of the world, the real power was all consolidated in masculine hands. It was even codified into law. Only in decreeing and enforcing the rules of etiquette and behavior did the women of Society have the opportunity to become "powerful," though men could still overrule them. Power was power, and no matter how petty the power was, some people just *had* to feel they had it over someone else.

"So, I must be quiet and meek and polite to a fault," she said, thoughtfully. "Well, it scarcely matters to me that some old harridan sees me as subservient to her."

"That is your best battle plan, my lady," Marie agreed. "Think what it is that most young ladies in Society are pursuing. Good marriages with someone richer or higher in rank than they are. They must put themselves forward without transgressing, or risk the ire of their families for not trying hard enough. But should *you* find yourself in need of functioning within Society—well, what is it that you will be there for?"

"Certainly not that!" she laughed, looking into Marie's face via the mirror. "Likeliest is that I will have strong need to keep myself from being noticed. I see what you mean. Because I do not need or want what Society is promising to an unmarried woman, there are fewer rules for me as well."

Marie nodded, taking down her hair and brushing it with firm, gentle strokes. "If you are endeavoring to keep from being noticed, I recommend no powder or paint at all, and only the most simple and modest gowns of your wardrobe. You will be taken as lately come from school, and if you apparently have no fortune, will be of no interest to anyone. You may observe from the sidelines, among the wall-flowers."

Rosa sighed with regret, though she could see the logic and had come to that conclusion herself. If she were on the Hunt, as Fritz had been, her best defense would be invisibility. Absolutely logical—but she had been enjoying herself so very much being the center of attention tonight.

Marie pursed her lips, and raised her eyebrow. Rosa waited to see what witty thing the maid would say. Marie was proving to be highly entertaining. Rosa was quite certain that this was not the normal relationship between maid and mistress (even if she was only Marie's temporary superior) but she was also quite certain that the shrewd young woman would never behave like this with anyone who was not a fellow magician. Probably not even then, unless she had been invited to do so, as Rosa had invited her.

"You have proven yourself tonight to be a valuable and entertaining guest, and as you master Society, the Count will expose you to those who would be more critical of your behavior than this lot. Rest assured, you shall have plenty of opportunities to be the toast of gatherings as long as the Count is alive," Marie said with a wink. "And probably well beyond that, as long as you are willing to come out of that benighted forest of yours."

"The Schwarzwald is not benighted!" Rosa protested, stung at the implied insult to her home, and rushing to its defense.

"Any place where one cannot have a single meal without being stared at by beheaded beasts is benighted," Marie replied with a shudder. "I shall never forget that so-called hunting party the Count attended with his mistress five years ago—it was hunting, in the sense of pursuing deer and boar rather than magical foes. It was being held by the Count von Willensdorf, and intended as a retreat for several powerful men and their mistresses."

"Really?" Rosa blinked. "They do that?"

Marie nodded. "Generally, the wives are sent off to the spa towns to be pampered and fussed over, so that the men are free to enjoy a week or more of discreet dalliance in the company of other men and their mistresses. The Count's inamorata of the moment was someone who had never been outside a city, and had no idea what a 'hunting lodge' looked like—and neither did I! Even the bedrooms had dead deer in them! Fortunately the lady had hysterics and demanded we all go home, and the Count has never again ventured to do such a thing."

Poor Count, she thought, then laughed at herself. Of course if the Graf actually wanted to go for a game-hunting trip of *that* sort, he could. All he needed to do was to go without his mistress, or find a mistress for whom such things were more to her taste. It wasn't as if he had to please anyone but himself!

"Well we are not in a hunting lodge, we are in the Count's manor. If this were anything but a party of magicians, I would now be telling you everything the other servants said in downstairs gossip, in order that you could learn everything I could glean about the other guests." Marie continued. "That, however, is not necessary. Instead

I will tell you what tomorrow's daytime entertainment will be. Have you ever played at Hounds and Hare?"

Rosa laughed with delight. It had been one of her favorite childhood "games"—although it was as much training for her position in the future as it was a game. "Of course! Who hasn't, among our kind?"

"The Count would like you to provide a real challenge to the adults, and play the Hare for them. Markos will be the Hare for the children. Whichever group catches their Hare first, wins a prize."

Now, by this point, Rosa had walked or ridden over nearly every inch of the Graf's grounds since she had arrived here, and she beamed with glee at Marie at this news. This was going to be great fun!

She didn't know how familiar Markos was with the property, but he would be leading the children on a chase, so not knowing it well would only give him a little bit of a handicap to make it a fair contest.

Marie smiled back. "I thought you would like that," she said. "The Count will announce it at breakfast. It is a good thing that you decided to retire early—you are going to need your sleep!"

Rosa was prepared for the surprise, dressed in her Schwarzwald gear, when she came down to breakfast. The Graf smiled at her with a twinkle in his eye when he saw her and recognized that Marie had told her what was to come. When all the guests had assembled for breakfast, and knives and forks were busy, he stood up and called for their attention.

"My good friends," he said. "For your edification and enjoyment, I have organized a competition of Hare and Hounds, divided between the children and the adults. Markos Nagy will play the Hare for the children, and our good friend Gunther will supervise the children's group to help them if they become truly stuck. Rosamund von Schwarzwald will play the Hare for the adult group, and I expect her to challenge your tracking abilities. If anyone wishes to sit the game out, I will provide a fire-scrying overview of the progress of both groups."

The enthusiasm with which this announcement was met left no question as to whether anyone was going to remain behind. "The children will be mounted, and I have had ponies brought up for them," the Graf continued, when the hum of conversation had stilled a little. "The adults may have the choice of being mounted or going afoot. I expect you to work together this morning on your Hunting Party and strategy, and selecting your Hunt Master. Gunther will help the children do the same. After luncheon, we will give the Hares their start, and the Hunt will begin."

The prospect of doing something Hunt-like without the danger and risk of a real Hunt was almost always appealing to the magicians associated with White Lodges. It was the fellowship and challenge of the Hunt, without the prospect of someone dying, or the need to work with fellow mages you might not particularly care for. As a result, everyone except Markos and Rosa hurried through their meal and adjourned to the library for the adults, except for Gunther, who took himself to wherever the children were being assembled.

"Well, my lady," said Markos, when the dining room was deserted by all but a lone servant, waiting for a signal that they wanted anything else. "What do you think our plan should be? I am very familiar with the Count's estate." Although she knew he had gone to bed later than she, he looked just as well rested, and quite cheerful at the prospect of entertaining the children of the group.

"Ah good! I am as well. And you should call me Rosa, fellow Hare." She smiled at him as she moved to sit across from him and cleared objects away from the tablecloth between them. "In that case, I think, for maximum confusion, we should deliberately cross our trails several times."

Markos chuckled; it was the first time she had heard him laugh, and it was a pleasing, low-pitched sound. "That is an excellent plan. So . . . let us let this butter dish represent the manor, here—and let me outline the gardens with these knives." He placed the dish, and between them, they soon had a tolerable map laid out on the table as they plotted their paths.

The servants were very patient about not taking away

the breakfast things until they were finished—even though it was nearly lunchtime before they were satisfied. The Graf's estate was not only the palace and grounds, but included several hundred acres of farms, forest, grazing, and an entire village. There had been plenty for them to work with. By the time the chase was over, everyone should be weary.

They were able to join the others wearing satisfied smiles, which invoked answering smiles from some, rueful expressions from others. But everyone was ready; the others had taken the opportunity to change into clothing suitable for riding or walking across rough land. Which, as Rosa knew, was prudent. While Markos was not going to subject the children to anything like a punishing Hunt, Rosa had no such intentions, and there were plenty of places on the Graf's property that were nearly as wild as her own Schwarzwald.

"Rosa, Markos, are you ready?" the Graf asked them, when a light luncheon had been cleared away.

"We are," Rosa replied, after a glance at Markos, who nodded at her.

"Very well. Rosa, your group will be riding, so please go to the stables and choose your mount first. You may leave as soon as you are ready." The Graf gave her a little bow, and she ran off to do as he directed. She did wonder about Markos for a moment, and why the Graf had not directed *him* to choose a mount, but now was not the time for her to think about anything but her own Hunt.

There was a lively young Arab mare that was her favorite in the Graf's stables, but she passed by her stall and went straight to another—a big coldblooded hunter, a heavily dappled gray gelding. There were times when her path was going to double back on itself and she might find herself waiting in cover until the hunting party had passed. If that happened, she needed a horse that would blend into the bushes. With that dapple pattern he would look like sun on leaves.

One of the stable hands tacked the gelding up for hunting, and with a saddle for riding astride. The man knew better by this time than to offer her a sidesaddle, a mounting block, or a hand up. She mounted up on her own, chirped to the blunt-headed gelding, gave him a touch of the heel, and they were off. She left a clear trail at first, galloping down the Graf's beautifully manicured lane at a brisk pace, just enough to let the horse work off his initial impatience. Once the tree-covered lane reached a little stone bridge over a stream, she sent the gelding plunging down the bank of the stream and into the streambed. Willows overhung it on both banks; here it was part of the landscaping for the Graf's palace. She could not bring herself to think of so vast a building as a mere "manor." But eventually, it would lead her into the part of the property where "grounds" became "farms and forest" without the need to find a gate in a fence or a wall.

The Hounds would be following not scent, but the traces of Earth Magic she was deliberately throwing out behind her. But these traces worked just like scent, and running water confused or washed them away.

Markos would be doing the same as she, but he would be leaving a clearer trail, and nothing near as lengthy. *Her* trail would cover most of the many hundred acres that were personally owned by the Graf. His would stay mostly inside the grounds. This was not only a game for the children, it was an educational exercise. One day, perhaps sooner than their parents would like, they would be on a real Hunting Party, and what they learned today might bring that Hunt to a successful conclusion.

The water splashed around the gelding's knees, and he snorted, but not in dissatisfaction. He plowed willingly upstream until they came to a fence that ended on either bank. Once past that, she signaled him to climb the bank and work his way along a path on the bank barely wide enough for him.

She caught neither sign nor sound of Markos, and she wondered where he was. If he was riding, he'd have to choose a much slower horse than hers, or even a large pony, to make the Hunt fair for the children, but surely he wasn't going afoot, was he?

Well, it was possible. He certainly looked supremely fit. He was Hungarian, but she didn't know which part of

Hungary he was from. If the plains, well, the plainsmen were practically born in the saddle, but if he was from the mountains he might well be accustomed to going afoot.

A path led away from the one along the bank, and she followed it until they broke out of the trees into the open. Here, there was an open meadow around a ruin—most would take it for artificial, but its real age cried out to her as she and the gelding galloped past. The Graf had left this meadow to grow freely rather than mowing it, and long grass swished just below her feet as the gelding surged through it. She threw out a particularly strong trace in the direction of the ruin as she passed it; they might waste time looking for her in the ruin when she was long gone.

By now the horse was well into the spirit of the exercise and responded instantly to whatever she asked of him. This was the other reason why she had chosen him; the mare sometimes turned contrary, and she didn't want to have to fight a sudden fit of contrariness at a bad time.

Back into the woods on the other side of the meadow they went, working their way to the eastern border of the estate lands. When they struck the orchard, she took a path that wove among the trees in a deliberate pattern that she had worked out ahead of time. She knew the pattern; her pursuers wouldn't, and as she crossed and recrossed her own trail, she knew she would be confounding them. She skirted the edges of the orchard in several places so when she exited, it wouldn't be obvious. This was a tactic that one of the werewolves she had hunted in the Schwarzwald had used—while it was a truism that the more a shifter went to the beast, the more of the beast took over the man when he took beast form, this particular magician had retained a high level of human reasoning. He had been particularly hard to Hunt, and in the end, she'd employed not only her own senses, but the help of a pack of Earth Elementals to decipher the trail. *They* were much better at seeing the "age" of a trace than she was.

The trees were full of little green apples, and there was a very, very faint apple scent in the air. She finished her pattern and exited at the south side of the orchard, but neither in the middle, nor at the corner. Then she took a straight gallop across another open space, a field left to go fallow with a fine flock of goats grazing on the weeds. From there, she galloped along the edges of a planted field, staying far enough away from the actual plowed and planted rows of rye that there was no risk any of the crop would be trampled by those behind her.

Back she dove into a little copse of trees, jumped the gelding over a hedge back onto the grounds of the palace, then she hit the first place where her path would cross the one that Markos was laying.

There was no outward sign of him, but she immediately detected a trace of Earth Magic, weaker than hers, but distinct. She was astonished. How had he gotten so far ahead of her?

Well good for him that he had. There was no way for her to tell how long ago he had passed; it could have been mere moments or a quarter of an hour. In either case, he was surely leading his young pursuers on a merry chase. She reined in her horse a moment and strained her ears, and sure enough, she heard, faint and far, childish shrieks and wild laughter in the distance. She sent the gray on his way, jumping back and forth over the hedge three times before striking a road that led through a proper gate in the hedge. She didn't bother with the gate, since the gelding was having no problems with jumping the hedge. Instead, she made a final leap, and ended up on the "farm" side.

The Hunt was supposed to last all afternoon, and she and Markos had determined to make sure that it did. They had minimized the amount of time they would be on open ground, but there were *some* places where that would work to her advantage. And one of them was coming right up.

She sent the gelding onto the road and trotted right into the Graf's village, where those who worked his farmlands lived. In the old days, before the Graf's ancestors had replaced it with the palace, the castle that guarded and ruled these lands had stood here; now there was a ruin on a hill in the midst of the village. Watching carefully for children darting out in front of her, she trotted around the village as she had trotted around the orchard, and then through as much of the ruins as she could, leaving liberal samples of

magic and encountering Markos' traces more than once.
Clever! The village wasn't *that* far outside of the grounds,
and using it would give the children a challenge.

Once clear of the village, she galloped across another
meadow filled with dairy cattle, startling the cows who gazed
at her in astonishment, heading for the wildest part of the
Graf's lands. She didn't bother to confuse her path this
time—the fact that the hunters would have to search for
widely-separated traces would be difficult enough. This cor-
responded to a place where the quarry was running away,
and it would be a good exercise for those following her. The
faster a hunted thing ran, the lighter its mark on the land.

She was heading for the woods at the farthest southern
edge of the Graf's property, a substantial tract of primeval
forest, carefully preserved by the Graf's ancestors for centuries. She expected to encounter a host of excited Earth
Elementals here, all eager to help her with the Hunt.

But as she plunged into the shadow beneath the trees,
without warning everything changed.

It felt as if she had plunged into icy water, but it was
water that wanted desperately to murder her.

There was not a trace of any Elementals about, and the
instant they had crossed the invisible boundary and the inimical power touched them, her horse screamed in panic
and fought her, rearing and bucking furiously. Whatever
was in that power had sent him mad with terror, and she
had no more than a second to react.

She kicked her feet free of the stirrups and leapt free of
him, aiming for a clear patch with a forgiving juniper bush
in the middle of it. Whatever had been lying in wait here
had gotten into place, here on the Graf's farmlands, without
the Graf or his people detecting it. Its animosity felt in-
tensely personal, and she didn't need to have to fight a hysterical horse at the same time something was trying to kill
her!

As well that she made her leap off the horse, for as soon
as she left the saddle, a spear of ice lanced through the air
where she had been and shattered on a tree-trunk. She tumbled out of the prickly branches of the juniper bush and
whirled to face the direction from which it had come.

She found herself face to face with a woman.

A blond woman, all in white, whose expression was distorted with fury and a hint of madness. A woman who stood in the middle of an iced-over pond in which undines struggled frantically to escape from ice closing around their waists. Rosa barely had a chance to register both Air *and* Water, and the impossible presence of a second spirit beside—or was it *inside?*—the woman, when she found herself dodging more icy daggers.

The pain and fear of the trapped and tortured undines added fuel to the woman's magic, and her accuracy and speed kept Rosa from bringing up the shields that might protect her from the attacks. All she could do was tumble and dodge, and curse herself that she had come out here unarmed. If only she had her knives, or her coach gun, or even her crossbow!

She dove and rolled between two trees, and the bark scraped bits of wool from her jacket as another ice-dagger shattered over her head, raining shards down on her. Chill pain lanced her face as one of them cut her, but she kept rolling into the temporary cover of some bushes. Her heart raced, and her breath burned in her lungs with cold. Air and Water . . . Air meant lightning!

A moment later, she felt the earth beneath her cry with jagged agony, and she lurched out of that cover and into the open in time for a lightning bolt to slam down where she had been.

A sharp scent burned her lungs and she staggered back and forth, trying to keep moving, half-blinded by the light. It hadn't been a huge strike, but it certainly had been enough to kill.

She felt, rather than saw, another ice-dagger impact her, but the thick wool of her jacket kept it from penetrating too far.

She blessed the hunters of the Schwarzwald for coming up with a garment that was as much protection from sharp objects as it was protection from the cold.

Through the glowing orbs that obscured her vision, she spotted the woman, and in desperation, Rosa ran *toward* her rather than away, leaping forward in an attempt to grapple as she felt the earth under her feet change to the ice of the frozen pond.

She didn't so much tackle the woman as crash into her, but it was enough to interrupt her attack. Rosa and her foe both tumbled together down onto the ice.

But Rosa didn't hit her squarely, and ended up bouncing away, sliding out of reach before she could pin the woman down. She slammed into the bank with her shoulder, seeing stars of pain as well as glowing orbs, and dug her nails into the earth, screaming her outrage and a warning into the land for as far as her magic would reach—more than enough to cover every inch of the Graf's estate. If she didn't survive this, the rest of the Graf's guests would turn from a Hounds and Hare hunt to a real Hunting Party and put an end to this monster! And if she could just stay alive until they got here—

She rolled to one side as she felt the earth and water cry again, and this time the lightning bolt hit so close she smelled burned wool from her jacket as well as the sharp lightning smell. But this time she kept her eyes closed, and didn't even try to get to her feet. Instead, in the moment of respite after the lightning struck, she slapped her hand down on the bank again, drawing on the raw power of the ground, and called up shields composed of Earth energies; shields both magical and physical. The Earth energies enveloped her like a cocoon, and a moment later she heard, rather than saw, a shower of ice-daggers shatter against the magic shell around her.

A howl filled with rage split the air as she staggered to her feet, bruised and bleeding, but now protected.

Her adversary ignored it.

The woman's attention was entirely riveted on Rosa; it was as if nothing else existed, and once again, Rosa had the disconcerting impression that there were not one, but two spirits staring at her out of those rage-filled eyes.

Again the earth cried out, but now Rosa stood firm, eyes narrowed against the glare, protected inside her shields. Earth energies grounded Air—and her foe might not know that.

The lightning struck—distinctly weaker this time—and

disintegrated into a tracery not unlike white-hot veins that ran along the outside of her shields into the earth at her feet.

Then a black, furry projectile rocketed out of the bushes and hit the woman like a bullet from an elephant gun.

Unlike Rosa's clumsy attempt at a tackle, the beast struck true. They both crashed to the rock-hard ice. The woman's head hit the ice with a sickening *crack*, and for a moment, Rosa thought that the fight was over. Surely no one could remain conscious after a blow like that!

But she was down for only a moment. With a shriek like a harpy, she flung the beast off her before Rosa could even decide what it was, and redoubled her efforts, sending ice-daggers and smaller lightning-bolts after both of them. The beast, whatever it was, was unprotected against the assault and dodged into the cover of the brush, leaving the woman free to attack Rosa again.

Bargeist? It was possible. Woden's bargeists were known to run through the Schwarzwald on stormy nights, and she suspected after her Hunt in Romania, she still had Woden's favor . . .

The undines entrapped in the ice struggled weakly, growing ever paler and more translucent. The woman was killing them, something Rosa hadn't known was even possible, and which made her furious and nauseous at the same time. She exploded her outrage outward, and her own Element answered, bringing a small—literally—army to her side.

A rock flew unerringly toward Rosa's adversary from the bushes, cracking against the side of her head. Not a second later, a dozen or more followed it, pelting her from all directions. As the woman ducked and tried to protect herself with upraised hands, Rosa got a glimpse of a little faun popping up out of cover, no trace of sleepy mischief on his face, whirling a sling over his head and letting fly at the magician before dropping back into hiding again.

Then the beast leapt from out of the bushes and struck her again, knocking her off her feet. This time he didn't pause to use those formidable jaws; he scrabbled back across the ice and into cover before she could get to her feet.

This gave Rosa the breathing space to expand her shields, and her fauns gathered to her, continuing to rain rocks on the woman, who had finally erected her own shields. The two of them stared at each other as the rocks and ice daggers shattered harmlessly on their shields.

The two women stared at each other, ignoring the missiles.

Why ice-daggers and lightning and nothing else? Why not call in boreals to attack me through the shields and try to freeze me the way the undines are being frozen? Why doesn't she switch to some other form of attack?

Of one thing there was no doubt. There was a second spirit inside that woman. And now Rosa recognized the energy signature of the second. Small wonder she hadn't known who it was till now, for after all, she had only ever seen it once.

But the shape of the ice-daggers should have given her a clue.

She knew that shape. She had helped to forge one in exactly that pattern, blade and hilt. It was her own throwing knife in ice form, one of a set of four, that differed from each other only by the sigil on the pommel nut.

The ice-dagger was identical to Zephyr, the knife that had killed the Air Mage that had tried to murder the Graf's agent, Fritz. The spirit inhabiting her attacker was that of the Air Master who had called himself "Durendal."

The man's face was etched in her mind, as were the faces of every human she had been forced to kill. There were, thank the Good God, not many of those; most of her Hunts were against things other than human—or against those humans who no longer wore a human face. But she remembered him; oh yes, she did. And now she could see the family resemblance in this woman's features. She even looked as if she was the same age as the man that Rosa had killed.

Twins?

Probably. It would explain how he had come to possess this woman's body, and why she had let him. Twins had a special bond, and Water was a pliant, yielding Element. It would have been easy for someone like the arrogant Durendal to bully and dominate a female twin whose power was

Water, making her totally subservient to him—easy for him to forge an emergency path to her body, so that if anything ever happened to his physical body, his spirit could leap to hers and take it over completely. Small wonder Fritz had been unaware of the girl's existence; Durendal would have kept her isolated, cloistered, hidden away. The only reason Rosa was still alive was that his control over his sister's magic was limited, and as he was in a foreign body, his control over his own magic was just as limited. That was why he only seemed to be able to ice over the pond to trap the undines, forge shields, ice-daggers, and wield weak lightning.

If he'd taken the time to gain true Mastery over both his sister's power and his own, she wouldn't have had a chance without a full Hunting Party. But he had let the burning desire for revenge drive him, and not good sense. He must have set out to find her as soon as he was able to completely control his sister's body.

They might have stood there forever, locked in stalemate, except that at the same moment Rosa recognized the situation for what it was, one of the little water nymphs, the undines, gasped and died. The transparent body slumped to the ice that held her, and faded into nothingness.

A stab of fury and fear coursed through Rosa.

The woman's shields shivered, and one of the fauns' rocks sailed through it, catching her on the cheekbone. *This* time she let out a little cry and one hand went to her face. She'd *felt* that, as she had not felt the blow to her head when she fell to the ice. The death of the undine had weakened her!

The shield shivered again.

And Rosa suddenly felt the ice underneath her vibrate with furious pounding . . . exactly like the pounding of dozens of fists from the water beneath.

"The ice!" Rosa cried, "Attack the ice at her feet!" And the fauns redirected their deadly fire to the ice where the shields ended. The remaining undines suddenly seemed to gain in strength, and the ice-daggers dropped out of the air and shattered on the ground.

The ice at the woman's feet cracked. She started and stared downward.

The ice at her feet spiderwebbed, and she took a slow step backward, a look of disbelief on her face.

With a sharp *crack,* the ice before her disintegrated into a mass of chunks.

With a shrill cry, the woman tried to turn and make for shore, but it was too late. The ice fell apart beneath her. And as she dropped into the water, dozens of scaled arms reached for her.

But not to save her.

She—or her brother in her body—had abused her power and murdered those who would have helped her. The vengeful Water Elementals called the nix claimed her for their own.

7

THE Hunting Party—now a Hunting Party in truth—arrived just as the last bubbles broke on the surface of the rapidly thawing pond. The fauns had vanished, as had the undines and the nix, and there was no evidence of the Water Master or the spirit of her presumed brother who had possessed her. Rosa could not see or feel any other energies but the ones that should be there; the slow pulse of natural Air, Earth, and Water.

Nevertheless—and rightly—the Hunting Party spread out over the forest and the land around it, checking everything twice and three times, to be sure there were no left-over Elementals, trapped or coerced, and above all, nothing left behind by—well, really, what would you call the thing she had fought? Had it been Durendal alone? Durendal and his sister? The revenant of Durendal, composed of rage and magic?

Well no matter what you called it, since Rosa wasn't in any danger, the priority of the Hunting Party was to make sure there was no other danger lurking.

Eventually, by ones and twos, they came back to her. Rosa sat on the bank of the pond, dabbing at a cut over her eye with a pocket-handkerchief. This was by no means the most she had ever been injured in a fight. She had a couple of shallow cuts, and a good many bruises, but no broken bones, no serious wounds, and nothing worse than a foul ache from where she had hit her shoulder against the bank. It hadn't dislocated, but it hurt almost as much as if it had.

Still, the Graf and the others fussed over her until Gunther waved them all off with irritation, helped her to her feet, held her out at arm's length to examine her, and nodded.

"You'll do," he said brusquely. "What did you learn?"

"Never to go unarmed, not even on a friend's estate," she replied, with great irritation at herself. "I should not have been so great a fool. If I had had a pistol, or a knife, this would have been cut much shorter."

"We will speak of this later," Gunther replied. "Markos has caught your horse. Let us return to the manor, and you may get a bath and change of clothing and have your injuries tended. Are you feeling well enough for dinner?"

"I could eat a boar," she said, knowing that once she had conquered her aches and pains, all that expenditure of energy, magical and physical, would have to be repaid. Gunther chuckled, and squeezed her shoulders before letting her go.

At that exact moment, the last two of the party returned. "You must come see this!" one shouted, as soon as he was within hearing distance. He beckoned, and of course, everyone traipsed toward him, including Rosa.

The two—the professor and one of his students—led the way through the forest tract to the other side. And there, just off-center in the meadow and sticking up out of the long grass as if a gigantic child had set it down there, was—a wicker basket.

A basket trailing strings further on into the meadow. Rosa finally realized what it was just as the Graf uttered an astonished exclamation.

"By God, it's a *balloon!*" he gasped.

And so it was. Those strings led off to an enormous, and

now deflated, balloon made of varnished silk. There was no mechanism for producing hot air, so this must have been a gas balloon.

"Well, that explains how the cad was able to get here without anyone noticing," the Graf said. "He was an Air Master; he could have traveled as fast as his captive Air Elementals would take him, and once here, all he had to do was empty the balloon."

"Oh! And that would be how he got ahead of the train!" Rosa exclaimed. "I knew he must have used Air Elementals somehow—I do not know enough about what they are capable of to have guessed *how* he used them."

"There are legends that very powerful Air Masters could somehow fly with the help of their Elementals, but—" The professor shrugged. "Legends only. No details on how that was possible." He looked thoughtful. "Archytas in ancient Greece was reputed to have built a bird-shaped flying device. And of course, we have gliding, fixed-wing machines that can carry a passenger. I myself have ridden in one that is pulled into the air by a team of horses. But using a balloon—that is very clever indeed."

"He obviously did not intend to return the same way," the professor pointed out. "There is no way to fill the balloon from here, and it is not a hot air balloon."

"I presume he did not care." The Graf and the some of the others prowled around the little basket, which was just big enough to hold a single person, but no more. "He must have had more than one of these things stored away in case he required them. And perhaps he also had one or more gliders as well, but a balloon has the advantage of being able to land vertically."

The professor shook his head. "So much intelligence. So much ingenuity. Such a waste."

Rosa found a large boulder in the grass to sit down on. Her shoulder really did ache abominably. "We should tell other Lodges about balloons and gliders," she pointed out. "Even though such things would probably entail gaining the cooperation of a great many Air Elementals at once, surely there are *some* Air Masters that can coax such cooperation out of their allies."

The Graf nodded. But Gunther made a face. "I should not care to trust my safety high in the sky on the fidelity of flighty Air Elementals."

"Nor would I," said one of the students. "Perhaps that is another reason to use a balloon. Even if you lose control of the Elementals, you still have the gas to keep you aloft safely and you can land safely in the usual manner."

"A wise precaution for someone who is coercing his Elementals," said Markos, who came up at that moment leading Rosa's horse.

"And it would be a wise idea for all of us to return to the manor," Gunther pointed out. "Your people are wise enough to collect this contraption and any clues Durendal might have left behind."

That was the best idea that Rosa had heard since the trap had been sprung on her.

"You will have a whole new story to tell us," the Graf said, as Markos brought her poor, tired horse to her. *This* time she did not disdain the stirrup he made for her with his hands, and gratefully used it to get into the saddle.

"Yes, sir," she replied, taking the comment for the order it actually was. "As soon as I am bathed and changed."

The lot of them rode slowly back to the palace, taking the direct way, and as they approached the gardens, Rosa sensed all the anxious eyes peering out of the windows, though at this distance it was impossible to make out any individual forms behind the glass. She also sensed the relief and the lowering of many shields when the party had been counted and the correct number arrived at.

Markos was riding a tall pony, which had to work hard to keep up with the horses as they scented their stable and picked up their pace. The pony's gait didn't look to be very comfortable for the poor young man, and Rosa got the feeling he didn't ride very often.

She, however, spared very little energy worrying about him; she gave her tired gelding a little heel, and encouraged him into a canter. She wanted to be in the ministering hands of Marie before she fell off his back. The very first thing she wanted was something for the vile shoulder-ache she had.

And the next was a hot bath for that and for her bruises. And after that?

Well the Graf had promised them all a sort of *bierhalle*. She wanted a mountain of bratwurst, and a pail of beer!

"The grand thing about living in a Fire Master's home is that one never lacks for hot water," Marie said, somewhere past the steam rising from the bath Rosa was soaking in. The Graf had turned what might have once been a maid's room into a bath room. Water came from cisterns on the roof, and was heated by a cooperative salamander. Rosa reclined in an enormous bathtub of carved marble with absurd clawed feet. The hot water felt impossibly good on all her aches. In the Lodge that the Bruderschaft shared, one had to bathe in the kitchen, in an ancient brass bathtub that might have dated all the way back to the days of knights. It was made to sit in, not recline in—though one certainly did get hot water up to one's chin.

This tub, however, also allowed you to have hot water up to one's chin, but there was plenty of room to stretch out. And Marie had put in scent, a sort of honey-rose. It was wonderful. She'd never bathed in scented water before.

"That alone could convince me to leave the Schwarzwald if we didn't already have a Fire Master among the Bruderschaft," Rosa replied. "Is my jacket utterly ruined?" She was going to be irritated if it was. It was her favorite hunting coat.

"I don't believe so," Marie replied. "I believe we—and by 'we,' I mean the laundry maids—can get the scorch marks and mud out of it successfully." The maid loomed up through the steam and looked down at Rosa. "Are your bruises soaked enough you feel ready to join the others?"

Since tantalizing whiffs of frying sausage had somehow been making their way to the bath room for the last half hour, it would have taken more than a few bruises to keep Rosa away. "Quite," she said, firmly, and rose from the bath like a weary undine. Marie wrapped her in one enormous towel, her hair in a second, and helped her out.

She bit back a few groans as the maid also helped her into fresh clothing; for once, having Marie help her dress was welcome rather than faintly embarrassing. The willow tea Marie had given her in the bath was finally doing something about her aching shoulder.

Well, tonight's "theme" was a *bierhalle,* and that meant she would be able to dress comfortably. She only had the one loden jacket, but there was the jacket from the riding habit that was similar, and evidently Marie judged it to go well enough with her divided skirt that it would pass muster. At this point, Rosa was putty in the maid's hands when it came to a clothing selection. All she wanted was a plate of sausage and kraut and a stein of beer. Preferably a very large stein of beer.

Marie probably sensed her impatience, because all she did so far as a hairdo was concerned was to braid Rosa's long hair and coil the braid into a knot at the nape of her neck. "There!" she said, when she had driven the last hairpin home. "Go, and I advise that you do not polka, unless you want your shoulder to complain mightily about being bounced about."

Since Rosa had absolutely *no* intention of dancing, that was going to be a very easy order to obey.

Her arrival at the ersatz *bierhalle* that the Graf had set up in the morning room was greeted with mingled enthusiasm and concern. A comfortable, heavily padded chair had been brought from another room for her, and she settled herself gratefully into it at the end of the table rather than taking a place on one of the benches.

This wasn't a bad imitation of a *bierhalle.* The servants were wearing what looked like their second-best clothing for holiday and fair days, and the ones in the brass band even boasted Bavarian *lederhosen,* fancy suspenders, and dashing hats. Garlands of ivy had been looped over the windows, and all the furniture had been taken out and replaced with tables and benches. Literally all the furniture, down to the rugs; it would have been a daunting task for just a single evening's entertainment by Rosa's standards, but ... this was the Graf, and his palace alone had more people living in it than many villages in the Schwarzwald.

Grilled sausages warmed over chafing dishes, and barrels of beer were lined up on stands along one wall. Of course, a real *bierhalle* at home would also have had deer, bear and boar heads, and mounted deer antlers stuck up wherever there was room on the walls, and the floor would *never* be so polished, but these were minor things and did not at all detract from the general atmosphere of great cheer. A servant brought her bratwurst and sauerkraut on a tray for her lap; another set a gratifyingly large stein of beer on a little table at her elbow. The little amateur brass band was reasonably in tune, and made up in enthusiasm what they lacked in skill—reminding her strongly of the band her Vati played in. She devoured her plate of sausage and kraut, and was brought a second, which she likewise demolished, and finally was brought a plate of sliced apples and cheeses—sweet cakes not going very well with beer. The children were alternately romping to the music and devouring sausage—the littlest ones eating with their fingers, while their mothers indulged this momentary lapse in table manners. There were larger chunks of cheese and bowls of apples on the tables, and anyone who wanted to could just carve some cheese off with the huge knives placed nearby and help himself to apples.

By now, Rosa was basking in the warm glow that surrounded her thanks to some really excellent beer. The company was good too; she had Markos on one side, and the Graf's secretary, Rudolf, on the other. Rudolf was regaling the company with a story from his university days, a complicated tale of getting a donkey into a professor's rooms that had *nothing* to do with magic. Both young men were paying her flattering attention, and she had drunk just enough to lose her self-consciousness about that, but not so much that she would say or do something stupid. It was a fine balance, but nothing like as hard to keep as balancing magical energies. Perhaps the only fly in the ointment was that she really *liked* to dance, but she knew it would be a very, very bad idea. Her shoulder was just beginning to settle down to a dull ache, and it was definitely not going to cope well with dancing.

Rudolf finished his tale to applause and laughter, and

Rosa sipped her beer and nibbled a little truly excellent cheese to balance it out. The band returned from having devoured their own mountains of sausage and sauerkraut, and headed for the bandstand. *This can't possibly get better! Good food, tolerable music, good beer, excellent company . . .*

"*Ho! Markos!*" An exuberant shout from the door turned all eyes in that direction, and Markos shot to his feet, waving at the figure that stood there beside the impassive footman.

"*Dominik!*" Markos called back happily. "You are here at last!"

The dark young man who came striding into the room was just as handsome as Markos and a great deal more flamboyant. He could not ever have been mistaken for German, not even by a blind man.

Anyone with an eye to costume would recognize him as Hungarian, with his red vest, black trousers tucked into shining black riding boots, and red, fur-trimmed coat worn on his shoulders like a cape, rather than with his arms in the sleeves. He had an impressive moustache, his hair was slightly long by Rosa's standards, and his eyes glowed with good humor.

Or perhaps it was just that all of him glowed with Earth Magic.

And even those two words, "Ho, Markos!", had been infused with a rich Hungarian accent. *Has the Graf responded to Gunther sending three of the Bruderschaft to Romania by importing mages from Hungary, now?* Rosa thought to herself with amusement. *Well if all of them are going to be handsome young men, I am not going to object!*

The two young men embraced, and Markos turned to the rest of the company. "This is my cousin, Dominik Petro," he said, proudly. "The best man with horses in all of Hungary! And an Earth Master."

"Now, now, don't give me such flattery, I might get used to it," Dominik laughed, mock-cuffing him.

The Graf rose; Dominik clicked his heels together and bowed. "Count. It is good to meet you at last. I—"

The Graf held up his hand. "Is your business so urgent that it cannot wait a few hours?"

Dominik shook his head. "If it were, I would have come faster," he admitted. "We have had this mystery for years and have put off dealing with it because—"

"Then sit. Don't think about it for now. If it has endured for years, it can endure a few more hours." The Graf waved at the table. "Enjoy the food, the beer, and the company. You are just in time to listen to Hunt Master Rosamund tell us what she encountered invading my property. By balloon, no less!"

"Balloon!" Now Rosa definitely had the young man's attention, and he eyed her with speculation . . . and something else that made her flush a little. The Count gestured for him to take a spot on the bench next to Markos, and one of the servants brought him food. "This sounds like a fantastic tale from Jules Verne! I am eager to hear it!"

"Well, we are getting a little ahead of ourselves," Rosa replied, giving her empty plate to the servant that had brought Dominik his food. "We didn't know there was a balloon involved until the end, and I need to begin at the very beginning."

She described very briefly why she and Hans had gone to Romania, then in more detail how she had met Fritz when the train had been stopped, and how she had killed Durendal—"Or so I thought," she told her audience. "I sent the body off with a minotaur so there would be nothing in this world to hold a spirit—and so there would be nothing for any followers to find." She looked to Rudolf and the Graf. "Did anyone know he had a sister?"

"Until Fritz found him, we didn't even know who he was," Rudolf said for both of them. He craned his neck upward. "Fritz? Can you join us?"

Rosa expected Fritz to come from the other end of the table, but to her delight, the tuba player put down his instrument—and it was Fritz! He walked toward them, looking very self-conscious in his *lederhosen*. "What is it that I can contribute?" he asked diffidently.

"Did you have time to learn that Durendal had a sister?" Rudolf asked.

Fritz shook his head. "I am afraid that everything I learned, I learned in the course of no more than three hours.

I managed to isolate Durendal's magic signature over the course of a few days, and eventually connected the signature to the living man. I followed the man to his home, asked a neighbor who lived there and described the man I had seen, and got his name. I was actually going to the telegraph office when I was attacked by Air Elementals and fled." He hung his head. "I am very sorry—"

"Really, Fritz, if you keep saying you are sorry that you retreated in the face of great peril, I am going to have to become quite cross with you," the Graf interrupted. "You are no good to me or anyone else dead, and dead you would have been if you had stayed. So please, stop apologizing for not being dead!"

Fritz looked relieved. "If the Count does not object, may I go back to the band?" he said meekly.

"Your tuba playing is excellent, and please let the rest of the band know that I am very much enjoying the music," the Graf replied, and gave him a kindly pat on the shoulder as he passed.

The attention turned back to Rosa.

"Does anyone know about possession?" she asked.

The professor cleared his throat and came to the fore. "In theory. I have studied such things."

"We are all ears, my dear Professor," said the Graf, leaning on the table. "Enlighten us."

"According to my studies, it is easier when one is either a blood relation, or has been in close proximity to the possessee." The professor pursed his lips. "It can be accomplished with various spells, but it can also be accomplished by persuading the—well, I will call her, 'the victim'—to invite possession. The nearer the relation in blood or proximity, the easier the possession."

"The young lady had the same cast of features as Durendal," Rosa observed. "And she seemed to be about the same age."

"Then until we learn otherwise, I will speculate that this was a twin sister, and one he kept under his constant control. And evidently he had prepared her to become his vessel if anything ever happened to his physical body." The professor nodded. "It is often the case with twins that one is very much the more dominant of the two. And we know nothing of Durendal's upbringing. His family has not been known to us as one that contains mages, so — "

"We must assume he was taught coercive magic by someone in his family. His father, probably," said the Graf. "This may go back generations, but only with Durendal did they produce a Master, or we would have uncovered them before this."

"I suppose," Rosa said, slowly and reluctantly. "It is even possible the sister was so devoted to Durendal that she not only cooperated, she actually called his spirit to herself when he died." She frowned; the mere idea revolted her.

"Is that even possible?" asked someone behind her.

The Graf answered for her, mouth set in a grim line. "Oh yes. Very possible. The nearer one is in familial relationship, the easier it is. And the more that the primary can mentally dominate the secondary, the easier it is."

"Such devotion is not unheard of," the professor seconded. "Lovers calling back the spirits of their loved ones, siblings doing the same. Usually, however, the spirit wishes to be set free, not remain bound to this earth."

"It could easily have been both. Durendal prepared his sister, both as his vessel, and fostered a slavish devotion to him to cause her to actually open herself to his possession," Rudolf said, dispassionately. "Twins often have a spiritual bond and know when something has happened to each other. If she felt him die — and if he had prepared her both to receive his spirit and to call it to her — it would not have mattered if they had been half a world apart. It would have happened."

"I've read of such things, but this is the first time I actually saw a possession," Rosa confessed. "And it didn't immediately occur to me that this was what I was seeing. Still, the fact that I was running for my life should be some excuse."

She described how the trap had been sprung, how she had seen both Air and Water Mastery in her attacker, how she had been confused at first, then realized there actually were two spirits in the same body. She related how the dark beast had given her the openings she needed to get her defenses up and to call her allies, and how she and the fauns had fought the revenant.

"It was the death of the undine that weakened it, though," she continued. "I am not sure why."

"I think it was probably because Durendal was too distracted," the Graf said, as Gunther nodded agreement. "Too many attackers at once. It kept him from using the energy released as the poor undine perished; possibly at that point he was having to stave off the nix as well. Instead, when the undine perished, he found he then had *less* of the pain and fear energies he needed. That loosened his hold a little on the undines, the nix attacked in force, which strengthened the undines, and—"

"And the fauns and I directed our fire at the ice, rather than Durendal. We broke the ice, allowing the nix to seize their prey, and that was the end of it. I *hope,*" she added, looking to the Graf.

"I have people out at the pond, still. There is no sign of Durendal." The Graf grimaced. "I find it unlikely that he could have a *third* vessel waiting, but we are on the watch for anything of the sort. I must see about setting up a Lodge in Vienna."

"Well, that is all the tale there is," Rosa concluded. "I regret, Master Petro, that there is absolutely nothing of Jules Verne about it. Except that after the rest arrived and we did a search for any traps, allies or other mischief, we found the balloon. It was a gas balloon, and the Count believes Durendal had such things on hand in case he needed to travel swiftly. He was an Air Master, after all. And wealthy enough to afford such things, it seems."

Dominik nodded. "Rather than being at the mercy of the wind, he would be the *master* of the wind, directing it to take him precisely where he wanted to go, and as fast as he cared to, with only needing to keep in mind how fragile such constructions are. Which would explain how he was able to get ahead of the train and set up the ambush there."

"And he always intended to abandon the contraption, both here and at the train, I suspect," Rudolf said, looking very thoughtful. "I wonder if he didn't intend to take Fritz's ticket and board the train in our friend's place, then take the return train to Vienna."

"And Fritz would simply—vanish." The Graf nodded. "But—here? He was setting down in the middle of territory belonging to the enemy! And how did he—"

"His Elementals probably told him all of our plans; it wasn't as if we were keeping anything about this party a secret," Gunther pointed out gruffly. "And they would have kept him informed as he drew nearer to your estate, old friend. By the time he was ready to land, he would have known exactly what Rosa was going to do. It isn't as if we guarded against errant sylphs when she and Markos were planning their trails."

"But how, in the name of Heaven, did he think he was going to get away?" the Graf protested.

The professor held up a finger and they all turned toward him. "Mind you, this is all speculation—" he said, after clearing his throat.

"But—" the Graf prompted.

"But my studies of the supernatural seem to indicate that spirits without their proper bodies degrade over time, as it were," the professor said, gravely. "This is why haunts repeat the same actions over and over. And the more of themselves that spirits devote to a highly emotional task, such as revenge, the faster that degradation occurs."

The Graf looked impatient for a moment. "I do not see why this is relevant," he complained.

"It is relevant, my dear host, because I don't think that Durendal was thinking of escape *at all,*" the professor replied. "His ability to think was severely compromised. He could hold only one thing in his mind at a time. That is, if the theory of spirit degradation is correct."

"It's as good an explanation as any," rumbled Gunther.

"So it seems that all our puzzles are answered, or at least have *an* answer, though we can't know if it is the right one—well, except one." Rosa looked to the Graf. "Have you any old churches near that forest? *Very* old, I mean, old enough to have had a dog buried at the foundations to serve as a bargeist? I don't recall any ruins, but if it had not been for that bargeist distracting her—him—I would not have been able to get my own shields up and mount a counterattack."

Markos coughed politely, as the Graf, somewhat to Rosa's puzzlement, looked amused—and so did Dominik. "You might as well tell her, Markos," Dominik said. "Tell them all, since it seems only the Count knows."

"That wasn't a bargeist, Hunt Master," the young Hungarian said diffidently. "That was—er—me."

At first, Rosa wasn't sure what he had said. Then she wasn't sure she had heard him correctly. Then—

"Oh, you mean you spirit-rode a dog?" she said, puzzled. "But where did you get a dog of that size? Or did—"

"No, I don't mean that at all, Hunt Master," Markos replied. "I mean, that really *was* me. In my shifted form. I am a werewolf."

"What?" Rosa was not the only one exclaiming over that, though she might have been the only one wishing for a coach gun and cursing that, once again, she was unarmed.

Or, judging by the hubbub that ensued, perhaps not.

When the clamor finally died down—and it did so *only* when the Graf himself got to his feet and ordered them all to "Cease your bawling!"—Markos spoke again. At this point, every drop of alcohol in Rosa's body had been burned away by fear and alarm and she was on a hair trigger, which was not improved by the fact that now she hurt all over again.

The Graf was standing at this point. "Sit down, all of you," he ordered, and when they all took their seats again, reluctantly, he glared at them. At that moment it was easy to see how his ancestors had won their title and estate. He was every bit the warrior that Rosa considered *herself* to be, and then some.

"I invited the boy here, knowing exactly what he is, as I have known of his family all my life," the Graf barked. "Do you think I would have brought anything dangerous into my own house? Now think, all of you. You've all heard, and read, of shape-shifters that work with the White Lodges. Well, they are real. And Markos is one of them. Hear him out."

Markos licked his lips, nervously. "It's the Nagy blood-line, or rather, my branch of it," he said. "We are not sorcer-ers, we are hereditary shape-shifters. The ability goes back centuries, probably before Christ. In some of the oldest books in my house, it is said we are the children of the god-dess Asena, but I don't know about that. Our tradition is that we have always used our ability to help us destroy the *vampir,* even though some people think we are associated with them."

Seeing that Gunther was not at all alarmed by the pres-ence of—one of *those*—in their midst, Rosa had fought her immediate reaction to a standstill, and calmed herself down somewhat. Though she still wished for a coach gun, or at least, a pistol loaded with silver shot. Just in case. Because you never knew. . . .

And it was Gunther who spoke up when Markos fell si-lent, speaking directly to Rosa. "I have told you that not every shifter is evil, Rosa," he chided gently—though Rosa noted that she was not the only person in the room to look dubious. "I told you that from the time I began to teach you, did I not? And you never questioned me. I have known of the Nagy family for all my life, though I have never met one of them until now, and I know them to be good allies of the White Lodges."

"Yes . . . well," she muttered, and favored Gunther and the Graf with a glare. "You might have told me before this!"

"And spoil the surprise?" the Graf said, blandly. "This has been highly informative. I commend you all for being perfectly willing to bash out the brains of a fellow guest if he or she suddenly turned dangerous. It is a useful habit to be in, although the emotions are entirely misplaced this time."

At that moment, Rosa realized that she had been hold-ing the handle of her stein all this time as if she was prepar-ing to use it as a weapon. And so was everyone else. She flushed a little—but did not let go.

"So, tell us about you, and your bloodline, and what you can do, Markos," the Graf continued, with a wave of his hand. "This is all very instructive. Like Gunther, of course, I knew *of* you, but I have never met a Nagy that I know of."

"I can shift at any time, so long as I do it in shadow, because direct sunlight interferes with the process," Markos continued. "It doesn't depend on moonlight—but that is just my family. It takes longer when it is daylight, except for those of us who, like me, are Earth Magicians. We can draw on the power of the Earth and speed the process along."

"Or another Earth Magician like me can offer assistance," Dominik said genially. "I can help, when someone needs to grow fur in a great hurry."

Now Rosa stared at *him*. An Earth Master? Helping shifters to shift?

"And shall I expect you to grow long ears and teeth as well?" she blurted.

Dominik chuckled. "No, not at all, that talent is in the Nagy blood, not in the Petro side. A pity, because it meant that I had to travel at man's and horse's pace to get here, and I couldn't run across country with a change of clothing tied to my back."

"Is that how you got here?" Gunther asked, looking only very interested.

Markos nodded. "Wolves can run for miles without stopping. That was how I got from my homeland to Budapest, where I caught a train like anyone else."

Rosa now found herself distinctly torn. On the one hand, this was fascinating, and she envied him being able to run free on four legs and not have to depend on horses and carriages and trains. On the other—

He was a *werewolf*.

"And I, who have also come to the Count with the same request, was forced to ride to Budapest, suffering flea-infested piles of straw that cheating innkeepers dared to name 'beds,' truly *terrible* food, and worse beer." Dominik sighed theatrically. "Oh, how I would have liked to be able to run as a wolf! I have other talents, however, and quite useful ones. For instance, Fraulein Rosamund, I assume you would like to have that injured shoulder of yours back in condition by morning?"

What did that—oh!

"Your Mastery includes healing?" she asked.

"It does, if you will trust me to do so." Dominik's eyes

twinkled. "After all, I am in league with a werewolf. Worse! He is my cousin! Who knows what terrible things I might do to you?"

Rosa was torn. This was a very good test of their sincerity. But on the other hand—

She glanced around at the rest, who seemed to have decided to give the two young men the benefit of the doubt and looked much more relaxed and accepting of them than she was.

Even Gunther. Even *Gunther.* Well, it was true that Gunther had been insisting from the time she had been rescued that not *all* shape-shifters were bad.

Well, Dominik Petro—or to use Hungarian fashion, which placed the family name first, Petro Dominik—was an Earth Master and there was nothing about him that set up alarms in her. *Be polite. After all, you have silver knives, and you know how to use them.*

"I would very much appreciate that, Master Petro," she said. "Very much."

"Before you go to bed then, I would rather not make you move from that comfortable chair," he replied, with a hint of a laugh. "And I would rather not perform like a dancing bear in front of everyone, so perhaps a place with less of an audience."

"We'll get you a quiet corner," the Graf promised, then added, wryly, "I think we can find some privacy somewhere."

"Really?" Dominik responded, feigning shock, and looking around at the ersatz *bierhalle.* "I cannot imagine *where!*"

When everyone laughed at that, Rosa decided, with only a little reluctance, that she was beginning to like Dominik very much. *And I liked Markos very much until . . .* Damn it all. Should she trust her knowledge or her instincts? Should she trust everything she had learned, often the hard way, or the Graf and Gunther?

She listened to the music, took part in the conversation, drank the Graf's truly excellent beer, and watched the cousins, trying not to look as if she was planning where to stick her silver knives into them.

Then, finally, the obvious occurred to her. If there was

anyone likely to tell her the absolute truth about the two, it was her little allies, the Earth Elementals. And this was protected, sheltered ground for them; everything that could be done to make Elementals feel welcome on the Graf's estate had been done. *So, do the obvious. Go ask the creatures that you know you can always trust in matters of magic.*

The room was getting a bit warm, so she used that as an excuse to lever herself up out of the armchair and go out onto the terrace.

"I need some fresh air and a short walk before I fall asleep here," she said, with a little smile as she got up. She winced a bit at the pain in her shoulder; had she dislocated it? It felt as if she had, and then popped it back in again. It wouldn't have been the first time she had done such a thing.

"I've ordered the gardens to be illuminated," the Graf said, with less than half his attention, as he watched two of the professor's pupils dancing a polka in a manner that could only be described as "wild." "They are lovely that way, if I do say so myself."

Well that was the perfect invitation, and Rosa walked slowly to the doors to the terrace—taking with her a napkin full of cheese, of course. And from the terrace, she took the steps down into the garden, finding a quiet spot surrounded by the Graf's beloved roses. There she settled down on the perfectly manicured lawn, and drew a circle around herself with her finger in the grass, watching as the line of power followed her finger and enclosed her. This was not to keep anything *out,* it was to provide an even more protected space for whatever chose to answer her invitation.

Then, with a few sigils sketched in the air, and a warm glow of welcome, she issued that invitation.

She hoped, mostly, for one of the little *alvar.* There was no telling what—or even whether—an Elemental would actually come when called like this. She'd never had the invitation fail, but then, there was always a first time.

But it wasn't a moment later, before she found herself swarmed, not only by *alvar,* but by *haus-alvar,* a couple of fauns, and even a sylph, who darted in, dropped a rosebud in her lap, and vanished before she could say anything.

She shared out the cheese as equally as she could; normally at least some of the Elementals would have snatched the treat and run, but tonight, they all arranged themselves around her as if they were having a picnic together in the grass. There must have been three dozen of the little *alvar,* and as she looked about her, it came to her that this looked exactly like one of the happier illustrations in a fairy tale book. Some of the *alvar* were actually leaning against her, and all of them were on the charming side of grotesque. Most of them were dressed in garments made of flowers, leaves, and moss. Their little faces were all pleasant, and they spoke softly to one another in voices that sounded like sleepy birds. One of the fauns looked up at her expectantly.

"Well, my friends," she said, looking down at their strange faces in the moonlight. "I called you because I need to know something, and I think you can tell me."

That occasioned more soft twittering. They seemed to be quite pleased that she would ask them something. *But the Graf is a Fire Master, so I suppose even though he makes his gardens welcoming for them, the Earth Elementals are rarely called on.*

"Is it the answer to a riddle?" the faun asked, nodding his curly head. "We know a great many riddles!"

"Not that kind of riddle," she replied. "It is a riddle in the shape of a man."

But the faun laughed. "Oh!" he exclaimed, as if she had delighted him. "We already know what you want! You are the Master of the Hunt, and there is a shifter up there in the Big House! You want to know about him!"

She sighed with relief. The Elementals could on occasion be extremely obtuse. Tonight it seemed they were in a mood to be direct. "You are right. There is a shifter there that the others think is—"

One of the *haus-alvar* interrupted her by shyly putting its sticklike hand on her knee. This one was very thin, and seemed to have somehow created clothing out of broom-straws. "The Wolf-Runners are good," it whispered to her. "My cousins' cousins' cousins know them. And this one is very good. But—"

She waited, while it struggled for words. No use in trying to rush the little creatures, nor prompt them. Their minds didn't work the same as humans, and if you tried to get them to say something before they were ready to come out with it, you often got nothing you could use. Possibly because they were so used to speaking in aphorisms and riddles that when they wanted to say something directly, it was very difficult for them to do so.

Finally it seemed to figure out what it wanted to say. "There is a danger. If the man runs as a wolf for too long, the man is lost forever in the wolf."

Her mouth went a little dry. This was exactly what she had been afraid of—that the mere act of shifting shapes itself was dangerous to the shifter and those around him. "Is that a danger to me, or to him?" she asked, managing to get the words out.

"Both," the *haus-alvar* said solemnly. "The wolf may not know you. The wolf may be afraid. Bad things could happen."

Suddenly, all their heads came up at once, alert and alarmed; Rosa bit back an exclamation of pain as she wrenched herself around to see who or what had alarmed them.

But they all relaxed again and settled, and slow, steady footfalls—the footfalls of a man who was deliberately making his approach known—heralded the arrival of someone she knew immediately by the unmistakable silhouette of his Hungarian coat against the light from the garden lamp behind him.

"Well, having a feast and didn't invite me?" Dominik said, feigning hurt, and making the *alvar* giggle and the fauns laugh aloud. "Maybe I won't share what I brought, then."

That caused all the Elementals, who were extraordinarily relaxed in his presence, right to their feet, clamoring to see what treat it was he had brought with him.

He finally relented, sat down on the grass across from Rosa, and opened the parcel that someone had made up for him out of a breadbasket and covered with one of the enormous napkins. The bundle was full of more cheese chunks and bread, and the *alvar* and fauns swarmed it so thickly nothing of the contents could be seen for a moment.

When they cleared away, their arms were full of "loot," and there was not so much as a crumb left in the basket. Dominik made a little shooing motion as they waited to hear what he wanted of them. "I am going to heal this lady. Leave a bit of magic for me to use, if you wish to, and go enjoy your treats."

He didn't have to tell them twice. Before Rosa could blink, the circle was emptied of Elementals, but full of Earth energies. Elementals liked things in balance; if they hadn't managed to *steal* something, if they accepted a gift, they were uneasy until they gave a gift in return.

Dominik gave her a long and measuring look. She returned it.

"You don't entirely trust us," he said. "Me and Markos, that is. But you trust me a little more than Markos."

Well if he was going to be candid with her, she would be just as blunt with him.

"I've been killing shifters for a long time now," she pointed out. "And when I was a young child, one tried to kill me, and did succeed in murdering my teacher. I found the mangled body in the pantry I tried to hide in. This is the first time I've seen one that didn't want to kill me first."

"A good point." Dominik nodded. "Well, since you are not drawing a knife on me just yet, let me address your injuries first. Then, when that is done, we can speak of other things."

That was, to her mind, a perfectly reasonable response.

"As you will," she replied.

8

USING Earth Magic to heal, as Rosa was well aware, was generally not that ... impressive. It certainly wasn't as impressive as making lightning strike, or controlling a wildfire. Dominik simply muttered a few things under his breath, and sketched a couple of sigils in the air, while she sat where she was and watched, with interest but not a lot of comprehension, as the golden glow of the magic somehow drained *into* her. She didn't feel any immediate relief, either—but she hadn't expected to. She had been worked on by a healer many times in the past, and she knew that in most circumstances, a healer merely helped your body to heal itself more quickly. She'd heard of healers doing more than that in great and desperate situations, but she had never seen such a thing, nor spoken with anyone who had.

On the other hand, she had never met a "good" shapeshifter before either, so ... it could be possible.

When the last of the golden glow was gone, she flexed her shoulder experimentally. "Well, I can see that by morning that *will* be better," she remarked, pleased. She knew her body well enough to be able to tell when even the smallest improvements had taken place. Already there was a little less pain and a little more free movement. That was a sign she was healing faster than she would have on her own.

"Good. Now, about my cousin . . ." A couple of the little *alvar* crept close again, and settled down politely near them, watching their faces and listening. Dominik coughed politely. "You know, the Nagy family is very well thought of where we come from. They perform exactly the same sort of tasks that your Schwarzwald Brotherhood does—they keep the land healthy, they hunt down magicians gone to the bad and evil things, they find lost children. It is just that some of them do so on four legs, at need."

The light from the garden lamps fell clearly on both of them, so she studied his expression. It was open and honest, and the way the *alvar* were at ease with him just reinforced the fact that they had vouched for him, and for his cousin, Markos.

The only possible conclusion was that she needed to make some fundamental changes in her outlook, at least where the extended Nagy family was concerned.

She took a long, deep breath to calm herself. "I understand that is your reality. But you must please understand that this is very difficult for me to believe. My reality is that I have never once encountered a shifter that was not murdering people, Elementals, or both. I generally ended up fighting for my life when I encountered one. And the few times that I did not, it was because I killed them before they knew I was there."

"But!" Dominik said, raising a finger. "Wait! Have you ever encountered one that was *not* either a sorcerer, or cursed, or infected? I would think not. The ability to shift from birth is confined to a very few bloodlines, and every one of those I know personally is . . . moral to a fault."

She thought about that for a while. "I believe you are correct in asking me that question. I don't think I have ever encountered one that was born to the . . . would you call it a talent?"

"I certainly would," he said emphatically. "Absolutely. And absolutely, I would trust those I know under any and all circumstances. I *mean* that, Fraulein, and I have done so. I have spent time utterly alone with Markos when he was shifted and never had a moment of unease. And as for the rest of his family—well! I have known Nagys to go out into howling blizzards, into conditions that would kill a man, and patiently herd cattle, sheep, or goats into shelter, thus saving the herds and the livelihoods of their neighbors. I have known them to search for missing children until their paws bled. I have known them to search for missing men, and when found, hold bears or boars off wounded hunters all by themselves. And I have *never* known them to harm so much as a hair on the head of someone who did not deserve punishment."

Every word rang of conviction. More, every word sounded like something he actually had witnessed for himself.

She blinked, taken a bit aback at his vehemence. "You are very eloquent in their defense," she managed. She went from sitting cross-legged to hugging her knees, glad that her clothing allowed her to do so. She was feeling defensive, and was not used to feeling that way during a . . . discussion.

Then again, she had never had a discussion quite like this one.

"Because they deserve defending." He shrugged, but she got the feeling that was a kind of habit, rather than an expression of indifference. "I want you to understand that the Nagys are the allies of humanity, not predators. I want you to understand that Markos in particular is a good, honorable warrior in the service of the right. That he happens to wear fur to go to war is irrelevant."

"This seems very important to you," she observed. *Which is odd, considering that we've only just met, and may never meet again . . . unless you know something I do not.*

His next words confirmed that guess. "Yes, this is important to me, because the reason he and I are here is that we need the help of someone from the Count's White Lodge, a Lodge he can introduce us to, or your Bruderschaft—and that someone might well be you."

"Me?" She managed not to squeak the word, but it was

a near thing. Was this a consequence of all those introductions the Graf had been making? Or was it something else entirely?

"Possibly. We will not know until we speak at length with the Count and Master Gunther." He shrugged again. He got to his feet and offered her his hand. She put out her good hand, he grasped the wrist, and helped her to her feet. He was as strong as he looked. She let go of his hand as soon as she was on her feet. "And we will probably talk about it for several days yet. As the Count said, this is not—as yet—an emergency or a crisis. In fact, we have reason to believe the situation has persisted for decades, so a few days more will be of no matter."

Well, that truly got her interest. A situation that had persisted for decades? She could think of a few things that the Bruderschaft had dealt with that matched that description. It seemed that the Schwarzwald liked to hide secrets that were revealed only when someone stumbled upon them. Once, it had been a colony of particularly nasty little goblins that had been invoked by a long-ago Master gone bad, and had been left behind to work as much undirected mischief as they cared to when he died. More than once, it had been an evil magician who was also cunning enough to keep his depredations at such a low level that he remained unnoticed until he happened to choose the wrong victim— someone or something that had been missed.

That was the most likely scenario here. The most successful villains were those who kept their ambition and greed within bounds—who practiced self-restraint, and did not allow their emotions to get the better of them. Who, like wise predators, did not kill indiscriminately. Such were, thankfully, rare. But when they did occur, they were all the harder to find.

Gone, thank the Good God, were the days when the likes of Countess Bartholdy could keep an entire fiefdom in silent and abject terror. But that only meant that great evil had to exercise great cunning.

"I could eat another plate of sausage after that, I think," Dominik said, abruptly changing the subject, and smiling at her with great charm. She usually did not care for men with moustaches, but she thought Dominik looked rather dashing. "I hope there is still some left."

"I am not in the least surprised that you are ravenous," she told him lightly, sensing she would not hear another word out of him on the subject of why he and Markos were here until he was ready. "The healers of the Bruderschaft generally eat twice as much as the rest of us, and stay lean as a staff." She gestured up at the terrace and the ersatz *bierhalle*. "Shall we go and let your cousin know he can pull his not-so-metaphorical tail from between his legs, and that I will not be hunting for my coach gun or my knives?"

"So, have I persuaded you already that we are on the side of the angels?" He sounded surprised.

"I would not go so far as that," she cautioned, "But it is truce between us for now. It is not that you are not persuasive, Herr Petro. It is that I have much to overcome before I am trusting. The habits and fears of a lifetime are not overcome by a few words, no matter how well chosen."

"Point taken. Truce and at least the appearance of friendship will be enough." He gestured to her to proceed. They climbed the steps to the terrace to find that the party had spilled out into the fresh air and the band had retired. Some servants were already dismantling the *bierhalle* and restoring the furnishings. Others were waiting attendance on the terrace. Since the terrace was supplied with summer furnishings, no comfort was lost in coming outside into the balmy night air.

"Rosa, and Dominik, we were just discussing what should be the entertainment for tomorrow!" the Graf said as they climbed up onto the terrace and looked about.

"Something not so strenuous as today, I think," Rosa said feelingly. "Other than that, I fear I am at a loss to suggest anything. We tend to spend what leisure time we have in the Schwarzwald very quietly."

Really, whenever she thought of *free time,* the first thing that sprang to her mind was reading. A pile of cushions between the roots of a tree in summer, or warmly toasting by the fire in winter with a new book—this was her notion of a fine way to spend a few hours.

"If I may suggest, my lord?" The butler, splendidly attired in old-fashioned livery that included knee breeches, was supervising the servants out here on the terrace, standing not far from the Graf, and interjected his few words diffidently and with profound respect.

"By all means, Bergdorf, suggest away!" the Graf exclaimed.

The butler bowed. "There is a band of gypsies camped down at the meadow you reserve for them. I could send to see if they would be willing to provide some entertainment on the morrow, in the evening."

Rosa perked up at that suggestion. The Bruderschaft and the Romany got along well together, as did most Elemental Magicians—magic ran strongly in the Romany blood, and while the Roma did not scruple to work their tricks on most *gadjo,* they never would do so on fellow magicians. That was probably why the Graf had a designated safe area for the Roma to camp in; it kept them secure from persecution, and discouraged mischief on the part of the Roma, who would not bring trouble to one who was willing to host them.

"That is an excellent plan; please see to it, Bergdorf. And even if they are unwilling or have nothing to entertain us with, make sure you tender my respects, and deliver the usual provender." Rosa smiled at that last, for the Graf was wise. Offer the Roma hospitality and they would confine themselves to gathering what they could find in the forest and setting snares for rabbits.

She liked gypsies, and yet felt sad for them at the same time. Very few cared to host them. They were persecuted in nearly every land. And you could go on about "the romance of the road" all you liked, but the road was a very, very hard life and there was nothing romantic about being crammed, entire families, into a wagon the size of her bedroom. She hoped they would come, for she loved to watch gypsy dancing, and to listen to their melancholy, yet defiant, music.

"Since the children were essentially deprived of their Hunt today, why not arrange some contests for them during the day?" she ventured to suggest, as she took a lounging chair near the Graf and Gunther. "Archery, perhaps. Croquet and shuttlecock. Footraces? That sort of thing? There could be prizes. That way they would get over not winning the Hunt prize."

"Another excellent suggestion." The Graf nodded. "Wear the little creatures out all afternoon so that supper makes them sleepy and we can send them off to bed at sunset and get them out from underfoot."

"My dear Count!" exclaimed one of the mothers, half laughing and half in reproach, "You have such an unromantic view of children!"

"Children are unromantic beings, my lady," the Graf retorted, waggling a finger at her. "Little savages, in fact. There is not a sentimental bone in a child's body, I do assure you. The best thing one can do for them on a daily basis is wear them out so they sleep well at night, and by way of education stuff their heads full of what you would like them to know in the fond hope they will actually retain some of it."

Evidently the lady in question knew the Graf well enough not to be offended, because she laughed. "A good thing you never had any of your own, then," she retorted. "That is an appalling way to raise a child! Oh, fresh air and sunshine and a great deal of exercise, but if you wish a child to learn, you must find a way to make him love to learn. Stuffing their little heads full will only make them sick of learning and turn them into very dull adults."

Torches had been set up all around the terrace, and each of the little tables had its own lantern, so there was plenty of light. The Graf had remarkably comfortable outdoor furniture, not stiff wood or wrought iron, but yielding wickerwork with cushions. She wished she could whisk some of it away to the Lodge.

The men were drinking port and smoking cigars now, while the ladies sipped sherry or coffee—thanks to Marie, Rosa knew that if this had been a "real" gathering, the men and women would be divided into two different rooms. The men would be smoking and drinking in exclusively male company, in the billiard room, while the ladies occupied the parlor. Perhaps some of the younger men—especially if they were interested in the young ladies—would adjourn to the parlor, but only after a suitable interval in exclusively masculine company.

What a ridiculous custom! Marie said it was because men would use the opportunity to speak of "serious" topics, politics, business, and the like—as if women weren't just as interested in those things as men! But there it was: outside of the circles of the Elemental Mages—or the circles of the bohemian artists and writers and musicians—such topics were not thought "suitable" for female minds.

Rosa hoped profoundly that if she ever *did* need to operate in "Society," it would not be for long. She wasn't sure she could bear the boredom.

One of the professor's students, though only an Air Mage, had somehow persuaded some sylphs to send all the smoke away from the ladies, and a good thing, too. Although Gunther and some of the other men of the Bruderschaft enjoyed their cigars of an evening, Rosa could not abide the smell of the things and generally left for her own room when they lit up.

She had found a very comfortable lounging chair, and the lassitude that usually came on her after a difficult fight made her disinclined to move. From here, the garden illuminations were quite beautiful, especially around the fountain, where the water sparkled in the light like a continuous firework display.

"Are you longing for your forest, Master Rosa?" asked Markos diffidently. He was not smoking a nasty cigar, so Rosa beckoned him to come closer. He pulled up a wicker chair near her and took a seat.

"Not at all at the moment," she replied. "The Schwarzwald is more than a little intimidating by night, and I generally don't venture far from the Lodge unless I have to. The forest grows so closely around the Lodge itself that we have no pretty view at all by night, much less an illuminated landscape like this one. I will probably miss the forest soon, but right now, there is a great deal to be said in favor of a tamed and domesticated garden."

"Not all that tamed." He peered down below him. "The Count has made it a home for all sorts of our allies. I see an undine or three in the fountain, lots of small things scurrying in and out of hiding in the garden, and sylphs and salamanders playing about the lights."

She shifted over to mage-sight, and saw what he had, although the Elementals were being cautious about revealing themselves too much.

"You have sharp eyes. Does that come with being a shifter?" she asked. She tried to keep her tone neutral so he would not take that as some sort of attack.

"On the contrary, it is just practice at looking for the signs of our allies in any environment. Like most canines, the wolf's vision is restricted; I tend to be able to distinguish movement better than a human, but that is all. Shifted, I hunt with my nose rather than my eyes." He turned toward her, slightly, examining her expression. Probably looking for disapproval.

"Your cousin spoke eloquently on your behalf." She waited to see what his reaction to that would be. "On behalf of your entire family, in fact, but particularly for you."

"My cousin is a very good friend, and has been for all our lives," said Markos. "I could not ask for a better. Although we are only distantly related, he was in and out of our house as much as his own. And that is despite a difference in rank and circumstances. His father is a wealthy merchant; mine is a sheep farmer. He persuaded my father to let me go to university in Budapest when he went."

"Oh really?" That was unexpected. *Why would a were-wolf wish to go to university?* "And what did you study?"

"Latin, Greek, and History." Markos shrugged, an expression nearly identical to the one his cousin used. Rosa got the impression that they shrugged when they were at a momentary loss for words. "Not at all practical, I fear, but it was the knowledge that I craved. I attained a degree. Dominik studied medicine but didn't stay long enough to be given a Doctor of Medicine degree, and I left when he did." Markos smiled. "We were both homesick, we were both very, very tired of the city, and he said he had learned all a healer needed to know from 'scientific' medicine."

If he attained a degree, he must have been there three or four years at least. How could an Earth Mage live in a city that long? "I wonder that he tried at all. So much of what passes for medicine is torture under the guise of helping,"

she observed. "In many ways we are no better than the an-
cients in how we treat injury and illness. But I am surprised
that two Earth Mages could abide the city for any length of
time at all."

"Budapest is pleasant, for a city." Markos looked over
the low wall around the terrace for a moment. "And the
university is a green haven inside it. We had plenty of opportunities to go on short trips to inns just outside the city,
thanks to his father. Although—" He paused for a moment,
and laughed. "Well, you are no delicate flower. Many of
those inns were used by wealthy men to entertain their mistresses, in the pleasant months. We often found our entire
bills taken care of by gentlemen who feared we had seen
something they didn't want us to see."

"I don't think I could bring myself to live there, regardless," she replied, though she was highly amused at the con-
fession about the inns.

"I don't know how Dom did." He looked down into his
port glass; the wine seemed to be mostly untasted. "I at least
could always shift and run out into the countryside whenever things grew too oppressive. He didn't have that escape.
And he is a Master. It must have been terribly difficult for
him, yet he never complained."

Her curiosity became unbearable. There was something
she had always wanted to know, and never had the chance
to ask, since asking questions of a beast that is trying to
murder you is not likely to elicit answers. But here she had
a "beast" captive, so to speak, so she asked it now.

"What becomes of your clothing? When you change, I
mean." She looked into his startled eyes fearlessly.

He blushed a bright scarlet.

She was puzzled for a moment—then the answer hit her
and she laughed out loud. Fortunately everyone else was so
involved in their own conversations—many of which were
eliciting laughter—that no one looked over at them.

"You shift nude!" she chortled.

He flushed even redder. "Well...er...yes...Wolves
don't wear clothing, after all," he stammered.

"But what do you do when you shift back?" she wanted

to know. "Didn't your cousin say you had run here as a wolf? I can't imagine turning up at the Count's door without a stitch on!"

"I would never be so rude!" he exclaimed indignantly. "There is a—a protocol for this. When we are just making a local run, we shift in private, such as in our rooms. If we are going somewhere, we carry a change of clothing in a harness on our back. If we are hunting, we arrange for a change of clothing to be with us—usually with our companions. We *never* hunt alone. That would be foolish."

Clearly, when he said "hunt," he wasn't talking about game-hunting. "But what if you—I don't know—want to chase rabbits or something?" she asked.

His color normalized, and his expression grew very serious. "Unless we absolutely must, we *do not* hunt for game," he replied. "That is . . . it is not advised. The more we act like wolves, the more we allow the wolf instincts to run free, the harder it is to remain human within the wolf. Hunting—and especially killing—these evoke particularly powerful instincts. So we don't risk it. I had money with me when I ran here. When I got hungry, I shifted, found an inn, and ate like a civilized man."

She remembered then what the *alvar* had said when she asked it for its opinion of Markos. *"There is a danger. If the man runs as a wolf for too long, the man is lost forever in the wolf."*

"Is the danger the same for those who shift by sorcery?" she asked.

He nodded. "And the more closely entwined with blood magic the sorcery is, the more likely it is that when the shift happens, the wolf becomes the dominant personality. As for those poor souls who are infected—" He shook his head. "—the poor wretches have no chance. When they shift, because they have not been trained from birth the way my family has been, it is worse than just the wolf overcoming the man. It is the worst of both man and beast. Every violent thought the man has ever had is acted upon. The wolf has no fear of man, and only knows that such-and-so is an enemy and must be destroyed."

"And those who are cursed?" she asked.

"The same. It takes a will of iron to fight down the beast within if you have been infected or cursed." Again, he shook his head. "I personally am glad I have never been forced to deal with either. I would feel guilty for a very long time for having to, essentially, punish a victim."

She nodded, and tried not to think of the werewolves she had *not* determined to be blood magicians, who she had been forced to put down. And she cursed him, just a little, for planting such disturbing thoughts in her mind.

"I see I have upset you," he said, interrupting her thoughts. "I beg your pardon, I did not intend—"

"Do not apologize for the truth," she said, with a little, abrupt motion of her hand. "It is better to know it and face it." She shrugged. "Besides, even if I had known that some of the beasts that I dispatched were, themselves, victims, what else could I have done? So far as I know, there is no cure for such things. And all of them had killed. All of them would have continued to kill. I had to stop them, and there is no prison I know of strong enough to hold one of these beasts forever. Either the man will escape through magic or guile, or the beast will, through force and violence."

He sighed. "No, there is no cure for infection. For a curse? I do not know, and I am afraid I could not tell between an individual who was cursed and one who had been infected. Possibly there *is* no such thing as a curse; that it is just a poetic way of describing the infected. And ..." He paused for a very long time before continuing. "And in all of those that I am aware of, who had any morals at all, who knew they had been infected, and knew what they had done—that knowledge was such a terrible burden that it drove them to suicide."

The night darkened for a moment, and a cold chill settled over Rosa. It was interrupted by Gunther and the Count, who called to them both to come and join the professor and Anna, the brilliant soprano, in an impromptu game of cards. Eager to leave behind their dark thoughts, they both did, and soon Dominik joined them as well.

By the time, Rosa was ready to take her leave for the evening, all such depressing reflections had been driven from her mind, and what she shared with Marie were nothing gloomier than speculations on what, if anything, the gypsies might be persuaded to perform for the company.

The children, when presented at breakfast with the idea of contests, had an idea of their own—and it was quite the clever one.

"We want an Olympics!" proclaimed the eldest of the boys. "Peter and Tobi and I have been studying the Greeks, and we want an Olympics!"

At that, the rest of the children all bounced in place or leapt to their feet. "Yes, yes!" they cried out. "Please, Uncle Heinrich! We want an Olympics!"

Rosa had the distinct impression that several of them had *no* idea what the Olympic Games were, but the three older boys wanted such a competition so badly that they wanted it too.

"It must be a proper Games," Johan said, with utmost seriousness. "We must invoke the Gods, and we must have chitons and tunics, and laurel wreathes and everything. And we must have an Olympic Torch to light! And we must have a marathon—"

The Graf embraced the plan with as much enthusiasm as the children, and sent his housekeeper running off to find pillowcases and sheets that could be sacrificed to make chitons and tunics. "But I think running twenty-five miles may be a bit much for a marathon," he pointed out gently. "It will take you a long time, possibly all day, and that would not be fun. So let us make our marathon—hmm—shall we say once around the palace and grounds?"

After due deliberation, and assurances that the Gods would not mind if children did a rather shorter marathon than the ancient Greeks had, the entire company pitched together to design the games. Marie and two of the laundry maids volunteered to make costumes of the sheets. Marie did the designing, and the laundry maids, accustomed to running up linen hems very quickly indeed on their treadle sewing machines, sewed the few seams needed.

By midmorning the preparations were complete. The girls all elected themselves as representatives of the goddess Athena and the god Apollo, and had a solemn procession, ending with the oldest of the girls calling upon Apollo. "Oh Apollo, god of the divine sun and idea of light, send your rays to light this sacred torch!" she called, and the Graf obliged by doing so. When the torch had gone up with a satisfactory *whoosh,* she continued. "Now you, god Zeus, bless all those here with peace and crown those who have mastered the sacred contests."

That was the signal for the release of a cage full of doves hidden in the bushes, to the applause of all. Then the games themselves began. There was no wrestling, in part because none of the children actually knew how to wrestle, and in part because there was such disparity in ages and sizes that no fair contests could have been staged. The same went for boxing, and of course chariot racing was completely out of the question as much too dangerous.

But before lunch, there were races in plenty; short sprints, longer races on courses laid out through the garden, and long jumps. And after lunch, there was pony racing, archery, throwing of a ball, and discus, hammer, and javelin. Two of the boys wanted to exclude the girls from these activities on the grounds that women were barred from the original Olympic Games, but the Graf pointed out sternly that the women of Sparta participated in *all* sports, and it would be counter to the spirit of the Olympics to exclude them.

The adults had cunningly planned the contests so that even the youngest children had a chance of winning at least one, and everything turned out as they had hoped. And it was all unexpectedly entertaining, at least for Rosa.

The conclusion of the Games was the "marathon," and as it turned out, it was one of the girls who won it, she having the best endurance of the lot.

The games concluded with the presentation of "laurel" wreathes and the prizes the Graf had intended to give for the Hunt. The prizes themselves were rather nice, Rosa thought; really *good* books, not silly moralistic ones, but rousing things with ancient gods and myths, pirates, knights and American cowboys in them. And good sets of bows and arrows, proper ones, of the sort that she would have loved to get.

Uncle Heinrich might say he doesn't like or understand children, but unless someone else chose those prizes, he knows exactly what children like. Or at least, the children of Elemental Mages, anyway, who were encouraged to think for themselves and be active regardless of whether they were boys or girls.

And the games had the desired effect of making the children so weary that a couple of them nearly fell asleep over their dinner, which, in deference to the entertainment, was laid at the highly unfashionable hour of six. They were all placed at a sort of head-table, still wearing their Greek costumes and their laurel wreathes, and were served before the adults. They even had wine, though it was well-diluted with grape juice, and got to eat with their fingers in supposed "ancient" fashion.

And all of them were quite willing to go up to bed, clutching their prizes, long before the gypsies arrived.

And arrive they did, just at sundown, without any fanfare at all. Just a single wagon and a trio of riders, each with a second person riding pillion.

They came up the drive to the palace, looking altogether out of place in front of the majestic building, moving slowly, as if uncertain of their welcome. The Graf had called everyone out to wait for them as a show of courtesy, and they assembled at the door.

The Graf went down to welcome them in person. He went straight to the first rider, a venerable, white-haired man with a truly epic moustache. *"Romale tai Shavale akarel tume o Heinrich,"* he said, spreading his arms wide.

I had no idea he spoke Romany! Rosa thought, pleased. Once again, Uncle Heinrich had proven himself able and willing to do the entirely unexpected.

The Roma gentleman smiled, and there ensued a conversation entirely in Romany, which ended in the Graf pressing upon the man a pouch. The man pocketed it without looking at it, and waved to his fellows who waited behind him. The procession went around to the back of the palace by means of a graveled path; Rosa and the other guests went back through the house to the gardens, where the entertainment was to be held. Servants had already brought down the garden furniture from the terrace and arranged it in a half-circle; everyone took a seat. Rosa obtained one of the lounges she had sat in last night, and waited with great anticipation for the Roma to set themselves up.

The wagon drove in, and was carefully positioned like the backdrop of a stage. Then the riders arrived, now smiling. The Graf gave them all a bow, said something else Rosa couldn't hear in Romany, and took a seat himself.

The riders dismounted, and it appeared that the wagon had been stuffed *full* of more Roma. They swarmed about the designated spot in the garden, and within moments, had transformed it into a cross between a circus ring and a stage. Occasionally one of them would ask something of the Graf, who would say something and point, but mostly they handled it all themselves. They were certainly costumed colorfully, in nearly every color. The girls wore enormous skirts with ruffled hems, embroidered blouses with bell-shaped sleeves, and wide belts or sashes, and shawls, sometimes tied at the waist, draped over their shoulders, or both. The men wore black or brown trousers with shining black boots, and embroidered shirts with high collars and gathered sleeves, with vests of red or black and wide sashes.

Rosa was very near the wagon, and she was not surprised to see the Roma giving her occasional nods and salutes of respect when one of them passed by her. After all, *she* could see the auras of power about all of them, though there was only one for whom the aura was very strong, a fine and dignified old lady swathed in many shawls. Rosa didn't doubt for a moment that they could tell she was an Earth Master; the old lady was, without a doubt, an Air Master. Sylphs practically swarmed all over her.

Her speculation proved true when Dominik finally found himself a seat, and got a similar salute.

A group of Roma arranged themselves in front of the wagon, the old lady and the old man in their midst. These were the musicians; it appeared that the old lady and gentleman were the singers, since they did not have any

instruments—there were two fiddlers, a fellow with a concertina and another with a guitar, a young girl with a tambourine and a man with a hammered dulcimer. As soon as
they were settled, they struck up a czardas, as the rest continued to arrange matters.

Rosa listened to the music with immense pleasure, tap-
ping her toe against the lounge chair and softly clapping her
hands in time to the rhythm, and she wasn't the only one.
The musicians played three songs while the others arranged
things to their liking, and then the entertainment truly
began.

In the reddening light of the sunset, another young girl
rode into the center of the grass on one of the horses. The
two came to a halt in complete silence, and paused there for
a moment, like a statue. Then, as the band struck up another
melody, the horse began to dance.

That was the only way that Rosa could think of it; the
horse truly was dancing to the music, picking his feet up
gracefully, turning in place, circling the "ring" one way, then
reversing and going the other, passing across it in a sort of
sideways motion that involved him crossing his legs in a
most remarkable manner.

The Graf, who was on one side of her, leaned over and
whispered. "I have seen students at the famous Spanish
Riding School in Vienna perform like this. I have never
seen anyone else do such riding before. This is most remarkable!"

Rosa nodded in agreement, unable to take her eyes off
the graceful horse and his utterly motionless rider. She
sensed the horse's immense enjoyment of all this, pleasure
in his own ability, pleasure in the admiration he got, even
pleasure in the music. It was completely wonderful!

Nor was that the end of the equine entertainment; the
girl rode out of the "ring," and two of the other horses, rider-
less but in harness, trotted into it, and three boys proceeded
to do the most amazing acrobatics around, and on, the moving horses that Rosa had ever seen. They jumped on and off
in the most astounding ways; stood on the backs of the
horses and jumped through hoops, and jumped from one
horse to another. They rode *under* the bellies of the horses,

dangled off the tails, and draped themselves under the horses' necks. And just as astonishing were the horses, who reacted to these antics not at all. The boys might not even have been there; the patient creatures kept their steady trot around and around, while the band played and each new trick brought a new burst of applause.

The band ended the song, and the horses trotted out of the ring, taking that as their cue to leave, she supposed. The boys bowed to tremendous applause, and one of the Graf's servants went around the ring, lighting more torches, now that the light was fading into twilight. As he did so, the old man sang in a powerful voice while the fiddler and man with the concertina played. Rosa could not understand the words, but the meaning came through clearly enough; it was so deeply, passionately sad that it brought tears to her eyes that she wiped away without shame.

But the audience was not left to wallow in sadness; the three boys came back, this time with metal rings, which they juggled amongst each other; the rings flashed through the air, reflecting the light of the torches, making all sorts of patterns among the three boys. Nor were the clever fellows done; when the song ended and the rings were all caught, they threw the rings to two girls standing on the sidelines, and got balls in return. Another display of amazing juggling took place, with the balls moving so fast it was hard to keep track of them.

Then the boys finished their turn, and retired. Their place was taken by the two girls.

They literally leapt into a lively series of dances, involving a lot of skirt movement and fast steps. The skirts almost seemed to be alive, in the way that the girls swirled them and made patterns with them. It was so *very* lively that she found herself clapping in time with the music, and the music itself was so joyful that she found herself not just smiling, but laughing. After three dances, two of the boys joined them, and if the girls had been lively, the boys were acrobatic. There was a great deal of heel-clicking, foot stamping, clapping, knee-slapping, and wild leaps as the girls capered around them saucily. Then the girls retired and the boys stretched their dancing to the limit and beyond.

It was marvelous. She had never seen anything quite like it.

"This is how our gypsies in Hungary dance," said Markos, from the other side of her. "In Romania the dancing is quite different."

"And in Spain, it is different as well," the Graf put in. "The dancers keep their upper bodies very stiff, and the footwork is not to be believed until you have seen it."

When the boys tired out, the grass was cleared, and the musicians began another slow, melancholy song. This time it was the old woman who sang, and again, although Rosa could not understand the words, she again found herself moved to tears.

When the old woman was done, each of the instrumentalists (except for the girl with the tambourine) took the star turn in a different song. To Rosa's mind, the most marvelous, and most magical, was the player of the hammered dulcimer. She had heard one once before, but not as good as this fellow. His hammers flew over the strings, which were in pitch-perfect tune, creating waterfalls of music.

When he was finished, the musicians put their instruments down, and the Graf signaled to the servants to begin filling mugs of beer from the barrel he had had brought down into the garden. One of the gypsy girls came to take the mugs and bring them to the others as they rested from their exertions.

"That last—that was the most amazing melody!" said Anna, the soprano. "I wonder if it has words. I *must* learn it!"

"That was a Hungarian song from the countryside, *Fölszállott a páva*," said Dominik. "It means 'The Peacock.'"

Anna frowned a little. "What a strange name. Is it a love song?"

"Well, the peacock *is* a symbol of love, but to us, it is also a symbol of freedom," Dominik replied. "The song tells the story of a peacock who visits a prisoner who is longing to be released so that he can be reunited with his love. Each day the peacock flies to the prisoner's cell and serenades him. The peacock's song sustains the prisoner in his ordeal and gives him hope." He grinned a little. "Although if you have listened to the Count's peacocks while you have been here, I think you will rather doubt that part."

They all laughed, because the cries of the peafowl, as they *all* knew, might have been wild and free, but they were scarcely melodious.

"Still!" Dominik continued, "It is the symbolism that counts, not the reality. I can teach you the song in an hour, if you like. The verses are simple variations on the words, 'Fly peacock, fly, to the prison, to sing to the poor prisoner, to sing to him of freedom.' For someone with your training and experience, it can be mastered quite quickly."

"I should love that," Anna replied, giving him a sweet look through her lashes that amused Rosa no end and made Dominik stroke his magnificent moustache, just a little. She happened to glance at Markos, inadvertently catching his eye, and he rolled his eyes a little. It took a great deal of self-control not to laugh.

The musicians were setting up again, and they all fell silent to listen respectfully to the music. The second half of the entertainment seemed to have been devised to fit into the calm of the evening, for there were no more wild dances and fast songs. The dancers swayed and circled rather than clapping and stamping; the songs were all slow, some clearly love songs, some pure, aching melancholy. When the echoes of the last song drifted over the garden, they all rose to their feet, and applauded with such enthusiasm that the Roma grinned to each other.

After that the servants brought out more beer and cooked sausages, bread and cheese, and the guests mingled with the Roma. The Graf and the old man fell immediately into a serious conversation all in Romany. Anna went to question the musicians. Dominik and his cousin got into an animated discussion in Hungarian with the three boy acrobats. Rosa found herself drawn, for some reason, to the old woman.

She wasn't sure how to approach the lady, until she realized that the old woman's mug was empty, and that gave her the opening she needed. She secured another mug of beer and a little basket of bread, cheese, and sausage, and brought them to her. The old woman looked up at her with bright, knowing eyes, and accepted Rosa's offerings wordlessly.

"Your songs made me cry," Rosa said, in slightly stilted Hungarian, since she did not know nearly enough Romany to even attempt to hold a conversation.

"The songs of the Roma are mostly sad, even those that do not sound so," the old woman said, with a little nod. "The ones that are not sad and full of tears, are sad and full of defiance. We sing to keep from weeping, we laugh to keep from weeping, we dance to keep from weeping. I am Mother Lovina."

"I am Rosamund, Master Lovina," Rosa said, with a little bow of respect. The old woman's eyes twinkled.

"You are Master Rosamund, modest one," Lovina retorted. "Your power is clear to anyone with eyes to see it. And these eyes are still clear, if old." She peered keenly at Rosa. "You are concerned with the young shifter. Do not be. His people have a reputation with mine, and it is unfailingly good."

Does she see my thoughts? How is that possible? Rosa felt a little chill, and hesitated. She thought back on that conversation, on the first evening of this party, with the professor and his students. How they said there were *psychical* abilities, not magic at all, that could account for things like—seeing things happening from afar, or into the future, or—

"I am Master of more than Air, my child," Lovina said, calmly. "I am Master of *dook,* of *drab* and *draba,* and I am *drabarni.* Many gifts run in the blood of the Roma, you see." But then the old lady smiled, and shook her head. "And yet, I do not need to walk in your head to know you are concerned with the shifter. It is all there to read in how you look at him, how you hold yourself when he is near. *I* know *your* reputation, Red Cloak. You once saved some of my people from a sorcerer who would have made them her slaves. You were younger then."

"I did!" Rosa exclaimed, then blushed. "I am sorry I did not do more for them—"

"They were too busy running once freed," Lovina replied shrewdly. "We Roma are more used to blows than pats; they were taking no chance that you might prove worse than their captor. But what one of us knows, eventually all of us do, and your reputation as a hunter of the dark is strong with us."

She hesitated, wondering if she dared presume to ask more questions, for here was someone who was *not* related to Markos, but seemed to know of the shifters, his family. If anyone was likely to be unbiased, wouldn't it be these gypsies? "I—mean no disrespect to you concerning what you say about the shifter, but—"

"But you are apprehensive. All your life, you have hunted the shifters, and the shifters have hunted *you*. They knew, from the moment you came into the dark forest, that though you were but a child, you would grow to be a deadly hunter of their kind. That is why they tried to slay you as a child." As Rosa's eyes widened that the old gypsy knew all these things without being told, Lovina nodded. "They can *scent* what you are from far, far away. And the evil ones will try to kill you before you can kill them. Believe me, had this young Nagy been evil, he would have found a way to slay you even beneath the Count's roof." She spread her hands wide. "But—you live. You need never fear a Nagy, I tell you this. A Nagy would throw himself over a cliff before he spilled a single drop of human blood."

Rosa let out her breath, unaware that she had been holding it all this time. It was one thing to hear such words from Markos' cousin, who, after all, was strongly prejudiced in his favor. It was quite another to hear them from the lips of a Roma Master, who had absolutely no reason to volunteer them.

"I thank you," she said. And smiled. "I must admit, it is a comfort to hear that I am not going to have to keep my guard up against another guest, even if it is one that I probably will never see again."

"Ah, now that is unlikely," the old woman said unexpectedly, and a chill went down Rosa's spine, as if someone had stepped over her grave. "No . . . your fate and his are firmly entwined."

The old woman's eyes had grown distant, and the chill at

Rosa's back strengthened. "You will be leaving here to-gether, and going into great danger. You, and he, and his cousin. The danger will be even greater than you suspect. I see a terrible darkness, and my sight cannot penetrate it . . ."

Then the old woman shook her head, as if to clear it. "That is all I can see, young Master. The future is nothing like as clear as those who would flatter young women with sweet words of lovers and weddings would like you to be-lieve." Then she smiled slightly, and the chill eased. "And even though I see great darkness ahead of you, it does not follow that this darkness will descend upon you. The future is not fated. It can always be changed."

She patted Rosa's hand, and Rosa smiled back. "And even if it is not, you have given me warning and I won't go into it blindly," Rosa replied, as bravely as she could man-age.

"Well said," Lovina applauded. "So. What can you tell me of fishing hereabouts? There is a fine pond in the meadow where we camp, and I am partial to a bit of fish."

9

THE palace seemed very quiet without all the visitors in it. Even though Rosa now knew that the building and grounds literally swarmed with servants, the only ones she could actually *see* at the moment from her bedroom window were the gardeners. They were putting the grounds to rights after several days of children romping through the garden, the Olympics, the Hunt, the several nights of gypsy entertaining, the masquerade....

All that had ended with the last of the invitees leaving yesterday afternoon; the professor and one of the poets. Poor poet! *It must be hard leaving the literal lap of luxury to go back to a little garret apartment.* At least she knew he wasn't starving; the Graf was kind and generous to his friends, and made sure the young man had enough to live on and even share.

It is a good thing for him that he is an Elemental Magician, however. He would never have wandered into the Count's purview if he hadn't been. Well, he could always move to the Schwarzwald and join the Bruderschaft. I don't imagine that hunting, tending a garden, chopping wood or any of the other things we do would interfere with the ability to write poetry.

What did other impoverished poets do? Ones that weren't in the same position? *Become café waiters? Clerks in stores?*

It was a sobering reflection. She knew what her fate would have been, had she not been what she was. Still in a city, and hoping for a husband, or possibly trying to get a position as a nanny, governess, or teacher. Or a nurse? *I could have been a nurse, I think. I would be better with sick people than children.* There were not a lot of options for a girl who was only the daughter of a schoolteacher.

She didn't really want to think about what she would have been like. She'd gotten glimpses, in the village, and on the train on the way to Romania, when she and Hans had traveled in the second and third class carriages. The lives of the girls her age—many of them with children in tow—seemed so confined! Their conversation was all about their children and husbands if they were married. She didn't really know *what* the unmarried ones talked about . . .

Well, there were, maybe, hints in her mother's magazines and newspapers. There were advertisements for "improving" lectures, lending libraries. There was church work, of course; there was always church work. Would that have been her life? Penny lectures, Altar Guild, charity sewing, the occasional exciting novel from a lending library? Gossip?

I'd have been living in the city. What would Vati have been doing? Presumably the same as now, a schoolteacher. Not a schoolmaster, surely; he was only a schoolmaster now because the school was so small. When she tried to imagine herself as the teacher's daughter, it felt as if she was smothering.

But I would have been used to it. I would have had no notion that anything other than such an existence was possible. Would I have been content? She could not imagine herself contented with such a restricted life, and yet, she could not see that she would have had any other choices. Her father could not have afforded a university education for her.

And without that, her choices were few: store clerk, nanny, governess, teacher, nurse, factory worker, waitress, wife and mother.

She shook the thoughts away. They were, after all, only speculation. She was here, in the Graf's palace, and she was what she was. Elemental Master. Hunt Master. Respected and listened to, even by men.

Now the only visitors were herself, Gunther, and the two Hungarians. And now—or rather, in a few moments, after Rosa presented herself after breakfasting in her rooms— they were all about to address what it was that had brought Dominik and Markos here in the first place.

She found herself eager, rather than apprehensive. Whatever unease had been engendered by Mother Lovina's precognitive moment was long gone—perhaps chased away by several days' worth of reflections on what an "ordinary life" would have been like.

Rosa's only unease now was that if she got used to all this pampering and rich living, she'd never be content in the Bruderschaft Lodge again. So now was a good time to leave, before she was used to it, and while she was able to think of the hard work of life in the forest with pleasure rather than distaste.

This morning she, not Marie, had picked out her outfit, her own, well-worn and familiar clothing. She wanted to be Hunt Master Rosa; she didn't want to be the lace-draped creature that had waltzed in Dominik's arms and felt like an enchanted princess. She didn't want to be the delicate girl in muslin who had dreamily discussed Hungarian poetry and music with Markos beside the fountain. She wanted to be the girl she *knew* when she looked in the mirror.

So now, she looked in the mirror, and saw just that; Rosa, with her hair braided and anchored firmly on her head, in her no-nonsense loden wool jacket with the modest shirtwaist and a neat green bow at the collar. The Rosa whose mind was firmly on her job, and not wandering away elsewhere to merry eyes and fine speaking voices, and who most assuredly was *not* wondering what it would be like to be kissed by a man with a moustache.

Another Rosa would be thinking of the young men instead of whatever peril had brought those young men here. Maybe the store clerk, working in a bookstore and daydreaming over sensational novels.

That Rosa was not her.

Until this moment, she had, because it was with the Graf and Gunther's tacit permission, allowed herself to set aside the concerns that had led Markos Nagy to come a-running to this part of the world. (And why not to Budapest? There was a White Lodge there . . .) It was now time to address those concerns. With a nod at herself, she strode out the door and into the hallway, soft boots making no noise at all on the marble floor.

Last night, the Graf had suggested they all meet on the terrace, taking advantage of the fine weather while they still had it. Markos and the Graf were there already when she arrived, the two of them in what appeared to be in earnest conversation as she passed the terrace doors. A fresh breeze met her, carrying the scent of late roses.

"Ah, Rosa, good. I expect Dominik and Gunther to be here at any moment, but we can begin now," the Graf said, rising and giving her a little bow. That alone told her that rank had been discarded for this conversation, and that meant it was quite serious. Whatever Markos had told the Graf thus far warranted weighty consideration. "Please repeat for Rosa's benefit what you told me."

"It is pathetically little," Markos confessed, as Rosa took a seat. "And the only reason that *I* know about this is because Dominik and I went to visit relatives—his, not mine—near Marosvásárhely."

"Transylvania . . . again." Rosa looked sideways at the Graf, who nodded. "I was lately there, as you know. It is a troubled place, and by stranger things than bandits, wild beasts, and revolution."

"Well, you see . . . this is my problem." Markos shook his head. "Let me begin at the beginning. Obviously we had to travel a great distance by horseback to get there. And as you already know from your travels to and within Romanian lands, in those wild mountains, often there is no direct road to get to where you need to go. The same is true in

Hungary. We ended up overnighting in the village of Casolt, and we were warned not to take the road to Cornatel, but instead detour to Sacadate—" He laughed weakly, and interrupted himself. "This means nothing without a map, I know. Let us just say it was a considerable detour out of our way. We asked why. We were told that the road was perilous, but when we asked further, we got strange evasions. No one would answer us straightly; no, it wasn't bandits, they would say. It was not rogue soldiers. And bears, wolves, and wild boars were no worse there than anywhere else. People just . . . disappeared. No one knew why. And when we got the locals deep enough into their cups, we heard that it was not just travelers who had disappeared, that people within and outside the village of Cornatel sometimes just . . . vanished . . . if they were out alone. And that children had been taken from farms thereabouts. When we asked what had happened, all anyone would do was shrug."

"True, true!" said Dominik, coming onto the terrace and taking another seat. "So, naturally, Markos being what he is, could not resist shifting and running the road to find what he could find."

"It was frustrating," Markos said. "It was more than frustrating. There is a great deal of the remains of terrible magics in those mountains. Well, Vlad Dracul came from thereabouts, his soldiers actually burned Cornatel to the ground in his time. It is very difficult to separate the traces; there is old magic evil, recent magic evil and old and recent evil of the ordinary sort. They are all layered atop one another."

"It is like that in the Schwarzwald," Gunther observed. "This is why the work of the Bruderschaft is often difficult."

"But I did determine that the record of 'disappearances' is a very, very long one. It goes back as much as forty years, and the *known* number of people who have disappeared over that time is *at least* one every two weeks." Markos waited for their reaction , and it was immediate.

"What?" exclaimed the Graf. "But—the authorities—how can so many—"

Dominik shrugged, his mouth taking on a cynical expression. "Because they were all people who are invisible to great men in cities. Peasants, gypsies, travelers. Peasant children. People who don't matter. There are all manner of rebels still in those mountains, *and* robber bands, and it is easy to blame them for the missing adults, and as for the children, well, children wander away, children run away, and there are plenty of wild beasts, holes to fall down, rivers to fall into. In short, no one important has ever disappeared, so the Hungarian authorities do not care. Frankly, if Markos and I had not spoken the dialect so well, we probably would never have been told about it. The local people have given up on anyone listening to them."

"So what did you *find,* Markos?" Rosa urged. "Obviously something that disturbed you."

"Blood magic. I think it is new, although it is hard to tell. I never did trace it to its origins. And . . . maybe . . . shifters." He shook his head. "The trouble is, shifters are seldom that methodical, or, frankly, that clever. The beast overcomes the man, in most cases, and I have never heard of a shifter who was able to keep his presence a secret for four years, much less forty. And where are all the bodies? With that many kills, surely bodies would turn up at some point."

"All good objections, to be sure," the Graf pondered, pulling a little on his chin as he considered the little that Markos could tell him.

"And the amount of territory involved—that is an objection too," Dominik put in. "Are we simply seeing a pattern where there is none? It's certainly an area much larger than a single shifter could cover. Are we seeing a single cause, where in fact, the authorities are right and the causes are many?"

"Yet the local folk are convinced it is *one* cause," Markos objected. "Even if they couldn't identify it. And . . . my instincts say it is one cause."

"It's hard to argue with your instincts, cousin, they are generally sharper than mine. Which is why I came with you to plead our case with the Count." Dominik bowed a little to the Graf. "You were the White Lodge Master we thought we were most likely to convince that this is something that needed looking into. The rest . . ." he shrugged. "We asked for help at the White Lodge in Belgrade, and they referred us to Budapest. At Budapest, the Master shrugged his shoulders, muttered something about peasants with too many children, and referred us to Austria and Germany. *They have more time to deal with matters of superstition and legend. They even collect such things,* I think is what the Master at Budapest said."

The Graf pulled a sour face. "No need to tell me, my young friend," he said. "As you say . . . to many of my fellow Hunt Masters, *no one of any importance* has fallen victim to whatever this is, and therefore, it is of no importance to us. An execrable attitude, and one that is echoed in the halls of mundane power as well as magical power. And an attitude I fear will cause us grief one day." He shrugged. "But, as the linnet said, when trying to put out the forest fire, *I am doing what I can.* Rosa, my dear, does this sound like something you would care to help these young men with?"

"Sir, I do not believe I have a choice," she said, slowly, once again feeling that chill running down the back of her neck. "Mother Lovina said something to me on the first night that the Roma entertained us, that my fate and that of Markos and Dominik are intertwined. I think this is something I must do."

"Oh . . . really?" The Graf, gave her a strange look. "What exactly did she say?"

"*'You will be leaving here together, and going into great danger. You, and he, and his cousin. The danger will be even greater than you suspect. I see a terrible darkness, and my sight cannot penetrate it . . .'*" Rosa quoted. "Then she told me she could see nothing more."

The Graf and Gunther exchanged a long look. Gunther shrugged, and turned to Rosa. "This is your choice, not mine, to make. Mother Lovina is unknown to me, but many of the Roma are gifted—or cursed—with clear sight into the future. Just remember that the future can always be altered."

Rosa thought about that for a long moment, while the soft sounds of the gardeners at work drifted up to the terrace, and a bold little sparrow came looking for crumbs. "In a sense, no matter what I do, it has already been altered by the fact that she said 'The danger will be even greater than you suspect.' I have been warned, and now I will be a hundred times as vigilant."

The Graf nodded. "You have a very good point."

"The only difficulty I can think of will be finding a way to bring all the things I think I might need," she said, with a wry smile. "Now that I have been warned—well, there are things that are common enough, like salt and holy water, that I can get them in Transylvania as easily as here. But there are others—not so common—"

"Ah!" the Graf said, with a faint note of triumph. "That, I think, you can leave up to me."

Once again, Rosa found herself traveling by train in the height of luxury. But this time it was not alone.

Ostensibly, they were a sister and two brothers, and given the cut and luxury of their clothing, there was not so much as a hint that anyone doubted the story. Not that it much mattered. Thanks to the Graf's largesse, for the first several days of the journey, by day they shared a private compartment that they left only to dine, and by night they slept in what amounted to tiny, exquisitely appointed bedrooms, so there really was no one to remark on the fact that they looked nothing at all like each other.

Privacy was paramount, because the discussions they had during the day were not the sort of thing they would have wanted anyone to overhear, obviously.

"I didn't even know there *was* a rail line to Sibiu," Rosa marveled, bent over the map on the table between them. This was not exactly a parlor car, but it *was* a very nicely appointed private compartment. Outside the handsomely curtained window, a landscape rolled by that she wished she could explore. Were there any Elementals, new to her, out there?

"Well it is still going to be a roundabout journey," Dominik pointed out. His finger traced their journey. "First we get off at Bucharest and take the train up to Medias by way of Brasov here, and from there literally circle around the area we need to get to, like this, in order to reach Sibiu." He traced the circle with his finger. "It's partly the mountains, and partly that there isn't a lot of demand for a railway on the direct route. They are not good trains, I am afraid. Not like the German and Austrian trains."

"How, not good?" she asked.

He shrugged. "Small. Smaller than this train, smaller engine, not able to pull as much. The cars are smaller, not as wide."

She nodded. "We have them too. The Kandertalbahn is one I know. I am no stranger to such things."

"Well, you know how it is, then." Dominik rested his finger on Sibiu. "These trains, they don't run regularly, and you never see them from the road. And without this map and timetable you would not even know they existed unless you crossed the right of way, which doesn't happen very often. The roads go one way, railway takes a different route."

"Not that the timetable is of much use," Markos sighed. "It is more of a suggestion."

Dominik laughed. "Well, we are not efficient and methodical Prussians, cousin. We are grateful the train gets us there at all."

Rosa rolled her eyes a little, but she understood.

"The best place to abandon our current status is at Bucharest, which was what I had planned, if that is all right with you," Markos said diffidently, looking at Dominik and Rosa in turn. "The last thing we want to do is look out of place—although I had considered that if we looked wealthy, we might make ourselves an attractive target. The problem is, we might make ourselves an attractive target for everything *except* what we are hunting, if that makes sense to you."

"Perfect sense." She nodded. "We should blend in as exactly as we can. We want the local folk to be willing to talk to us, as well, the way they spoke to you and Dominik."

"We would have to overnight at Bucharest anyway," Dominik pointed out. "Possibly, depending on how the trains are running, spend more than one night." He cast a reassuring glance at Rosa. "Bucharest is a very green city. You will have no difficulty there. We can stay in a hotel in Little Paris."

"Should we store our aristocratic belongings in Bucharest somewhere, or send them back to the Count?" Rosa asked.

"Store them," Dominik said immediately. "You, at least, are going back to the Schwarzwald, and you can take our borrowed finery back with you. We can leave the trunk indefinitely at the hotel, and make our transition there."

What? What on earth are the people at the hotel going to think, when aristocrats arrive and peasants leave? Won't we run into difficulty? Might someone even call the police? Rosa blinked in confusion. "But—are we not going to—"

"My dear Hunt Master," Dominik drawled, "We are wealthy, aristocratic and eccentric. We merely tell the concierge that we are going on an adventure in the mountains, and have no wish to make ourselves the targets of bandits. He will not blink an eye when we leave a trunk with him—and leave wearing . . . more plebian garments than we arrived in. The concierge will be happy to help us, and think that we are being quite sensible. We are going on an adventure, after all, not being *stupid*. No one with any sense would dress like *this* in the Carpathians."

"We are also two very able, and well-armed, young men with their sister, who will also be well-armed." Markos shrugged. "We will be seen as eccentric, not idiots. People will approve. In fact, I would not be the least surprised if the concierge arranges for us to leave the hotel by a back entrance to avoid even the chance of unpleasantness."

"You are eccentric when you have enough money to not be considered crazy," Dominik laughed. Rosa laughed with him.

"So that is the difference! I always wondered." She pondered the map again, as the train rocked gently. "Then we become our normal selves, so to speak, in Bucharest, and get the train to Brasov. I am going to miss first class . . ."

"So will I." Dominik pulled a long face. "But at least we can travel the best class available and not have to sit on hard benches next to chickens. Even our common clothing will be good enough that no one will look askance at us in the car. The wagon will be waiting for us in Sibiu, thanks to the Count's money and our family. Now, this is what I had in mind when we arrive in Sibiu. We can get the wagon right away. Markos or I will go fetch it when the train arrives; whoever is left at the railway station can get the luggage to the curb."

"You go. Strange horses don't like me," Markos said, instantly.

Dominik raised an eyebrow. "So you want to have time all alone with Rosa, cousin?" he said, with a slow smile. "But what if I don't *want* you to?"

Rosa flushed and kept her face down. Were they actually competing over her? It gave her a strange feeling. "How fast are these trains?" she asked, trying to keep all their minds on business.

"Not very. Maybe ten miles an hour. We'll have to overnight in Brasov, and probably do the same in Sibiu, since I expect we will arrive after dark." Dominik tapped the map. "Once we have the wagon, we can go where we like in Sibiu. I know good hotels in both towns."

"You would," muttered Markos.

"Just because some of us haven't the ability to curl up in any available stable and be comfortable . . ." Dominik *tsk*'d. "It is no crime to like comfort. We'll be camping soon enough, or staying in dark old village inns, with boxes full of straw for beds. I'll take a nice featherbed every time I can get one."

"If we are going to arrive after dark and wind up making an overnight stay at Sibiu, why don't we just go to the hotel first?" Markos continued, reasonably. "We can have all our luggage brought there instead of having to sit there waiting in the cold and dark on a mound of luggage at the curb. Then, you can get the wagon in the morning, and we can load it all from the hotel in the daylight, instead of getting it all stowed badly in the dark at the station. *And* we will have the help of porters instead of having to load it by ourselves."

Rosa nodded eagerly in agreement. After her travels with Hans, the prospect of sitting curbside on a mound of trunks in the dark, waiting for a wagon to arrive *long* after all the porters had vanished was not a pleasant one. And knowing she would have to help with the stowing, or risk not knowing where her things were for days. . . .

"You are infuriatingly logical, cousin." Dominik laughed, and winked at Rosa. "Very well then. That will be our plan."

"I would rather not load a wagon in the dark either. I am not certain what our reception would be if we came driving up to a good hotel in what is obviously a trader's van. And I will readily admit that an easy night in a good hotel is much to my liking. That will give me a chance to coax up a *haus-alvar* to teach me the local dialects overnight," Rosa said with relief. "We will do best if we can all speak like natives, not just you two."

"You are as clever as you are pretty." Dominik replied admiringly, setting his chin on his palm and gazing at her warmly across the table, making certain to catch her eye and hold it. Did he flirt with *every* young woman like this?

No, he didn't flirt with the other young ladies at the Graf's party. Just me.

She flushed. Markos scowled, and looked as if he was going to say something cutting. The luncheon gong rang just in time to prevent anything more than a moment of irritation on Markos' part, and discomfort on hers.

After luncheon, they decided that they had done all the planning they could for now. Dominik elected to go to the parlor car where he could smoke and doze in a comfortable wing chair. Markos and Rosa went to their private compartment. The upholstered couches were not as comfortable as the chairs in the parlor car, but Markos didn't smoke, and Rosa preferred the view and the privacy.

"You never did tell me," she said, once the door was closed and the curtains on the corridor side drawn, so that the steward would not disturb them unless they rang. She was of a mind to stretch out in an unladylike sprawl. "I asked you, and you never did tell me about it. When I asked you a few days ago about shifting."

"Tell you what?" Markos asked, looking at her oddly.

"What happens to your clothing when you change?" she persisted. He flushed, clearly embarrassed.

"I ... ah ... I don't wear any," he stammered. She giggled, and hid it behind her hand. "That is, I find somewhere that I won't be disturbed. Quiet barns are usually good for that. Stables are chancier, horses that don't know me tend to be uneasy about me, but cattle seem to take me as a dog, not a wolf. I bundle the clothing up and strap it to a harness that fits me as a human or a wolf. I put on the harness with the bundle on my back. Then I change, and when I get where I am going, I find another barn, or a good thick lot of bushes, I change back and put on my clothing."

"That's clever, and practical. Do all shifters do that?" She was slowly getting over the unease caused by merely being in the presence of a shifter, and allowed her curiosity about shifters to awaken.

"Well, they do in the Nagy family. I can't speak for all of them." Markos had commandeered feather pillows out of one of the car stewards; he put his in one end of the upholstered bench and sprawled out over the length of it with his back wedged against the pillow. She put hers in the opposite corner, and half-curled up against it with her legs up on the bench. "We don't have a half-and-half state. We go straight from human to wolf, and back again. I've heard of some that do, though. Have you ever k—seen a shifter that does the half-and-half?"

Rosa nodded. "The very first one I ever saw, did. The one that murdered my teacher and tried to kill me," she replied. The memories flashed behind her eyes. "I eliminated two more like that, over the years. I think they do it because it gives them the mind of a human but the weapons of a wolf and entirely supernatural strength."

For a long while she had been sure she would never, ever get past the terror those memories induced in her. But she had. They even began to fade—and now, from the perspective of the Hunt Master she was, she wished in a way that they hadn't. Every encounter meant she had a little more information about the shifters, another thing she might be able to use against them. But she would never be able to mine that first one thoroughly, for it was too long ago.

She remembered the terrible strength, though. How the creature's claws had ripped through the door; how it had nearly destroyed a fully grown elk. That was not natural strength.

Markos pondered that. "It must be the magic that gives them that strength. *I* don't get that sort of strength as a wolf, just the supernatural healing. And only when I am a wolf." He frowned.

She rested her elbow on the table and her head on her hand and regarded him thoughtfully. "But you don't shift magically. The really bad ones practically stank of blood magic."

He nodded. "At least, not as far as my family knows. *If* we are born with the ability to shift, it comes on us as soon as we are weaned. We stay the same weight as a wolf that we are as a human, too—shifting doesn't make us any larger. We stay cubs a lot longer than wolf cubs do; we mature at the human rate."

But the ones that shift using blood magic—I know they can be bigger as wolves and half-wolves than they are as humans. There must be something special about the power that comes from killing that gives them extra strength and extra size.

"Does it hurt?" she asked, after a moment of silence.

He thought about that for a moment. "Well, that is ... complicated. Have you ever seen a contortionist? One of those performers that can twist his body into impossible positions."

She nodded. "Once."

"Well, they are born with incredibly flexibility, but they have to train and keep training to keep that flexible, and to keep it from hurting when they take those positions. As long as they do that, it is difficult, and takes effort, but it doesn't hurt, or at least, not enough to keep them from wanting to perform. Shifting is like that. If you do it often enough, it doesn't hurt. If you don't shift for years, then suddenly need to, it does. Quite a lot." He leaned back, and closed his eyes. "Truth to tell, I like being a wolf. Sometimes I like it better than being a man. Things are simpler as a wolf."

"In what way?" she asked, even more curious now.

"In every possible way." He chuckled. "As my dear cousin pointed out, as a wolf, I don't need a house or even a bed to be comfortable. A nice den dug into the ground suits me fine. I obviously don't need clothing. I don't care who the Emperor is, I don't care about politics. You can't collect taxes from a wolf."

She had to laugh at that one.

"It's easy hunting, with a wolf's instincts and a man's brain, and obviously, once I catch my dinner, I eat it right there with no fuss. But it goes deeper than that." He licked his lips, and glanced at her, as if wondering how she was going to take his next words. "Wolves don't have any— moral questions. Everything is simple, and even if I have a man's mind, I tend to look at everything through the eyes of the wolf. If someone attacks you, you run from him, or you have to kill him, and if you have to kill him, well, that is that. You don't wonder if he has a family waiting for him somewhere . . . if he could be a good man if you just gave him a second chance."

But she did understand, actually, because she had spent years and years studying and coming to understand how her Earth allies thought and acted, so that she could predict what they would do, and steer their behavior.

"Elementals are like that. Exactly like that. Well, you saw what happened when the revenant of Durendal was taken by the nix. All they cared about was that he had attacked and murdered one of theirs, and the moment they could take revenge, they did." She'd had her share of regrets in the night over that one. Wondering if Durendal's sister had been coerced after all, or if she had known what she was getting in for when she "invited" him. Wondering if she'd had second thoughts after he took over. Wondering if she could have been freed, ever. *I don't know how to banish a revenant. The only way I know to be rid of one is to kill the vessel.* "Sometimes I'm relieved when they take things into their own hands like that." But she could hear it in her own voice, when she said it—the doubt. Wondering if she should have interfered. Wondering if she *could* have interfered. Water Elementals didn't answer to her.

But maybe I could have gotten an Earth Elemental to save her. . . .

He opened his eyes and looked at her for a moment. "You are having second thoughts about how Durendal died. Don't."

"Why not?" she asked. "It wasn't Durendal whose body died. I have no second thoughts about ending *his* life, but what about the girl whose body he claimed?"

"To begin with, nix are often murderous, and what he did to the other Water Elementals probably drove them right out of his control. In the end, they were merely the judges and executioners for someone who had murdered one of their own kind. Durendal was *evil* and I think he got what he deserved."

"But . . . it wasn't *just* Durendal," she objected. "There was the girl—his sister, I think. What if she did not deserve to die?"

He folded his arms over his chest and thought for a moment. "To be possessed by a revenant, one must consent. Yes?"

"Yes," she admitted. "But—"

"Oh it is possible that Durendal somehow persuaded her, or had her under his thumb. But I think that unlikely. And I will tell you why. I have a theory. My feeling is that she and he were two of a kind, struggling for ascendancy while pretending to be allies, and perhaps—the shoe, as they say, was on the other foot." He raised an eyebrow. "I actually believe that she invited him to inhabit her, even *called* to him when she felt him die, thinking she could subsume him and hold *him* captive while enjoying his power."

Rosa held his gaze, not hiding her surprise. "Really? What makes you think that?"

"Just a feeling." He shrugged a little. "I am not much of an Earth Magician, but the wolf in me . . . senses emotions quickly. That is what the wolf thinks. And to be honest, there is absolutely nothing to indicate which of the two of them, Durendal or the sister, was truly in control."

Well, that was true. She had *assumed* Durendal, based on the few moments when she had looked into the Air Master's eyes. But she didn't know the sister at all. That cold, angry persona that had stared out of the girl's eyes—it might have been Durendal. But if the twins had been like-minded—it might have been the girl herself. Or some unholy mating of the two.

He smiled wryly at her. "You forget, this country not only spawned Vlad Dracul, it also spawned Countess Bathory. Both utterly ruthless. Both willing to use blood magic to get what they wanted. Both Earth Masters, did you know that?"

She shook her head.

"In the wolf pack the most dominant is the primary male, but the *second* most dominant is his primary female, and the wolf in me never forgets that a female can be just as strong, as deadly, and as clever as a male. In the shifter packs, when the eldest is a wise, cunning, and experienced female, it is she who is the prime, since strength and endurance are the least of the things that makes a prime shifter." He tipped a little salute to her. "My cousin sometimes forgets that. My cousin was not brought up in a pack, a pack where it is my grandmother who leads."

She grinned a little at him. "I knew there was a good reason why I liked you, Markos."

"You would very much like my *Bunica*, I think. I know she would like you. When this mystery is solved, I would like you to meet the pack." He stretched a little; he seemed more at ease with her now than he had been before.

She had to smile at that. Whatever else he was, Markos was a typical male, and didn't think about "implications." "It would be better if I asked Gunther to invite you to visit the Schwarzwald and you persuaded her to come," she suggested. "Otherwise it will look as if you are bringing home a potential bride for examination."

At his startled look she smiled a little more. Clearly, the thought had never occurred to him. But she knew "grandmothers" as a breed very well indeed. Her home village was full of matchmaking grandmothers, and even the Bruderschaft had a share of them. Mothers, too, were prone to matchmaking but in her experience, it was grandmothers that were truly obsessed with it.

Now he was flushing. "You are right. That is exactly what she would do, and I was a fool not to think of it."

She had to laugh at that. "Not a fool, a man," she corrected. "You poor fellows are unaware of the machinations of grandmothers until it is too late."

"Perhaps I should ask you to enlighten me!" He joined in her laughter—and that is how Dominik found them, and the more quizzical he looked, the more they laughed, and were unable to properly explain to him just what was so funny.

10

THE hotel in Sibiu was possibly the best of the entire trip, so far as Rosa was concerned. Not because it was grand, or the rooms were grand—although it *was,* as Dominik had promised, the best hotel in the town. But because it was exactly the proper mix of everything to make her feel comforted and at home, and still feel a bit pampered.

The room was not large, perhaps a trifle larger than her room at the Bruderschaft Lodge. The bed was beautiful, all of wood, with a wooden canopy overhead, and the most wonderful featherbed! There was a gorgeous Turkish carpet on the floor, a fine fire in the fireplace. And silence! Which was exactly what she needed to call on the Elementals and ask for a *haus-alvar,* one of the little domestic Earth Elementals that enjoyed living alongside humans, bringing them luck and domestic peace.

For this, she needed only what she had brought up in her portmanteau, along with some sweet cakes she had bought from a vendor at the railway station. Not just *any* sweet cakes, of course; the heavenly aroma had lured her to the old woman's cart, and she had bought and tasted one before she purchased more. Markos called them *kurtoskalacs,* "chimney cakes," he said. They had been made by wrapping the dough around a wooden dowel and baking them that way, with a sugar crust. He and Dominik had eaten half a dozen between them; she had barely been able to save two for her spell.

She sat down on the Turkish rug in front of the hearth and traced a circle around herself. Then she opened her portmanteau and took out a flat, dished stone—her room was on the third floor, and she needed a more direct connection to Earth than was possible this far off the ground. She set the chimney cakes on it, and drew four symbols on the rug in between her and the stone—symbols representing the sort of *alvar* she was requesting, and specifying a feast in return for a favor.

Then she closed her eyes, and drew up the power from the Earth, through the stone, sending outward to create her shields—set to prevent only inimical things from coming to her. Helpful creatures, like *haus-alvar,* would be welcomed—and protected from things that might want to prey on *them.*

She opened her eyes when she felt a little tug at her sleeve, and looked down into the big button-black eyes of an *alvar.* But it was not like any she had ever seen before. This little creature had the head and spindly arms of a skinny little man, but the body of a chicken, and a red cap in the form of a comb.

But nothing with evil intentions could pass her shields, so as odd as the creature looked, she smiled at it, and it tentatively smiled back.

"I need to learn the way people speak here," she said, slowly and carefully. "While I sleep, will you give me all the languages, and all the accents and differences, for all the people between here and Casolt if I give you these two cakes? You must put all this into my mind so that it will be as if I was born in these parts." She nodded at the chimney cakes and the little creature's eyes bulged with greed and delight. It nodded quickly, and she erased one of the four symbols protecting the cakes from little thieving *alvar.* Just in case. Because *alvar* were as mischievous as they were helpful, more often than not.

The funny little fellow leapt on the cakes and began breaking pieces off, stuffing them into his mouth as fast as he could. When he was done, his stomach bulged, and his odd little face bore a blissful expression before he vanished.

Rosa banished her shields, put the stone back in her portmanteau, and got out her nightdress. That feather bed looked absolutely heavenly, and this last leg of the trip had been on a train that swayed and rattled for most of the journey—traversing some amazing scenery, but also taking a toll on most of the passengers. She could not wait to take the bed warmer out and tuck herself in.

She blew out all the candles in the room, and changed by the light of the fire. The bed *was* heavenly, and beautifully warm. And the last thing she saw as she closed her eyes was the chicken-bodied *alvar*, sitting solemnly on the footboard of the bed, braiding Earth Magic. . . .

There was a moment of confusion as Rosa awoke with words swirling in her head. But a moment later they sorted themselves out, as they always did when she got a new language magically, and she smiled into the sunshine pouring into her room. Strange that little house-spirit might have been, but he kept his bargain.

She washed herself in the warm water from the pitcher left on the hearth, dressed quickly, packed her portmanteau and hurried down to the dining room. Markos was there already, devouring eggs, pork sausage, and a sweet bread.

"Good morning, that looks fantastic," she said in Romanian. Markos raised an eyebrow.

"Your accent has improved out of all recognition. I take it you had good luck last night," he replied in a slightly different dialect.

"Very much so. The chimney cakes were greatly relished. Where is Dominik?" she asked in the same dialect.

"Getting the wagon; he's already had breakfast. The concierge of the hotel is putting our good things into storage in the attics. Dominik picked the perfect hotel." Markos paused for a few more bites. "This one gets all manner of summer visitors, some who come here every year and simply leave their things over the winter. The request didn't even raise an eyebrow."

"Your cousin is a valuable fellow to have around." A waiter arrived at that same moment, and Rosa turned to him. "What my brother is having, please," she told him.

The waiter bowed slightly, with a smile for her, paused only long enough to pour her a glass of milk, and went off. Rosa reached for it; she would miss her coffee, but she did like milk in the morning, and evidently that was the custom in these parts.

Dominik returned just as they were both finishing.

"Ready, you two?" he said in German.

Rosa laughed and stood up. "More than ready," she told him in Romanian, making his eyes widen with amusement. "Let's go see to the wagon before someone stores something too heavy to move on *my* trunk."

The porters were just bringing out the luggage that had been stored overnight. With a little input from her, everything was soon stowed away.

This was an enclosed wagon, a little like a delivery van, not much like a gypsy wagon, for it was a very utilitarian brown and had no carvings or bright paint. Inside it was just as utilitarian; the trunks were stowed along the walls with just enough room to walk from the front to the back, narrow bunk beds could be lowered down on chains for sleeping, there was a tiny metal stove at one end, and no windows. It would certainly be much more comfortable to sleep in than camping when the weather turned bad, but it was small and light enough to be pulled by a single horse, although a second was tied to the tail of the wagon.

Markos was right; the horses didn't care for him much. They didn't rear or try to run, but they rolled their eyes at him and sweated when he was too near. He kept away as much as he could, helping to arrange things inside the wagon.

With the help of the porters, things were ever so much easier; within the hour, Rosa was driving the fully loaded wagon out of the stable yard, waving a cheerful goodbye to their satisfied and well-paid helpers.

Rosa was driving, because it became clear that while Markos knew how to drive, the horse would not tolerate him on the other end of the reins, and Dominik had never driven outside of a city in his life.

She, on the other hand, had over a decade's worth of experience taking the Bruderschaft supply wagon to and from the village market in all weathers and all conditions. So before the two of them could get into an argument, she simply hopped into the driver's box and solved the problem. She elected to get used to the horse in the traces now, where it would be easier to control him than out on the open road. By the time they got out of Sibiu, she should have the measure of him, and might even consider turning the reins over to Dominik.

It was, after all, not going to be a problem to get to their first destination, the village of Casolt. Just travel straight east, or as "east" as the road would let them.

She let the horse amble along at the same pace as the rest of the traffic on the main road, which was leisurely; letting the horse get used to her hands on the reins, and taking the sense of the animal she was driving. He was neither a good, nor a bad horse; he had no bad habits that she could tell, but he didn't seem particularly bright, either. Rather like the cart horse the Bruderschaft owned. It would take a horse-mad little girl to be in love with a stolid beast like this one, but on the other hand, that meant he should get used to Markos fairly quickly, and shouldn't give them any problems. Well, other than the usual. She had no doubt that he'd wander or even run off if he wasn't hobbled and tethered, and that, given the option, he'd eat himself to foundering. Best to make sure the grain stayed well out of his reach.

All the buildings here were quite close together, and most of them were the same light stone or brick, some with whitewashed walls. All seemed to have red-tiled roofs. It made for a cheerful aspect, but was very different from the white walls and black beams of the buildings in the Schwarzwald villages, or the dark wooden Lodges deep in the forest itself.

She heard a half a dozen languages being spoken in the streets, with Romanian, Hungarian and German predomi-

nating. Half the signs said this was "Hermannstadt" rather
than Sibiu. A very handsome church dominated the skyline
with three towering spires, the middle one taller by far than
the other two. *Gothic?* she wondered. She was only vaguely
familiar with church architecture.

Dominik opened the little door into the wagon and
joined her in the driver's box. "Handsome town," he said.

"I agree," she nodded.

"It will probably seem very familiar to you—the language, anyway. There are a lot of Germans and Austrians
living here, and in fact, it was originally built by Germans."
He glanced sideways at her. "Not too many problems since
1867 and the *Ausgleich.* It also was once the capital of Transylvania. Which would be why the Turks burned it to the
ground."

That must have been a very long time ago, since all the
buildings seemed centuries old. *The time of Vlad Dracul, I
suppose,* she thought.

"Fagaras Mountains *there*—" he pointed with his chin.
"Cibin Mountains *there,* and Lotrului Mountains *there.*"
The mountains, which towered over the roofs in the distance, had snow on them. She hoped they weren't going to
have to travel too high into them, although she had brought
all her warmest things.

"I've often thought about living here," he continued, as
the horse made his way down the cobbled street, which was
certainly less crowded than she had expected. "It's tolerable
for an Earth Master, there are a great many cultural events
here, plays, concerts, even operas."

"It would not be tolerable for me, except for a few days
at a time," she replied, for already she could feel the faint
unease she always had in cities, no matter how green they
were. "Too much dead stone, not enough green and growing
things. But at least, it's not *poisoned.* If all that dead stone
and brick doesn't bother you, you should be all right."

"Maybe I'm not as sensitive as you are," he said, sounding faintly disappointed.

"Sensitive in a different way, I expect." The horse had
decided to go from an amble to a slow walk; she popped the
reins on his back and chirped to him to remind him that she

wasn't asleep on the box. Reluctantly, he sped back up to match the traffic. "Healers don't seem to be as bothered by dead stone as my sort. Maybe because we need to see different things."

"That's as good a theory as any." He coughed a little. "At any rate, we should be out of the city soon, and on our way straight to Casolt. It's just a village. From there, we try to get ourselves into trouble."

"That's a nice way to put it." She glanced at him. "What are we supposed to be, anyway?"

"Oh, don't worry, Markos and I picked out something very logical, and I promise, this won't be any trouble for you. We're folklorists, like the Grimm Brothers." He grinned. "That way it's our *job* to listen to peoples' stories. I hope you can take notes quickly."

"I'll manage." It was a brilliant idea, actually. She liked it. People *would* talk to them; folklorists were proud of their role in preserving culture, and it was a point of pride for many to help with that. "Besides, we of all people should know those tales have a lot of truth in them. The more we can get written down about Transylvania, the better it will be for other Masters who might have to come in from outside."

He laughed. "Just like I said, as wise as you are pretty."

This time she slapped his shoulder. And not playfully, although it was not very hard either. "And that is enough of your nonsense, Master Dominik! Do you think I am going to respond to your flirtations as if I was any waitress in a café?"

He just laughed again. "Now, Master Rosa, flirtation comes as naturally to me as breathing! I could no more stifle one than stifle the other!"

Ah, now there's the truth at last, she thought, and yet she was a little disappointed to hear it. She would have liked to have thought that he didn't flirt with *every* female he encountered.

"So, we are folklorists? Does that mean just you and Markos, or does it include me as well?" she asked. They had finally moved out of the city, and she slapped the reins on the horse's back to make him pick up his pace. The horse sighed gustily, but obeyed. The transition was fairly abrupt. One moment they were on a cobbled street surrounded by houses, the next, they were on a packed dirt road with hilly fields to either side. The hills were as often wooded as they were cleared; wooden fences marked the borders of fields, and it appeared that half of those were used for grazing, while half were cultivated. Her experienced eye picked out that while the cultivated fields were not suffering, they also were not as fertile as the ones in Germany. Probably the ground was harder here, with more stones. The grazing animals seemed to be predominantly sheep and goats, although cattle weren't rare. Nor were horses. But Transylvania was not only the land of the Romanians, it was the land of the Hungarian Magyars who prided themselves on their horsemanship.

"Well, that depends," Dominik replied.

"Depends upon what?" She looked at him curiously, wondering what, exactly, was going to come out of his mouth. And whether or not she was going to be annoyed with him over it.

"On whether you think you'll be able to move and act more freely if you are 'just' our sister, pretending to be a mere girl bored with us and our fascination with stupid old tales, or if it will be better for you to be the equal partner in this scholastic fishing expedition." Dominik shrugged helplessly. "I haven't a good answer either way."

"Why not both?" she suggested. "When we get to Casolt, I can see what happens when I play the scholar. If we happen across a village on the way there, I can see what happens when I'm the bored sister. We'll use whatever works best."

"Well said, O Solomon," Markos put in from inside the wagon. "Selimbar is on the way, and it is a good place to stop and eat and make some inquiries."

"Well that was unproductive." Rosa glanced back at Selimbar, and pulled a sour face. Not because of the village—but because the town of Sibiu was clearly visible in the distance, visible enough to make out the spires of that impressive church.

The difference from Sibiu could not possibly have been more obvious however. Out here, white, brick buildings were nowhere near as common as wooden ones, and tile roofs gave way to shingle and thatch. Many houses had a beehive-shaped oven near the kitchen door. And these looked like German villages.

That makes sense . . . with the houses so close together in the city, fire could easily leap from one to the other if they were wood—and thatch and shingle can catch fire quickly from a single spark. And in the city, it is easier and cheaper to buy bread than make it yourself.

"Well I certainly heard enough stories of wolves carrying people off in winter to fill ten books," said Markos, who had taken Dominik's former spot beside Rosa in the driver's box by the simple expedient of getting there first. Dominik was sulking in the wagon itself. "Lots of stories of witches and ghosts, too. Oh, and did you know Vlad Dracul's bad son was the ruler back in Sibiu until he was stabbed to death?"

Or perhaps she was doing him a disservice. He might actually be writing their notes up in a more legible format . . .

In a moving wagon? Not likely.

"Well I got nothing except questions about my dowry and attempts to find out if my virtue was negotiable," she replied, and made a rude noise. "More of the latter than the former, so pretending to be a modest and bored sister was no defense. I think the assumption was that you two were trying to market me."

Markos made a choking sound; she pounded him on the back when it appeared he actually *was* choking. "I am . . . very sorry I was not aware of that," he managed. "You should have said something! I would have—"

"Dear heavens, I wasn't going to tell either of you until we were well away!" she retorted. "I've killed *vampir,* I've killed shifters, I've turned trolls to dust. The day I can't deal with some idiot who thinks because I come from a city I have never seen a *real man* before, the sun will probably rise in the west! The only time I suspected the cad would not take no for an answer, I spitted a fly on the table between us with my dagger, then sweetly apologized. That shut him up."

"Um," Markos said, after a moment. "I expect it would shut me up, too."

"What did you learn, besides tales of wolves?" she asked. The road wound its way along the valley between the hills. There were a lot more woods than fields, now. It was beginning to feel like home, actually.

"Mostly that wolves are bad enough hereabouts in the winter that a real shifter could probably kill at will and no one would notice," Markos said, thoughtfully. "Summer is different, though. The wolves go back to the steppes; they come with the snow and leave when it is gone. So all those disappearances in summer are definitely not natural."

The wagon jounced and swayed over ruts in the dirt road, despite Rosa's careful driving. This was very pretty country; it was a pity she couldn't take the time to appreciate it. She was too busy trying to keep the wagon on the best bits of the road. It seemed to be hay time here; many of the fields were either full of drying hay, or there were hay carts gathering the dried fodder up. It would not be stored in barns, however. All up and down the road, there were peculiar haystacks in various stages of formation, from the foundation of tree branches around a center pole, to the tripod of crude racks upon which the stack was formed, to the finished stack, tall and conical. They were carefully raked before they were considered finished, groomed so that rain would run right down the outside and not spoil the hay, then topped with a heavy wreath and perhaps some branches to keep the stack from blowing away. Rosa had never seen haystacks like this. It made her want to burrow into them like a child.

"The road will get better soon," Markos promised. "Not as much traffic. These roads get churned up near a village in summertime."

"I hope so; we are making wretched time," she grumbled. "At this rate, it will take us two days to get to Casolt, and I had thought we would be there by nightfall. So tell me more, if there is anything."

"Nothing, except 'unnatural' things that are strictly related to the village. Local haunts, local curses, local witches. And that tells me that the predation hasn't gotten this far—that outside of Casolt is probably where it starts." He tapped his finger on the side of his nose. "And since *I* know how much territory a shifter can cover, that gives me a good idea of the spread."

"If it is a shifter," she pointed out.

"If it is a shifter," he admitted. "It's just within the realm of possible that it is a real wolf pack that remains here in summer, having discovered that humans are easy to hunt and tasty."

She raised her eyes from the immediate mess that the road was, and saw, to her pleasure, that things did get a little smoother a little further ahead. "It could be something else entirely, too," she replied absently. "Is there anything—well—local that *you* know about that it could be?"

"These mountains hold a lot of secrets, but everything I can think of is a variation on a *vampir* or a shifter," Markos said, after a moment. "I can't imagine it could be a *balaur,* I should think someone would have noticed a dragon with more than one head."

"I would think someone would have noticed a dragon with only *one* head," Rosa said dryly, as the wagon finally got to a part of the road that was not as rutted, and she clucked to the horse. "And it would take an awfully powerful one to manifest physically enough to eat people."

Markos was silent. "We keep coming to the same conclusion. A shifter," he said, finally. "The only question is, what kind is he?"

"What have you got that is native—besides your family?" she asked. "The *vampir* I killed was a little different from the ones I hunted in Germany."

"*Moroi,* maybe," Markos mused. "I don't know, some of our *vampir* are also shape-shifters, like the *strigoi.* And, of course, there are completely human sorcerers that use blood magic to transform . . ."

"That could be why all the killing. He has to keep killing to renew and power the transformative spell." She let go of the reins with one hand to rub her temple. "If so, he'll be the most powerful shifter I've ever seen. It will take all of us to track him and kill him."

"If he's too much for us, I could call on the family, maybe," Markos said.

"Then we'd take the chance that by the time they got here, he'd flee or go into hiding. The reason this is working for him is that he's in a remote area where wolves kill people all the time, and his chances of being discovered were almost nothing until you and Dominik showed up." She frowned. "If he retreats into Russia, we'll never find him again."

"And he'll know who was hunting him." Markos went a little pale. "It wouldn't be that hard for him to pick us Nagys off one at a time. We don't have that much *magic.*"

"And by the time you'd gotten help, he could be gone again." She nodded grimly. "The one advantage we have right now is that he doesn't know he's being hunted. We have to get him before he realizes that. My mentor told me about a *vampir* once that not only figured out he was being hunted, but by who and what, and over the course of a century completely destroyed a White Lodge and every family that ever had a member in it. On the whole, shifters aren't nearly that smart, and they tend to succumb to the beast the more they shift and the older they get, but if this one has been killing for the past forty years—he's not the usual sort of shifter."

"And . . . maybe it *is* just wolves, robbers, and anarchists," Markos added, after a long silence.

"There's one other possibility . . ." she said reluctantly. "The God of the Hunt taking sacrifices."

That happened sometimes—mostly in England, Scotland and Wales. Even Ireland. Never in living memory in Germany or Austria, but—

But to her relief, Markos laughed. "We don't have any such thing," he assured her. "You go back to the Dacians, and we have the god Heros, who never hunts humans, only beasts. The goddess Bendis was a huntress too, but she never hunted humans either."

"Well that explains why the being I called up before was so willing to help me," she replied.

Markos nodded. "He'd have been irked at the shifter in his woods, a thing that is unnatural, a hunter that kills without discrimination and wastes what he kills. Both he and Bendis aided human hunters. But of course, Heros had to play with you a little before he helped you, that's just how supernatural creatures are. Especially gods, though I have to say, our gods were never as fickle or contrary as the Greek and Roman ones. Simple people, we Dacians, and we had simple gods. Give them their sacrifice, and they were right on your side, and no trickery about it." He paused a moment. "The Nagys—my family anyway—are almost pure Dacian."

Rosa shook her head. "I'm no scholar, I have no idea what that means."

"Well, when the Greeks ran into us, they called us the 'people of the wolf,' and although most historians think that's because we had wolf battle standards, or wolf totems, or some wolf-inspired warrior society, my family knows better. We were of the Appuli tribe. We were never conquered by the Romans, for obvious reasons. Hard to exterminate a village that can turn into wolves and run away, harder still when we can load everything onto our horses and donkeys and drive them ahead of us." He chuckled, and her eyes widened.

"That far back?" she exclaimed.

He nodded. "We became part of the 'free Dacians' eventually, although the family always stayed a little apart. That's why we are different from most shifters. It's in our blood. It's a lot harder for the beast to get control—not impossible, but a lot harder. That's also why my people supposedly told Alexander the Great that we could not die, it was mistranslated. What we told him was that his people could not *kill* us, which in wolf form is certainly true."

"How do you know all these things?" she demanded, a little suspiciously.

"Because when Dominik went off to study medicine and I came to join him, it wasn't as if I needed to learn a—a trade or anything. We don't need a lawyer, or a doctor—just shift, and almost anything heals, even most illnesses." He raised an eyebrow at her. "So I decided to study history, *our* history. I put together what I was taught with what our family traditions were, and suddenly a lot of things in the oral tradition made a lot more sense."

"You're going to make a convincing folklorist," she observed. "Which is good, because now that we are on a better road we might well make Casolt just after sundown." She glanced back the way they had come. *Finally* the spires of Sibiu were out of sight.

"I've had some practice; when I first came back home, I went around to all of the oldest people in the clan and collected stories." He shrugged. "Mostly, you listen and take a lot of notes. If something isn't clear, you ask questions. And if anyone asks you why you are doing this, you tell them *it's because young people don't listen anymore.* That's something that has *always* been true."

She laughed, and the horse flicked his ears back at her. "Old people like to hear that. That's something that has always been true, too."

"Oh hey, look!" He pointed ahead. There was a clearly artificial point showing at the top of a hill far ahead. A steeple.

"Basilica?" she asked.

He shook his head. "Saxon church. There are a lot of Saxons hereabouts. You might get more out of the locals if you speak German than if you speak Romanian."

"Well we can try both." She clucked to the horse, who seemed a bit more eager to move ahead. Maybe because it was afternoon and he was hoping for a stable.

Sheep, a few cattle, herds of goats. Fewer animals than there would have been in the fields of home. "Why Saxons?" she asked.

"The Hungarian Kings—including dear old Vlad!— invited them to come as mercenaries," Markos said. "The commanders and officers got land and titles, the rest got land. Thanks to the Turks, there were no living Hungarians or Romanians to claim it, and that meant there wasn't much intermarrying and the old customs were held onto. That was a long time ago, of course, so no Lutherans here, just good Saxon Catholics."

That could be very advantageous, since living in the Schwarzwald meant Rosa was more Catholic than Lutheran. She pondered all the ways she could use that as they slowly neared the distant steeple, and the sun passed behind them.

It was down by the time they reached Casolt, and they arrived in the village in the blue dusk. The church was high on the hill above the village itself, and unlike Sibiu the houses were painted in many colors and seemed to be wooden. Some had tiled roofs, but most were shingled. As they drove along the main road, with the houses all about them, a few people came out of their doors at the sound of cartwheels, but most probably thought they were fellow villagers, late-come from the fields.

The horse picked up his head and his feet, and a moment later Rosa saw why. There was a tavern or an inn ahead of them, people sitting outside at little tables drinking the *incredibly* potent plum liquor that was ubiquitous in this part of the world. Rosa had already encountered it in Brasov and knew to be wary of it.

Even though the horse was moving faster than he usually did, it still wasn't anything like a headlong gallop, and the people sitting about had plenty of time to take them in, recognize this wasn't a farm cart or a Roma wagon, and call to the people inside to come and look. So by the time the horse stopped, looking about eagerly for a stable, everyone was out and curious. But in time-honored tradition, they waited for the innkeeper in his long white apron to come up to Markos.

"Welcome to Casolt, strangers," he said. In German.

"Thank you very much," Rosa replied. "My brothers and I are scholars." Then she nodded to Markos to indicate he should say something.

But that was when Dominik popped his head out of the door behind them. Exerting himself to the utmost, he described their little group, and somehow, from the bare bones of "we are going to be folklorists," he managed to construct an entire history for the three of them as Rosa sat there, astonished.

It seemed they were not just scholars themselves, but the children of scholars, and their father was associated with Budapest University. Which presumably accounted for the *extremely* eccentric notion of a female getting a university education and traveling with her brothers to collect stories. Rosa could only marvel; it was a good, strong, simple story, and having him pop out and tell it right now meant he wouldn't have to repeat it. Nor would they, which also meant there was far less chance they would contradict each other.

Dominik continued to elaborate. Their mother had died young, so their father had brought them all up alike. He was not wealthy, so he augmented his income by writing, and particularly wanted to collect tales from around Transylvania so they wouldn't be lost. He couldn't go himself, so he sent his children out. They'd had great success west and north of Sibiu where people were universally friendly and helpful.

Oh that is good, Dominik! That puts them in competition to show us equal or better hospitality.

By this time, most of the villagers at the inn had gathered about them. "We were hoping that either there were rooms to be had, or that we could put our wagon somewhere and sleep in it," Dominik concluded. The innkeeper eyed them all dubiously.

"I am not sure fine young gentlemen and the lady would care for my rooms," he said.

Markos chuckled. "We are all hardier than you think," he said. "We are not soft, even though we have lived in cities! As long as the weather holds, we have traveled for three years now, and camp like shepherds in the hills as often as not."

Rosa noted he didn't say "like gypsies;" the poor Roma had a poor reputation among village folk. Though it had to be said; there was some truth in the reputation. They certainly did steal whenever they got a chance.

Some clans did, anyway.

Now the innkeeper brightened a bit. "Well, if you would come see the rooms . . ."

"I will," said Rosa, handed Dominik the reins, and jumped down off the box. The innkeeper led her into his unprepossessing building, while presumably Dominik maneuvered the wagon into a place where it was safe and stabled the horses.

The main room was dark, and held the ubiquitous aroma of meat and vegetable stew heavily seasoned with paprika that she expected. But beneath that, was the smell of cleanliness, which was a good sign, and the place had a good wooden floor, which was another good sign.

There were two tiny rooms, with beds taking up most of the space. But the linens were clean, the beds were featherbeds, and there was no sign of lice or other undesirable bedfellows. So Rosa set to bargaining with their host, and by the time the young men came in with the two small bags they would use for overnight, she had struck a deal.

"Supper then!" the innkeeper said jovially, no doubt very pleased to have his rooms so unexpectedly occupied. *"Sărmăluțe cu mămăligă,* my wife's specialty!"

Relieved that it wouldn't be *papricaș,* which she liked, but had had far too much of already, Rosa followed him to an age-polished table in front of the fireplace. There was wine—real wine and not *țuică,* the plum liquor, or worse, *turt* which was twice as strong—and a plate of pickled vegetables to eat while they waited. Then came the meal, which was a pork-stuffed cabbage leaf with sauerkraut. Rosa felt right at home; this was nearly identical to things she ate or cooked at the Bruderschaft Lodge, except for the spices. There was a lot more cabbage than meat, but that was to be expected; they were no longer eating at the Graf's table, after all!

When they were done, they went outside to talk to the locals. Here, the talk was in mixed Romanian and the local German, so the village wasn't *entirely* German. Rosa surveyed the tables and benches scattered about the little inn yard, assessing the people who were sitting out there. There was good light from a couple of torches and a lantern hung just at the inn door. Ideally she wanted someone who wasn't sitting and gossiping with anyone else, but not someone who looked disagreeable. Although if she could find a couple of approachable women without any men—they might be a good source of stories. But right under the lamp, on a bench where she could lean her back against the wall of the inn, Rosa found an old lady nursing a small glass of that potent plum liquor and, after getting a nod of permission, sat next to her. She warmed up her shields; an Earth Master was not as good at projecting emotions as a Fire Master was, but an Earth Master could always make herself "feel" cozy and comfortable, and the sort of person that other people would like to talk to. She hoped the old woman was not impervious to that sort of thing. Some people were, particularly unpleasant people and bad-tempered people. The old lady seemed quite friendly and approachable however. And all of the villagers outside the inn had heard their little story, so the ice had been broken.

It was a lovely evening, in a nice little village. Some houses had lanterns out at the front door. Some had a torch stuck at the road. Most had nothing but the soft light of their windows. Some people were sitting on benches by their front doors, but most were making their way here.

There seemed to be a hundred thousand stars out, and it was a cloudless night. Rosa was fairly sure she wouldn't want to be here in the dead of winter, but now, in late summer, it was lovely. There was a scent of all the drying hay on the breeze, and a soft hum of talk from all the people gathered in the inn yard.

The old woman next to her was dressed in what Rosa now realized was the Saxon variation on the local clothing; instead of a white skirt, she wore a black one, with embroidery, a black embroidered vest, an embroidered white apron, and a plain black blouse, with a black bonnet of some sort over her gray hair, and two embroidered ribbons trailing from it, over her shoulders and down her chest. She was a little bent, but not much, and slender. Her face was not very wrinkled, and it was possible to see she had been a great beauty in her youth.

"It's a pity," the old lady said, without preamble, in German.

"What is a pity, good lady?" Rosa replied. "Oh, my name is Rosa Nagy. Dominik and Markos are my brothers."

The old woman nodded. "And you are the scholars, so I heard. Your father must be very odd to raise a girl as a scholar." Rosa stifled a smile; it seemed that the old were universally allowed to be as rude as they liked.

"He is. Very odd. But I like it, and a scholar's daughter

doesn't have any dowry so I have no prospects!" she replied
cheerfully. "I might as well be useful, and I like traveling
and even living in a camp. When my father dies, or grows
too old to teach, Markos or Dominik will take his place and
I will go out with the other to collect stories. I think only the
one that becomes a teacher will marry, so I will probably
keep house for the one that doesn't in winter, when we can't
travel. Was that what the pity was about?"

The old lady seemed to like her attitude. "I am Frau
Schmidt. No, the pity is we have no music tonight. The gypsies are off hunting for a missing boy, who they already
know will not be found." She lowered her voice in a conspiratorial fashion. "That's not so bad for Casolt. It will be
a while before we need to be vigilant again. Months, if we're
lucky. If we're even luckier, it will take a gypsy again and
not one of us."

"Vigilant against what?" Rosa lowered hers, too, and
leaned toward the old woman—who smelled, oddly enough,
of peppermint, and not the cabbage or garlic that Rosa expected.

The old lady shrugged. "Against what no one wants to
talk about. Something out there—" she pointed her chin
eastward "—likes to hunt people. No one has ever seen it
and lived to tell about it. Back when I was a girl, they tried
hunting for it, and got nowhere. Now no one tries anymore.
We just know it moves around, and once it's taken a person,
it moves off to hunt somewhere else. So it can't be a beast,
now, can it?"

Rosa pretended to think about that. "I wouldn't imagine
a beast would be that clever," she said, finally. "Does everyone know about this?"

"Most do," Frau Schmidt said flatly. "They just won't talk
about it. I think they are afraid that if they do, the thing will
come hunting for them, or someone in their family."

"And you aren't?" Rosa dared.

The old lady laughed. "I've outlived my whole family,
and the thing never comes into the village, so I am safe
enough. I rent out my farm to Iliescu's boy and his wife, I
have my little garden, I don't need to leave. When I die, the
boy hopes I will leave him the farm so he treats me fair, and

brings me good things. As long as he keeps doing that, keeping me happy and comfortable as if he was my own boy, I'll leave him the farm, and he knows that, and I know that he knows, and he knows that I know that he knows, so we are all settled."

"You, Frau Schmidt, are a very wise woman," Rosa declared, and the old lady laughed. Rosa had the feeling that hardly anyone ever talked to Frau Schmidt, but that she *listened* to everything, so it seemed that Rosa had found a good source of information. "You get the income, you get good things to eat, and you know the farm will be in good hands, even if they aren't of your own blood."

"Oh, Iliescu's boy is near enough. Cousin of my mother. That will do, since the farm came to me as my dowry. My little cottage I live in now was Erik's from his parents. They lived in it until they died. We kept it up and never sold it, and when Erik left for the next world, I let Iliescu's boy rent the farm from me, and I moved there." That set Frau Schmidt off on a detailed rundown of the pedigree and degree of relationship of everyone in the village. From there, she dove with great relish into village scandals. Rosa listened with amusement and interest, because, from investigations in the past, she knew this was part of the bargain when you got things you could use. When you found the person in the village who knew everything, the price of learning what you wanted to know was to listen to everything. Rosa was the perfect listener for someone like Frau Schmidt. *All* of the village scandal could be laid out like a feast before the two of them, without worry that the wrong story would get back to someone who could make trouble out of it. So Rosa *ah'd* and *oh'd* and *tsk'd* at the right moments, while the village's recent and current history was unveiled in all its tawdry glory.

Predictably, said history was just like the history of every other village its size. Girls who had gone to the altar pregnant, boys with reputations, unfaithful husbands, unfaithful wives . . . and sad things, like boys who were snatched up by the Hungarian army never to be seen again, or not to come home until they were half forgotten by everyone.

And, of course, a forty-year litany of the missing. Young

men mostly, occasional girls, and too-adventurous children. All of them taken while alone—alone in the field, alone hunting, alone gathering mushrooms, wandered off from the safety of the farmyard. Frau Schmidt was very shrewd. She not only included missing villagers, she included the missing that had passed *through* the village and never turned up down the road. Gypsies, lone travelers, peddlers.

"But you'll be all right," she would say, nodding wisely, each time she added another to the toll. "You'll be fine. There are three of you. It never takes anyone who is *with* someone. Just don't go strolling about alone."

During this time, Rosa refreshed her glass of plum liquor three times. Frau Schmidt showed absolutely no signs of intoxication, which Rosa could only marvel at. *You would think she was drinking water,* Rosa reflected. But then again, after a lifetime of drinking such powerful liquor, maybe it was like water to her. Rosa kept to her much milder wine. The Romanians made decent wine. From the look of things, it was perfectly acceptable for a woman to drink wine, but there was not one of the men that was not downing glasses of the potent plum. Evidently, if you didn't, you weren't a man.

Dominik had taken up with a group of young men, Markos with what looked like a couple of farmers. Markos and the farmers were seated, bent over a small, sturdy, rough wood table, while Dominik and the young men were standing together near the entrance to a low stone wall that separated the drinking area from the rest of the street. They had been laughing, earlier, evidently at Dominik's jokes. They weren't laughing now. Markos and the farmers had been serious all night.

Now the farmers stood up, and bade farewell to Markos, who stood up with them, took his glass, and went over to join his cousin. The innkeeper came by and offered to refresh Frau Schmidt's glass again, but she handed it to him instead.

"I know my limit, old friend," she said, with a smile. "I've had enough to make me forget my aching bones and go to sleep. Be good to this nice young scholar girl. She listened to my tales as too many youngsters don't do, and laughed at all the right places."

"I will, old mother," the innkeeper said, offering her his hand so she could get more easily to her feet. "Dream well."

"With your good *țuică* in me, that won't be hard," she chuckled. "I shall dream of when I was young and skinny and Schmidt and I danced the *Învârtita* until the sun came up or the gypsies stopped playing."

With that, she turned her back to them and made her remarkably steady and stately way out of the yard, and down the street, until she moved out of Rosa's sight.

"A good woman, Frau Schmidt," the innkeeper said aloud, and winked at Rosa. "And all her tales are true, except the ones that are not."

Rosa chuckled. "She reminds me of the good old lady across the courtyard from us at the university. She makes the best *clătite!* I have never mastered making them so thin."

The innkeeper made a sympathetic noise, perhaps reassured by the fact that the odd "lady scholar" was also domestic enough to lament her inability to make thin pancakes. That probably put his world back upright on its feet for him. Or rather, if he still believed that the world was flat (and he might!) it flipped the world right-side up for him. "If you stay long enough, perhaps my Maria will show you," he said in a kindly tone.

"I would like that very much," she said sincerely, because to be honest, having tasted the Romanian version of pancakes, she was not at all sure she would ever be satisfied with the German ones again.

Besides, it would be a good opportunity to coax more stories out of another village woman, this time the innkeeper's wife, who probably heard as much, if not more, than Frau Schmidt.

Meanwhile, she glanced at the cousins, who appeared to be deep in some sort of conversation with the knot of young village men. And two more of the customers called farewells to the innkeeper and departed.

"The boys will probably be talking half the night, if your young men let them," she said indulgently. "I will go to bed, write up my notes, and sleep like a sensible person. Thank you for your most excellent hospitality."

"You paid me well enough for it, Miss," the innkeeper laughed. "Good night!"

She went into the inn, to the right hand room where her bag had been left, fetching a burning straw from the fireplace to light the candle on the wall. Once there, she sat cross-legged on the bed, writing out everything pertinent that Frau Schmidt had told her. There was quite a lot of it, and it was a good thing Rosa had an excellent memory. The only detail that had been left out was the identity—or presumed identity—of whatever "it" was that was killing so indiscriminately. She debated leaving her notebook in the cousins' room, then decided against it. They might well be too tipsy to read it, and although she knew Markos could throw off the effects of even complete drunkenness by shifting from man to wolf and back again, Dominik couldn't.

Better to catch them in the morning.

So, with that, she changed into her nightgown and snuggled into the featherbed. She didn't even hear when the cousins came in.

11

Breakfast was *mămăligă*, a porridge of cornmeal, which Rosa found very tasty. Rather than coffee or tea, she was offered milk so fresh it was still warm. She was the first one awake, and it was the innkeeper's wife and daughters who greeted her and presented her with a hearty bowl and cup, and seated her at the same table they'd had dinner on.

"Did the gypsies ever find their lost person?" she asked, casually, before they could escape back to the kitchen.

"Oh Frau Schmidt told you of that did she?" said the wife, waving the two daughters back to their work. She, too, was wearing the Saxon costume; this time a blue skirt and vest rather than the black of a widow, and a white apron. The Romanians wore white skirts with an embroidered black apron fore and aft, presumably in an attempt to keep a white skirt clean.

"She told me about *many* things," said Rosa, with a faint smile, as a chicken wandered in the open door, looked disappointed that there was nothing on the spotless wooden floor to eat, and wandered out again. "But yes."

The innkeeper's wife sighed. "The gypsies have never done us any harm, and their playing makes folks stay and drink longer than they would otherwise," she said, which relieved Rosa, who was afraid she might have to somehow justify her concern. "It's a tragedy. There's always one of those too-bold little boys in every family or clan, you know?"

Rosa nodded, and decided to make up some family history of her own. "Dominik was like that. Up on the roof, up in a tree, over the wall—no matter what anyone said to him, he was always sure they were just nagging him to keep him from having fun."

"Exactly! It makes me glad I only have the one boy, and he's as careful as a sheepdog," Maria said fondly. "Well that was what Shandor was like, reckless beyond belief. Ten years old, and no one could tell him anything, and if he hadn't been the sweetest-natured child who almost always managed to charm his way out of trouble, he would never have been able to sit for all the whippings. And not one whipping changed him, either, he was that headstrong. Day before yesterday, he took his pony when he was told not to, and headed out for Avrig, which he was told he could not go to. The pony came back, covered in lather, without him." Maria stopped, and wiped her eye with her apron. "Well, there, I am a mother too. He might have been a gypsy scamp, but he had a mother and her heart is broken, and I, who buried two babies, I can feel that."

"And all credit to you, for the Good God made all of us, even gypsies," said Rosa, heartily. "We are all of us His Children."

Maria smiled wanly. "There are plenty who would say the Devil made the gypsies, but—well there you are. And no, they have not found him, some of the men came at dawn to beg of me *țuică* for the funeral feast. I gave them a little barrel, and also cornmeal and a chicken, for as I said, they have never stolen from me."

She hesitated a moment, and Rosa said, shrewdly, "And you might as well give them what you could spare, so they wouldn't steal *more* than you could spare."

Maria smiled thinly. "My husband said you were clever.

Yes, there is that, and after they left there was a mark in chalk at the gate which I have not washed off. There may be food and animals missing from the village today, but the mother in me finds it hard to fault them. They have no body to mourn over, they will have to make it up somehow."

Rosa got an idea then, but kept it to herself for the moment.

"Well, there you are. At least the good will come of it that our youngsters won't go wandering off alone for a good long while, and God willing, that will keep them safe." She sighed, and picked up Rosa's empty cup and bowl. "Would you like more?"

"Yes, please—" Rosa began, and just then, the cousins emerged, with sleepy, sheepish expressions and neatly combed hair, from their room. "—and my brothers will want some too!"

With a nod to the boys, Maria went to the kitchen, and came back with three bowls and three cups of milk, and a round of sheep's cheese. Markos and Dominik sat across from her and ate with a good appetite, which meant at least they were not suffering from any ill effects of drinking. Maria and her daughters busied themselves in the kitchen and the oven in the back; from the smell of things, the day's bread was coming out.

"I think we all have news, yes?" Dominik said, as soon as they were alone.

Rosa nodded. "You know about the gypsy boy?"

Markos made a face. "Yes. The fellows we were with were saying *one less gypsy is a good thing,* but that might have been stupid talking. They got a little into their cups, though, and it was pretty clear they were relieved, and I can guess why."

Rosa nodded. "It means no one from around here is going to be taken for a while. Even the innkeeper's wife came close to saying that, although she puts it down to the youngsters being too scared to run about alone. But I had an idea. I know something of Roma customs. Even without a body to mourn, they'll be having a funeral feast, and then burning everything the boy owned to keep from being haunted. What if one of you bought a couple of hens or ducks or even a young pig and took it out there to them, say we are paying our respects. *I* can't do that, I'm a woman, but you can. And we can get away with being nice to gypsies, we're folklorists, we're trying to collect stories. No one will be the least bit surprised that we are trying to make up to them."

The cousins exchanged a look. "I can do that," Dominik said. "I've had a bit to do with the Roma."

"That leaves me free to shift and see what my nose can pick up," Markos said with satisfaction. "It's harder by day, but I can manage, and given what just happened, I am not sure I want to run around alone at night, even shifted. The boy was carried off in broad daylight, after all. Heavens only knows what could happen at night."

"And I can find another lonely old woman to get stories out of," said Rosa. "Or maybe I can get some out of the innkeeper's wife. If I can find a single moment when she isn't busy, that is."

So the three of them parted company. Rosa got the book of blank pages she was taking notes in, Dominik went to go find someone willing to sell him something for the gypsy funeral feast, and Markos just . . . vanished. Rosa suspected he was using magic to do it; there was a spell that even simple magicians could work that tended to make people look right past you even when they were looking *at* you, that she and others used to good effect. If you didn't guard against it, it worked even on Masters.

So, assuming that this village was like most villages, and that eventually all the old men and women and gossips would end up here in the yard of the inn, drinking beer or a kind of tea made of elderberry flowers, she set up at one of the sturdy little tables, writing out some of the folktales she had heard in the first village. There had been a variation on one of the Grimm tales she knew, which in German was *The Goat and Her Seven Kids,* but in this version had only three kids. In the German version, the kids were a little smarter than the Romanian version, and were only fooled by the wolf at the door after he had whitened his paws with flour and softened his voice with honey.

As she wrote, slowly, a few old men began to appear,

doing their best to look entirely incurious. *Just like my home village, the old men turn up first, then the old ladies. An old man has "nothing to do," when he is too old to work. An old woman is still expected to keep the house*... Two of them set up a chess board, deliberately not looking at her. This, as Rosa knew, was not snubbing her. She looked busy, they were leaving her alone. They all ordered beer.

Time passed; Rosa used her ruse of writing to extend her magical senses through the village. She might be able to coax one of the *haus-alvar* equivalents to appear in her room tonight, if she made it clear she was friendly and prepared to "pay" in bread.

She was so intent on this that she scarcely noticed how much time had passed until one of the two daughters put a warm flatbread crowned with melting cheese and sour cream on the table next to her, along with a glass of beer. She looked up, realized she was hungry, and thanked the girl, who craned her neck to look at the notebook curiously, giggled at Rosa's sketch of the kid and his mother roasting the wolf, and went to serve the men.

Rosa continued writing—or in this case, sketching—in her notebook with one hand, while breaking off bits of the bread and eating them with the other.

That was when she felt a tugging at her skirt.

She looked surreptitiously down.

There was a *haus-alvar*—a German one!—tugging at her hem.

...oh, of course. These people are of Saxon German blood. They speak German. Their haus-alvar *probably followed them here, packed up in their belongings, sort of...*

Then she got a second shock, as someone at the chess table bit off an exclamation.

She glanced over at the old men, all of whom were staring in shock at the *haus-alvar*.

They can see it?

Obviously they could, as they looked from the *alvar*, to her, and back again.

Making up her mind quickly, she leaned down to speak to the Elemental. "Yes, what is it, my friend?" she asked quietly.

"You must come to Markos, quickly!" the little fellow said, and ran off. She didn't even bother to keep up the ruse that she couldn't see him, she just grabbed her notebook, picked up her skirts, and ran after him.

He led her to a stable on the south side of the village; when she got there, Dominik was just running into the stable, and as she joined them both, Markos had only pulled on his trousers.

"I found the boy's trail," he said, without preamble. "I found the scent of what took him—a shifter, as we had expected. I tracked the thing to its den, or at least a temporary den." He held up a hand. "Before you ask, he had the boy, and the boy was dead. But he's sleeping now, and we have a good chance of trapping and killing him if we move fast."

Dominik nodded. "Our horses are trained to ride as well as haul. Rosa, let's move. Can you ride b—"

"I can ride any way," she said, already heading out the stable door. She was running so fast he never even caught up to her until they reached the inn.

"Get the horses," she said shortly. "I'll take care of the weapons. I think I'm the only one that brought any, anyway."

She climbed into the back of the wagon and felt in the half-dark for her keys that she kept in a pouch under her skirt that she could reach through a slit-seam. The chests all had the same lock, and she knew where everything was; in a moment she had two of them open and started pulling out weapons. Her coach gun, of course, and the silver buckshot loads. Two silver daggers. And a weapon that she, personally, had never had occasion to use . . . but that Dominik just might be able to wield.

A folding, silver-headed boar spear. The three segments locked in place, and the cross-guards behind the head folded down and locked. This would be ridiculous to use against a *boar,* since the locking segments would probably fail. But against a werewolf in wolf form, or half-form, it could prove very potent. And if Markos and the unknown shifter got into a fight, the spear would be safer to use than her coach gun, at least until you could get the two separated.

Just in case, she also got out a flask of holy water and a bag of blessed salt. You never knew when those would come in handy.

She locked the chest that she had taken the weapons from up, pulled off her skirt and petticoat right there in the wagon, and pulled on her divided riding skirt over her drawers. Then she locked her clothing chest, gathered up the weapons, and jumped down out of the wagon.

Dominik was just bringing up the horses with their bridles on, and short reins clipped to the bits instead of the driving reins. Rosa strapped the sheath for the coach gun onto her back and the belt with the silver dagger and the ammunition pouch over her jacket. She handed a second belt and dagger to Dominik and unfolded the boar spear for him. He watched attentively and nodded. She folded it and stowed it in a sheath not unlike her coach gun's and handed it to him. He armed himself, then offered her his cupped hands to assist her onto the horse's back. She really didn't *need* them, but smiled and put her foot in his hands anyway, vaulting easily into place on the horse's bare back. He used a bit of fence to help him mount, and the two of them cantered toward the stable where they had left Markos. They didn't meet anyone; at this time of day, almost everyone was in the fields, working. Just as well; explaining where they were going and why they were armed to the teeth would be a complication she didn't want right now.

Markos was waiting in wolf form, lying outside of the stable in the shadow, where he could see anyone approaching and slink into hiding before they could spot him. The horses snorted at the scent of him, but didn't act up. As soon as he spotted them coming, he ran off; they urged their horses into a gallop to follow. He quickly outdistanced them, but that didn't matter; his track was as clear as if he had left prints on the ground in red paint, thanks to her ability to see magic. Even if Dominik couldn't see the track himself, which she doubted, he could follow her.

They were tearing across hilly fields lately mown for their hay, which at least meant they weren't destroying any crops as they galloped—and meant they could cut straight across, too, avoiding the conical haystacks. There was no one working out here now that the hay was mown, dried, and stacked. There were people out in distant fields, but they were too far away to be more than little dots, and it wasn't likely they'd notice the two of them tearing across the countryside.

This was easy country for a gallop; the hills weren't so steep as to strain the horses going either up or down. The fences were more of a suggestion than anything, being as they were made mostly of sticks and old boards nailed to a support. They weren't even waist-high, most of them, and the horses didn't hesitate to jump them.

Rosa didn't often ride bareback, but it was in the nature of an Earth Master to be able to work well instinctively with almost any animal. She settled her shields about her and her horse and settled loosely into the gelding's mind, until she was moving with him as closely as if she was his other half. He accepted her in his mind stoically; he noticed her there, but it didn't trouble him. She could even see through his eyes if she cared to, but that would be far too disorienting for both of them; being able to move with him, encourage him over jumps, and calm him at need was quite enough.

Markos' trail led straight over these hay meadows, past weathered old storage barns gray with age, toward meadows where sheep, goats, and cattle grazed, and beyond that to steeper, thickly forested hills, with some sheer rock faces showing above the trees.

The sheep scattered before them, but quickly formed back into a flock under the wise eyes of the goats when no one chased them. The cattle just looked up, then went back to grazing.

He did say . . . the shifter was holed up in a den. There would be caves there, and dens dug by badgers, wild wolves, and bears. The shifter could have taken any of those. She hoped it was a cave, or a bear den. If he was holed up in a badger- or wolf-dug den, getting him *out . . .* that could be tricky. And hazardous. There wouldn't be any room for a human to move in there, and Markos in wolf form was the only one who would be able to get in. *I have to get there when Markos does. We can't try and dig him out of a wolf den. We'll have to smoke him out, or use some other ploy, and I am not sure Markos is thinking clearly enough to realize that.*

She urged more speed out of the horse. She didn't think Markos would attack before they arrived, but his blood was probably up, and she knew he was angry. Both his human and wolf sides were angry, and of the two, the wolf was going to be the most reckless. If the wolf took over—

Wasn't that what that little alvar *said? He would be in danger if the wolf won?* It was impossible to tell when the *alvar* were talking in general, or making actual predictions about the future. She had the feeling that time wasn't quite the same for them. She bent down over the horse's thick neck and dug her heels into his sides. He was barely damp; after pulling a wagon all day, a gallop with a single human on his back probably wasn't a lot of work for him.

The tree line loomed, and it was clear, even at a distance, that these were "wild" hills, hills the local villagers and farmers never went to except to hunt. And this was very foreign territory for a horse who traveled open roads all the time. The horse didn't want to go in there; instinctively he knew he would be at a disadvantage in there, that predators like wolves and bears could ambush him and his one advantage, speed, would be gone. She sensed his resistance, and overrode it. He wasn't like her faithful hunter back in the Schwarzwald; he was a creature of open meadows and open skies—and the occasional comfortable barn and stable. He didn't at all like this thing they were riding toward, which was not like a stand of two or three trees in a meadow that provided shade in summer. This was . . . a green wall. He didn't *like* it, and he didn't want any part of it.

He didn't have to like it. He just had to go in, following Markos' trail, and ruthlessly, she guided him in.

He immediately dropped from a gallop to a reluctant walk, even though Markos had found a relatively clear game trail for them to follow. There were *things* too close on either side of him. He hated it, and if there had been room to shy sideways, he would have! She had to fight him until he finally understood he had no choice but to do as she demanded, and he finally moved into a stiff, jouncing trot,

determined to make things as uncomfortable for her as
they were for him. But shortly he realized that since there
was no saddle to cushion his back, *he* was being punished as
much as she was, and gave over.

She couldn't get him to gallop on this trail, no matter
what she did, but then again, that would be a very dangerous thing to do. There was a lot of leaf litter, and no telling
what was under it. She would do Markos no good by driving
the horse until he fell and broke both their necks. So they
moved along at what was not quite a trot, and not quite a
canter, with her staying low on his neck to avoid the
branches that lashed at them, his hooves thudding dully on
the ground. She kept her arm up to shield the side of her
face from all the *other* branches they pushed past, and was
very glad of her thick wool jacket and moleskin skirt, both
of which could shrug off such punishment. Unlike her skin.

She sensed Dominik close behind, so at least he was having as much luck with his horse as she was with hers.

The trail led into a steep, rocky defile, and she tensed, for
she could feel Markos up ahead, not very far at all. It was
cool and damp in here, cool enough she was glad of that
jacket, and the defile was entirely in shadow, with the gray
walls standing stark and unforgiving, and the undergrowth
limited to spindly trees and stringy grass. This was both a
good and a bad place to meet the shifter. Good, because
they could easily pen him here and he couldn't get away, not
with sheer rock walls on either side of them. Bad, because
there wasn't a lot of room to fight—

And the moment she thought that, she felt the magic
around Markos flare.

"He's attacking!" she cried out, and dug her heels into
her horse's sides. Startled, he leapt forward, with Dominik's
horse's nose in his tail, giving him further encouragement to
move.

They broke into a tiny, open area, sloping downward,
with a rocky scree in front of them, slippery and treacherous, and a rough cave entrance at the back of it. The entrance was at least as tall as two men and wide enough to
admit the horse. Two wolves were fighting in the middle of
the open space, and if it had not been for Markos' clear,

golden aura of Earth power, she would not have been able to tell them apart. Their snarls echoed off the rock walls, and the loose stones rattled and cascaded under their feet.

They charged and broke apart, charged and broke apart, each of them trying to get a lethal hold on the other, leg or throat. Their snarls echoed off the rock walls as Rosa launched herself off her horse's back and pulled her coach gun. But they were too close; she couldn't hit the shifter without hitting Markos too—

Her horse screamed in fear at the raw wolf-scent and the shifter's head moved in their direction. The horse bolted toward the cave's entrance; it didn't matter. She could either find him later and persuade him to come back or—it wouldn't matter, and the villagers would find him wandering back alone, like the gypsy pony.

Markos took immediate advantage of the momentary distraction, dashing in and getting his jaws on the shifter's foreleg. A shake of his head, a wet-sounding *snap,* and he leapt away, leaving the shifter with a broken leg. His legs fought for purchase on the treacherous scree, and stones rattled down the hill.

The shifter snarled, made a three-legged leap backward—

And his whole body writhed, obscenely, nauseatingly, as he reared up on his hind legs. He howled in pain, and the injured leg twisted and straightened, then hind and forelegs both flexed in an unnatural way and become distorted parodies of human arms and legs. The head bulged, the muzzle shortened—

And Dominik charged before he could close in on Markos again, in this more powerful form. In the interval between when he'd jumped off his horse and now, Dominik had snapped the boar spear together, and now he ran straight at the shifter, shouting hysterically at the top of his lungs.

The shifter recognized the silver spearhead for what it was, instinctively perhaps, for he leapt backward, and Dominik skidded to a halt on the stone, barely managing to keep from plunging down the slope and into the cave.

But that gave Rosa all the opening—and range—she

needed. The coach gun was in her hands without even thinking about it, and as Dominik scrambled backward, she emptied the gun into the shifter, broke the breech as he staggered back, reloaded, and emptied it into him again. She was so keyed up she didn't even register the kick of the gun against her shoulder.

The first took him in the chest, the second in the stomach. He uttered a strangled gurgle and fell, sliding down the slope, leaving a trail of blood on the rocks as he slid. He stopped sliding a few feet short of the entrance.

Markos dropped to the ground, panting, and licking his front paws. Dominik approached the body, warily, boar spear at the ready.

"Make sure of him!" Rosa called, reloading again, and making her way carefully down the scree. Nothing loath, as soon as he got within reach of the body, Dominik stabbed the spear down into the remains of the chest. She presumed that, as a healer *and* a doctor, he would know where the heart was. . . .

And she didn't want to waste another of her precious shells. Making them wasn't easy *or* cheap.

"It's dead," Dominik said flatly. "I'm going to see what's in the cave."

He left the spear sticking out of the carcass, and edged his way down the loose rock. She holstered her gun on her back, making sure it was safe first, then scrambled up the loose rock and went to check on Markos.

There were some gashes on his neck and legs that he allowed her to examine gingerly, but they were healing even as she poked at them. "Do we have to worry about you being bitten by him?" she asked.

He shook his head in the negative. Presumably he would know if it was possible to be infected by the bite of a shifter.

"I've found what's left of the gypsy boy!" Dominik called from inside the cave, his voice sounding strange and hollow, as if he was calling from the Underworld. Well, in a way, he was. "It's ugly, but it's definitely him."

Dominik emerged from the cave, looking shaken, but not ill. Well, he was a doctor. Presumably he had seen dead bodies before, even mutilated ones. "Do you think you'd be able to run back to the village?" she asked Markos, who looked at her with his head to one side, puzzled, but nodded.

Dominik slipped and slid his way up the slope and joined them. By this time she already had her plan in mind. There was no point in pretending they were anything other than what they actually were—not after the way those old men had reacted to the *alvar.* She could use that to their advantage.

Well . . . except for Markos. He had better not be known as a shifter. But there was no reason why he could not reveal he was also an Elemental Magician. "I'd like you two to go back to the village where Markos left his clothing," she said. "The villagers all know we went tearing out of there, and they're going to be wild with questions—and a couple of the old men at the inn *saw* that *haus-alvar* you sent for me, Dominik. So they know, or some of them do anyway, that we're not just folklorists. Markos, you shift back and make sure they don't see you until you do, and then the two of you get the gypsies and any of the villagers that want to come. I'll stay here and see what I can learn until you return."

Dominik nodded, and after a moment, so did Markos. "How do we explain—" Dominik began. She cut him off.

"We explain nothing. If they ask questions about how we knew where the beast was, we look inscrutable and say that's a secret we can't divulge." The long tradition of the Bruderschaft in keeping the curious from getting *too* curious stood her in good stead, now. "If they had a Master, or even a magician here, we'd have sensed him, and *they* would have known where to send for help when these killings started forty years ago. All they have are sensitives, maybe some hedge-wizards and herb-witches. So any time they start to ask a question that we don't want to answer, that's what we say. We're not at liberty to divulge that information."

"But how do we explain why we're here?" Dominik asked—then before she could reply, she saw him come up with the answer himself. "Of course! The truth! We passed this way, found out about the killings, and sought out a monster-slayer: you."

She nodded. "Exactly. And we don't have to be too exact about where you found me, or how. Just say that because you are magicians, you know monsters exist, and you know how to find people that can kill them."

"And our motive?" Dominik persisted.

"To please the Good God," she said firmly. "As the properly pious knights of old did. That's one motive they won't ever question. And it has the added value of being true as well. The Bruderschaft was originally a small order of knights who were also Masters. We found we could move about more easily, and do more good, if we left off the knightly trappings and became foresters."

Markos stood up, and shook himself all over; from all that Rosa could see, his wounds were completely healed now. The foolish horses, too stupid to find the game trail in their state of panic, had crowded together into a little side passage. They had at least jammed themselves in with their rears to the rock wall, and they seemed relieved to see Dominik and Rosa. Both of them were foaming with nervous sweat, but were otherwise all right. Dominik got the reins of his without any problem; Rosa saw the horse calm instantly when he touched its nose, so he was using his own Earth powers on it. Rosa imposed a firm mental control on hers, despite some resistance. Once it was tractable, she led hers over to a tree where she tied it, taking no chances on its running off in case the silly thing decided to take fright again.

Then again, running off was probably the smartest thing they could have done, and it certainly got them out of the way of the fight. Having a couple of rearing, thrashing horses in that melee would have been very. . . .awkward.

Dominik mounted his horse, and he and Markos trotted off down the game trail; the thudding of hooves in leaf litter quickly faded to nothing. Now alone, Rosa went to examine the bodies.

First she slid and scrambled all the way down into the cave; there wasn't much light coming in from the entrance at all, and she didn't have the advantage of Markos' superior night vision. So once on relatively level ground, she closed her eyes for a moment and concentrated. This spell didn't come easily to an Earth Master; it was generally more of an Air or Fire ability. A simple Earth Magician couldn't have done this, it required a disproportionate amount of power than an Air or Fire Mage would need to supply. *Come on. You've done this before.* Earth power didn't *want* to produce visible effects. Earth power preferred to make things grow, not glow. But when she opened her eyes again, her hand was glowing as brightly as a lit candle, or two.

She held it above her head, so as to avoid blinding herself, and waited while her eyes adjusted to the cave. It wasn't a very deep one, and after a moment, it was easy to see the gypsy boy's body, brought unceremoniously down into the cave and left in the middle of the floor. *Brought,* not dragged: an important distinction. There was no sign of dragging at all, no smears on the rock, and given how the throat had been torn out, there would have been. And the body itself was in a heap, not pulled straight, as it would have been if it had been dragged. She moved to the body, knelt beside it with her hand casting light on it, and examined it. The shifter must have brought the body here in its half-form, then dumped it.

Then fed. That was what Dominik had meant by "not pretty." It looked as if he had done the feeding in full wolf form, which would correspond with Markos finding him asleep. Wolves generally slept after a heavy meal.

But there it was. The creature had not just killed the boy, it had fed on him. *Fed.*

This was the worst sort of shifter. One that not only killed humans, but ate them. And given that the beast had brought the boy here in half-form, he didn't even have the poor excuse that the wolf had taken over. He had knowingly brought the body here, knowingly gone full-wolf, for the purposes of feeding on the body. Obscene. Cannibalistic.

She had seen all she needed to see. She extinguished the light on her hand, and made her way slowly, slipping in the loose rock, back up the slope to where the shifter lay.

She paused beside him, and examined him with a frown on her face. He looked ... wrong. Not in the way that shifters always looked in the half-form, twisted, warped amalgams of beast and man, but wrong in other ways. Diseased. As if, even in human form, there would have been things obviously wrong with him.

The fur was patchy—*mangy,* she would have said, if it had been a true wolf or a dog. The skin where there was no fur had swaths of red, roughened, flaking areas. The face— she was used to the half-wolf, half-human faces of the shifters in this form, and this creature ... the skull was strangely flattened in front, and the eyes set too close together. The claws were yellow and brittle, and looked unhealthy. The tail had lost half its fur. In fact, the *only* area of fur that looked healthy was the band around its torso that represented the wolfskin belt that all sorcerous shifters used for their transformation.

She caught a glimpse of something glittering around its neck, and reached down, fingers catching on a thin chain hidden in the patchy chest fur. She pulled. It broke. And as she pulled it off the body, she was strangely unsurprised to find there was a little copper medallion dangling from it.

A medallion that showed the Stag of St. Hubert, with the inverted cross between its horns.

That was two of these medals now. Both found on shifters in Romania—in Transylvania, to be precise. There was something going on here, something *besides* the usual "sorcerer uses blood magic to become a shifter."

One such medal could have been a fluke, but two?

One—well, a sufficiently motivated magician could very well have had the medal made just for himself. Or he could have made it himself. It wasn't that hard to carve wax into a medal form, press it into clay, and pour in some molten copper.

Two identical medals meant someone had made a more permanent mold, one that could be reused, and then had them cast or cast them himself. Two identical medals, found miles and miles apart, meant someone was giving them away to shifters.

Why?

Just how many more were there?

And what did this mean?

Was there a sorcerer out here who was taking like-minded fiends and teaching them? Turning them into—what? A kind of counter-Bruderschaft?

Or had the plot to do so only just begun?

12

THE sound of many horses pushing through the forest alerted her to the arrival of Dominik, Markos and ... whoever they were bringing with them. They were coming at the trot, so there was a dull rumble of hooves on the ground, and the noise of horses that were less skittish than the cart horses pushing their way through the underbrush on either side of the game trail.

Dominik was in the lead as they came up the defile, with Markos on a borrowed horse behind him. The borrowed horse was even more stolid than the two cart horses were; it clearly did not care what was on its back, as long as whatever was there wasn't actively sticking teeth or claws into it. When Rosa invoked Earth Magic to touch its mind, she was amused to discover that all it was thinking about was whether there might be something to eat when they got where they were going.

And behind him was a procession of mixed gypsies and villagers, mounted singly or double on horses and ponies. They gypsies all looked stricken; the women were weeping, and the one woman that Rosa thought was the boy's mother was nearly collapsing with grief.

At least she'll have a body to bury now. Cold comfort, but what was worse? Always wondering what had happened, or knowing the truth? In Rosa's experience, it was uncertainty that was the harder of the two.

Rosa moved off to one side, discretely out of the way, as soon as Dominik came into view. Really, at the moment, she didn't want to be seen at all. It wasn't that she felt at all guilty—how could she have done anything, when they hadn't even reached the village when the boy was killed? But *her* presence was a complication that simply didn't need to happen, and wouldn't, if she stayed out of the way. She let Dominik be the one to show them the shifter, and take the gypsies down to the cave to deal with the boy's body. Dominik had been the one who had been talking to them after all . . . and if they assumed that Dominik had been the one that killed the shifter, that was fine with her.

They all left their horses at the top of the scree tied to a couple of scrawny saplings there. Then they divided into two parties; Markos led the villagers, and Dominik led the gypsies. The gypsies solemnly got torches out of bags tied to their saddles, as the three village men huddled in subdued and nervous consultation around the shifter's body. Two of them were the old men who had seen her talking to the *haus-alvar.* She had a pretty good idea they knew exactly what they were looking at. In the folktales she had collected, there were plenty of stories of shifters.

It must be a shock to actually see a dead one.

Dominik got out a little tin matchbox, pulled out a lucifer match, and struck a light to one of the torches; the rest lit theirs from the first once it was properly burning. They all made their way gingerly down the scree and into the cave—and as she had pretty much expected, almost immediately wailing and lamenting echoed hauntingly out of the cave mouth and up the slope. It put a cold chill down her back to hear it, for it sounded as if spirits were crying from deep inside the earth.

Well, at least now they have a body to mourn. Dominik

emerged from the cave mouth and scrambled his way up the slope, as Markos joined the three villagers at the shifter's body. Dominik paused there as well, and that was, she considered, her signal to join the group.

They all turned to look at her as her feet rattled a little stream of stones down toward them. From the looks on their faces, the three village men expected some answers out of her. But they waited until she had joined them before speaking.

"So . . . you are the monster hunter then?" said one of the two old men, looking at her with a piercing gaze. "The one that Markos Nagy told us about? Even though you are a woman?"

"I am," she affirmed, and turned the lapel of her coat so they could see the Bruderschaft badge pinned there. "I have been with the Brotherhood of the Foresters in the Black Forest since I was a child." At their puzzled looks, she realized that their knowledge of geography probably didn't extend past Sibiu. "That is in Germany, a long way to the west past Sibiu, past Budapest."

That got nods of recognition, and she continued. "The Brotherhood was formed to kill monsters. They rescued me from another like this one—" she toed the dead shifter. "It had murdered my grandmother. They learned that I was born with the magic of the Earth, which is what they use to fight these creatures, and took me in. I have been one of them ever since."

Another frown of puzzlement creased all three brows. "But . . . you speak as if you come from here—" said the second old man hesitantly. "Your speech is just like ours, and even people from Brasov sound different from us."

She nodded. "Magic gives me the gift of tongues," was all she said. They all nodded sagely. So . . . they were all familiar *enough* with magic to accept that statement—or else they were just going by "the gift of tongues" mentioned in their tales and in the Bible.

Then again . . . there was a half-wolf shifter at their feet. How was the "gift of tongues" any harder to believe in than *that?* It was actually not so bad having to explain all of this to people who were "backward" and "old fashioned" if not "medieval" by the standards of the folks living in cities. *If I ever need to hunt a shifter or other terrible creature in a city, I could have a hard time keeping out of trouble with the police.* How would you explain to a policeman in, say, Hamburg that you were hunting something out of what he considered to be a fairy tale?

Well, even if one or two of these men had had doubts about what was roaming their hills, they had none now. Something that solid and real lying at his feet was likely to make a believer out of the most hardened of skeptics.

And this is a part of the world where they take witchcraft seriously.

"And you—studied to do this sort of thing?" asked the third, and slightly younger man. He was middle-aged, rather than old, and seemed a bit dazed by all of this. "You are a woman!" He said it as if it was an accusation, which was—well, it was something she had heard before when hunting. As if a woman was completely incapable of doing anything other than being a victim.

At least he didn't say, "You are a girl!"

"The Brotherhood has several women in it," she said, and pulled the coach gun from the sheath on her back. "I don't need to be strong, I just need to be properly armed, trained, and prepared to kill. It doesn't take being a man to shoot, and shoot well. And like a gun, magic does not care if the person using it is a man or a woman."

The first of the old men burst into laughter at that, and slapped his leg. But the laughter cutting across the gypsies' mourning sounded brittle and fragile, and the old man cut himself off rather quickly. "Pardon," he said. "That was unseemly, and rude, even if they are gypsies down there. They still have feelings, and they have lost a child. But she certainly put you in your place, my friend! She reminds me of my Tatya! Especially the day I found her skinning the wolf she had shot at the back door! *'Do you think I was going to wait for you to come home, old faker?'* she said, *'The wolf wouldn't!'*" He laughed again, only this time, more of a hearty chuckle behind a formidable moustache.

"This is Petrescu," Dominik said, quickly, nodding at the first old man. "And Vasile—" the second "—and Lungu."

That was for the middle-aged man. "Petrescu is the mayor of the village."

Markos nodded. "I went to the inn to see who in the village wanted to come to see what we had killed, because there was always the chance that this *thing*, when it was a man, had lived in the village. These three thought they had the best chance of recognizing it, if so."

"And I saw you speaking to the—" Petrescu paused, and shrugged. "Well, you know. At the inn. So I knew you were a magician. We have not seen a real magician, not a good one anyway, for a long, long time. We had a witch—a good witch—" he added hastily. "But she died before she could take anyone as her successor. Some of us can *see* things, the little things that aren't animals, but no one has been able to use any magic here for a very long time."

She thought about that a moment. "Fifty years?" she guessed. "Fifty years since you had a magician, and not a witch?" She thought that the "witch" had probably been a herb-wife with a little Earth Magic. Just enough to make her medicines more effective, and to allow her to get advice from Elementals, when they chose to speak to her.

He nodded after a moment of thought. "Probably that much. It was in my father's time, for sure."

"And you don't see anything familiar in this creature?" she asked.

All three men shook their heads vigorously. "Nothing about it," Petrescu said for them all.

"Do you know anyone in the village with a habit of wearing a copper saint's medal?" she asked cautiously.

That elicited a laugh and headshakes. "We might be poor by what city folk have," Vasile said, with a snort. "But we have our standards! No one here would make a saint's medal out of *copper*. That would be an insult to the saints!"

So . . . whoever this was, he didn't hide himself in the village. He either lived in another village, or more likely, had a cave somewhere in these hills.

That might be the explanation for why the killings started forty years ago; a shifter had arrived here from somewhere else, then discovered the area was fundamentally unguarded. With no one around who could see magic to track him, as long as he retained human intellect and muddled his trail accordingly, he would have been safe from purely human hunters. But could this shifter be *that* old?

She looked down at the body. There was no sign of graying hair, but that didn't mean anything, not really. Old wolves only got gray around the muzzle, and this thing's muzzle was all but bare.

But age had other signs. The skin got delicate, easily bruised. Old people lost hair. The regenerative capabilities of the shift wouldn't be able to fix all that—shifting didn't make you younger. And maybe that was why this shifter looked so . . . shabby. The scaly, rough and red patches of skin, the patches of lost hair—even the deformed-looking skull—those might all be signs of age. It might be that the half-form, the one that was the strongest, but was also the hardest to control, was showing the similar signs of age that the human form would.

It seemed that Petrescu was thinking the same things. "This creature could be that old," he said. "It looks like an old man that is falling apart, in a way. But if it *is* that old, how could it manage to kill?"

"It only killed a boy," she reminded him. "The other victims, at least the recent ones—they were undoubtedly alone, but were they also young?"

Petrescu pulled at his moustache, and turned to Lungu. "Well, we know it was killing people on the road, and from other villages, so we don't know exactly, but—"

"Even an old wolf can kill a man if he sneaks up on him," Lungu said with authority. "I am the best wolf hunter in the village, and I have seen wolves with gray muzzles tear the throats out of strong young men who were not wary enough."

"There you are, then," Petrescu said, with a nod. "This thing could be that old, maybe. How young can they turn, like this?"

The horses stirred uneasily where they were tied. They didn't like being this close to the shifter corpse . . .

Or maybe they didn't like being this close to Markos.

"This is a sorcerer," she explained. "Or—was. I was taught that they shift by means of spells, spells that take blood. Human blood, for a spell this strong." She sheathed her coach gun, dropped down beside the body, sitting on her heels, and drew her knife, pointing out the wolfskin band around the thing's waist. "You see this? See how it is different from the rest of his hide? When he's a man, that's a belt, a belt he keeps next to his skin, under his clothing. They use a wolfskin belt, blood, and a magic ritual, these shifters—I would rather not go into any more detail than that. But that is how they become the wolf and the half-wolf, and I have heard of sorcerers as young as fifteen being able to transform. So if you are asking me, could *this* creature have been the one responsible for forty years of killing, all by himself?"

She looked up, to see all three of the men nodding, and looking anxious.

"Well then, I have to say it is possible." She stood up and sheathed her knife, then rubbed the back of her neck under her hair. She was constrained to tell the truth. It was possible. But there were a lot of things wrong with that theory. "I have never *heard* of a single sorcerer being able to kill one human a week for forty years—and yes, that is how many deaths there have been, that is why we are here—but it isn't impossible."

"That many!" Vasile swallowed hard. "But—why?"

"Well . . . there are other reasons for killing besides feeding, as this one did." She wondered if they thought she was somehow inhuman for being able to discuss such a thing dispassionately, but the truth was, this was all old to her, where it was new and raw to them. "The spell to shift requires blood constantly to renew, and the strongest for that is human blood. That is the likeliest answer, but there are others, as well."

"Such as?" Petrescu asked. Of the three of them, he seemed the most interested.

"It depends on what other magic he was doing. He may have been paying some demon in blood and lives for protection, and that might be why you were never able to catch him," she pointed out. "Once a sorcerer has shifted like this, he keeps shifting. I have never heard of one who shifted only once, then stopped. But when you start killing your fellow man, you attract a lot of attention. Protecting himself with the help of a demon might be why you were never able to find him."

"Any other reasons?" Petrescu wanted to know.

"Well . . ." She looked down at the corpse. "Aside from the shabbiness—there was no sign of weakness. He fought and moved like any other shifter I have ever fought. And if he *is* that old, there might be a reason for that, too. He was a sorcerer, after all. There are spells for increasing one's life and strength that require human blood, and if he was here in these hills and killing for so long, he may have been doing those sorts of spells as well. All that—all that could explain his forty years of success."

It all sounded very plausible. So why was she not convinced, herself?

Because of what is in my pocket . . . That—evil version of the St. Hubert medal. She could not believe that it was coincidence that this shifter was wearing one too. And where there were two, it stood to reason that there were more.

The problem was, she had no other evidence than that. And it was perfectly easy to come up with reasons *why* that other shifter could have worn such a medal.

This one could be the father, and the other, the son. Shifters won't share territory; the human side of him would have protected and taught the boy until he was old enough to fend for himself, old enough to know the spells and be able to shift as well as his father, but then—he'd be driven off. And it would be natural for a young sorcerer to look for protection from something older and stronger, like the vampir.

It all sounded perfectly logical. She just couldn't actually believe it. And she could not put forth an argument for why she didn't believe it. All she had was a feeling. Even *she* would not have urged any sort of action just on the basis of a feeling.

I am not sure I would even act alone based only on a feeling.

She wished she could consult with the Graf, or better still, Gunther. They would be able to tell her if it was just needless worry, or her instincts were correct.

But Dominik and Markos seemed to approve of what

she was saying. Dominik actually beamed at her for a moment, then wiped the expression from his face, when a particularly heartrending wail came from the cave. The three villagers nodded solemnly, looking relieved.

She couldn't, she just couldn't, let this go without warning them as strongly as she could without looking like a nervous . . . female. "I just find it very difficult, myself, to believe that one sorcerer could have been responsible for all those murders for all those years," she cautioned. "Now, you know this part of the world much better than I do, and you are in a better position to judge than I am, but I would strongly advise you not to let your guard down—"

"Miss Schwarzwald!" Vasile exclaimed, throwing his hands up in the air, making the horses shy and dance a little. "We are in the Transylvania! Steppe wolves come down on us every winter! There are our own wolves here all the year round! There are bears! There are robbers and thieves and deserted soldiers in these hills and mountains! And on top of that, our young men have to dodge conscription gangs for the Army! Why would you think we would ever let our guard down?"

She grimaced. He had a point. Still . . . there was a chill sensation in the pit of her stomach.

"Those are all things that answer to a bullet or a knife or even a pitchfork," she pointed out reluctantly. "Well, maybe not the conscription gangs, but, the rest certainly do. This—"

"But *now* we know of you and your Brotherhood!" Vasile beamed, and looked as if he was contemplating patting her on the head. Or at least, on the shoulder. "If we suspect there is another such, we can send word, yes?"

Markos looked pointedly at Dominik, who shuffled his feet, thought a moment, then said, "I can tell you how to get a letter to me. Or where to send someone as a messenger if a letter is not fast enough. Or both. And if for some reason, Fraulein Rosa cannot come, then Markos and I can find another hunter . . . if it is needed."

"But it probably will not be," said Petrescu, dismissively. He looked like a man who had had all his questions answered. "Everything this young woman has said only convinces me that we had one, single, evil man plaguing us for decades. It is the simplest explanation!" He took out his handkerchief and mopped his face. "And now thanks to you, the evil man is dead."

To Rosa's hidden dismay, both Markos and Dominik agreed. And what could she do? She couldn't challenge them in front of the village men; it would undermine their authority. She had to nod reluctantly. And . . . Petrescu was right. This part of the world was very dangerous, if you were not careful all the time. No one was going to go out frolicking alone in the woods just because they thought *this particular* danger had been put to rest . . .

But she didn't believe this shifter had been alone. She just didn't.

This, obviously was not the time and place to argue about it. The gypsies were deep in their own mourning ritual, and they would probably bury the boy here where he was—in their belief, you wanted to bury your dead as far away from your camp as you could, for fear the ghost would follow you and haunt you. In the Schwarzwald, gypsies that had lost a member of the tribe sometimes asked the Bruderschaft for permission to bury their dead in the bit of hallowed ground where they buried their own. Permission was always given.

But it was highly unlikely the villagers would give the same sort of permission—and this cave was remote enough both to confuse the ghost, and to ensure no one would come profane the grave.

It seemed Dominik had some of the same thoughts going through his head. "We should give them some peace," he said, nodding his head toward the cave. "Let them bury their dead without us around."

The villagers nodded. There was a long moment of silence, broken only by the horses snorting and moving a little. But being, for the most part, cart horses, they took their rest when they could get it, and didn't waste energy on jostling one another or trying to pick fights.

"Is there anything anyone wants to do with this?" she asked, toeing the corpse again, distastefully. There was no more information *she* could extract from it, that was certain.

The three villagers looked at her as if they thought she

was insane. Markos and Dominik shook their heads. "Well," she said, "I didn't know if you wanted to drag it back to the village and . . . display it?"

"I think not," replied Petrescu after a moment. "There are some people in the village who should know the truth of this, but most would only be frightened to no good effect. No, there is no reason to take it back. And the horses might refuse to carry it."

"They probably would," she agreed. "In that case, I think we should be rid of it. If we burn it, that will purify it. I think by the time the gypsies come out there will be nothing but bones." She pulled her metal bottle of naphtha out of the pouch she kept the ammunition in and unscrewed the top, pulling the cork out. The sharp, heavy scent of the naphtha wafted up out of the bottle. "I hope you still have matches," she said to Dominik, and began pouring it over the body.

"I have something that will add to the burning." Petrescu went to his horse, and returned with a leather wine-bag. "I thought . . . well, I thought if I needed to join the gypsies as mayor in mourning their boy, I well . . . needed to have something along. If you understand my meaning."

He pulled the stopper out of the flask, and poured the contents over the body as well. A smell of *very* strong liquor rose to join the scent of the naphtha. Rosa coughed a little and stepped back—whatever was in that wine-bag was a great deal more potent even than that wicked plum liquor!

They all stepped back as Dominik produced his box of lucifer matches, struck one, and tossed it on the body. The flame spread with a little *whump* as even the vapors caught fire.

When the body was burning well—aided by whatever it was that Petrescu had doused it with, as well as Rosa's naphtha—the five of them collected their horses and rode off, making sure first that the gypsy horses were all well tied up. There was no telling how long they would be in that cave.

By the light above the defile it was no later than mid-afternoon at most. Rosa felt astonished. With everything that had just happened, it seemed as if it should be nightfall at least!

The wailing of the gypsies faded behind them, and was soon muffled by the forest.

"Well, I didn't expect that to be over so soon," Dominik said, happily, when they were finally alone. After a generous meal served up by the innkeeper, they were all in the wagon, as it seemed the most private place to talk. Dominik and Markos were sitting on one of the pulled-down beds while she cleaned and replaced her weapons in their proper places.

On the ride back, they had agreed with the three village men that the villagers would only tell those who could see Elementals about the truth of the situation. The rest would be told that the gypsy boy had been killed by a gigantic and cunning wolf, a true rogue of its kind, and that Dominik and Markos had tracked and killed it.

This was another situation Rosa wasn't happy about, but what could she do or say? This wasn't her country, much less her village, and Dominik and Markos seemed content with the plan. Of course, she wouldn't have told the unwary and unmagical about the shifter, but if it had been her, she would at least have claimed the boy had been killed by—

Well, by what, exactly? What could she have invented that would have made them wary, in case the shifter wasn't alone?

Maybe . . . a bandit? And that there might be more?

But Petrescu had already made the point that the villagers all knew there were bandits about, that they expected bandits about, and they watched for bandits. A shifter wasn't a bandit. A shifter—

There was no good answer.

While the men busied themselves with oiling harnesses, she cleaned her coach gun, preparing to store it again. Markos had made an abortive move to take it and do so himself, but she had given him a sharp look, and he had made a little gesture of apology and withdrawn his hand. No one touched her gun but her. That way she always knew that caring for it had been done right. If an ordinary hunter of ordinary beasts could not afford a misfire, how much *more* important was that to her?

"I'm not sure it's over," she said, flatly. "Wait a moment and I'll show you why."

She had finished her cleaning; the gun had been properly put away, the naphtha bottle refilled from the jug in the corner of the chest, corked tightly and the lid screwed on just as tightly, and tucked in its proper place. Now, with all her gear in readiness again, she could put her hand on any of it in the darkest night; she closed and locked the chest.

She pulled down the bunk from the wall over the chests she had just closed, and sat down on it across from the two cousins. She fished the medal out of her pocket and handed it over.

What might have been the strangest thing about the medal was that there was ... nothing to distinguish it from any other bit of jewelry. No feeling of evil. No residual magic. It might have been just—a badge, a simple means of identifying someone. Like the St. Hubert's medal that she herself wore. The Bruderschaft only used these medals as a means of identification, not as talismans or anything of that sort.

That was just common sense. While ordinary magicians could play at investing power in objects they might use later, a society of hunters and warriors knew better than to do anything so foolish. The Bruderschaft generally did not invest magic in any object—because such objects could be lost, stolen, or taken away, and in the wrong hands, be used to harm their creators. As hunters, descended from warriors, they knew better than to put weapons in the hands of potential enemies. Especially not magical weapons, which could strike from hundreds of miles away, and with little or no warning.

Well, maybe these shifters are the same ... they are sorcerers, after all. They would know the risks. And they would know that every man's hand would be against them. All the more reason to refrain from creating talismans.

Oh granted, you *could* sever the link between the object and yourself, but first, you had to be aware that it was gone. And the ritual to do such severing was tedious and taxing.

Better not to have to do it at all.

Dominik looked at it, turned it over in his fingers doubtfully, then passed it to Markos, who did the same.

"I don't feel anything from it," Dominik said, frowning. "Oh, it's definitely a thing that is meant to identify the holder as someone who holds God in contempt. Why else make a blasphemous version of a holy object. You are right in that the inverse cross is certainly nasty enough on its own, but . . . I don't see why you think this means we didn't just remove the problem at the root."

"Because this isn't the first medallion I've found like that," Rosa replied flatly, and went on to describe the shifter she had killed in another part of the Carpathians—and the medal she had found on him. "That's two, absolutely identical. One, I could believe was merely intended as a way to spit in the eye of the Brotherhood, or of White Lodges in general. But two? Identical? I *cannot* believe that is coincidence."

"Perhaps not, but it could have been father and son," Dominik pointed out, as Markos held his peace. "That makes more sense than . . . than some sort of shifter Black Lodge. And shifters won't share a territory," he continued, in an uncanny echo of her own thoughts on the matter. "You know that. But he could have given his son a token he could be identified by later, so they didn't accidentally fight each other. A young shifter, under the influence of wolf instincts, would have gone looking for someone strong to attach himself to. And we know that *vampir* like to lure in shifters as servants. It all falls together very nicely, without inventing a whole . . . group of these madmen."

"Well . . . we always say that shifters won't share a territory because they won't, not with a stranger," she pointed out, her unease not easing even a little bit. "But we've never seen a *family* of the sorcerous kind of shifter before! And shifters *do* share a territory, don't they, Markos?" She gazed at him, willing him to say something. "Your family shares a territory, just like a wolf pack shares!"

He grimaced. "Well . . . that's true enough. But . . . we're a family, and I have never heard of a *family* of sorcerers. . . ."

She sighed gustily. "And just what is Dominik's family, then? Or mine? Or the Count's? Maybe not sorcerers, but magicians, certainly. The magic runs in the bloodline. Maybe sorcerous magic can run in the bloodline too!"

"But where was the evidence that there was more than one of these fiends?" Dominik countered. "Markos?"

"I only scented the one," Markos admitted.

"And none of us saw any sign back at that cave that there was more than one," Dominik said firmly. "Rosa, seriously, the work here is done. And if you are looking for an excuse to stay around us for a while longer, you don't need to make—"

She stood up, red-faced. "Excuse?" she retorted angrily. "You think I'm some sort of lovesick village idiot? You flatter yourself!"

"He does that quite a lot, actually," Markos muttered. And when Dominik turned to glare at him with mingled astonishment and accusation, he shrugged. "You *do*. Every time a pretty girl looks at you, you're certain she's interested. And if all she does is say a single kind word, you're certain she's in love with you."

"Now look here—" Dominik began, heatedly.

"No, you look here," Rosa interrupted, anger burning high enough to bury all the feelings of undoubted attraction she'd had to both of them. "You think I am being unreasonable. Fine. I'll take one of the horses and the cart, and drive back to Sibiu. I can pick up all the gear we left, and head home. You can have the other horse to ride back to wherever you're going. Markos can run on his own four legs. If you want to stay here a while and be the heroes, and have girls fawning all over you, you go right ahead and *do* that. Just make sure that Petrescu has a way to get word to you when *more* trouble surfaces!"

Markos looked extremely worried at that statement, but didn't say anything. She pushed past them and headed for the inn. It was too late to leave today, but she could get a very early start tomorrow morning. As she entered the inn by way of the stable door, she heard Dominik and Markos. . . .

Well, they weren't *quarreling* exactly, but their voices were certainly raised. And the word "women" was playing a prominent role.

She was met in the common room by the innkeeper's wife, who looked worried. "It is not business of mine but—"

"It is a difference of long standing between my . . .

brothers," she said, making an effort not to snap. "About ladies."

The innkeeper's wife snorted. "Oh yes. Master Dominik. Doesn't come over too strong, but it's clear that he fancies himself the answer to a maiden's prayer, and sadly, there are enough maidens who feel the same, which just confirms his notion."

"Well, they are going to go on to visit some distant relations; we have enough tales for me to take them back to Father, and I really want to get there before autumn weather starts. So I am taking the wagon and leaving in the morning," she said, making up the story on the spot.

"Meaning, now that the quarrel has broken out into the open, you had rather not be stuck in a wagon with the two of them fighting," the innkeeper's wife said shrewdly. "I don't blame you. The chicken *papricaş* is done; I'll fix you a dinner you can eat in your room, and in the morning you can be up and gone before those lazy louts think of stirring."

She bustled off to the kitchen, and came back with a tray, following Rosa to her room and setting things up for her, before winking and closing the door.

Outside, through the tiny window at the end of the bed, the sound of voices raised in a real argument came floating. She got up and closed the window.

Fine, she thought, as she dug angrily into her meal. *Now they'll probably forget everything I told them and warned them about, arguing over this idiocy. As if it is more important than the idea that there might be more of those shifters out in the mountains!*

And the idea that *she* might be so in love with one of them that she would actually jeopardize everything she had worked for—to be taken seriously, to be taken as an equal— to *make up* a story like that just to stay near them! It made her blood boil!

Men! She thought, stabbing at an inoffensive piece of chicken. *Who needs them? Not me!*

13

EITHER the liquor was even more potent than she had thought, or the long, hard ride and the fight with the shifter had taken a great deal out of her. Or the argument with the cousins had distressed and exhausted her far more than either.

Possibly all three, for she did not sleep well for what seemed like half the night, and when she finally did fall asleep, it was to be lost in vague and unpleasant dreams.

The long and the short of it was that Rosa slept much longer than she had intended. For the first time, her inborn sense of time had failed her, or perhaps the evil dreams had ensnared her so much she could not break free of them.

She had intended to be up at dawn, in order to avoid having to argue with Markos and Dominik. She didn't want to go through it all over again—and when she had been tossing and turning last night, it had occurred to her that there was no reason why she could not stop in Bucharest, discover who the Master of the White Lodge there was, and lay it all at his feet. After all, it was one thing to ignore the deaths of mere peasants and gypsies with no clear witness to the fact that those deaths had been caused by a rogue sorcerer. It was *quite* another to ignore the word of a Hunt Master—

And she had a notion that she could shame the Bucharest Lodge into mounting a true Hunt out here, purely on the basis of the fact that she, a mere female Earth Master, had been the one that found the first shifter and dispatched him. They wouldn't like that; they'd want to have some sort of triumph that rivaled hers.

If only she could be clever enough to figure out just how to manipulate them....

As for Markos and Dominik, she figured that by the time they woke, she would have their gear unloaded from the wagon, the horse harnessed, and be ready to be on her way. All she needed to do would be to wake at her usual time.

Which, of course, she didn't.

In fact, she only woke when someone was frantically pounding on her door, and, opening sticky eyes, she saw to her dismay that it was easily midmorning. There was bright sunlight outside the embroidered curtains of her little room, too bright for it to be anywhere near dawn. She flung the covers off herself, pulled a skirt over her night shift, and opened the door.

It was Dominik, and he nearly fell into the room as she pulled the door away just as his fist was about to strike it. "What on earth is the matter?" she asked crossly, and before he could answer, making sure no one was in the immediate vicinity, she pulled him in and closed the door after him. "What?" she repeated, putting her fists on her hips and glaring at him.

"It's Markos!" he choked. "After you left, we kept arguing, only it was him and me, because he took your side. He kept on and on about how you had the better instincts of the three of us, as well as far more experience as a Hunt Master, and that even if we hadn't found anything, you were probably right and there was more than one of those shifters. Finally he said that he was going to go back out as soon as the sun went down and give the hills a really *good* hunt, looking for more shifter scent."

Well! So Markos was on *her* side? She forgave him for not supporting her in the first place when the argument had begun.

"And?" she prodded. If Markos had gone out, why had Dominik come pounding on her door? Had he found something?

"And he isn't back yet!" Dominik said frantically, and her blood ran cold. "He said he'd be back by dawn!"

She opened her mouth to say something, but Dominik had the proverbial bit between his teeth and was rattling on.

"He had it all planned out! He was planning on us spending at least a couple more days here, and he finally argued me down, because, why not? The food is great here and the liquor is better, and the beds are comfortable—if he wanted to run around the hills like a wolf for a week, that was all right with me! I figured I would be staying here and kind of educating Petrescu and a couple of the others in some basic magic . . . find out what Element they were, then give them a way to get in touch with me or Markos if something turned up after we left. We agreed on that, and Markos went out . . . but Markos didn't come back this morning!"

Her head had cleared as soon as she opened the door; she always was one to wake up instantly, or nearly so. The instant she had an opening when he took a deep breath, she snapped out her answer. "Then we'll go look for him."

He opened his mouth and she *knew* he was going to cry *But how?* and she forestalled that. "Magically, of course. But not here. I'll find Petrescu and ask him if he has a space he can lock people out of for a while, otherwise we'll ride out and find some place in the hills where we won't be disturbed. Give me a moment to get ready."

She opened the door and shoved him out, then closed the door behind him so she could change into proper clothing. No one was going to take her seriously if she started running about in a skirt over a night rail.

A few minutes later she opened the door again to find him still anxiously standing right outside her door, all but wringing his hands. "Follow me," she said, "First we need the mayor," and pushed passed him to check the open-air tables for Petrescu.

She was deliberately sitting on any emotional reaction, because emotions would not help the situation at all. There was absolutely no point in *two* people getting wrought up.

Besides, if there was one thing she knew beyond a shadow of a doubt, it was that allowing her emotions to get the better of her was not going to help Markos in this situation. She knew what she needed to do first. *Find him. Find out if he is in danger.* If he wasn't, well she would let his cousin yell at him when he came back. But if he was—

If he is in danger, we need to find out exactly what the danger is, and how to get him out of it.

And if he was dead—

If he is dead, I shall raise a Hunt the likes of which has never been seen since the days of Vlad the Impaler.

Petrescu was there at one of the outdoor tables with his two cronies from yesterday, all three of them discussing something intently. Without a doubt, they were still talking about the shifter Rosa had killed; that would probably remain the topic of their discussion for weeks. They looked up as she approached, and must have seen by her face that something very bad had happened.

"Markos went hunting out in the hills last night to make certain there were no more of those shifters out there," she said, obviously not explaining *how* he went out. She had to tell the truth—but nothing compelled her to tell *all* of the truth. "He's not what we call a Hunt Master, but he *is* as experienced at hunting game as I am hunting evil things—and he certainly does have some experience of his own at hunting evil things. I was—I *am*, as you know—not convinced that there was only one *vârcolac*. According to Dominik, Markos agreed with me. He felt that if there are more out there, they would probably come looking for the one we killed." Not exactly a lie—it was what she would have said if she had thought of it instead of being angry. "So he went out to set up an ambush. He was supposed to come back at dawn and didn't. There is no point in scouring the hills for him, since that would only waste time—but if I have a private space, I can look for him with magic."

Petrescu's eyes lit up at that. And before he could ask the inevitable question, she answered it for him. "Yes, you can watch. You ought to, you do have Earth Magic enough to see the spirits, so in fact, it might be something you can learn to find missing villagers. I don't *know* that you can, for sure—" she cautioned, as he looked even more eager. "It might be like the difference between someone with good vision, and the sort of woman who has such extraordinary vision that she can embroider designs with single hairs. But you can watch me now, and when we have found Markos and gotten him back safely, I will help you and we will see if you can do this too. But finding Markos is more important right now."

"Yes, yes, of course," Petrescu said, and as his two companions remained quiet, he thought very hard for a moment, his brows creasing and his formidable moustache quivering. Then his face brightened. "Ah! I know! My hay barn. It has nothing in it at the moment, we have just cleared all of last year's hay out before we put in this year's. Will that do?"

"Beautifully," she said. "Let me get my things from the wagon."

Now I am so glad Gunther always drilled organization into me, she thought, as she ran around the side of the inn and hopped into the back of the wagon. She knew exactly where the bag of items she needed for various magics was stored, and she knew where every item *in* that bag was. It was just a moment to unlock the chest, seize what looked for all the world like a black leather doctor's bag (because it was), and lock the chest again.

She was back before Dominik could even start wringing his hands again.

"I have everything I need in here," she said, lifting the bag. "Let's go."

"We'll be off, mayor," Vasile said, looking more than a bit uncomfortable with all this open talk of magic. "If you need us, you know where to find us."

Petrescu just nodded as his two cronies walked off, clearly trying to look as if they were strolling away and not escaping from a situation they really didn't want to get involved with.

Petrescu waved them out into the street. "There won't be

any fire, will there?" Petrescu asked anxiously, his moustache bristling with sudden anxiety at the thought. "You
don't want a fire in a hay barn, even if it *is* cleaned out."

"No, no fire," she promised, and then, as they trotted
down the village street to his home, she explained, briefly,
the four sorts of Elemental powers. "Just like the old Greeks
said. Air, Water, Fire, and Earth. Each one has its own Elemental creatures, and depending, you might be able to see
all of them, or might not. And the magic of each Element
has its own particular strengths and weaknesses. I'm Earth,
and so are Markos and Dominik," she said, just as they
came to Petrescu's home and left the main street, going to a
path around the side of the house that would lead them to
the paddock where he would winter his cattle and sheep
and where his hay barn would be. "Everything that I do,
everything that I use, is of the Earth. So no, I won't be using
any fire."

She knew that Dominik must be thinking she was mad—
or not taking this seriously enough—because she was
talking so much. But she had a reason here; she didn't want
Dominik talking, for fear he would blurt out that Markos
was a shifter too. And she didn't want Petrescu asking questions. So far as Petrescu was concerned, Markos was just the
"other young stranger lad" who had helped kill the *vârcolac*. He didn't know Markos; he wasn't all that concerned
about Markos. Her chatter about magic would interest him
more than enough to keep him quiet.

As befitted the mayor of the village, Petrescu's house
was larger than many, and had two stories; it had a fine tiled
roof rather than thatch, and unlike some of the other houses
in the village, the wood had been stained a dark brown
rather than painted in a pastel color. The lower story was
walled in stone and had a wooden door in the front of it,
and very tiny windows, currently shuttered. The upper story
was wood, and was reached by two staircases framing the
door of the lower story. That lower story would probably
have a dirt floor, be used for food storage, and possibly to
shelter delicate or sickly animals during the winter, while
the upper story was for the people.

They rounded the back of the house, passed a beautifully

built bread oven and outdoor kitchen, and Petrescu opened
a gate in a proper, tall fence and let them into the barnyard.

Petrescu had both a very impressive animal barn, strong
and well built, and an equally well-built hay barn, both built
of heavy wood with a stone foundation. It was to the latter
they headed.

The hay barn had no windows at all in the walls, but it
didn't need any, for the upper part of it was open, allowing
air and light in. Petrescu opened the plank door for them,
and when they were all inside, closed it and dropped a bar
into supports to keep it shut—and to keep nosy people
out.

Rosa took a long look around, breathing in the slightly
dusty scent of old hay. There were still little piles of it here
and there, and wisps caught on every splinter. No one bothered to plane the planks smooth for a hay barn.

This would a good place to work. Growing things (like
hay) were of Earth, the floor was Earth, the plank walls
were wood, which was of Earth. The only things lacking for
properly shielded Earth Magic were things she had brought
herself. The Earth Master in Rosa approved. The upper part
of the walls of the barn were open, so that the hay stored in
here could breathe and would not rot. That gave them
plenty of light to see by.

"This is good," she said aloud. "This is perfect. Come,
and sit where I show you." She led them all to the center of
the barn, indicated to Dominik and Petrescu where they
were to sit. Dominik just dropped down where she pointed;
Petrescu considered, went out, and came back in again with
a little three-legged wooden milking stool.

"Would it be all right—?" he asked.

"Perfectly all right," she said, and sat down, as he positioned his stool and lowered himself down onto it while she
carefully laid out her tools.

They were few, for something like this.

Knowing that she might have to do some sort of "finding," she had packed the best map of the area she could get,
actually better than the one they had been using all along.
She got out a jar full of sand, and from a little vial, a strand
of hair.

Dominik's eyes grew big when he saw that last. "Is that—" he asked, pointing, sounding shocked.

"From Markos? Yes," she replied. If the situation had not been so serious, she might have smirked at his shock. "I have some from you, too. Any time I am working or traveling with someone, I make sure to get something of theirs early on just in case something like this happens. The fact that you didn't *know* I did so should show you that I am *very* good at getting things like this. And it should make you a good bit more careful about making sure no one else does."

She turned to Petrescu. "This is very old magic, and it is often something that anyone with a bit of magic, especially Earth Magic, can do. Witches sometimes use this magic, if they are good people. You need something that was part of the person you are looking for, like hair, or a bit of cloth from something he wore all the time. Once, when I was hunting for a child, I scraped some sawdust off a little wooden toy he always played with. You have the priest bless your sand—have him do about a bucket full, so you always have some ready when you need it."

Petrescu nodded. "I see. Sand is earth—"

"And the closer to pure earth your spell ingredients are, the easier it will be for you to work the magic." She shook out a little of the sand in a linen handkerchief. "Don't be tempted to use silk cloth, though. Stick as close to common stuff as a you can." She looked up for a moment, and caught Petrescu's gaze. "That is a very lucky thing for us Earth Magicians. We don't need sapphires or expensive incense or gold chalices. Earthen cups, sand, linen cloth, all work wonderfully for us. Now, first, you cut up the hair or cloth as fine as you can—"

She'd done this so many times she didn't even need to think about it. She could cut a hair into pieces so tiny they looked like specks. She made sure to do so as close to the sand as possible, and quickly mixed the bits into the sand with her finger.

"You might as well see if you can see what I am going to do now; I don't know if you *will*, but if you can, that will mean you have more than just a thread of Earth Magic in you," she explained patiently. "I am going to make a protected space around us, and it will look like half an eggshell, and we will be inside. It will keep anything bad from seeing that we are doing anything. When you work magic, other magicians can see you doing it, unless you protect yourself. But the protections fool their senses into thinking nothing is going on."

This didn't require any special preparation on her part, just breathing in, concentrating, and then breathing out. As she breathed out, she pushed her personal "shields" as she called them, outward. To the eyes of another Elemental Magician, it would look as if she were inflating a sort of gold-colored soap bubble outward from herself, until it was just big enough to hold all three of them.

Petrescu's eyes got large and round, and his mouth under that brush-like moustache dropped open a bit before he snapped it shut.

Well! He saw that. She'd have to make sure he got teaching, then. He could do a lot for his village with a little magic.

"Now, you make a barrier around the area on the map you think the lost person is in," she continued, and called up Earth energies into her hand. To her own eyes, her hand glowed so golden it seemed to be wearing a glove made of light. "You see the power in my hand?" she asked.

Wide-eyed, Petrescu nodded.

"So, you draw with the power on the map." A wolf could travel fifty miles in a day, so that was the distance she drew, a circle with a radius of about fifty miles, with the village as the center of the circle.

Dominik was staring intently. This must be all new to him, too. *Well, he's a healer. I don't suppose anyone ever thought he would need anything but the knowledge of how to drive out sickness and speed up healing.* That wasn't how it was in the Bruderschaft, but the Bruderschaft had once been a society of knights, hadn't it? And in a society of fighters, even the healer needs to learn all the tricks.

"Now this is the tricky part. You put more power into the sand, but you have to concentrate and put *intention* in there too. You . . . you tell the sand you want it to show you where the person whose property is mixed with it is. That takes a lot of practice and a hunter's concentration."

"What do you mean by that?" Dominik finally spoke up. "Is this something to do with being a Hunt Master?"

"No, actually. I mean it literally," she said. "It's exactly the way you concentrate when you are lining something up for a shot. And you know that moment when you know the shot is going to be good?" she asked.

Petrescu nodded. So did Dominik.

"Well that is exactly like the moment you know the sand is ready to do its work. You *feel* it, the moment it is ready. And it's like letting an arrow loose. It's not a pushing, it's a letting go."

She held the handkerchief with the sand in it in the palm of one hand, cupped her other hand over the top, and poured Earth Magic into it. The sand didn't have to be blessed, actually, just clean—but Petrescu was a very good and pious man, and having a priest bless something he was going to use for magic would make him more comfortable with doing the magic. And that would make it easier for him to make it all work.

As for her—she always had *everything* she used blessed by the priest that served the Bruderschaft. You never knew when you would come across something so evil that a blessing would make the difference between success and failure.

When she felt that the sand could not possibly absorb any more power, she "told" the power what she wanted.

Find Markos. Show us where he is. Find him.

Then she trickled a little of the sand down onto the map, and gently began to shake the piece of paper.

This was why she had put the power barrier on the *map* rather than on the ground. *She* didn't actually need to shake the paper to provide the motion to the sand; if she continued to *will* the sand, it would move of its own accord. But there were several reasons why that wouldn't be such a good idea.

First of all, it was a waste of magical power, power she might need later. She didn't have an unlimited store of it, after all; no magician did—unless one of the Great Elementals happened to choose that magician as a channel. Anything she wasted now, she might regret having used later.

Second, this was a sufficient amount of uncanniness as it

was for the village mayor. She didn't need to spook him by having him watch sand crawl across the paper on its own.

And third—Petrescu would probably never be able to make the sand move himself. So she was using the method he could use, since both were equally efficacious.

Slowly, as she shook the paper back and forth, the sand began to migrate to one side of the map—deeper into the hills, and past the point where they had found the first shifter. It started sticking onto a single spot, and once there, it was as if it had been sprinkled onto glue, for it would not move. When she stopped moving the paper, all the sand was packed onto that one spot, like a hard little rock glued down onto the paper.

"Holy Mother!" Petrescu exclaimed. "It worked!"

But Rosa frowned, and then bit back an exclamation of alarm. For the pale sand was darkening even as they watched, until, within a minute or two, it had turned a dark red.

"What—?" Petrescu said, puzzled.

"That means—that means that Markos is in great danger," Dominik said, bleakly. "Doesn't it?"

"Yes it does," she replied, and "told" the sand to fuse itself to the paper, just to be sure. "He's still alive, or it would have turned black. But we need to get to him, quickly."

She tied up the rest of the sand with the dust-of-hair in it in the handkerchief; she might have a use for it later. Then she folded the map, pulled her shields back into herself, and got up off the floor before either of the men thought to do so.

"I'll loan you my horses," Petrescu said. "They're Magyar riding horses; they'll get you there faster than your old nags." He used his walking stick to lever himself up off the milking stool, and stood up. Dominik picked it up and handed it to him.

"Dominik, you go with the mayor to get the horses; meet me at the inn. If you've got sheathes for guns, or saddlebags, or both, sir, please put those on when you saddle the horses up." Petrescu nodded. She stowed her things away in the satchel and they all hurried out of the barn. As soon as she was in the clear, she started running, counting down the things in her head she thought she might need.

What's the worst that could possibly happen? She asked herself as she ran and, ignoring the startled looks around the inn, scrambled back into the wagon. *The worst would be—an entire clan of shifters.*

If that was the case, there was no way on Heaven or earth they would be able to survive in a straight fight. They'd have to find out where Markos was, how he was being held, *why* he was being held, and figure out some way of getting out without it turning into a straight fight.

Then they'd have to get the White Lodge at Bucharest, any Elemental Magicians at Sibiu, at Brasov—was there a White Lodge at Belgrade? Probably. But that many sorcerers—it would mean the biggest Hunt in five hundred years. Maybe more.

Unless they are all very weak, or inexperienced . . . they only know a handful of spells, and the shifter spell. . . .

That would, more or less, fit. After all, you would *think* that a large number of sorcerers would have taken over a town, or something, by now. And yet they seemed to be keeping their depredations to solitary victims.

Hope for that, but don't count on it.

And hope for help from the Elementals. Once she got out into the countryside, she would be dealing with the native Romanian creatures, not the Saxon imports here and in Sibiu. Maybe—no, definitely—it had been a very good thing that they'd had that stop to collect folktales.

Meanwhile . . . she knew silver worked against these shifters, whether they were calling themselves *vârcolac,* or "werewolves" or whatever. The rules she had learned still clearly applied. So—

She opened a very specific chest, one with three locks on it, because besides being valuable in the hunt, these objects were valuable in their own right. She actually wished she'd had them on the Hunt with Hans, but she'd had no reason to suspect a shifter when she'd packed.

From now on, she thought grimly, *I am never leaving home without them.*

They were peculiar garments that she took out of the chest. Her special leather gear, and Hans', which would fit Dominik. Two leather collars with skirts that protected a bit

of the chest, back and shoulders. Two leather vests—one
fitted to her, like a corset, and one a good bit looser. Two
pairs of leather gloves with *long* cuffs that reached to the
elbow. And two pairs of very tight-fitting leather pants—the
larger of the two had lacings up the outer sides so Dominik
could get them on over his own trousers and snug them
tight. Hers were form-fitting, again, fitted to her. Dominik
would have to make do with his own boots. She had a pair
that went with this outfit.

This outfit, that weighed far more than it should have.

Because sandwiched between the silk lining and the
leather was another layer: a layer of cloth of silver.

If a shifter tried to bite, he'd get a surprise.

This was not to say that the shifter wouldn't be able to
kill them some other way. He could slash the vests to ribbons with enough swipes of his claws. He could break their
backs, or their necks. He could smash them into a cliff or a
tree, or bash out their brains with a rock.

But at least he wouldn't be able to tear their throats out,
or rip open any of the major arteries with his teeth.

She stripped and changed right there in the wagon, and
never mind that someone might come by. Then she armed
herself up.

Silver daggers for both of them. Coach gun on her back.
Ammunition pouch with every shell she had. Crossbow
with silver-headed bolts for Dominik. Pistols with silver
bullets for both of them—one for him, two for her. The
boar spear for Dominik, and a shorter spear as well. Then
the pouch she slung over her shoulder, and began loading.
Bottles of holy water—you never knew, sometimes it
worked on shifters, sometimes it didn't. Blessed salt. Wolfsbane oil that she rubbed all over the outside of the leather,
hers and Dominik's. It would last a day and a night, and
then it would have to be renewed to be effective, so she
tucked the bottle into the pouch beside the holy water and
the salt. The map went in there too, and the sand, and a
good compass. Every other bit of magic she did out there
would have to either rely on raw power or the help of Elementals, because she would not have time for any elaborate rituals.

Food: dried beef and hard biscuit. Water bottles, though she hoped they wouldn't need that, in those hills. The horses could subsist on grass for a few days without coming to harm, but she picked up a bag of oats anyway.

Is that all I need and we can carry? This was the first time she was not going to have the backing of a nearby Lodge, and ... that made things a good bit more complicated than she would have liked.

Then she sat down and spent the time writing a letter, expending a little energy to duplicate the contents on four more blank pieces of paper beneath the one she was writing on, as if she were using carbonic paper between them.

If you are receiving this, it means that something has gone terribly wrong, and if I am not already dead, you must put your mind to the fact that you might be forced to kill me.

Then she outlined everything she knew, as briefly as she could. Sealing the letters, she addressed them to Gunther and the Graf, reserving copies for Dominik to address to his and Markos' fathers. She signed and sealed hers, put postage on all four, and jumped down out of the wagon, striding out into the street and ignoring the startled looks of the villagers who were trying to get their minds reconciled to seeing *a woman in tight black leather trousers.* Part of her mind, divorced from the worry of what might be happening to Markos, was amused by the thought that they would probably one and all accept seeing *vâlvă* and *iele* in the streets and *balaur* overhead, but could not encompass the notion of a woman in trousers.

She didn't run, but only because she saw Petrescu and Dominik astride a pair of exceptionally handsome horses, both bays with black manes and tails, coming toward her.

When they saw her, they urged their horses into a canter and pulled up next to her. Petrescu's eyes boggled, but he said nothing about her attire. He dismounted, and took some of her burdens from her, stowing oats and water bottles and bags in the saddlebags.

"Dominik," she said, sternly. "You need to dismount too. Put these on."

He didn't argue. She handed Dominik the leather garments and the weapons she had brought for him, one by one. He checked the pistol for being loaded, and strapped on all of the leather right there in the street.

"Now sign and address these," she ordered, handing him the two letters. "One to your parents, one to Markos." He looked them over soberly, took the lead pencil she handed him and obeyed, sealing them with the gummed seal she had left inside the envelopes.

She gave all four letters to Petrescu. "If we are not back within three days, put these in the post," she told him.

Petrescu's moustache quivered, but he took them and tucked them inside his vest. "I will go and pray to the Virgin and her Son that I may burn them tomorrow," the old man said, fervently.

Dominik nodded, soberly. Then he distributed his weapons around himself and remounted. She was very glad that she'd taken the time to pack Hans' extra leathers along. She had hesitated for a moment at the time, but now she was glad she had left the weapons chest intact.

Petrescu offered her his cupped hands. As weighed down as she was with weapons, this time she accepted the help with no second thoughts about it making her look weak.

"Go," was all Petrescu said. "Come back safe. God and the Virgin guard you."

Wordlessly, they turned the horses' heads and cantered out of the village. She would have *liked* to gallop, but they needed to save the horses. They wouldn't gain anything by driving their mounts to exhaustion, then being forced to dismount and walk them the rest of the way.

They rode in silence. She didn't know what Dominik was thinking, but *she* was trying to figure out ways of tracking Markos down once they got close to the spot where he was, presumably, under siege—or being held captive. She hoped it was captive. Unless a miracle happened, and he was fighting from a protected spot, they would never get there in time to save him if he was under siege.

Or better still, let him be hiding somewhere, nursing his wounds and healing.

She unfolded the map and checked the little hard button of sand. It was still the same color. So at least things hadn't gotten worse for him.

If he's aboveground, I can borrow a bird's eyes to look for him. A raven would be best. She could bargain with one of those; they were intelligent enough to understand the concept. And they loved dried meat.

But if he was underground? Because if, for some reason, he had taken to a cave—maybe to rest from an attack—how would she and Dominik ever find him?

Are there dwarves here? Gnomes? Surely there is some cave-dwelling Elemental I can call on . . .

The horses were magnificent, and if she hadn't been fretting herself to bits, she would have loved the ride; they had a canter that absolutely ate the miles. Soon the village was completely out of sight in the distance and they were long past the spot where the *vârcolac* had taken the dead gypsy. She consulted the map, and, now that it had been imbued with magical power, she persuaded it to actually reflect their surroundings, as well as giving their own location as two little dots moving across the parchment. It wasn't that hard, this was a little thing practically everyone in the Bruderschaft knew how to do, and it didn't take but a thought. *Be as we see. . . .*

The parchment populated itself with pale grey mounds for hills and mountains, and little green spikes for trees. When that was done, it made two dots, one red, one black, for her and Dominik. She saw that they were about halfway there, and put it safely back inside her vest.

About ten miles; another ten to go. A bit more than half an hour. It seemed that they had been riding for an age, and that they would never get there in time. Her insides knotted up. If they weren't in time. . . .

She glanced over at Dominik, who paced her stride for stride, grim-faced. He looked over and caught her eye.

It was hard to communicate when pounding across the hills, and neither of them, she suspected, wanted to shout. But he managed to get his face into an expression of inquiry that was pretty easy to read. *Do you have any idea what we are facing? Any plans?*

She shrugged. He nodded.

They both turned their attention to getting as much out of their mounts as they could without exhausting them.

Finally they found their path taking them into deep woods, among hills almost tall enough to qualify as mountains. They followed streambeds and game trails, whenever they found something going more or less in the direction they needed. It was easier to follow the streambeds than the game trails, but it was rough going either way. They *had* to slow now, but the map was no longer nearly as much help, since they were practically on top of the sand-dot.

And that was when she had a brainstorm, and reined her horse in at a slightly clearer spot in the woods. Dominik immediately did the same. His horse blew out its breath in a snort, impatiently.

"What—?" Dominik asked, in a harsh whisper. She held up her hand, then pulled off her right glove with her teeth, and gently detached the sand-dot from the map. Leaning forward, she carefully transferred it to the center of her horse's browband and made it fuse there with a little magic. Keeping her fingers on it, she concentrated, willing power and intention not only into the bit of Markos-infused sand but into the horse's mind as well. *Follow, my four-legged friend. Follow where that leads.* She tickled the part of her magic that allowed her to get inside the horse's mind, and commune with him without words. She sensed he understood, and withdrew a little.

Around her the forest was—itself. There seemed to be nothing whatsoever sinister lurking within it. If she had not known better, she would never have guessed this was a place where Markos could be in danger.

Maybe whatever it is is very, very good at hiding.

She patted the horse's neck, trying to communicate her anxiety for a herd-mate without frightening him. Then she slacked the reins, and gently nudged the horse with her heels.

He threw up his head, a little startled for a moment, then, tentatively began to move through the trees, forsaking the game trail altogether. Dominik followed right at her horse's tail. She figured he knew enough about magic to have understood what she was doing when he saw it, and didn't want to break the silence with voices. Human voices had a nasty tendency to carry quite far in the forest.

One great advantage of being Elemental Masters in a situation like this was that wildlife tended not to call the alarm on their approach. An Elemental Master—especially an Earth Master—could move through a forest and attract less attention from wild things than a large predator, like a bear. And since their horses were not much bigger than deer, the soft sound of their hooves on the ground was not likely to give them away. Unless this peril had a nose keener than anything else in the forest, or was using birds to stand guard, it was unlikely they would give themselves away.

She linked herself to the little dot of sand as well, allowing herself to feel the "tug" as it tried to reach Markos. If the horse needed a little extra guidance, she would be able to give it. She kept the reins slack, and her hands light on them, for this fellow had shown himself to have a sensitive mouth.

But this horse was as clever and willing as their cart horse had been dull and recalcitrant. Now that he "understood" what was wanted, he was completely attentive to the signals to his mind, and stepped carefully among the undergrowth to find the easiest path to get where the sand was taking him.

She kept her eyes half-closed, trying to be as sensitive to the forest around her as she could, looking and "feeling" for trouble—was there any chance, any chance at all, that whatever Markos had encountered would have been careless enough to leave traces of itself?

Oh, may it be so, she prayed fervently.

And then, as if her prayer had been answered, she saw it.

Unmistakable, and just joining their path ahead, barely visible through the trees. She would have seen it, regardless, once they had gone a little farther, but since she was looking hard for it, the signs screamed at her with their wrongness. She reined the horse in on pure reaction, her heart in her mouth.

Energy trails, like dried blood. The visible traces of *vârcolac,* shifters, users of blood magic. Not one. Not three or four. This was . . . a lot. Weaving in and out around each other, all going in the same direction. A dozen, maybe more.

Dominik pulled up beside her, and when she glanced at

him, she saw his eyes were wide with shock. He looked over at her.

"We need to rethink this," she whispered. She had not anticipated there might be *this* much opposition. She had never heard of that many shifters working together, like a real wolf pack.

Not ever.

This was unprecedented.

"Whatever we were thinking of doing," she continued, her mouth dry, "Is clearly out of the question. We need some really original plans."

Wordlessly, he nodded.

Rosa and Dominik lay side by side above a crack in the hillside. They were belly-down on sparse grass over a scant layer of soil, which in turn topped granite. Sun shining down on them seemed to give no heat, at least not to Rosa. She suppressed shivers at the sheer level of dark magic she could sense beneath them. A thin stream of somewhat noisome smoke barely wafted out of the crack in the rock. That crack served as the "chimney" to a cave somewhere far below. And in that cave was Markos.

That was what the sand-dot told them; the energy traces of the shifters told them that there were . . . a lot of them. It was like a murky, polluted cesspit down there.

There were so many of the shifters that, near the entrance of the cave, their trails all got muddled into one solid wash of horrid, sickening power, and all that Rosa knew for certain was that there were far more than a dozen.

Another problem was that there was no way to tease out individual trails without actually having something belonging to the shifter. So there was no way of picking them out individually to count them, either.

And there was the problem of traffic in and out of the cave. Energy trails faded after about a day, but who knew how many times the shifters had entered and left the cave during that time? All she could tell for certain was that there were far more of them than she and Dominik could handle with a straightforward attack.

By the smell coming up from that chimney-crack . . . this was their home den, the place from which they staged all their attacks. And they had been living there for a very long time. The stink of unwashed bodies, human and lupine, was enough to gag a goat. It was flavored with the smoke, hints of old blood and a touch of rotting meat. She wondered how they could *stand* it. Wolves had incredibly sensitive noses.

But maybe, since it was *their* stink, they liked it.

This was definitely where Markos was being held, and they knew, now, that he must be being held as a prisoner. There was no way a pack of shifters like this would have allowed him to join them, no matter how cleverly he tried. In fact, that might be how they had taken Markos prisoner in the first place.

She and Dominik couldn't tell exactly where Markos *was* in there, and all they knew for certain was that he wasn't dead yet. She felt her gut clenching, and forced back tears. To be so close to him, and not be able to think of a way to rescue him! This would need a full Hunt, and he would be dead long, long before she could bring a full Hunt here. Never had she felt more helpless—

Well . . . not quite never. The last time she had felt this helpless, she had been trapped in the pantry, with a shifter clawing through the door. . . .

. . . shifter, clawing through the door. All alone. Desperate. And reaching out, fueled purely by that desperation . . .

Wait . . .

It wasn't so much an *idea* as a . . . feeling.

Could I? Should I, that's more to the point.

What choice do we have?

"Let's get back to the horses," she whispered. She wiggled backward from the crack until she was well away, then got carefully to her feet and stole quietly through the forest. Years and years of practice, plus her soft-soled boots, made her so quiet that she didn't even snap a twig. Dominik was a little more clumsy; despite his best effort, he kept stepping on branches, and rustling leaves—but he was smart enough to make his movements slow and deliberate, so that they sounded rather like a bear shoving his way through the brush, and not like a human at all.

Once they were well away from the—well, she could only think of it as a "den"—she broke into a trot. There was no point in being quiet now, and she wanted to get back to a safe point before she spoke aloud. Dominik did the same and followed right behind her, trying to put his feet in her footsteps to confuse their path, until they got to the little cleft where they had left the horses.

It was not unlike the cleft in the rock back at the first shifter cave, except that it was shallower and there was no cave at the back of it. They had left the horses tied up to a young tree about the girth of a bracelet, right beside a trickle of water, and there was enough grass beneath it to keep the horses satisfied for now.

When we have to leave them . . . I must tie them loosely, scatter the oats around them, and give them orders to pull free and run by sunrise. She hoped this cleft was far enough from the shifter den that the shifters wouldn't scent the horses. She hoped no bears or real wolves would get them overnight.

Then again, she doubted that bears or wolves would come this close to the shifter den. Likely the only animals around here were things the shifters wouldn't trouble to kill.

"I need to do a magic working. This isn't going to be like anything you have ever seen before, Dominik," she said, as they paused and took some deep breaths, leaning a little against the horses' rumps. "It—it isn't even exactly a ritual, or a spell, or anything of the sort. I'll tell you the truth; when it comes to all the magic that I actually know, I'm completely at my wit's end for remembering *anything* that will do us any good at all."

He nodded. "Nothing I could think of would, either," he admitted, grim-faced. "We need a Hunt, but—blessed Virgin, how could we ever be so cruel as to try and make one up out of Petrescu and his villagers? And nothing we summoned, not even from my family or Markos', would get here in time."

She nodded, lips compressed into a thin, hard line. "But I finally remembered that I did something by accident, once upon a time when I was a child and as desperate as we are now, that worked beyond anything I should have been able to do. I'm going to try something of the same thing, this time on purpose. And we'll see what we get." She took a deep breath, and dropped her hands to her sides, shaking them out. "This probably isn't even going to *look* much like magic. So . . . well, all I can do is try."

She dropped all of her shielding. After all, she hadn't even known what shields *were* back then, much less been able to raise them. She needed to be the opposite of what she usually was; she needed to return to that pure, innocent state of childhood, when she had no idea that—some things weren't possible.

Maybe . . . maybe in that state of purity and innocence, anything was possible.

And she closed her eyes, made herself entirely still, and . . . opened herself to the forest, to the hills and mountains, to the earth beneath her. Opened herself to all the life around her—which was the thing she had done instinctively and in a panic as a child.

This time she had no fear that the *vârcolac* would sense her. She knew now what she had not known then—that the shifters were entirely *un*natural. That they were not in tune with the Earth, because their magic, like the magic of all of those who used blood-engendered power, was the opposite of Earth Magic. That they divorced themselves from the Earth, in a sense—attuning themselves only to the opposite powers of corruption, evil, and decay. What she did . . . well, they wouldn't even know she was doing it. The only reason that shifter back in Grossmutter's cottage had known what she was doing was because, untutored child that she was, she had called for help to anything that could hear her. This time, she was going to call for . . . only good things, wholesome things, anything natural, and tied to the Earth, that might be inclined to help her.

But it would leave her completely open and at the mercy of whatever answered her. Back in Germany, she knew what she would get. But this was Romania. And what answered her might not be friendly to her. The Saxons— Rhenish in her case, but spirits and Elementals wouldn't know the difference—might not be regarded kindly by the native Romanian spirits and Elementals. She hadn't sensed any animosity, but the truth was, she just didn't know. The Saxons had brought their own creatures with them when they arrived centuries ago. Had they displaced the natives? Did the natives resent that? Never mind how long ago it had been, Elementals remembered favors and grudges for millennia. . . .

She was counting on Dominik's presence—and the fact that they were trying to rescue Markos from something utterly foul—to temper that. But there were no guarantees. And if whatever came decided she needed punishment as an interloper rather than aid as an ally, well . . .

Well, then I will beg for help for Markos and submit to any punishment it might deem my due, she thought, reconciling herself to it. There was, after all, no choice. This was their best chance to save him. Probably their only chance. He had believed in her, and stood up for her, and taken her side. She could not do less for him.

She gathered all the power that was within her, as she had as a child. She tried to put herself in the attitude of supplication—not groveling, but as one who has exhausted all other options, and will accept with an open, grateful heart whatever might come to her aid. And she waited, until the moment felt right, as the tension built, as the metaphysical arrow waited, and the bowstring was drawn back, until the mystical quarry was in her sights, and the arrow was ready to leap from the bow, and the moment was *just right*—

And the moment came, single, whole, and perfect.

Please! she called out, making her whole, body ring with their need. *HELP US!!*

Just as it had that moment, so long ago, the entire forest seemed to ring like a bell. It was as if a shudder, an earthquake—no, a *power* quake—went through everything, and a moment after that . . . came an enormous *silence.* Nothing made a sound, not a bird, not a leaf, not the horses next to them. Not even the wind. For that moment, everything in the forest was completely, utterly still, and everything that had breath, held its breath—

Dominik looked as if she had struck him between the

eyes with a hammer. Even his handsome moustache had lost its life, and drooped as if stunned.

She, too, held her breath, staring at the opening to the cleft in the hill where they had taken shelter, wondering what, if anything, was going to answer her.

Then, she had her answer.

There was light, golden light, building out there in the forest. It was a clear, pure light, of a sort she had never seen before. For a moment, it looked as if the most perfect sunbeam ever created had pierced the canopy and was illuminating a spot right where the cleft opened up into the woods. But then the light got stronger ... and stronger ... and began moving toward them.

Rosa clutched the saddle, knees going weak. She hadn't exactly hoped for this ... she hadn't allowed herself to hope for anything.

But whatever had answered her, it was powerful. More powerful, maybe, than that avatar of the Great Hunter that had appeared to help her with the first Romanian shifter, the one that had worn the first copper medal. But there was more than just *one* being answering her call this time.

The light formed into shapes, and then into solid creatures. Human-formed, but definitely not human. The power played around them like a halo.

It was a procession of maidens, pacing two-by-two toward them.

But oh! Such maidens as these she had never seen in her life, and reckoned she never would again.

The first lot were the most impressive, and most beautiful of them all. There were two of them, with long hair flowing down to the ground, hair the actual color of gold, golden gowns, and eyes the color of the sky. Their faces were impossibly beautiful, and still—like statues come to life. "Zâne," whispered Dominik, eyes bulging, moustache bristling, as they neared and then divided, facing and standing one to either side of them. "They are like—guardian angels."

Before she could respond, more paced forward out of the light. The second lot, six of them, walking toward them in a line of three pairs, were also beautiful, but dressed in

mail coats over white gowns, and their hair was more the
color of white gold. Their faces were *anything* but still. They
smiled, lazily, and even though they were wearing armor,
they swayed as if they were dancing, seductively. *"Iele,"*
Dominik said, and shivered, as they cast voluptuous glances
at him. He looked as if he was torn between fear and longing for them; being a woman, Rosa was immune to their
seductive power, but she could sense how hard Dominik
was fighting to resist. They seemed to find that amusing. She
sensed that if they had wanted to, they could have brought
Dominik crawling to them on his hands and knees. But they
were here for another purpose, and were not inclined to toy
with him. This time, anyway.

The last lot, another set of two, were two beautiful girls,
a little less beautiful than the *iele,* with hair the color of
wheat-straw. They were the most human looking of the
lot—which was to say, not all that human, but more approachable. Their expressions were grave, and their eyes
were dark, like bottomless pools of water. Both wore golden
gowns. There were blue flames hovering just above their
heads. *"Vâlva băilor,"* said Dominik faintly. They did not
look at Dominik, though they nodded at Rosa. She thought
they looked faintly friendly.

The girls arranged themselves in a semicircle with an
open place exactly opposite the two of them. And now the
light playing around them became too bright to look on for
a moment; Rosa and Dominik had to close their eyes. The
light seemed to burn through her closed eyelids, and when
it faded and she opened them again, there was a man standing in that gap. An old man, dressed in white like the first
two girls, like several of the Romanian men that Rosa had
seen in Sibiu. He wore baggy white trousers, a white shirt,
both not just white, but dazzlingly so. He had plain brown
boots, an embroidered belt at least a hand's-breadth wide
around his waist. He had very long white hair, far longer
than anything she had seen in this country before, with a
long white beard, formidable white moustache, and a wise
and kindly look on his face. He faced both of them, leaning
on a staff, his bright blue eyes twinkling a little.

"Moşul!" gasped Dominik, and went to one knee. Rosa

didn't go that far—strangely, the name only meant "old man"—but she did bow with profound respect. *Moşul* seemed to find this amusing.

"We have come to aid you, children," the Old Man said, with a chuckle. "Your simple and heartfelt call for help touched our hearts. And we, too, wish to rid our land of the foul and unnatural creatures that have infested it. It is just as well that you did not seek to rescue your brother-in-power by yourselves. The evil *vârcolac* in that cave number three and forty. You would never have escaped alive."

They both gasped; Rosa felt the blood draining from her face. "What do you advise, Wise Elder?" she asked, humbly. "We cannot leave him there, but as you say, we cannot hope to rescue him alone."

"Most assuredly not, you must not leave him in their hands!" the Old Man exclaimed. "No, it is more than time that the foul creatures were scoured from that den, and as I said, we have come to aid you. And we intend far more than advice. Do we not, my daughters?"

"They have plagued the people of this land long enough, and have not repented of their ways," said one of the two *zâne*, sternly. Well, if they were a sort of guardian angel, they were surely offended by the forty-year reign of the murder of innocent people, half of them young people and children. "Too many innocent souls cry out to us, restless because they cannot sleep while these creatures roam free, and kill, and kill again. This cannot stand."

The *iele* just looked eager, and didn't say anything. Truth to tell, they seemed just a little bloodthirsty, to Rosa.

But the Elementals sometimes are bloodthirsty, especially the nature spirits, she reminded herself. *Most especially those that were once gods. The old gods were not single in nature, they had their light and dark sides.* She regarded the Beings lined up before her. *Our luck they are showing us their bright sides.*

Now, there was always, *always,* a catch, when supernatural beings like this—Greater Elementals, in fact—came to aid an Elemental Master. As Gunther often said, "All that the Great Ones do is to give you the tools. It is up to you to wield them correctly."

So Rosa bowed again, and said, "Then if you have brought these wondrous creatures to be our army, I beg you, tell us what your strengths and weaknesses are, that we may all emerge victorious." It was the *weaknesses* that concerned her the most. Although the *iele* might be dressed in armor, it didn't follow that they were actual *fighters*. And if the *zâne* were a sort of "guardian angel," it might be that all they did was defend, and not attack. "And if this aid comes at a price—"

"There is no price," said the same one that had spoken before. "Not for this. This is . . . proper work for us all."

The Old Man laughed. "Oh, Little Red Cloak, the girl in the cloak as red as blood, there is wisdom in you, wisdom as well as spirit. Come, let us sit together and we will all talk."

The opening of the cave looked as if someone had hewn an irregular hole in the rock. It was probably natural, but looked unnervingly man-made, as if something big and with tremendous strength, but rather clumsy, had cut it out with a hammer and chisel.

That evil blood magic muddled all over the ground before it made her just a little sick. She was beginning to wonder if that might be entirely on purpose, to keep things away from the cave. Would they be that clever?

Dominik was on one side with the crossbow, which he said he was "good" with, and one pistol. Rosa was on the other side, with the coach gun, pistols, boar spear, and her knife. They didn't have any plans to use the firearms though, not yet.

The *iele,* as she had suspected, were not fighters of any sort. They had worn their mail coats as an indication that they were coming to Rosa and Dominik on a mission of revenge—presumably for the victims of the shifters, who thanks to the Old Man, Rosa now knew numbered in the thousands. But their work would be done—stark naked. That was their nature. They were supreme seductresses. It was a feral, yet innocent seductiveness, as natural and careless as a cat in heat. That was the weapon that *they* would be using.

It was daylight, and all of the shifters were in the cave.
Most of them were asleep, thanks to the work of the Old
Man. He had contributed some initial magic; small, yet
powerful. He had put it into the heads of the creatures to
seek their separate dens within the cave, alone, and had sent
them drifting off to sleep. And then he had left, after Rosa
had questioned him one more time as to the abilities of the
maidens. It was clear he had done all he intended to do; that
was fine. Her plans were based on what the maidens had
said they would do, and every tiny bit of help was a vast
blessing which she was deeply, deeply grateful for.

Technically, she should not have had the aid of the *iele* at
all. They were Great Air Elementals, not of Earth. But the
vâlva băilor, the Great Elementals of the Earth, had begged
their sisters of the air to come when Rosa had asked for
help. And Rosa had, after all, opened herself to *all* of nature
when she had begged for aid. So they had agreed to come,
and when they understood what it was that was being asked
of them, they had become avidly eager. It was clear that
they had wanted revenge for a very, very long time. But the
shifters were sorcerers, and they knew how to protect themselves. They had not, in the past, left themselves open for
the *iele's* usual mode of attack. Only thanks to the Old Man
were the *iele* going to get their chance.

They would not follow her orders, however. It was left to
the *zâne* to intercede for her, and beg them to do certain
things, in a certain order, for the *zâne* were of a fifth Element, that of Spirit, and Spirit ruled over all. Rosa had
learned *of* that Element, from Gunther, but he had told her
that there had never been a Master of Spirit, and never
would be, for such a Master could command the very angels
and that could not be permitted. She was, truth to tell, more
than a little stunned that the *zâne* had come to their aid at
all. She could only think that they had really come for two
reasons: because Markos was worthy, and because it was
past time for the shifters to end their reign of terror.

So now, she and Dominik were positioned just outside
the cave, and it was time for her to put her plan into motion.
The two *vâlva băilor* had already done their work; they had
impressed the image of the cavern before them firmly in

their minds, and given them the gift to see in the dark as clearly as the Elementals themselves could. Both Dominik and Rosa would know every inch of that cavern as if they had spent every moment of their lives in it. And the shifters would have no advantage over them when it came to the ability to see in the darkness.

Now the two *vâlva băilor* were gone, gone wherever the Old Man had gone. It was time for the next phase.

Rosa bowed to the beautiful, ethereal woman waiting beside her, bowing as deeply as ever she could. "Great One," she said, formally. "If it be your will, would you speak to your sisters of the air, and say that we would, at their pleasure, have them begin their dance?"

A faint smile creased the spirit's lips, though she did not unclasp her hands. "You speak with great courtesy, little sister," came the reply, as sweet and soft as a flute played by a lover. "And they are pleased to dance, now."

A faint hint of music came from the cave mouth. It was hardly more than a hint, and if Rosa had not been listening for it, she certainly would not have paid any attention to it. But in listening to it . . . there was something about it that was wild and . . . lusty. She sensed that if she listened closely enough she might start to be affected by it, as she had been affected by the Wild Hunter.

It did not grow stronger, so much, as nearer.

It was very hard waiting, but the *iele* were not to be hurried. Rosa had more than a suspicion they were enjoying playing with their victim; Dominik had whispered at one point that they had a very cruel streak to them, like the *wilis* she had encountered, the spirits of young girls who had killed themselves over love, or had died of broken hearts. Like the *wilis*, the *iele* were dancers. Like the *wilis*, when they got hold of a victim—in the *wilis'* case, any man, and in the case of the *iele*, virtually anyone who dared to spy on them dancing—they would dance their prey to death.

The compulsion to dance, once the *iele* or the *wilis* got hold of you, could not be denied. And unless another spirit took pity on you and protected you, it could not be broken, either.

Somewhere, inside the cavern, the *iele* had found one of

the shifters sleeping alone; half-waking him, they cast their spell over him. And now they were luring him, step by step, into the open. The spell of the Old Man would keep the rest of the shifters asleep as long as nothing louder than the music of the *iele* disturbed them. But it would not be the *iele* dancing him to death that would kill him. The truth of the matter was that the *iele* could not hold him for very long; once one of the others realized something was going on, as a sorcerer, he could break their magic. That was why the Elementals had not been able to take their revenge before now.

Rosa tensed as the form of a beautiful girl dressed only in her hair came spinning and weaving out of the entrance of the cave. She was followed by another—then a third— and finally, the shifter, going through clumsy, slow dancing motions, as if he was dancing half asleep, followed by the last of the four.

He was . . . hideous. The same malformed head as the shifter they had killed, only fully human now. The same scabrous skin and patchy hair. He was filthy, and stank; his finger- and toenails were untrimmed, thick, and yellow, with filth and blood crusted under them. His facial hair was as patchy as the hair on his head, and he wore little more than a rag wrapped around his loins. He moved, or rather stumbled, through a kind of mockery of a dance. His eyes, a filmy blue, were wide open, and his mouth was agape with terror. His teeth were the only part of him that looked healthy. Rosa didn't want to think what his breath and body odor must be like—

The *iele* drew him further out in the open. They needed to get him far enough past the entrance that any noise he made wouldn't echo down into the cave. And just when Rosa was wondering what in God's name Dominik was waiting for, she heard the *snap* of the crossbow, and a silver-tipped bolt impacted the shifter right in the heart.

She ran out and made sure of him with the spear, as the *iele* stood around them, giggling.

This was why they couldn't use the guns. They didn't dare use anything that made that sort of noise, to wake the other shifters. They *must*, at all costs, whittle the numbers down as much as possible. It probably was not going to be possible to take them all down this way—the older the shifter, the more powerful he would be, and the less likely to be snared by the *iele*—but the fewer there were when the time came for a straight fight, the better.

She and Dominik pulled the foul body out of the entrance and into the brush where it could lie concealed, and took up their positions again. She was unsurprised to find he was wearing a copper medallion, like the others she had found. The *iele* clapped their hands with childlike glee, then skipped back into the cave, looking as innocent as the dawn.

The *zână* looked after them, and sighed. "My little sisters are . . ." she seemed at a loss for words.

Rosa searched long and hard for something tactful. Finally she thought she had it. "Primal?" she suggested.

The *zână* regarded her with faint gratitude. "Yes," the spirit said, simply. "And they do take such enjoyment in what they do."

"The Good God made us what we are," Rosa said diplomatically, and set herself up for the next victim.

"Even so," said the *zână*. "Even so."

14

EVENTUALLY, their luck ran out, as they had known it would.

There were, according to the Old Man, forty-three of the shifters in the cave. Slowly, the *iele* had led twenty-eight of them out, and all of them had been wearing the evil St. Hubert's medallion. But when the time came to separate the twenty-ninth from the rest, the well-practiced maneuver failed. They picked one who was more than half awake already, and could resist their magic, and he was *not* pleased at them.

They knew their luck had run out when, instead of music, a bloodcurdling howl blasted out of the entrance of the cave, and a moment later, the *iele* fled. They poured out in a stream of breasts and hair, crowding past each other and taking to the sky as quickly as they could. Which was — very quickly indeed. Rosa could only watch them go, as they flew away on the wind. They would not be back; the Old Man had already explained this; they *could* be attacked and hurt by sorcerers, and wouldn't chance being injured, not even for revenge. She couldn't fault them for that. After all, while a human could be philosophical about death, knowing he had a soul and presumably would be rewarded in Heaven . . . the Elementals had no such security. Any priests she had spoken to either vehemently denied that anything other than a human had a soul, or considered the concept dubious at best. So, as far as the Elementals were concerned, death was extinction.

The *zână* at Rosa's side pursed her lips grimly, and vanished. She would join her sister in the cave, standing guard over a badly wounded, and slowly regenerating, Markos. Slowly regenerating, rather than quickly, because the shifters knew very well what silver did to their kind, and they had been torturing him with silver knives.

Or so the *vâlva băilor* said, and Rosa had no reason to doubt them.

They would not get any more chances at harming Markos. Not with two *zâne* standing guard over him.

Or at least the spirits would guard him for as long as Rosa and Dominik survived this—

So we must survive this!

The aroused and offended shifters were taking their time about showing themselves now that the *iele* had fled. That was fine; it gave them a little time to prepare.

Fifteen shifters, though . . . we have got to thin the ranks more. She felt her muscles tense and her insides clench up. She refused to give in to fear, but she could feel terror lurking just beyond the wall of her will, waiting to pounce. This . . . this was far, far more than she had ever undertaken without a full Hunt behind her.

Or even with *a full Hunt behind me.*

As Rosa pulled her coach gun from the sheath on her back, another howl split the air and a shifter in full wolf form—which was, of course, immune to the *iele's* magic— exploded out of the cave entrance. Before Dominik could even take aim, Rosa gave him a welcome of silver shot to the head.

The coach gun roared and kicked; she broke the breech and reloaded, and aimed again.

The blast shredded the beast's skull; it traveled forward

another couple of paces on its momentum, then dropped to the earth with a messy *splat*. But before it hit the ground, another leapt from the entrance, and now it was Dominik's turn to take it in the eye with a silver-tipped bolt, thriftily saved, for he had pulled every arrow out of the bodies they piled up to the side.

There followed a cacophony of enraged howls and growls from inside the cave, but nothing ventured out. The shifters had learned their lesson quickly.

Rosa whistled, and Dominik sprinted across the distance between them. They tucked themselves, side by side, into a little alcove where their backs were protected by the cliff and they would just fit together without interfering with each other. They knew better than to think that they had the shifters penned in there. Rosa had never yet seen a cave used as a stronghold that did not have at least one back entrance. This was not likely to be the first.

By now, the sun was setting, for they had been slowly picking off the shifters all afternoon. And under ordinary circumstances, the dark might have favored the shifters, but the spell of the *vâlva băilor* would allow them to see in the dark like a pair of owls. The shifters would not know that, and Rosa hoped it might make them careless.

At least, for a time, anyway.

She and Dominik strained their ears, listening for a stealthy scrape of claws on stone, or a panting breath. But the shifters were old at this game, and the rush of two of them from around the side of the rock took both of the magicians by surprise.

The one that leapt for Rosa got a chest full of silver shot, but Dominik didn't even have time to aim. She just barely missed being spattered by blood and bits and other nastiness. Dominik got a lucky shot; at such close range, the pistol didn't make as big a hole in the creature's chest as it would have a little further away, but he managed to blast through the ribs and into the heart, and the shifter staggered back about two yards and dropped to the ground. She backed up a half pace, all the room she had, and slammed a shell into the coach gun, and waited, her heart pounding, while Dominik made a clumsier business of reloading the pistol.

"How many is that now?" she asked in a low voice.

"Four out of the fifteen left. That's eleven yet to go." He was breathing hard; from fear or fight-stress, she reckoned. So far as she knew, he had never fought, much less killed, anything before.

"Breathe deeply and slowly," she advised. "The tenser you are, the more like you are to miss the shot."

The cave had gone ominously quiet. The light was fading in good earnest now; overhead the sky had gone from light blue to the color that Rosa associated with the Virgin's robes, and there was just a hint or two of a star. It was rapidly getting cooler. But their eyes were having no trouble adjusting to the darkness. Curiously, it was nothing like the way she saw things outlined in Earth power—although that was definitely a component, with everything that was alive faintly haloed with golden light, the half-faded blood magic a kind of loathsome, black-red skin on the surface of the ground. No, this was very much like a bright twilight, except that everything was in its proper color rather than in shades of blue.

She picked up a faint scrabble of claws above them, and elbowed Dominik hard, jerking her head up.

They separated a little, both of them starting to breathe quickly. At the last minute, as if they were both thinking the same thing, she sheathed the coach gun at her back and he holstered his pistol, seizing the boar spear from where it was leaning against the rock while she drew both her silver daggers.

The scratch of claws *right* above them gave them a hint of warning; they flung themselves back and to the side, and an enormous shifter plummeted into the space between them.

He was in half-form; he had to have been to have been able to climb the steep side of the hill and negotiate the rock above their cleft. As he fell, or leapt, and landed between them, he lashed out with claws to either side of him. They were both immediately assaulted with an incredible stench. Rosa wedged herself against the rock as hard as she could to avoid his claws.

He was incredibly fast, even if he did look as malformed and sickly as the rest—misshapen skull, mangy fur, rough and patchy skin. He might look diseased, but he certainly didn't *move* like he was diseased. Rosa maneuvered for space and jumped back, but Dominik charged in with the boar spear.

Dominik either had incredible luck or incredibly good aim; he got the shifter right beneath the breastbone, and knocked him off-balance at the same time. Putting his back into it, Dominik ran the shifter into the rock wall; the spearhead bit into him and he screamed and clawed at the shaft. In half-form, these particular shifters seemed to have a particularly tough hide. Either that or the spear-point had dulled. Well, it was heavily plated in silver, and silver wasn't known for keeping an edge well.

Rosa had been keeping half an eye on the cave entrance, and dropped a dagger as another shifter, also in half-form, rushed out, coming straight at her. She didn't have time for the coach gun; she barely had time to reach for the pistol and shoot. And she wasn't nearly as lucky as Dominik; the bullet hit the creature's shoulder, eliciting a scream, but not dropping him.

He continued for her. On impulse, she dove straight at him, or rather, for the ground in his path.

That was the last thing he was expecting.

As he skidded to a halt and tried to grab her, her hands hit the ground and she tucked and rolled, somersaulted between his legs, and came up on her feet behind him. She had *just* enough time to unholster and unload her second pistol into his back, blowing a huge hole in his spine, when more scrabbling behind her made her whirl, pulling the coach gun off her back at the same time.

She caught a third shifter in wolf form in mid-leap with the blast of silver shot. She dodged to the side as the body hit the place where she had been standing.

Just as Dominik finished his with a savage twist of the spear. The shifter pinned against the rock choked, shuddered, and went limp.

She gathered up her dropped weapons, rushed back to him, and put her back to the rock as he pulled the spear loose and turned to face the open. She was shaking with fear now. She had never had to face this many foes with only herself and a partner. This would be the *perfect* time to rush them; all four guns were discharged, the crossbow was lying just out of reach, and all they had to hold shifters off was the spear.

Silence.

She quickly loaded the coach gun. "Get the crossbow," she whispered, and with the spear at the ready, Dominik edged over to where it was lying in the middle of the open space. Rather than pick it up, however, he kicked it over to her with a sideways boot of his foot.

It skittered across the rock, making an unnaturally loud clatter. She snatched it up, and waited for him to get back.

Dominik edged crabwise back to her, and under cover of his spear, she hung the crossbow on his belt, reloaded the pistols and thrust one back into the holster beside it. He might not be good with it, but so far, at the close quarters they had been fighting, it didn't matter.

The cave, the cliffs above them, and the area before them all remained still, and silent.

After a while, as her rapid heart rate slowed, she swallowed down nausea. It *stank* out here.

There was the horrible smell of rank feces from the gut-ruptured shifter Rosa had gotten in mid-jump, and from the one Dominik had stabbed. Virtually all of the shifters had involuntarily wet themselves as they died, so there was the stench of urine as well. The bodies smelled like the worst possible combination of unwashed human and filthy canine. And over all was the smell of tainted blood.

Dominik must have been thinking the same thing. "At least they're dead," he muttered under his breath. "I'm glad we dragged most of them away. I don't think we would be able to breathe otherwise. How many left?"

"Eight to go," she said loud enough to carry to the cave, making a strong effort to sound completely casual, as if this was something she did every day. And she took care to speak in Romanian. Time to see if she couldn't unnerve *them* a little. After all, they'd cut the pack down from over forty, although the pack would not be aware it had been with the help of Elementals. "I wonder if these idiots know that I am Red Cloak?"

"I'm not sure they'd know what that meant," Dominik replied, following her lead. "I think it's only the dogs of Germany, Austria, and Hungary that wet themselves when they hear that name." He *tsk'd.* "If they knew it, they'd have run before we even got here."

"If they let our friend come out, I *might, possibly,* pull back long enough to let them run for it even now," she said, carelessly. "That's not to say I wouldn't come after them eventually, but at least they'd have a head start." Was there any chance she could bluff them into abandoning the cave and Markos, and running?

Then again—how much of a bluff would it be? She and Dominik and the Elementals had whittled them down to a bare fraction of the original pack.

"And what do you want with the wolf-man?"

The voice that echoed out of the black cave entrance was deep, and angry, and very loud. She couldn't tell what emotions made it sound so tight and gravelly. *Fear? Maybe?* She could hope. Fear would be much better for her purposes than rage. But there wasn't any uncertainty there that *she* could read.

"He's my friend," she said. "And an Earth Magician. As, I have no doubt, you already know, sorcerer. You should have reckoned by now that we will do whatever it takes to win him free of you."

There was a very long pause.

"You have murdered my sons and my wives," came the reply. Ah, now she recognized the emotion. It was anger. But, unfortunately, not rage. Anger was something that fueled the ability to think as often as not. There was a calm underlying this anger, a deadly calm.

"And you lot have been murdering for decades. You have the deaths of hundreds on your hands. We have a long way to go before we're even," she called back, just as calmly.

But she whispered to Dominik when the silence fell again. "I think he's stalling for time, to get a better ambush

set up on us. We must stand back to back, and get a little
more into the open. I'll face the cave, you face the opening;
I don't think they'll try going over the top of the cliff again,
it takes too long and they can't see us as well. We might get
a rush, soon."

They edged together out into the space in front of the
cave. At least there was a breeze blowing now, blowing
some of the stench away.

"We must eat," the voice whined.

"Then eat deer, you rotten bastard," she snarled back.
"There's plenty of deer in these hills. Bears, too. That's no
excuse for murdering hundreds of innocent people, and you
very well know it."

A really sickening thought was rearing its head in the
back of her mind. *You have murdered my sons and my
wives, he said . . . but said nothing about daughters. Oh . . .
ugh . . .* Her gorge rose. *What if his daughters* are *his wives?*

She almost threw up a little. That would certainly explain
why they all looked . . . misshapen and sickly. Blood magic
tended to magnify everything, not just what you were trying
to do with it. You took enough risks of defects and sickness
when you mated fathers and daughters, anyone who bred
animals knew that. Add blood magic to the mix, especially
if he was doing blood magic to ensure fertility. . . .

Bile rose in her throat. So did the determination to not
let a single one of these monsters live, *especially* the leader.
He must not be allowed to get away, or he would find a way
to start this all over again. She got the coach gun in her
hands, and made sure the pistols were at the ready.

"He has to be getting more of his . . . gah . . . followers in
place," Dominik whispered.

So he figured it out too, and can't bear to say "children."

"The question is . . . how many, and where are they going
to come from?" she replied.

She had just finished that sentence, when she got her
answer.

"NOW children!" howled the voice from the cave, and
four of the shifters rushed from the cave straight at Rosa.

She got the first with the coach gun right as it cleared the
mouth of the cave, for the entrance was narrow enough that

only two could pass it at a time. She hit it in the head and shattered its skull, and dropped the coach gun at her feet as the body went down. The coach gun hadn't hit the ground before she had pulled both pistols and fired. The first pistol missed, the second hit the shifter's shoulder, and sent the shifter spinning into its sibling, knocking them both over into a tangle of limbs, and leaving her with only one to fight for now.

She had just enough time to throw up her left arm to keep it off her throat. It was small, no bigger than a real wolf, but that was big enough as it leapt for her. Its jaws closed on her arm as her right hand closed around the hilt of her dagger.

The jaws never clamped down far enough for the teeth to do more than bruise her flesh. As soon as it bit down, it realized it did *not* want what it had caught.

Between the cloth-of-silver and the wolfsbane oil, the shifter reacted as if it had gotten a mouth full of coals. It yelped in pain, spat her arm out, then frantically tried to leap away again as she slashed for its throat with her dagger.

She missed the throat, but got a good cut in on the shoulder. It yelped again, and scuttled back to the other two that were still standing.

Behind her, she could hear and feel Dominik fending off more shifters with his spear. She reached behind her for *his* pistol, blindly; got her hands on it, and pulled it out of the holster and fired it into the face of the unwounded shifter that finally untangled itself from the wounded one and rushed her. It went down and didn't move.

She got her other dagger into her left hand, and waited. The two shifters limped back and forth in front of her, warily; trying to work up the nerve to attack her, she suspected. They were both small. All four of the ones on her side were small. Females? Adolescents?

She heard the same sort of strangled yelp behind her as the shifter that had tried to bite her had uttered, and at the same time, Dominik was pushed back against her with a little grunt. That seemed to embolden the two facing her.

They both leapt for her at the same time. One went high,

going for her throat, and one went low, for a leg. Evidently they weren't too bright. Or they thought the protection on her arm was a fluke.

She let the shifter have the leg, and rather than trying to save her throat, she grabbed the other shifter as it impacted her, driving *her* back against Dominik's back, and pulled it into a one-handed bear hug as it tried to bite her throat out and had the same reaction the other'd had to her arm. Suddenly realizing she had the upper hand, it squirmed and kicked at her with clawed hind-feet. She plunged her dagger into its belly, cutting viciously downward.

It screamed, and ripped itself away, trailing intestines. She slashed at the face of the one trying to somehow bite her leg without getting a mouth full of silver and wolfsbane. She managed to cut right across its eyes, blinding it. *It* screamed and shook its head wildly, backing away until it ran into the cliff-face.

The one she'd disemboweled had fallen over. It was still moving. Shifters were resilient. It was trying to push its guts back into its own body with its nose . . . then it began writhing and spasming—

She snatched up the coach gun from the ground, jammed a cartridge in, and shot the blinded one. She broke the breech, reloaded and turned to the one she had disembweled. It had gone to half-form, and was using clawed hands to stuff its guts back in. If she gave it enough time—it *might* just heal, even though the wounds had been made with silver.

She didn't intend to give it enough time. She aimed carefully, and blew its back open.

Then she reloaded and turned to help Dominik.

He had three. Or rather, had had three. One was practically cut in half at his feet with the silver dagger lying on the ground beside it. One was impaled on the boar spear and was trying to claw its way past the guard to get to him.

The third was shaking its head and acting as if it was choking.

She shot the third one. At the same time, Dominik heaved the spear rapidly back and forth in a sawing motion, and the last shifter fell off it, spine cut.

They leaned together, panting. Now that it was over, Rosa felt as if she was going to drop to her knees and never stand up again. Her leg hurt. Her arm hurt. Her throat hurt. The shifters had not managed to mangle or crush what they'd bitten, but they had bruised her to the bone, and she figured Dominik was in the same shape.

And she was exhausted, so exhausted she was shaking.

They had been picking off the shifters for hours; that hadn't been so bad, really, it had been like killing birds chased toward you by beaters. But this—this had been a real fight, and the worst odds she had ever had in her life. *We did it. We actually lived through it . . .*

And then there was one.

But even though her limbs felt as heavy as if they were made of stone, and just about as responsive, she managed to reload the coach gun, then the three pistols, and pass one of those to Dominik. Because there was still one more shifter in there.

The leader. The father of the clan.

Her guts roiled and revolted at the thought.

But she stood up straight, and faced the cave opening. Dominik turned and joined her, shoulder to shoulder.

She swallowed hard, twice, trying to get her throat to work. It *hurt.* It hurt to swallow, and it hurt to talk. It was a good thing the shifter hadn't bitten down any harder. "Come—" she said, hoarsely, and scarcely above a whisper. "Come—"

She shook her head. She couldn't get a word out. Dominik patted her back with the side of the pistol he was holding, and took over.

"Come out, monster!" he called, defiantly. "Come out and face us! We've killed your children! Don't you want our blood?"

A snarl split the air like the sound of tearing cloth.

"Don't you want your friend?" the creature bellowed, voice choking with rage. "Come in after me! If you are lucky, you will see him die before I rend you limb from limb!"

"Can the *zâne* hold him off?" she whispered.

He shook his head. "I think so . . . but I don't know. And

anyway, even if they can, we can't let that creature escape. We have to go in there after him. If he gets away, he'll just go somewhere else, and breed himself a new pack."

Dominik was merely echoing her earlier thoughts. They would have to go in after the "father," the sorcerer who had started this all. They had no choice.

The shifter was not waiting for them in the entrance, but then, they hadn't expected him to be. Their mystically enhanced memory showed them that this cavern was more than just a simple cave, it was a cave complex.

From the entrance it broadened out into a fair sized room, one with three tunnel entrances at the back of it. There were a few thick piles of rags and bracken in here against the walls. There was no sign of the *zâne* or of Markos.

There was also no sign of the shifter.

The cave . . . stank. The smell was unbelievable in here, and she wondered how anything with a canine nose could bear it. Unwashed, filthy human; unwashed, filthy wolf. Rotting meat. Feces and urine—evidently when the weather was bad, they just picked a corner and relieved themselves in it. Smoke, from somewhere deeper in the cave. Blood. Old blood, and ominously, fresh blood. All of the stench concentrated by the cave's natural humidity.

Rosa looked to Dominik. "Right, left, or center?" she asked.

"We know he's going to try and kill Markos," Dominik replied. "We need to get to Markos as soon as possible. You know he's the one who is going to find us, not the other way around."

She concentrated on the images that the *vâlva băilor* had put in their minds. It took a moment to orient herself, but as soon as she had, it was all as clear as if it was her own memory. "Left," she said instantly, and Dominik nodded. Now that she had all the images sorted out in her head, she knew exactly where Markos was. They would have to traverse the left-hand tunnel, past one of the places where the shifters slept and ate, past one little appendix cave (and she had no idea what they used *that* for), and take a right. Markos was in a second little finger cave, off the main cavern tunnels.

And there were dozens, literally dozens, of places where the chief shifter could ambush them.

On the other hand . . . we know that. And we know where those places are.

Dominik closed his eyes a moment, perhaps to settle the path in his head as she had, then opened them. "Let's go," he said.

He took the lead; she let him. He had the crossbow ready and loaded, and had the good instinct or good training to keep it aimed where his gaze went. She had the coach gun; kept her eyes on what was behind them as well as what was to the side. The cave was as bright as if someone had illuminated it to their bespelled eyes, and there was no way that the shifter could know that.

But he had been killing for a long time. If he was the original shifter of this pack, he could have been murdering for decades. He had a lot of practice in dealing death.

So have I, she thought grimly.

Often in caves, there was the sound of dripping water. There was no such sound here. Possibly it was a "dead" cave, one where the water source that had formed it had diverted or dried up, leaving behind formations that had turned brown and lifeless. The floor was littered with trash, mostly leaves and branches; piles of what looked like leaves, dead bracken, and rags had been heaped against the walls to make what looked like crude beds. So, was this where some of them had slept?

It was hard to tell, but in the image in Rosa's head, this cave was huge, and there was enough room for a couple of hundred of the creatures to have bedded down comfortably without having to sleep in the entrance-room.

Maybe this is where the ones supposed to be on guard slept. That hadn't done them much good against the Old Man and the *iele*.

But there were those three entrances ahead of them, and the shifter could emerge from any of them at any time. So they made their way, eyes darting in every possible direction, listening hard for the slightest noise, step by cautious step toward their goal. Rosa had a certain amount of practice in keeping her heart from racing with fear, but poor Dominik must be having trouble hearing over the noise of his pounding in his ears. They both tried their best to walk silently, but the trash on the floor made it difficult.

I don't know how the shifter could do any better, though.

Nothing leapt out at them once they reached the leftmost tunnel entrance and moved into it. Rosa kept her eyes behind, though, since there was absolutely no reason why the shifter couldn't have been hiding just inside one of the other two tunnels with the intention of coming at them from the rear.

At least the floor was clean here. But again, that worked as much in the shifter's favor as theirs. He *could* slip up on them from the rear, silently.

At least the tunnel was narrow enough here that there was no chance he could be waiting to leap out of hiding from the side.

Rosa elected to literally walk backward, mere inches from Dominik, coach gun at the ready. Step by careful step they made their way deeper into the caves, until they came to a spot where the tunnel branched.

They knew from their implanted memories that the tunnel joined up again, not twenty feet later. The trouble was that this was an excellent place for an ambush.

Dominik stopped, uncertain. She moved up next to him, sideways, keeping a wary eye behind, and touched his arm. She pointed to him, and indicated the left hand side of the tunnel, then to herself, and indicated the right. He nodded, and she mouthed the single word "run." He nodded again. They separated, and at her signal each of them sprinted through the assigned segment, weapon at the ready.

She dashed the twenty or so feet, sweating, seeing nothing, but expecting to hear the sound of combat at any moment from his side.

But there was nothing but the sound of his boots on the stone. *Her* boots, of course, were soft-soled, and she had learned to run in a sort of gliding motion that barely lifted her feet from the ground. She startled him a little as they met at the join again, but not so much that she was in danger of a crossbow bolt in her direction.

She let out a sigh that he echoed, and they went back to their previous pattern, her walking backward, him forward, down the twists and turns of the tunnel. The floor had been smoothed and polished, but it looked as if it had been by water rather than by the work of man. When he stopped again, she knew they had come to the next obstacle. The cave would widen out into an actual room. There would be a rough stone platform in the middle, something like a table, except natural. Off to one side would be a narrow little tunnel the Elementals had, in their own wisdom about such things, assumed was a dead-end cavelet. That would be an excellent place for the shifter to be waiting.

Rosa had noticed, in the back of her mind, that the smell of fresh blood had been getting stronger as they approached the larger room. Now she suddenly heard Dominik making a strangled sound, and turned—

To see sheer horror.

There was a pile of bodies on that platform in the center of the room, and blood literally ran from the stone and pooled at its base. There were at least ten, because that was the number of heads she counted, in a state of numb disbelief. Possibly, there were more. The stumps of candles stood at the cardinal points around the stone platform. All the bodies appeared to be of women, most were young, and some appeared to be pregnant. None of them looked like the shifter-kin. All were dressed in rags and were in various stages of emaciation. Their faces were frozen in expressions of agony and terror.

And the effluvia of blood magic was thick on the ground and tainting the air.

Well . . . now I know where else he was getting "children" from, she thought, swallowing down her nausea. *And where he was getting the blood-power to keep fueling the shifts.* Because the power had to come from somewhere, every time one of these monsters shifted form. Probably they were using their wolfskin belts as the storage point, since the copper medallions hadn't shown any sign of being the talismans.

Scuff marks and bloodstains showed where the women had come from—that little side-cave that the Elementals hadn't troubled to explore. It must have been a sort of prison, where the shifters had held women they had somehow captured instead of killing.

All the other, terrible reasons to keep prisoners raced through Rosa's head, and she was pretty certain that all of them were right. But one thing was absolutely certain. The chief reason had been so that they would have a steady supply of sacrifices for blood magic.

And while his offspring had fought his battle, the chief of the shifters had been killing his captives on his altar. All of them.

So now, he had the power of ten, a dozen sacrifices, all in his hands. What could he do with that much power?

"This . . . isn't good, is it?" Dominik whispered in a stricken voice.

"No," she said grimly. "It's not."

But across the cavern, she could see the dim reflection of what must be an overpowering golden glow that was as healthy and beautiful and *sane* as the miasma of the residue of blood magic was sickening and hideous and insane. That was the *zâne*, who must have mounted an epic set of protections around Markos when the chief shifter began his slaughter. That they were still there and had not left was at least an indication that Markos was still alive and being protected. She took heart from that, and strength of will from that glow.

"You see where we need to go?" she breathed to him.

He nodded. She put her hand on his arm, briefly, trying to comfort. He turned toward her a moment, and she didn't think it was the strange Elemental sight that made him look green. She squeezed his arm.

"Then let's go."

It was hard, hard to turn her back on that light, on the promise of somewhere that wasn't a home to terrible slaughter, that wasn't literally awash with blood. But he needed that promise more than she did. He was not a fighter, he was a healer, a physician, and yet he had been fighting at her side for most of the day, only to be confronted by a sight that must be out of his worst nightmares. It was one thing to know *of* such atrocities. It was quite another to be thrust without warning into the middle of one. Every sense must be in revolt against such evil, and every instinct telling him to flee. He was probably holding onto courage and sanity by the thinnest of margins, and he needed that promise of goodness ahead of him.

Whereas she . . . well, while this might be the worst such slaughter she had seen, it was by no means the first. There were still patches of great evil in the Schwarzwald, in places where no man had ventured for centuries. The evil had slept, gone dormant, and almost undetectable—except to the evil that was akin to it. Man, or things that had once been men, still sought out those patches of evil, awakened them, and drew strength from them.

And then they strengthened the evil with death.

You never became inured to such sights, they never ceased to horrify, but they ceased to shock. And to a lesser extent, they ceased to sicken.

And at least those poor women are no longer suffering from their captivity at that beast's hands. She reminded herself that she had seen people "rescued" from similar situations, and they were never able to be made whole again. Many of them had been driven quite mad, and never regained their sanity. Those that were not mad were haunted for the rest of their lives. Sometimes those lives were very short indeed, for they could not bear the nightmares, the days haunted by fear, the nights when they could not sleep and every tiny sound threw them into a panic. There was never, ever any peace for them, and they killed themselves in despair.

The priests said that those who killed themselves could never enter Heaven—whereas these poor, murdered victims *surely* had, having suffered enough Hell on earth during their captivity to expiate any sin.

So . . . who was better off? Those who had died like this and gone to Heaven? Or those who had been rescued only to seek death at their own hands, and were doomed to Purgatory?

She dragged her attention back to the here and now, as

Dominik began his slow, painful traverse of the cavern. They were going to have to go past that dreadful altar in order to get to the next part of the cave, and the nearer they came to it, the worse *she* felt, and she assumed, *he* felt. If it had only been the emotional and the physical nausea and horror, that would have been bad enough, but they were both being infected by the spiritual horror, and, being Earth Magicians, by the defilement of the Earth itself. There had been deep magic here, that was now perverted and turned to wicked ends. They felt that and it sickened the power they held within themselves. She strengthened the shield around the two of them—suspecting that he had more than enough on his hands without trying to erect and maintain shields. That helped her; she hoped it helped him. Occasionally, they touched for a moment as they edged their way across the stone, and she felt him trembling.

Of course, that might just have been exhaustion too. It felt as if they had been battling forever. They hadn't eaten since they had started off from the inn—*she* had eaten before leaving, out of experience, but she doubted that he had—and they'd only snatched moments to gulp down water from the bottles at their sides. She knew hers was empty now, and his probably was as well.

All right then . . .

"Stop a moment," she whispered, and he obeyed. She couldn't do this any closer to that terrible altar than they were now, and she didn't want to wait until they were past, even though this would be much, much easier in the gentle protection of the *zâne*. But there was no telling what might happen between here and there, and they needed the boost now.

She strengthened the shield until it was as good as anything she might build ritually, and extended herself down, down into the earth at her feet, forcing her magic and her senses far past where the Earth had been profaned and polluted. She did not have to venture as deeply as she had feared she might. And to her weak-kneed relief, she was lucky; one of the great power-courses of Earth lay directly below them!

Small wonder these mountains were the home to so

many uncanny creatures, so many Elementals...small wonder they were far more numerous than in her homeland.

She touched that great power source, tapped into it, and brought it up as if she had tapped into a deep spring. She let the power flow through herself and into Dominik, taking the place of the food he had not eaten and the water they were both feeling the lack of. It wasn't a perfect replacement, but she sensed some of his trembling ease, and felt him standing up a little stronger, felt his stance firming. When she had brought up as much as her own power could safely control, she let go of that mighty stream, and she heard him sigh.

"Thank you," he whispered. She nudged him with an elbow to signal he should continue, and their painfully slow progress began again.

Past the altar, and she tried to look at it no more than she had to.

The floor of this cavern was clean of everything but blood. She suspected that the chief shifter deliberately kept his "family" out of here, to avoid having confrontations over his captives. That shifter she had killed in that other part of these mountains came from this "family"—so what had happened? She doubted he had gone on his own. This was too...ideal a haven for their kind. Plenty of victims, shelter, everything they could want. Surely he had been either driven out over conflict, or sent out to look for a new hunting ground and another secure cave like this one.

Driven out, I think. If this is like a wolf pack, a strong male will inevitably challenge the father, and his choices, if he lost that fight, would be to die, submit, or flee.

Just as she thought that, she caught a flicker of movement at the entrance to the captives' cave.

And that was all the warning she had.

One moment, that flicker of movement. The next, all the breath was driven out of her as something hit her across the midsection, knocking the coach gun out of her hands and sending it across the room. It hit the floor and discharged, knocking a shower of rock bits out of the ceiling as *she* hit the wall of the cave and saw stars.

She fought to get her breath, gasping with no result for several agonizing moments before she managed to get her lungs and chest muscles working. Then she sucked in a breath of air with a sound like someone dying; sucked in another, and frantically looked back at where she had come from.

The shifter was in the middle of the room, glowing a sickly black-red with blood magic. She had never seen anything moving as fast as he was moving, and had never seen anything imbued with that much blood-power. He must have slapped the crossbow out of Dominik's hands the way he had slapped the gun out of hers, because Dominik didn't have it in his hands anymore. Somehow Dominik had managed to get the boar spear off his back and was being chased backward by the thing.

The shifter must have been watching his children fight, and learning what not to do. He didn't try to bite Dominik. Instead, he kept raking his claws at the healer, forcing him back each time. It would probably hurt him when his claws encountered the cloth-of-silver, but nothing like the way it would hurt when he bit. She fumbled at her belt for a pistol, but her hands were cold, and she couldn't feel the butts, and for a panicked moment, she thought she had lost both of the guns.

As if in a nightmare she saw Dominik's foot slip.

"Hey!" she shouted, jumping to her feet as the shifter *instantly* reacted to her shout, just as she realized her belt had twisted and the pistols weren't where they should have been. *"Hey!"*

She pulled her pistols as the shifter whirled, saw her up, and launched for her. She fired both. The first missed completely. The second hit his shoulder. He yelped for a moment, but kept coming, and before she even had a chance to dodge out of the way, he backhanded her into the wall again. Both pistols went flying.

She hit the wall, and saw more than stars; for a moment she blacked out, and came around to the sound of a pistol firing. This time the shifter screamed, but there was as much rage as pain in the sound. The scream was followed by the meaty sound of flesh-on-flesh impact, then stone-on-flesh impact, and the clatter of metal on stone. She shook her head violently to clear the darkness from her eyes and saw Dominik slumped against the wall of the cave opposite her, head sagging forward on his chest. With a sensation of being stabbed in the heart, she saw he wasn't moving.

15

THE shifter turned, and she fumbled out her silver dagger. It seemed pitiful against something that could move faster than she, and had been able to throw a big man into a wall with a single blow. She was absolutely galvanized with terror now, energized rather than paralyzed. Her heart beat wildly, but her hands were steady, and she kept her eyes glued on her enemy. Chills ran down her back at the look in his evil, yellow eyes, and her clothing and hair were damp with fear-sweat.

She scrambled to her feet, and backed her way along the wall. The shifter seemed in no hurry to attack her this time. And despite runnels of blood dripping down its shoulder in two places, he didn't seem to be handicapped by his wounds at all.

It had to be the blood magic, keeping him from feeling much from his injuries, even though they had been caused by silver.

The same deformed skull that the other shifters had sported marked this one, although its fur and skin didn't seem diseased. Its muzzle was more human in the half-form than theirs had been. It lifted its lip in a snarl as it stalked toward her.

She resisted the urge to turn and run. If she did that, she had no chance at all. Her only option was to figure out where the boar spear had gone, and get her hands on that. Maybe—maybe she could fend it off long enough to back her way to the cavelet where the *zâne* were. They might protect her as well as Markos. Or they might not protect *her,* but the shifter might not be able to bear the power that surrounded them, and she would be safe. . . .

Safe? There was no place safe in this cavern! There might not be any place safe in the country with this thing after her!

Safer, then?

If she could just get to that possible sanctuary, it would give Markos time to recover, and maybe give them both time for the blood-born power imbuing the monster to wear off. Maybe time for her to think of some magical offense or defense. Maybe she could collapse the cave roof on him. Maybe—

"Oo a shpiri, 'irl," came from between the shifter's misshapen lips. He laughed, as she stared at it without comprehending what it had said.

He passed a blood-smeared paw over his face. As she watched in nauseated fascination—still moving backward, step by careful step—he pushed and pulled on his jaw, his teeth, and his lips. The flesh and bone deformed and reformed, and he continued to poke and prod at his face, until at last, he had something more like a human mouth—except for the pointed teeth—and less like a muzzle.

He yawned hugely, with a popping noise as if something was settling into place, then grinned hideously. "I shaid, you have shpirit, girl," he repeated, in a voice that was half the whine of a canine, and half a peculiarly unpleasant, nasal human voice. "You are the firsht to fight me off for more than a moment or two in fifty yearsh. And you have magic."

He laughed, as if that was uproariously funny.

She didn't answer him. In her experience, not talking in cases like this was the best answer. It made men want to fill the silence with their own voice, and she might learn something that would save her and Markos.

. . . her and Markos. Because Dominik still was not moving, and she feared the worst.

The beast yawned again, but this time he looked angry. Yet he kept his temper. "Shpeak up! No?" He snarled, a sound like rotten canvas tearing. "You don't want to know who I am? I will tell you anyway! I am Bertalan Kaczor!"

Hungarian? That was unexpected. . . .

Not that there weren't Hungarians in Romania. The Austro-Hungarian Empire claimed this part of the world, after all. But—this part of Romania tended to be mostly native Romanians, with little islands of German Saxons . . .

He peered at her, and his mouth turned down in a rictus of a frown. "What? A magishian, and you do not know my name?"

"Well, you don't know *mine,*" she retorted, hoping to keep him talking, rather than attacking, while she backed toward presumed safety.

He frowned. "Austrian girl—"

"German," she corrected.

"Aushtrian, German, all one," he snarled. "You think you have sheen shorcherersh, but you have never sheen one like me!"

He flexed the muscles of the uninjured arm, and laughed. "I am sheventy yearsh old! I have been hunting theshe parts for fifty yearsh! I have been building my pack for all that time, until we have become the shcourge of the land!"

She decided to dare a taunt at him. "I don't see a pack now," she stated, matter-of-factly.

The growl that rumbled up out of his chest made the hair on the back of her neck stand up, and made her insides turn to water. *"Peashantsh!"* he snarled. "I should have known better. You cannot build a palash out of mud!" He took three enormous steps toward her, making her back up hastily—but not in the direction she wanted to go. He had forced her slantwise, toward the cave wall and not the tunnel that led to where Markos was. "You, on the other hand . . ." He laughed. "You are a magishian! I will catch you, and break your legsh sho you cannot run, and make you my breeding cow! You will be a *fine* bitch for my new pack!"

The horror of it struck her like a hammer, and froze her where she stood. He howled with laughter to see it—literally howled, throwing up his head to let out a blood-curdling wail of triumph.

Which ended, abruptly, in a scream of pain and rage as Markos in wolf-shape slashed at his hamstrings from behind.

She threw herself to the side, rolled, and came up several feet away to see that Markos had dashed out of reach of those terrible claws, and toward where Dominik lay. She got to her feet and ran in the other direction, where she might, just might, find one or more of the weapons they had lost. Behind her, she could hear the combat as Markos used his lower stature and wolf-speed to good effect, not standing and fighting, but dashing in to slash with his fangs and dashing away again. In wolf form he was just as fast as the sorcerer, and he was harder to hit than a human, since he was lower to the ground.

She searched frantically for a weapon. *There!* The coach gun lay against the rock wall! She dashed for it, praying that nothing had been smashed out of order or blown up when it went off on impact.

The moment she put her hands on it, she let out a wordless prayer of thanks. It was intact, despite having discharged when it struck the rock. She broke the breech, fumbled out the spent casing and fumbled in a new shell, and looked up.

The shifter was trying to pen Markos into a niche near Dominik, and he was succeeding. His arms were long, and Markos couldn't get past them. And each time the shifter moved closer, he had a better chance of catching Markos.

"Hey!" she shouted. "Half-breed cur!"

He whirled and stared at her. She was on fire with terror, but she couldn't stop now.

"You want me?" she taunted. *"Nyald ki a seggem!"*

It was the worst phrase she knew in Hungarian. She prayed it would goad him into rushing her.

It did.

With a scream of rage, he charged. She held her fire. *I'm only going to get the one shot. It has to count. . . .*

Halfway to her, he flung himself into the air in a tremendous leap, arms spread.

She waited, watching him sail through the air. It seemed as if he was floating there, moving with impossible slowness, as she waited, her heart pounding in her ears, until the last . . . possible . . . moment.

Then her finger twitched on the trigger, and the coach gun roared, and kicked back into her side, discharging the entire load of silver shot into his chest, throat, and face from no more than a yard or two away.

Blood and flesh spattered her, and then he hit her.

Down they went onto the stone floor of the cave. She felt a blow to the back of her head, and saw nothing but black again.

But the terrible weight on her was smothering her, and she woke again with a strangled gasp, then began trying to push the impossible weight off herself so she could breathe. The stink of him was driving her mad, the effluvia of his blood magic so intense she wasn't sure if she was going to choke on her own vomit or from lack of breath.

Then a feral growl made her freeze. She looked past the mangled remains of the sorcerer's head and saw Markos.

But not the Markos she knew.

His eyes were mad, his hackles up, and his lips lifted in a terrible snarl. He stalked toward her, stiff-legged.

The words of the little *alvar* rang in her memory. *There is a danger. If the man runs as a wolf for too long, the man is lost forever in the wolf.*

"Markos!" she said, sharply, which only elicited a rising growl from him. She swallowed her fear and nausea. She *had* to reach him. "Markos," she said, as coaxingly as she could, around a lump of sick horror and bile. "Markos. It's me. Your friend. Rosa. Remember me?"

The wolf continued to stare at her, fangs bared.

"You believed me, when no one else did, when everyone else said we had killed the only shifter. Markos, you *believed* in me. And I believe in you!" She put all the pleading she could into those words. "I do *not* believe you are lost in the wolf! Come back, Markos! Come back! Remember who you are and come back!"

She kept repeating the words "Come back" and his name, over and over, and projected as much of the Earth Magic that allowed her to reach the minds of animals as she could, bringing up images of him at the Graf's parties, on the trains, laughing at jokes, reading something, looking thoughtfully out a window. She refused to believe he was lost. She refused to believe she would survive the shifter only to die at the fangs of—

Slowly, his lips dropped over his fangs. Slowly, a vaguely puzzled look crept over the wolf's face, as if he was hearing something he didn't . . . quite . . . understand . . .

And then—he leapt.

And covered her face with wolfish kisses, cleaning the blood from her cheeks and eyes.

That was when she let herself pass into unconsciousness.

"Rosa. Rosa."

Something was licking her face. No, it wasn't licking her face, it was—washing her face. It wasn't a rough wet tongue, it was a rough, wet cloth.

"Rosa. You must wake up. You must wake up now."

Feebly, but with irritation, she pushed the cloth away and opened her eyes. The spell must still have been working, for the cave was as bright as if daylight were pouring in.

Her head felt just as bad as she would have expected, from having been hit against a stone wall twice and a stone floor once. Markos was sitting next to her, or rather kneeling, a battered bowl of water next to him, and a bit of cloth in his hand.

He seemed to be—mostly naked.

Well of course he is. He was a wolf, and his clothing is somewhere else.

"Can you stand?" Markos asked her anxiously.

He looked terrible. *He looks as bad as I feel,* she thought. There were healing cuts and bruises all over his neck, face, arms and chest. Both of his eyes had been blackened. She levered herself up a little on one elbow, and saw that he had found the remnants of trousers somewhere, mostly rags, but enough to keep him from being completely naked.

They both stank. And she was covered in blood and bits of shifter. Markos had been cleaning her face off, for which she was very grateful now that she came to think about it.

"I think so," she said, gingerly feeling the back of her head, and relieved only to find a lump, and not anything worse. "But I'd rather not." She didn't want to get up. She really didn't want to be awake. She didn't want to think about Dominik. . . .

"You have to," Markos said urgently, his brows creasing as well as they could, with all the injuries to his face. "I can't get Dominik into the saddle by myself. His leg's broken."

"What?" she gasped, sitting up so quickly she got flashes in front of her eyes and her head screamed at her. *"He's alive?"*

"He has a harder head than you. He was just knocked unconscious," Markos replied, getting an arm behind her shoulders and holding her upright, as her head went from screaming to merely throbbing. "But I can't get him into the saddle alone. I wouldn't ask you to do this, but I really need your help. We have got to get the horses and get out of here to get him—you—me some real help. I'm afraid if we stay here much longer we'll be in no condition to leave."

He had a point. A good one. A broken leg was no joke, and neither were blows to the head. What she needed to do was get herself moving and figure out just how badly her head had been rattled.

Groaning, she turned herself over so that she was on her hands and knees, then slowly, carefully, managed to get to her feet, with Markos hovering anxiously as if he was unsure whether or not he should offer to help. Once on her feet, she looked around the cave.

Her head throbbed, still, but it wasn't as bad as it could have been. *All right then. I can get things done. Maybe Dominik can manage to make it a little better, too. . . .*

The dead shifter was over to one side; by the smear of blood, Markos had dragged him off of her, which was kind of him. She wasn't sure how she would have reacted if she had awakened under the body.

Probably screaming a great deal.

"Are you all right?" Markos asked anxiously.

"I have been better," she said, "But I have also been worse. But Markos, are *you* all right?" She turned her attention to her friend, and took his shoulders in her hands, turning him to one side and the other, a little to examine his injuries. Then she took his chin in her right hand and tilted his face about to get a good look at what had been done to him there. "In the name of God, what were they doing to you? And *why?*"

"I'm not sure," he admitted, as she let him go. He was a little flushed, but soon cooled down. "The chief one, Bertalan—he kept trying to get me to bite his children. He seemed to be under the impression that a bite from a true, born shifter would allow his children to shift without the need for casting the spell." Markos made a face.

"And does it?" she asked, without thinking.

"Of course not!" he said crossly. "They kept beating me and cutting me, to make me bite. I finally gave in and bit them, and of course nothing happened. The taste is something I thought I would never get out of my mouth. And when that didn't work, he talked about breeding me to his wives. Daughters. Ugh, they were both. Granddaughters, too. Actually I think the ones living that weren't his captives were all his granddaughters at this point."

Markos looked as if he was going to gag, or throw up, or both. She didn't blame him. She felt nauseous too, and it wasn't all due to the blows on the head.

"It was all just. . . ." He shuddered. "It was like a nightmare. It was worse than a nightmare. If I could have ripped open a vein with my teeth to make it stop, I would have. It wasn't even a day and a night, and I thought I was going to go mad. And then—"

His face relaxed. "Then . . . the *zâne* came . . ."

Tears began to fall from his blackened eyes, and he broke down. Awkwardly, she put her arms around him and he sobbed on her shoulder. "Rosa, you can't imagine what that meant to me. In the middle of this . . . this horror, these horrible, horrible people, in the middle of being tortured and told that a sorcerer was going to take my own mind away from me came—*cleanness*. Something clean, and good, and wholesome. . . ."

"You did amazingly," she murmured, meaning it. Poor Markos . . . and poor Dominik. This was a hard, terrible way to learn just how vile evil could be. At least she had been able to learn that lesson by degrees.

"And they drove those—half human things out of my prison," he continued, sobbing. "And stayed with me and tried to heal me. And they promised me that if they somehow got driven away, they would kill me. You can't believe what that meant to me!"

She shivered. She could believe it—and she only thanked God, silently, that she had never found herself in that position.

She patted his shoulder, self-consciously, and held him until he recovered himself. It was a little strange, holding him like this, because there was nothing *remotely* sensual about it, even though he was half-naked. "I'm sorry," he said, pulling away, and wiping his face with his hand, then wincing as he touched bruised flesh. "I don't . . . I shouldn't have lost control like that."

"Don't be sorry," she replied. "It's all right."

He rubbed his hands over his arms self-consciously. "Let's go get Dominik. He probably thinks we don't care about him anymore," he said, trying half-heartedly to make a joke.

"I can hear you both perfectly well, you know," came a cross-sounding voice from behind and to her right. "It's my leg that's broken, not my hearing."

Markos flushed. She noticed he blushed everywhere. It was rather charming, actually. She found herself blushing too, and sternly told herself to stop.

"I'm getting stiffer by the moment," came the increasingly irritated voice. "And if my calculations and my poor abused pocket watch are correct, it's almost dawn."

The two of them separated completely, and turned to make their way around the grisly altar and to Dominik's side.

"How are you not screaming in agony?" she asked, kneeling down to look at his leg. She might not be a healer, but she had splinted a leg or three in her time. But she didn't need to do anything at all. This was an expert job.

"Healer," he reminded her. "I can make most of the pain go away."

"I wish I could," she grumbled—and managed not to wince away as he reached for her temple. Almost immediately, the throbbing subsided.

"Don't move fast. Don't lift anything heavy. Don't strain. You've still bruised your brain," he cautioned. "And it will warn you if you are doing something stupid."

"So I will try not to do anything stupid," she replied, putting one of his arms around her neck as Markos did the same on his other side. "Does getting you to your feet count as stupid?"

He didn't answer . . . but her head did ache a bit, warningly, as she and Markos hauled him upright.

They managed to get him up on one foot between them, and with his arms draped over their shoulders, hopped him through the cave. "Who splinted your leg?" Rosa asked, as they passed into the outer cave.

"I splinted my leg. Once Markos dragged that disgusting creature off you and made sure you were only knocked out and would come around in your own time, he rooted through the trash out here and found me some sticks and rags to tie it up with." He glanced over at Markos. "And some rags to tie himself up with."

"I left my clothes hidden out there in the woods when I came to investigate the area," Markos said, going red all over again. "But I wasn't going to leave the two of you alone just to find them!"

They made their slow way out of the cave and out to the open area where they had fought the last of the shifter children. It was, indeed, dawn. That was where Rosa and Markos left Dominik, with some better branches to tie his leg up with, while Rosa went to get the horses and Markos shifted to wolf to find his clothing. By some miracle, the horses were still there, although they had eaten every scrap of food there was to find within reach of their reins, as well as the bag of oats. She filled her water bottle and Dominik's at the little stream, after drinking her fill. The horses regarded her with mild impatience, as she mounted one and took up the other's reins to lead him, as if to say "It is long past time you came to get us!"

She brought them to the waiting healer. Unfortunately the one thing she hadn't packed was anything at all in the way of medicine. But, well, there would be plenty back at the village. Her head throbbed dully, but incessantly, and she would have given just about anything to lie down and sleep it away.

Markos still was not back, so she gave some food, and most importantly, water, to Dominik.

"Shouldn't you rest?" he asked, when she had made sure he was as comfortable as possible—which was to say, not very—and headed for the cave again.

"If I stop, I may not be able to start again," she told him, over her shoulder. "And I need my weapons. They're too valuable to leave behind."

The weapons were scattered all over the cave with the altar, and she had to fight down nausea and avert her eyes to get them. But she found all of them, all three knives, all three pistols, the boar spear, and the coach gun. Fortunately they were not too heavy, but she brought them out in three trips, leaving them next to Dominik and the horses. Her headache was easing again, as long as she moved slowly.

The last knife was right beside the chief shifter's body, so, just to be sure, she checked it over. Sure enough, there was a copper medallion on a copper chain around his neck, the Stag of St. Hubert, with the crucifix between his horns inverted. She dropped it on his body. *Rot there with him,* she thought. That was all the evidence she needed.

She didn't think there would be anything else of any value in that cave—but Markos wasn't back yet, and how would it hurt to be thorough? So she walked slowly through the entire cavern complex, taking advantage of her dark-vision while it lasted. And that was where she got a surprise.

Besides heaps of trash and filthy rags, and stores of mixed sound and rotten food, there was one cavelet that was full of nothing but human bones—

She thought she had gotten inured to it all, after the slaughter on the rough altar. She hadn't. She stared in stark horror as she tried to take in the sheer volume of victims and . . . couldn't. It was impossible. The bones, scarred by tooth marks, were heaped in a pile that filled the little cave, which was at least the size of an average cottage, and in the back they were piled as high as her head. Decades upon decades . . . more victims than anyone had ever guessed, even her.

The horrid sight just unleashed everything she had been holding back.

She sat down on the cave floor, and wept until she was sick, then she threw up the water she had drunk, then she wept until she didn't have any tears left.

And at the very back of the complex, there was one cavelet, room sized, that was clean. And full; full of the belongings and treasures of all those people the shifters had murdered and eaten. There were not many of those who had been taken who had actually possessed much, but there had been *hundreds* of victims, and the accumulation . . .

She thought about throwing a torch in there and burning it all. But then she remembered. . . .

There are people alive right now who lost loved ones to these monsters. Somewhere in here are tokens to identify the victims . . .

That was when it dawned on her. *This is something Petrescu should handle. He probably won't want to—but he should, and he will understand that. And he will finally bring peace to so many . . . people will finally be able to put their loved ones to rest. People will have answers.*

Avoiding the cave of bones, and the cave of the altar, she ventured out—into sunlight.

Markos was waiting, clothed, and cooking rabbits over a fire. The horses were grazing on armfuls of grass he had brought them. Dominik's leg was re-splinted, and he was drinking something and making a face over it.

"What's the matter?" she asked.

"Willow bark tea. Not my favorite," he said. "But it is

helping. I just can't wait to get back and get some laudanum and a real bed, and be pampered by one of our host's daughters until this damned thing heals. The ride back is going to be a horror."

She had had a broken leg once, herself, and she sympathized. "Well, let's get food inside us all, then get you up on the horse and get the horror over with."

If the young men noticed her red and swollen eyes, they were tactful enough not to say anything.

She had thought she wouldn't be able to eat, but had been prepared to choke the meat down because she knew that she needed it. But to her surprise, she was starving, and finished her half and licked the bones clean. Dominik managed to get all of his down as well, although he was not nearly so enthusiastic about it. Markos wolfed his down—like a starving wolf. But then, he had been more than a day and a half without food.

They got Dominik up on his horse; as the lighter of the two, Rosa mounted up behind him. She would be able to steady him if necessary, and take the reins at need. He was paper white when she got up behind him, and she was feeling a little sick and sweating herself. But they both managed to stay ahorse, the other horse accepted Markos without too much fuss, and by the time the sun was over the trees, they were on their way.

It was not a pleasant journey, not for any of them. Markos was still covered in bruises and half-healed wounds. Rosa's head was aching abominably. And Dominik had both a battered head and that broken leg.

Mostly, they concentrated on the landscape immediately in front of them, guiding the horses over the smoothest parts and keeping them to a slow amble. It was marginally better once they broke out of the forest and into fields and meadows, but not by much. Rosa was about to suggest they stop and rest, when Markos suddenly exclaimed, "Look!"

She looked up, squinting against the sun, and saw nothing immediately in front of them. But then, she looked where he was pointing, off to the side, and toward a hill.

Just coming over the top of it was a group of mounted men, approaching at a canter. They dropped down between hills, but as they crested the one nearest, Rosa could easily make out Petrescu, kitted out with what must be every weapon he owned, however ancient, his moustache quivering with determination.

He saw them, and waved. A moment later the sound of his shout reached them. Dominik steadied the horse, as Rosa and Markos waved back. The group urged their horses into a gallop, and dropped behind a hill again.

But now, clearly came the sound of the thunder of hooves.

Rosa put her head against Dominik's back, and closed her eyes. *Now it truly is over, at last. . . .*

Dominik was ensconced in the best bed in the inn, with two of the daughters waiting on his every wish. Markos was asleep, after devouring another huge meal and drinking down as much of the potent plum liquor as possible.

Rosa was in Petrescu's house, lying on a featherbed that Petrescu's wife had brought down from the guest bedroom and placed beside the hearth, so that she could tell Petrescu the entire story while lying down.

She was back in "proper" women's clothing again, much to the relief of—well, practically everyone. They couldn't deny she was a heroine, but her outrageous leather clothing had made it very hard for the people of the village to keep their composure around her.

Right now, she wasn't in the mood to make anything more difficult on anyone than it had to be.

Besides, when they had arrived at the village, not only was she in her scandalous leather outfit, she was still covered in blood and other nastiness and wanted a wash, badly. So despite that every movement made her head complain in protest, she had stripped out of the gear, washed herself all over, and changed. The innkeeper's wife had even cleared the kitchen for her so she could do so comfortably, in private, and with warm water. She left her gear and the outfit she had loaned Dominik with the village cobbler to be cleaned and oiled. He took it with a bow that indicated that, now that she was no longer actually wearing it, he was going to treat it with the same reverence as holy vestments.

Petrescu's wife was something of an herbalist, and she had plied Rosa with a tea that was much more pleasant than willow bark, and much more effective. That, and lying down, made it possible for her to recite every detail Petrescu could have wanted. And probably quite a bit he really didn't want to hear, but knew he needed to anyway.

"So it's over, then?" he said when she finished, closed her eyes, and sighed.

"There may be some other lone shifters out there, somewhere," she said, waving her hand vaguely. The featherbed was heavenly, like lying in a supportive cloud. "But Markos can bring some of his family here to hunt them out. He was mumbling something about that when I left him."

"I shall let it be known in the other villages that we found—the *bandits* that had been preying on these parts," Petrescu said, finally. "We will burn the bodies of the shifters, and bring back the bodies and bones and the things you told us about." He sighed. "I suppose we must bury the bones in a common grave. I cannot imagine how we could ever sort them out. . . ."

"Let people sort them out for themselves. Even if they get the wrong bones, what would it matter?" she asked. "The old women that usually lay out the dead can probably do that for you. Then bury the unclaimed ones in that common grave."

"You're right, of course," he replied, and sighed again. "What a thing to come upon me in my old age. . . ."

"Stop complaining, old man," his wife scolded him, making Rosa smile a little. "Think of the honor that will come to you! Putting all those old griefs to rest at last! People will remember *you* as the mayor that solved the mystery of our vanished children."

"Would you care to spend the night here, instead of at the inn?" Petrescu asked, when Rosa was silent. "I would be honored to welcome you. And I could use your advice on what I should tell people."

Now that her head wasn't screaming, Rosa was acutely

aware of the fact that her body was one big bruise from head to toe. The inn was a good long walk away.

And Petrescu's wife was a very, very good cook *and* herbalist.

There was something to be said about giving up a little independence and being taken care of for a change. Especially by people who would be eager for her to take it back.

"Thank you," she said with gratitude. "I would."

Epilogue

MARKOS watched solemnly as the hotel porters loaded the cart with all of Rosa's luggage. Rosa stood beside him, looking every inch the fine lady, with her signature scarlet cloak over her fine merino gown. No one looking at her now would have any notion that three short weeks ago she had been the leather-clad, scandalous Hunt Master, spattered from head to foot with the blood of werewolves.

Then, again, no one would have any idea that the handsome young fellow beside her was himself a werewolf.

"I won't tell you to travel safely," Markos said, as the last of the trunks was stowed securely in the cart, and the driver clucked to the horses, sending them on their way to the train station. "I will tell you that I hope any adventures you have end with you triumphant." Then he blushed. "And that I shall greatly miss your company."

She smiled. "I shall miss yours, as well. And Dominik's too, I suppose. He won't miss me, though!"

They both laughed. Dominik was still luxuriating in his position as hero and invalid back in the village. There were many lovely maidens, including both of the innkeeper's daughters, who were eager to attend to his every whim. Markos, seemingly, had been perfectly willing to fade into the background as the "rescued," and as for Rosa, well, she was a rather *uncomfortable* heroine for the villagers, who were not at all sure what to make of her. It was much easier for them to have someone like Dominik to laud.

And she didn't mind that at all, no more than Markos had.

"As for me, if my intentions are carried out, I shall wield a silver knife against *nothing* more formidable than all the fine meals I intend to eat on the trains." The Graf's generosity had purchased the best accommodations all the way back to his estate, where he intended to grill her as intensively as he had the last time (if not more so) on her Hunt. She was looking forward to it. And, far from feeling homesick for the Schwarzwald, she was beginning to think it might be rather nice to winter over under the Graf's hospitality. And . . . perhaps longer. If she was going to make a habit of being sent off to far places to solve problems, the estate was far better suited to it than the Bruderschaft Lodge. And far more pleasant to return to.

"I hope, then, that is the only knife you wield," he said, and took her neatly gloved hand, and kissed it. "And here is your cab . . ."

Indeed, the cab, summoned by the hotel concierge, was just turning the corner.

"And so I must go." She squeezed his hand before taking hers away.

"Would it . . . be dreadfully presumptuous of me — assuming the Count is willing to host me — to take a trip to his estate in the hopes of — " He blushed again, and couldn't finish the sentence.

She laughed aloud, somewhat startling the cabby, who probably wasn't used to hearing a lady laugh so enthusiastically in public. "Of course not, you goose! I'll be there . . . well, I will confess to you, if the Count is willing, I should like to take up residence there instead of going home. I rather like the idea of being spoilt in between moments of having my life and limbs in jeopardy! So send word in a week or two, and I will tell you whether or not the Count agrees with my notion."

He flushed again, this time with pleasure. "I shall." But as the cabby was looking rather impatient, he handed her inside, and lifted her traveling luggage up to the rack.

"Goodbye, Rosa!" he said. "I hope to see you again soon!"

"Goodbye, Markos!" she called as the cabby pulled away. "And don't be too surprised if on my next Hunt I ask for you!"

She settled back into the cushions of the cab, grinning widely at the shocked—and delighted—look on his face. *One could do worse than having someone with Markos'— hrmm—talents—on a Hunt.*

One could do much worse, indeed!

MERCEDES LACKEY
The Elemental Masters Series

"Her characteristic carefulness, narrative gifts, and attention to detail shape into an altogether superior fantasy."   *—Booklist*

"It's not lighthearted fluff, but rather a dark tale full of the pain and devastation of war, the growing class struggle, and changing sex roles, and a couple of wounded protagonists worth rooting for."   *—Locus*

"Putting a fresh face to a well-loved fairytale is not an easy task, but it is one that seems effortless to the prolific Lackey. Beautiful phrasing and a thorough grounding in the dress, mannerisms and history of the period help move the story along gracefully. This is a wonderful example of a new look at an old theme."   *—Publishers Weekly*

"Richly detailed historic backgrounds add flavor and richness to an already strong series that belongs in most fantasy collections. Highly recommended."   *—Library Journal*

The Serpent's Shadow	978-0-7564-0061-3
The Gates of Sleep	978-0-7564-0101-6
Phoenix and Ashes	978-0-7564-0272-3
The Wizard of London	978-0-7564-0363-8
Reserved for the Cat	978-0-7564-0488-8
Unnatural Issue	978-0-7564-0726-1
Home From the Sea	978-0-7564-0771-1
Steadfast	978-0-7564-0946-3
Blood Red	978-0-7564-0985-2
From a High Tower	978-0-7564-0898-5

To Order Call: 1-800-788-6262
www.dawbooks.com

DAW 23